MUSIC AND THE PLAY OF POWER IN THE MIDDLE EAST, NORTH AFRICA AND CENTRAL ASIA

Music and the Play of Power in the Middle East, North Africa and Central Asia

Edited by

LAUDAN NOOSHIN
City University London, UK

ASHGATE

Published by
Ashgate Publishing Limited
Wey Court East
Union Road
Farnham
Surrey, GU9 7PT
England

Ashgate Publishing Company
Suite 420
101 Cherry Street
Burlington
VT 05401-4405
USA

www.ashgate.com

British Library Cataloguing in Publication Data

Music and the Play of Power in the Middle East, North Africa and Central Asia. – (SOAS Musicology Series)
   1. Music – Middle East – History and criticism. 2. Music – Africa, North – History and criticism – Juvenile literature. 3. Music – Asia, Central – History and criticism.
   I. Series II. Nooshin, Laudan.
   780.9'56–dc22

Library of Congress Cataloging-in-Publication Data

Music and the Play of Power in the Middle East, North Africa and Central Asia / edited by Laudan Nooshin.
    p. cm. – (SOAS Musicology Series)
  ISBN 978-0-7546-3457-7 (hardcover : alk. paper) 1. Music – Political aspects – Middle East. 2. Music – Political aspects – Africa, North. 3. Music – Political aspects – Asia, Central. 4. Music, Influence of. I. Nooshin, Laudan.

  ML3916.M873 2009
  306.4'8420956–dc22

                  2008047658

ISBN 9780754634577 (hbk)
ISBN 9780754693840 (ebk)

Bach musicological font developed by © Yo Tomita.

Mixed Sources
Product group from well-managed forests and other controlled sources
www.fsc.org Cert no. SA-COC-1565
© 1996 Forest Stewardship Council
FSC

Printed and bound in Great Britain by
MPG Books Group, UK

Contents

List of Figures

List of Tables

List of Music Examples

Notes on Contributors

John Baily is Professor of Ethnomusicology and Head of the Afghanistan Music Unit at Goldsmiths, University of London. He holds doctorates in Experimental Psychology (1970) and Ethnomusicology (1988) and is also a graduate in ethnographic film making of the UK's National Film and Television School. He has worked extensively on music in Afghanistan and in the Afghan Diaspora since 1973 and has many publications, including CDs and DVDs. His report *'Can You Stop the Birds Singing?' The Censorship of Music in Afghanistan* was published by Freemuse in 2001. Since then he has visited Kabul several times to assist with the regeneration of music in the post-Taliban era. He is also a performer and teacher of music from Afghanistan, playing the *rubab* and *dutar* lutes.

Ruth F. Davis is Senior Lecturer in Ethnomusicology at Cambridge University and Fellow and Director of Studies in Music at Corpus Christi College. She has published and broadcast extensively on music of North Africa, the Mediterranean and the Middle East. Her book *Ma'luf: Reflections on the Arab Andalusian Music of Tunisia* was published by the Scarecrow Press in 2004 and her critical edition of Robert Lachmann's radio programs 'Oriental Music', based on his research in Mandatory Palestine, is forthcoming with A-R Editions. In 2008 she organised the first international ICTM conference on Jewish music, 'Al-Andalus and its Jewish Diasporas: Music Exodus', at Corpus Christi College and she is currently editing a volume on this theme for Scarecrow Press.

Wendy S. DeBano completed her MA in Ethnomusicology at Arizona State University and completed doctoral coursework in the field of ethnomusicology at the University of Santa Barbara, California. She served as Co-Editor for the special issue of *Iranian Studies* – 'Music and Society in Iran' (vol. 38, no. 3, 2005). The research for this issue and the current chapter was conducted with fellowship support from the American Institute of Iranian Studies.

Michael Frishkopf is an ethnomusicologist specialising in sounds of the Arab world, West Africa and Islamic ritual, especially Sufism. His research also includes social network analysis and digital multimedia repository technology. He currently works at the University of Alberta, as Associate Professor in the Department of Music, Associate Director of the Canadian Centre for Ethnomusicology, and Associate Director for Multimedia at FolkwaysAlive! (in partnership with Smithsonian Folkways Recordings).

Rachel Harris is Lecturer in Ethnomusicology at the School of Oriental and African Studies (SOAS), London, where she teaches undergraduate and postgraduate courses in ethnomusicology and on the musics of Central Asia and China. She was co-editor of the journal *Ethnomusicology Forum* between 2004 and 2007. Her book, *Singing the Village: Memories, Music and Ritual amongst the Sibe of Xinjiang* is published by Oxford University Press (2004). Her current research specialism is in Uyghur music; she has published on aspects of the music culture from ritual contexts to globalisation, pop and identity politics, and is co-editor of *Situating the Uyghurs between China and Central Asia* (Ashgate 2007). Her latest book is on the Uyghur Muqam: *The Making of a Musical Canon in Chinese Central Asia: The Ughur Twelve Muqam* (Ashgate 2008). She has collaborated in the production of several CD recordings, and plays *dutar* with the London Uyghur Ensemble.

Tony Langlois lectures in Media and Communication at Mary Immaculate College, University of Limerick. He received his PhD in 1997 from Queen's University, Belfast, for research on the musical cultures of the Algerian/Moroccan border area. He has published several articles on UK dance music, Canadian cultural politics, popular Islam in the Maghreb and North African music videos, and has recently been making short ethnographic films in Algeria. He has taught at the University of Ulster and the Open University and has also worked in the cultural diversity field of conflict resolution in Northern Ireland. Tony performs experimental music with various Ireland-based ensembles.

Laura Lohman is an Assistant Professor of Music at California State University, Fullerton, where her scholarship and teaching span the disciplines of ethnomusicology and musicology. Her research addresses the music of the Middle East and early America. She is completing a study of Umm Kulthūm's late career and reception history for Wesleyan University Press.

Laudan Nooshin is a Senior Lecturer in the Music Department at City University London, UK. Her current research interests include contemporary developments in Iranian traditional and popular musics; gender issues, with particular reference to the work of women musicians in Iran; neo/post-colonialism, Orientalism and the politics of cultural representation; globalisation; music and power; and music and cultural identity. Her recent writings have appeared as book chapters and as articles in scholarly journals such as the *Journal of the Royal Musical Association*, *Ethnomusicology Forum* and *Iranian Studies*. She is currently Co-Editor of *Ethnomusicology Forum*.

Kay Kaufman Shelemay is the G. Gordon Watts Professor of Music and Professor of African and African American Studies at Harvard University. Her book *Music, Ritual, and Falasha History* (1986), won both the ASCAP-Deems Taylor Award (1987) and the Prize of the International Musicological Society (1988). Other publications include *A Song of Longing: An Ethiopian Journey* (1991); *Ethiopian*

Christian Chant: An Anthology (3 vols, 1993–97), co-edited with Peter Jeffery; *Let Jasmine Rain Down: Song and Remembrance among Syrian Jews* (1998); the revised second edition of *Soundscapes: Exploring Music in a Changing World* (2006); *and Pain and its Transformations: The Interface of Biology and Culture* (2007), co-edited with Sarah Coakley. A past-president of the Society for Ethnomusicology, Shelemay has held fellowships from the National Endowment for the Humanities, the Radcliffe Institute for Advanced Study, the American Council of Learned Societies and the Guggenheim Foundation.

Federico Spinetti is Assistant Professor of Ethnomusicology at the University of Alberta, Edmonton, Canada. He is a graduate of the University of Bologna, Italy (Laurea in Oriental History, 1999) and of the School of Oriental and African Studies, London (MMus Ethnomusicology, 2001; PhD Ethnomusicology, 2006). He has conducted extensive periods of fieldwork in Tajikistan and Iran, and his current research interests include the musics of Central Asia, Iran and the Mediterranean, popular music and the media, music and politics, music and architecture, and ethnographic film-making.

Martin Stokes is University Lecturer in Ethnomusicology at Oxford University, and Fellow in Music at St. John's College. He writes on various aspects of Middle Eastern, Mediterranean and European music, and social and cultural theory in ethnomusicology. Currently he is working on a book provisionally entitled 'The Republic of Love: Transformations of Intimacy in Turkish Popular Music'. His most recent publications are 'Adam Smith and the Dark Nightingale: On Twentieth Century Sentimentalism' in *Twentieth Century Music* (2007), 'Listening to Abd al-Halim Hafiz', in Mark Slobin (ed.) *Global Soundtracks: Music in World Cinema* (2008) and 'Shedding Light on the Balkans: Sezen Aksu's Anatolian Pop', in Donna Buchanan (ed.) *Balkan Popular Culture and the Ottoman Ecumeme: Music, Image and Regional Political Discourse* (2008). He shared the Jaap Kunst Prize from the Society for Ethnomusicology in 2005 for 'Music and the Global Order', published in the *Annual Review of Anthropology* (2004).

Acknowledgements

This book has had a long genesis and many people have been involved in bringing it to fruition. Amongst those who have given moral and practical support along the way, I would particularly like to thank Martin Stokes, Tina K. Ramnarine, Owen Wright, Katherine Brown and Richard Tapper for their valuable comments on several of the chapters and to Gage Averill and Reinhard Strohm for taking the time to share with me their thoughts on music and power. In addition, I owe a great debt of gratitude to the many musicians, colleagues and scholars whose work has inspired me over the years. Without the support of Heidi May at Ashgate and the SOAS Musicology Series Editorial Board, this book would never have come about. I also gratefully acknowledge the support of the Arts and Humanities Research Council, Brunel University and City University London, for providing research time towards the completion of this book.

To the fabulous team of authors whose work is gathered here, my profound thanks for your evergreen patience, your hard work and your faith in the project. And to my wonderful family for your love and support throughout.

The authors and I dedicate this volume to the musicians of the Middle East, North Africa and Central Asia, both at home and in diaspora, who, despite often overwhelming odds, continue to create music of great beauty and power.

Note on Transliteration

This book does not follow a standard transliteration system. The chapters in this volume cover a number of languages and each author has transliterated non-English text following established conventions specific to the language in question, and seeking where possible to convey the sound of the spoken words as pronounced in English.

Prelude: Power and the Play of Music

Laudan Nooshin

Introduction

> The apparatus is thus always inscribed in a play of power, but it is also always linked to certain coordinates of knowledge … This is what the apparatus consists in: strategies of relations of forces supporting, and supported by, types of knowledge. (Foucault 1980:196)

> All music, any organization of sounds is then a tool for the creation or consolidation of a community … noise is inscribed from the start within the panoply of power … And since noise is the source of power, power has always listened to it with fascination … (Attali 1985:6)

> whoever comes their way. Whoever draws too close,
> off guard, and catches the Sirens' voices in the air –
> no sailing home for him, no wife raising to meet him
> no happy children beaming up at their father's face.
> The high, thrilling song of the Sirens will transfix him
> (Homer, *The Odyssey* [trans. Fagles 1996:50])

The power of music to inspire, touch, influence, uplift, heal and transform has long been a source of wonder for human beings. In particular, music's close connection with the supernatural and the magical has for thousands of years invoked associations of power. Ethnomusicologists have, of course, long recognised and documented such power, and even sought to explain it. However, whilst questions of power were implicit in the work of many early ethnomusicologists, prior to the 1980s relatively few engaged directly with such questions, or sought a theoretical framework for their understanding. The emergence of Poststructuralism in the 1960s, followed by Cultural Studies, Critical Theory and Postcolonial Studies in the 1970s and '80s, were immensely important in bringing issues of power to the fore of academic discourse; yet, whilst writers such as Jacques Derrida, Roland Barthes, Antonio Gramsci, Michel Foucault, Edward Said and Jean Baudrillard were reshaping the scholarly landscape of the humanities and social sciences, only a handful of ethnomusicologists – most notably those working on Latin America and the Caribbean – were attending to the profound inscribing of power in every aspect of music production, dissemination, representation and reception. By the early 1990s, however, issues of power could no longer be sidelined, particularly with the emergence of the 'New Musicology' in the United States (and Critical Musicology in the UK) and the opening up of new arenas of music study, most notably in relation to gender and popular music. Moreover, the writings of scholars such as Kofi Agawu (1992), Martin Stokes (1992) and Philip Bohlman, particularly the latter's watershed article 'Musicology as a Political Act' (1993), required that we reflect not just on the power relations 'out there', but on our own scholarly entanglement in such relations.[1] Things have certainly come a long way since the early 1990s and ethnomusicologists today bring to their work a more nuanced understanding of the ways in which power is thoroughly implicated in the social practices of music as it 'comes to bear on every process of cultural creation and interpretation' (Averill 1997:3). At the same time, 'power' remains a relatively under-theorised concept in the ethnomusicological literature, including questions concerning the nature of power and our culturally-constructed understandings of it.

This volume explores various dimensions of power in music and music in power in the Middle East, North Africa and Central Asia, a region stretching from Morocco in the west to China in the east. Notwithstanding the divisions of geography and (post-)colonial mappings, this area shares a great deal in historical, religious and cultural terms, providing for interesting comparative perspectives. The idea for the volume emerged following the 2001 Annual Conference of the British Forum for Ethnomusicology, which I convened at Brunel University and for which the main theme was 'Music and Power'.[2] The richness of the topic and the direct relevance of so many of the issues to the musics of the region led to this volume, the first to focus on what I term the 'music-power nexus' in the context of the Middle East, North Africa and Central Asia. In this introduction, I explore a number of theoretical issues relating to music and power, and highlight some of the themes which run through the volume and which connect the chapters in

---

[1]   The reflexive turn out of which this work emerged dates back at least to the 1970s, as seen in the writings of Stephen Blum (1975) and Kenneth Gourlay (1978), both of whom sought to examine the role of the ethnomusicologist as a thoroughly socially-situated agent, and further to look at the ways in which 'all ethnomusicologists operate within the constraints of the "ideology" which influences concepts held about the aims and methods of the discipline' (Gourlay 1978:2). Also relevant here is the work of Jospeh Kerman (1985), one of the first musicologists to explore the ideological underpinnings of the discipline; and also that of Richard Middleton who implicates the terminologies, methodologies and ideologies of musicology in the exclusion (up until the time of writing in the late 1980s) of popular music from mainstream music studies (1990:103–26). For a specific and particularly stark example of the scholarly entanglement with issues of power and ideology, see Potter's (1998) illuminating study of musicology in Germany between 1918 and 1945, in which she explores 'the relationship musicology cultivated with the state, the party, and the German people' (xv) and how musicological work served to validate the ideologies and institutions of National Socialism.

[2]   This conference resulted in another volume on the same theme, edited by Annie J. Randall (2005).

various ways, before moving on to discuss each chapter in turn. As will become clear, the discourses of power in the region centre on some of the most contested social issues, particularly in relation to questions of nationhood, identity, gender and religion, all of which impact directly on music and its social meanings. The contributions to this volume explore the ways in which music serves as a medium for the negotiation of power; how music becomes a space for promoting – or conversely, resisting or subverting – particular ideologies or positions of authority; how music accrues symbolic power in ways which are very particular, perhaps unique; how music becomes a site of social control or, alternatively, a vehicle for agency and empowerment, at times overt at others highly subtle. What is it about music that facilitates, and sometimes disrupts, the exercise and flows of power? And who controls such flows, how and for what purposes?

What makes this region such an interesting focus for a volume such as this is that music itself represents a highly contested area. The long-standing and well-documented debate over music's permissibility, particularly within Islamic orthodoxy, provides an important backdrop to much of the discussion, and is explicitly foregrounded in a number of chapters. Above all, music is often taken to have an excess of emotional power that requires control for the well-being of society. As Hirschkind observes, the debate over music's theological-legal status has been partly 'Feuled by a concern with the ability of music to bypass the faculty of rational judgement and directly affect the senses of the listener' (2004:134). Moreover, across much of the region under discussion, social anxieties over music (and dance) are paralleled with anxieties concerning gender, particularly in relation to women. Thus, women and music both represent problematic areas and often share a positioning as discursive 'Other': in the case of women, in relation to the normative male domain; in the case of music, in relation to the rational, controlled domain of the spoken and written word. Thus, social controls on women often provide a touchstone for controls on music-making, and *vice versa*. Where the two coincide – women as musicians and dancers – one often finds the most contentious and tightly controlled arenas of social activity, at least in the public domain. Paradoxically, of course, some of the greatest singers in this region have been women, and indeed the volume begins with a chapter on arguably the greatest of them all, Umm Kulthūm. What ostensibly began as religious doctrine has in many cases become politicised, particularly in countries where theocratic rule has merged religion and politics or where the clergy is particularly powerful. Thus, control over both music and women become important symbols of social and political control and what is argued in the name of religious doctrine is, more often than not, a means of exercising political power.[3]

Questions of power have figured prominently in the social science and cultural analysis literature on the region, particularly in relation to the legacy of colonialism

---

[3]   McClary documents an interesting parallel situation in seventeenth-century France where the banning of Italian music for political reasons was justified through questions of aesthetics, thus cloaking the ideological nature of the ban (1985:155).

and post-colonialism, orientalism, geo-politics, and so on. Particular mention should be made of Lila Abu-Lughod (1983, 1989, 2004), Timothy Mitchell (1988, 2002), Walter Armbrust (1996, 2000) and Charles Hirschkind (2004, 2006), whose writings on issues such as orientalism and representation, modernity, nationhood, media technologies, globalisation and the place of Islam in social and political life resonate strongly with many of the central themes of this volume. Hirschkind's work is of especial relevance, specifically his writings on 'the politics of listening' which examine the impact of the nationalist-modernist project in Egypt on the organisation of sensory experience, including listening, particularly in terms of listener agency. He traces the emergence in the 1950s and '60s of a new collective 'modern national auditory practice that connected traditions of ethical listening with emerging media practices of political discourse and musical entertainment' (2004:145), experienced particularly through the weekly radio speeches of President Nasser and the broadcast concerts of Umm Kulthūm. Whilst Abu-Lughod (1983, 2004) deals primarily with Egyptian television drama serials and the ways in which these engage with the national imaginary, her work addresses many of the same issues discussed in the first three chapters of this volume (Lohman, Stokes, Frishkopf), particularly the relationship between the Egyptian state, media communications and Islam, and how relations of power and ideology are played out in the space offered by mediating technologies.

In terms of the delineation of the region, as Armbrust observes, the Middle East has become 'a lightning rod for anxieties about the reality of conceptual boundaries ... For some, the Middle East as a cultural entity is a prime example – perhaps *the* prime example – of how European discourse created the definitively non-Western and thereby defined the Western by distinguishing it from an opposite created by political and social convention' (2000:1). Clearly, the now-naturalised concept of the 'Middle East' as a geographical and cultural entity has moved well beyond its origins as a Western construct and forms an important focus for local notions of belonging and identity. At the same time, the historical, cultural and religious connections with the countries of North Africa (often, as in this volume, included in the category of Middle East) and much of Central Asia highlights the constructed and porous nature of its boundaries.

Theories of Power

Seeking to understand the nature of power has exercised the minds of philosophers and others for millennia. In his novel *Utopia* (1515), for instance, English statesman and lawyer Thomas More grappled with questions of power within his vision of the ideal state, a vision heavily influenced by the writings of Plato. In the nineteenth century, historians, political economists, philosophers and sociologists such as Karl Marx, Friedrich Nietzsche and Max Weber concerned themselves centrally with questions of power, and power has continued to provide a focus of interest for writers from a wide range of disciplinary backgrounds through to the present day. One of the central problematics in discussing power is the term itself, ostensibly singular and monolithic but which belies a plural, fluid and multifaceted phenomenon. Is power a 'thing'? a force? an idea? a quality? And what are the relationships between different kinds of power, whether political, ideological, social, economic, semiotic, psychological and so on? Political scientists often distinguish five forms of power: 'force, persuasion, authority, coercion and manipulation' (Allison 1996:398) and definitions such as those offered by the Oxford Dictionary – 'the ability to do or act', 'a particular faculty of body and mind', 'political or social ascendancy or control', 'authorization; delegated authority', 'an influential person, group or organisation', 'military strength', and so on (Hawkins and Allen 1991:1135) – tend to focus on public manifestations of power generally associated with the political, 'the strategies and tactics for gaining, maintaining and increasing power, especially (but not exclusively) in its more formal and public dimensions' (Averill 1997:1).

Central to any discussion of power is the concept of ideology, defined as 'Any comprehensive or mutually consistent set of ideas by which a social group makes sense of the world' (Jones 1996:233). Not only does the exercise of power almost invariably include an ideological dimension, but ideology in turn serves to 'legitimate a system of authority' (Ricoeur 1986:17), and from a Marxist perspective to mask the real state of power relations. In his *Lectures on Ideology and Utopia*, Paul Ricoeur traces the changing discourses around the concept of ideology, from 'ideology as distortion' (Marx) to 'ideology as legitimation' (Weber) and finally to 'ideology as integration' (Geertz) (1986:254). In contrast to the somewhat pejorative Marxian connotations of ideology, both Weber and later the anthropologist Clifford Geertz have argued that ideology is not inexorably determined by economic and material factors, nor should it be viewed solely as a distortion of reality, but as an integral, indeed necessary, aspect of the social fabric through which human beings attach meanings to practice in order 'to render otherwise incomprehensible social situations meaningful' (Geertz 1973b:220),

> Whatever else ideologies may be – projections of unacknowledged fears, disguises for ulterior motives, phatic expressions of group solidarity – they are, most distinctively, maps of problematic social reality and matrices for the creation of collective conscience. (ibid.)

Ricoeur also revisits the relationship between ideology and utopia first expounded upon by sociologist Karl Mannheim in his influential text *Ideology and Utopia* (1936), and discusses the implications for our understanding of power: 'the turning point of both is in fact at the same place, that is to say, in the problem of authority. If every ideology tends finally to legitimate a system of authority, does not every utopia, the moment of the other, attempt to come to grips with the problem of power itself?' (1986:17). Attempts to theorise ideology have inevitably had to grapple with the philosophical conundrum identified by Mannheim – and dubbed

'Mannheim's Paradox' by Geertz (1973b:194) – that there is no ideologically-neutral space within which such theorising might take place.[4]

Such dimensions of the power 'complex' are clearly relevant to music. A great deal has been written on the overtly political uses of music, particularly in relation to strategies for 'gaining, maintaining and increasing power' and also as a medium for conveying political messages whose verbal expression is otherwise proscribed. At the same time, considerations of power and music extend far beyond this to encompass the subtle and often less visible workings of power as played out in the musical domain, a domain which clearly transcends 'music as sound' to encompass the many non-sounded dimensions of music. These include the physical and gestural, both within music and dance performance, as well as the ways in which music is conceptualised and imagined, the discursive formations within which music is embedded and which saturate the spaces around it, tying it to the social fabric; and of course the social fabric itself – the specific social, political, economic and institutional structures through which music is shaped.[5] As Bohlman observes, 'Music is always far more than sound, for it ceaselessly strives to be more than itself. It is because music pushes beyond the bounds of the sonic that the aesthetic and the political accrue to it, affording it the multiple conditions of power' (2007). And this brings us to a central problematic at the heart of this book: the intersection of the aesthetic with the ideological, political and social. The aesthetic dimension is particularly tricky, since any discussion of music and power has to take account of the fact that experiencing music is above all (usually) a pleasurable experience, which can in itself serve a naturalising agenda by which the aesthetic camouflages the ideological or political by deflecting attention from intended meanings.[6] And yet, even where such meanings are hidden, music's very presence can be a sign of agency. In this volume, this can be seen in the somewhat extreme case of Afghanistan, as discussed by John Baily, whether in relation to clandestine music-making during the Taliban period or – albeit briefly – in the immediate post-Taliban period when music's very presence came to symbolise

---

[4]   See also Ricoeur (1986:159–60).

[5]   Whilst contemporary Euro-American concepts of music tend to privilege sound, there is of course a long tradition of European thought to which non-sounded dimensions of music are central, most obviously the Platonic concept of the 'music of the spheres', the 'unheard music produced by the revolutions of the planets' (Grout and Palisca 2001:6; see also Stokes 1992:220). This concept has proved highly influential and was expounded upon in later writings, including the work of the sixth-century Roman scholar Boethius, whose three-fold division of music comprised *musica mundana* (cosmic music), *musica humana* and *musica instrumentalis*. It was only the latter, the lowliest form of music, that encompassed music as sound (Grout and Palisca 2001:27–9).

[6]   In the words of Sullivan, 'music's ability to point to all things and, in that very gesture, distract the hearer and thus escape being called into question, may be the outcome of a spell it casts on listeners or a false consciousness that it conjures in order to distract from its true intentions and lull into silence' (1997b:8–9). See also Born and Hesmondhalgh (2000:45).

freedom; and to a lesser extent the case of women musicians in Iran as discussed by Wendy DeBano. If music's presence is an indicator of agency, then its absence is often taken to represent the opposite. But, as a number of commentators have observed, such absences are rarely absolute and, as will be discussed further below, one needs to be attuned to what James C. Scott terms the 'hidden transcripts' (1990) which are often absent from the public realm.

The subtle workings of power bring us to a scholar whose work has contributed significantly to our understanding of the nature of power (and as reflected in the title of this volume): Michel Foucault. Foucault's ideas are useful in a number of ways, most obviously his insistence on the all-permeating nature of power,

> Power relations permeate all levels of social existence and are therefore to be found operating at every site of social life – in the private spheres of the family and sexuality as much as in the public spheres of politics, the economy and the law ... Foucault shifts our attention away from the grand, overall strategies of power, towards the many, localized circuits, tactics, mechanisms and effects through which power circulates – what Foucault calls the 'meticulous rituals' or the 'microphysics' of power. These power relations 'go right down to the depth of society' (Foucault 1977a, p.27). (Hall 1997b:50)

> According to Foucault, power is not merely something that individuals, groups or classes exercise, though of course it can be this. Foucault argues that discursive formations are networks of power within which we are all enmeshed ... power is everywhere and everything ... can be positive as well as negative. (Apperley 1996:187)

This infusing of power in every social relationship and every social action provides a useful framework for understanding how music (in the broadest sense) is embedded in relations of power which impact directly on its social meanings. Many of the chapters in this volume are informed, more or less explicitly, by a Foucauldian perspective, central to which is a deconstruction of binary oppositions between the 'powerful' and 'powerless', between action and reaction, domination and resistance. As will become clear, the operations of power are much more ambiguous and slippery than this, as Averill observes: 'Power is far from being the property of the powerful; it is a pervasive quality that adheres to every action and interaction. It is sought, undermined, despised, ignored, resisted, and negotiated' (1997:1). Moreover, Foucault disengages power from concepts of directionality, suggesting instead what Stuart Hall describes as the 'circularity of power' (1997a:261) or, in Averill's conceptualisation, 'a spatial, radial vision of the distribution of power in society' (1997:9).

Other aspects of Foucault's work which are of relevance to the current discussion include the ways in which discursive formations are implicated in power relations, the interlocking of knowledge and power, and questions of power and representation, ideas which were also deeply influential on the work of Edward Said.[7] In the context of the current volume, we need to ask whose voices are privileged in the discourses around music and, conversely, who is denied a voice. Also significant is Foucault's focus on the body as a site of social and political control, which is especially pertinent to music in its performative dimension, particularly in relation to dance. As already mentioned, in the geo-cultural region under consideration, this can be seen most starkly in the ways in which social anxieties over gender, music and dance become projected onto the female body and translate into controls on women's music-making and dancing.

Whilst critiques of Foucault have focused on his somewhat totalising and reductionist view of power,[8] his theories would seem to have great applicability to music and the subtle, often hidden, agendas it can be used to serve. Moreover, from a reverse perspective, as an important 'medium for the negotiation and communication of power' (Averill 1997:210), music can itself perhaps contribute to a greater understanding of the nature of power. Since power is always relational and all social relations involve power, and since music serves as an important forum for playing out social relations, music may be 'crucial in helping us to understand and interpret how power is enforced as well as how it is challenged' (Shelemay 2001:283).

Another writer whose work has been influential, particularly on scholars of popular music and culture, is Antonio Gramsci. Among the chapters in this volume, Federico Spinetti draws most directly on Gramsci's work. To some extent, Gramsci's focus on class relations is of limited relevance to the case studies discussed here in which other 'axes of difference' take on greater significance, although class issues are often subsumed within these. Nevertheless, concepts of cultural and ideological hegemony and consent are absolutely central to some of the discussions around post-colonial nation formation and cultural ownership. Such hegemonies are persistent and become incorporated into new power structures which often endure long after the demise of the hegemonic regime. In the case of Tajikistan, Spinetti discusses the ways in which hierarchical regional and 'ethnic' power structures established under Soviet rule, and which continued in the post-Soviet period and partly led to the civil war of the 1990s, could only endure because they gained wide consent among people. Similarly, the enduring attraction of the cosmopolitan West to young Iranians is often portrayed as simply a manifestation of the continuing global hegemony of Western culture. However, as a number of scholars have pointed out, binaries of hegemony and resistance offer only a crude tool to understanding the complexities of real lives,[9] and I argue in my chapter that

---

[7]   For one of the most thorough and far-reaching applications of Foucault's ideas on power to the Middle East (specifically, Egypt), see the work of Timothy Mitchell (1988, 2002).

[8]   See in particular the 'debate' between Foucault and the German philosopher and sociologist Habermas, in which the latter questioned the philosophical basis of Foucault's thinking on the relationship between power and critique (see Kelly 1994).

[9]   See in particular Scott's critique of Gramsci (1990). Scott's view of resistance has been criticised for being as totalising as Gramsci's view of hegemony.

the aspiration to (Western) cosmopolitanism amongst certain social groups in Iran has as much to do with new notions of belonging and identification as it does with Western cultural hegemony. To dismiss such aspirations as wholly hegemonic is to deny agency to the musicians and others involved in shaping new identities and new visions of the future.

The Music-Power Nexus

Within ethnomusicological literature the concept of power was for many years invoked primarily in relation to music's affective power, including its role in religious and other ritual contexts, but also in contexts of (post-/neo-)colonialism, as well as the more or less overtly political uses of music.[10] In the latter case, discussion was often framed in starkly dualistic terms of hegemony and resistance. However, as already noted, questions of power were often implicit in the writings of ethnomusicologists, even where the concept itself was not invoked. To take one example, the negative discourses around jazz in the United States between *c.*1920 and 1940 – as reported by Alan Merriam in *The Anthropology of Music* in a chapter exploring semiotics and questions of musical meaning – depended on an understanding of music's power, in this case allegedly to corrupt and bring about social and personal decline (1964:241–4). Among the examples cited, one of the most striking is the *New York Times* article of 4 February 1926 which reported that,

> the Salvation Army in Cincinnati became exercised over the fact that a theatre in which jazz was played had been located near a maternity hospital, for '… we are loathe to believe that babies born in the maternity hospital are to be legally subjected to the implanting of jazz emotions by such enforced propinquity to a theatre and jazz palace'. (ibid.:242)

Such views remind one strongly of the ancient Greek philosophy of *ethos*, the belief 'that music possessed moral qualities and could affect character and behaviour' (Grout and Palisca 2001:6), and also resonate indirectly with the long-standing debate within Islamic jurisprudence over the moral standing of music.[11]

---

[10]   See, amongst many others, Sullivan (1997a) and Ralls-MacLeod and Harvey (2000) for discussion of music in religious contexts; and Berliner (1977), Erlmann (1985), Waters (1985), Kaemmer (1989:37–9), Glick-Schiller and Fouron (1990), Waterman (1990), Garofalo (1992), Lipsitz (1994) and Taylor (1997), for examples of music as direct political action and/or anti-authoritarian resistance or subversion.

[11]   Both Plato and his student Aristotle wrote about the role of music in shaping character (see Grout and Palisca 2001:7; also Strunk 1952:3–24 and Tame 1984:19). Plato's views on music's place in education were immensely influential on medieval and Renaissance writers (see Tomlinson 1994). According to Greek mythology, the positive power of music was embodied in the figure of Orpheus – musician, augur, healer, religious

Whilst Merriam's 1960s scholarly toolkit did not offer a link between music as symbol and questions of power, such a link is nevertheless implicit. The examples which Merriam cites constitute a Foucauldian discursive formation through which jazz's symbolic social meanings are shaped through relationships of power, in this case strongly tied to racial discourses of the time.[12]

The literature abounds with examples such as this, where the music-power nexus forms a taken-for-granted backdrop, rarely discussed explicitly. From the mid-1980s, however, issues of power started to come to the fore, most notably in writings on Latin America and the Caribbean, but also in the growing literature on urban and popular musics which increasingly required an engagement with issues of class, 'race' and ethnicity. In part, such writings represented a reaction against the functionalist and insular models of cultural analysis prevalent among some anthropologists and ethnomusicologists in the preceding decades. Significant at this time was the work of Thomas Turino (1983, 1984), John A. Kaemmer (1989), Gage Averill (1989[13]), Christopher Waterman (1990), Veit Erlmann (1991) and Martin Stokes (1992).[14] Turino, in particular, was one of the first to introduce

---

figure and practitioner of magical arts – in contrast to the potentially destructive power of music symbolised by the bird-like creatures known as sirens who, through their beautiful voices, lured sailors to their deaths. For an interesting exploration of the sirens from a ethno-/musicological perspective, see Austern and Naroditskaya (2006). In some cultures, the symbolic power/danger of the sirens has, over the centuries, been fused with the figure of the mermaid (thus, in a number of European languages the term for mermaid is *sirena*, *sirènes* and so on); see Turino (1983) for discussion of beliefs concerning the musical, magical, seductive and destructive powers of the *sirena* in southern Peru. Interestingly, the Renaissance scholar and physician, Masilio Ficino (1433–99), who attributed magical powers to music (see Tomlinson 1994), drew on ideas from the writings of the ninth-century Arab writer al-Kindi, and was in turn influential on the work of Foucault.

[12]   Mention should also be made of Merriam's contemporary, cultural anthropologist Clifford Geertz, whose interpretive anthropology drew attention to the role of the symbolic in creating systems of meaning through culture. Geertz was, of course, also interested in questions of ideology (see above) and indeed viewed ideology as a 'cultural symbol-system' (1973b:218).

[13]   This article developed from a paper presented at a landmark conference held at Cornell University in April 1988, and organised by Deborah Pacini Hernandez, Martha Uloa and Mary Jo Dudley on the subject of class and 'race' in Latin American music. Other speakers included Thomas Turino, Chris Waterman and Charles Keil. I am grateful to Gage Averill for bringing this conference to my attention.

[14]   See also Coplan (1985) and Peña (1985). Within dance scholarship, Jane Cowan's study of gender relations and power in Greek dance (1990) was an important contribution to the literature in this area. A parallel trend was of course also emergent within musicology at this time, for example see the work of William Weber (1975, 1992), L.B. Meyer, who was particularly interested in the relationship between cultural and political ideology and music style change, first discussed in 1967 (128–330) and explored at length in 1989 in relation to the ideology of Romanticism (see pages 161–352), the various chapters in Leppert and McClary's edited volume (1987), and Walser (1993). Mention should also be made of the

the concept of hegemony into ethnomusicology and to explore the relationship between the aesthetic and the political, as well as the interplay between what he terms the 'hegemonic factor' and the 'identity factor'. In discussing the impact of socio-economic-political factors on the *mestizo* tradition in southern Peru, Turino considers how shifting relationships in the hierarchy of social power between the urban-*mestizo* middle class and the ruling *criollo* elite on the one hand and the indigenous *campesino* peasants on the other, have effected changes in musical style, performance contexts, instrument structure (his discussion focuses on the *charango*) and choice of genre. As Turino observes, *mestizos* are caught between the 'need for a regional identity and the persistent force of dominant class values ...' (1984:258), and whilst they 'seek to differentiate themselves from the criollo by the ideological and symbolic identification with campesino culture [identity factor], they nevertheless remain greatly influenced by the cultural and aesthetic values of the dominant group [hegemonic factor]' (266). Each of these factors offer the potential for empowerment, whether through the use of indigenous elements as a form of identity politics or, on the other hand, by drawing on the cultural capital associated with dominant *criollo* aesthetics. Kaemmer similarly examines the ways in which changing configurations of social power impact on musical style and on music's symbolic meanings, focusing on the case of Zimbabwe from the pre-colonial period through to independence in 1980. Placing power at the centre of his arguments, he concludes,

> Instead of considering music as frosting on a cake, music would be better seen as one of the important ways in which humans manipulate each other and the world about them ... music as a form of symbol is often used either to consolidate power or to adapt to situations of powerlessness. The theoretical problems of music and society might well be more aptly considered as problems of music and power. (1989:42, 44)

---

significant contribution in this area of a number of popular music scholars and sociologists of popular music, including John Shepherd, Simon Frith, Richard Middleton and Peter Wicke, whose work was strongly informed both by Cultural Studies and by Marxist theory (particularly via Raymond Williams and E.P. Thompson) and which engages directly with issues of class and ideology (see Shepherd et al. 1977, Shepherd 1991, 1993, Frith 1978, 1983, 1988, 1989, Middleton 1990, Wicke 1990). Shepherd, in particular, highlighted the relevance of Cultural Studies to musicology and advocated a dialogue between the two disciplines. His work is interesting for its exploration of how ideologies and relationships of social power become manifest within the codes and structures of music itself (see 1977, 1987; see also in this regard the work of Susan McClary, specifically in relation to gender ideologies [McClary 1991]). Also of relevance here is the work of cultural theorists and sociologists Dick Hebdige, Paul Gilroy and Lawrence Grossberg, all of whom studied under Stuart Hall at the University of Birmingham Centre for Contemporary Cultural Studies and whose writings on youth culture, class and 'race' engage centrally with music (see Hebdige 1979, Gilroy 1987, 1993, Grossberg 1991).

Waterman's now classic text on identity and power in Nigerian *jùjú* music (1990) was the first extended ethnographic study to examine questions of power in musical performance. Against the backdrop of complex class and colonial relationships in Nigeria (and extending beyond the national to global networks), Waterman explores the relationship between music and social order in Nigeria and the ways in which popular music, specifically *jùjú*, mediates these relationships. Waterman is particularly interested in how *jùjú* presents an image of a cohesive social order in the context of apparent opportunities for all, but at the same time subtly perpetuates traditional social divisions, hierarchies and hegemonies. These arguments are elucidated most openly in the final chapter, 'Jùjú Music and Inequality in Modern Yoruba Society' (213–28). Above all, Waterman prompts us to 'rethink the role of performance in the construction, expression, and legitimization of power relationships in the modern world' (Erlmann 1996:21).

Such writings paved the way for a radical shift in the 1990s as ethnomusicologists developed a more nuanced and theoretically-grounded understanding of the complex and pervasive workings of power, and started to explore concepts of power and their culturally-constructed nature.[15] Particular mention should be made of Gage Averill (a student of Waterman's), whose work on popular music in Haiti examines 'music's role in enacting and negotiating authority, domination, co-optation, subordination, hegemony, and resistance … Popular music, as a discursive terrain, is a site at which power is enacted, acknowledged, accommodated, signified, contested, and resisted' (1997:xv, xi). Whilst Averill documents a situation in which music is, generally speaking, more openly politicised and where the central discourses of power revolve around 'race' and class to a much greater extent than the musics discussed in this volume, still much of what he has to say about music and power is of immense relevance. Averill suggests that music's close link to memory, nostalgia and collective social experience are important factors in its entanglement with power, 'The powerful appeal of music – its engagement with human emotions – is the reason it serves effectively as an instrument of politics and a medium of power' (1997:19). Among other things (and following the work of Waterman), he points to music's *status-quo*-affirming function, 'one enacted through myriad musical rituals of alliance and obeisance' (ibid.:9), something which can also be seen through many centuries of European music in the church and court,

---

[15]   In considering some of the earliest ethnomusicological writings to engage directly with questions of power and ideology, it has not been my intention to go beyond the early 1990s, after which such questions became much more central to ethnomusicological thinking. However, for an interesting volume which explores the impact of Marxist thought on ethno/musicology, see Qureshi (2002).

It is a general fact of musical life that the rank of a ruler is measured in part by the music he can command. For several centuries, rival European courts were involved in intense competition to attract the best composers and performers (Hogwood 1977). (Baily, this volume)[16]

Indeed, many earlier writers, including John Blacking (see Baily, this volume), noted the link between political power and music, pointing to the role of music in official displays which serve to legitimate those in positions of authority, their institutions and their discourses. Such displays 'openly affirm and perpetuate an existing power structure' (Shelemay 2001:283) through 'public transcripts' (after Scott, 1990); in this way, power and authority are literally 'performed'.[17] At the same time, there are the 'hidden transcripts' in which 'musical performances and repertoires ... embed messages through metaphorical or coded terms' (Shelemay 2001:283), often comprising indirect and subtle 'everyday forms of resistance' (Scott 1990:290; see also Erlmann 1996:xxii, 231). As Scott points out, both the 'powerful' and the 'powerless' have such hidden transcripts such that a 'dominant ideology can be encoded within ordinary objects of everyday life' (Lipsitz 1994:110), an idea explored further by Shelemay in this volume.

Other dimensions of power which have been of interest to ethnomusicologists in recent years include the intersection between music, power and place (see, for example, Lipsitz 1994, Stokes 1994a), particularly in relation to concepts of 'globality' and the growing economic power of transnational capital. The debate surrounding the global 'world music' industry is particularly interesting for the ways in which it brings together questions of representation, appropriation and the politics of 'hybridity'.[18] Whether the world music industry serves to empower musicians locally or simply perpetuates Western hegemony, it certainly bears the heavy imprint of well-established power relations, many of which date back to the colonial period, and which raise complex issues for ethnomusicologists regarding their own involvement in the industry. More broadly, global interconnectedness and the collapsing of time and space facilitated primarily by electronic communications is impacting on notions of belonging, of 'self' and 'other', all of which have far-reaching implications for power relations.[19] Increasingly, as 'shared cultural space no longer depends upon shared geographical place ... New discursive spaces

---

[16] See also Attali (1985:47–51). Pointing to the need of those in authority to control sound – including music – Attali quotes from the music master in Molière's *Le Bourgeois Gentilhomme* (Act I, Scene II), 'Without music no State could survive' (49).

[17] See also Kaemmer (1989:33). In terms of the possible origins of music, Nettl even suggests that the display of 'power by musicking (or pre-musicking) together – shout, sing, yodel, growl, beat drums and rattles – to scare neighbouring bands or enemy hordes, that would be a plausible beginning of music' (2005:264–5).

[18] There is of course a substantial literature on these issues; see in particular Feld (1994a, 1994b), Taylor (1997, 2007), Erlmann (1999) and Stokes (2003b, 2004).

[19] See, for instance, Bohlman (2002).

allow for recognition of new networks and affiliations' (Lipsitz 1994:6) and the emergence of new communities of identity. In relation to the nation state as a unit of identification, many commentators have pointed to the growing importance of other units, both smaller and larger, and even predicted the nation state's eventual demise.[20] This can be seen clearly in the various religious (Frishkopf, Harris), regional (Langlois, Spinetti) and transnational (Lohman, Nooshin) identities and affiliations – some long-standing, others more recent – discussed in the chapters of this volume. Whilst the discussions are rooted in quite specific local contexts, all touch in some way on the broader issues of the region as well as the increasingly global 'social imaginary' as articulated by anthropologist and cultural theorist Arjun Appadurai. Appadurai's ideas are pertinent here, most particularly the shift from thinking in terms of 'landscapes' towards what he proposes as the constituent elements of contemporary global flows: ethnoscapes, mediascapes, technoscapes, finanscapes and ideoscapes, 'the dynamic movement of ethnic groups, images, technology, capital, and ideologies allows us all to inhabit many different "places" at once' (Lipsitz 1994:5). In relation to the current volume, each of these 'scapes' facilitates the circulation of musical sounds, ideas and products, whether through the channel of diasporic networks or cosmopolitan social formations, through mass mediation and the internet, through the commodity economy including the world music industry, and so on.

Like much ethnomusicological writing, questions of power have been implicit in the work of those researching the musics of the Middle East, North Africa and Central Asia, whether in relation to musical aesthetics and the affective power of music – for instance within ecstatic practices such as *sama'* and *tarab* (for example, see Lewisohn 1997 and Racy 2003) or the close connection between music and healing in the Medieval Islamic world (see Shiloah 1995:49–53) – or in relation to theological debates on music (see al-Faruqi 1985, Nasr 1997) or broader socio-cultural issues including gender, discourses of nationhood, emerging modernities, and so on (see Danielson 1997). However, since power does not constitute a central focus of such writings, most depend on an assumed understanding of power and few scholars attempt to interrogate the concept. Among those who have focused more directly on power, mention should be made of Castelo-Branco's writings on various aspects of Egyptian music in the mid-twentieth century including government policies towards music, the institutionalisation of music, Western music in Egypt and the relationship between modernity and tradition (see, for instance, 1980, 1984). Also significant is Martin Stokes' work on the Turkish urban popular genre *arabesk* (1992) in which he addresses a wide range of issues including the competing discourses within which *arabesk* operates (both official and unofficial, and including complex discourses of power and powerlessness), as

---

[20]   See, for instance, Steger (2003:61–8). At the same time, as the chapters in this volume testify, the nation state concept has proved a particularly powerful and tenacious one; thus, most of the discussion presented here deals with discourses in which the nation state is an unquestioned given; few problematise the concept itself.

well as such issues as migrancy, urbanisation, peripherality, emotionality, gender, nationhood, the role of technology and the media, and the interplay between secular and religious domains, all within the broad context of state cultural policies in Turkey. Many of the same topics are discussed by Marc Schade-Poulsen (1999) in the context of Algerian *raï*, but with a particular focus on gender, the latter also being central to Veronica Doubleday's writing on musical instruments and power (1999, 2008).[21]

Music, Power and Meaning

So what is it about music that lends itself to the expression, negotiation and circulation of power? Opinion certainly seems divided as to whether power can ever be a quality of music itself or whether it is more a question of the uses to which music is put. On the one hand, there is the view expressed by Randall in the introduction to her edited volume: 'None of the authors makes a claim for the power of music *itself* to persuade, coerce, resist or suppress; rather they address the uses to which music is put, the controls placed on it, and discursive treatments of it' (2005:1). This view accords well with an understanding of power which is fluid and relational, rather than an inherent quality 'possessed' by music. On the other hand, conventional wisdom as expressed widely in both academic and lay discourses across the centuries and in many societies unquestioningly accords agency to music. Indeed, sound itself is often accorded elemental power and a number of creation stories invoke the power of sound, and particularly music (Sullivan 1997b:7). Where these two views intersect, one might suggest, if one cannot claim for music that it *possesses* power, that it possesses qualities which make it a particularly suitable channel for power. As noted above, the intensity and immediacy with which music evokes emotion and memory are no doubt important factors, but these in themselves depend on something else. Whether power is something that music is born with, achieves or has thrust upon it, the music-power relationship can only be understood in relation to a third, crucial, element: meaning. Much of the discussion in this volume revolves around questions of music's social meanings and how such meanings are shaped by – and in turn shape – power relations. But there is a paradox. Whilst writers such as Randall argue that power only accrues to music because of particular associative meanings, music's power arguably lies in its multiple layers of meaning and the often *ambiguous* nature of its messages, as well as its apparent ability to accrue meaning whilst simultaneously denying that it means anything other than itself.[22] This partly

---

[21] Somewhat tangentially, but also of interest, is Stokes' critique of orientalist musicology with specific reference to scholars of Middle Eastern musics (2002).

[22] There is of course an extensive musicological literature on questions of musical meaning, discussion of which lies outside the scope of this introduction. It should be stressed that the primary focus of the current discussion is on music's *social* meanings, for

explains why, although music is so thoroughly implicated in the exercise of power, we often fail to recognise its operations. As suggested above, music perhaps serves as the ultimate naturalising mechanism; and power is nowhere more insidious and pervasive than when it becomes accepted as 'the way things are'.[23] Whilst the naturalising tendencies of music may support a conservative agenda, its semantic fluidity also allows it to be used in ways which challenge the *status quo* and which are often hard to control. As Stokes observes, 'Whilst metaphors of power transfer easily into brick or stone ... sound is more difficult stuff to handle' (1994c:32). Not only does music's semantic ambiguity allow it to simultaneously convey different meanings, to the extent that 'texts and musical messages [can] themselves contain inner voices, contradicting or subverting the overt messages' (Stokes 1992:14), but such meanings often arise from, and come to represent, competing positions of power, particularly in relation to the control of social space. One sees this, for instance, in the various social meanings which became attached to Iranian popular music during the 1980s and early 1990s (see Nooshin 2005a and this volume) at a time when government discourses, which sought to represent this music as a form of Western cultural imperialism, competed with unofficial discourses, particularly among young people for whom the music had quite different meanings.

Like power, meaning is always relational. And as with spoken language, musical meaning operates through structural difference, often at the level of musical style, as discussed by Michael Frishkopf in relation to Egyptian *tilawa* (Qur'anic recitation). As Frishkopf argues, the connection between sound and meaning is often arbitrary; but meaning depends on *difference*. Similarly, Langlois explores the ways in which the social meanings of musical genres in North Africa are largely defined through practices of differentiation, specifically in relation to social categories. On the one hand, differentiation is essential for musical meaning; on the other, such differentiation is rarely neutral, particularly when binary concepts are involved. Difference inevitably invokes dichotomy; and dichotomy invokes hierarchy. As Solie observes in the introduction to *Musicology and Difference*, 'Politically, then, difference is about power' (1993:6), and Bohlman goes further, 'alterity was not just created but enforced through the exercise of power' (2002:35). Significantly, it was mainly through gender studies of music in the late 1980s and early 1990s (including publications such as Solie's) that ethnomusicologists, and indeed musicologists, first became attentive to the ideological implications of difference and 'otherness'.[24] That ethnomusicologists should have come to this

---

the understanding of which the work of Timothy Rice offers a particularly useful framework (see 2001). In the same volume, Clayton (2001) explores some of the connections between the physical and physiological powers of organised sound and questions of meaning.

[23]   For discussion of the ways in which naturalising mechanisms, most notably as found within semiotic systems of representation, can serve to obscure relationships of power, see the writings of Roland Barthes (particularly 1972).

[24]   The work of Koskoff (1987) was seminal in this; see also the chapter by Robertson (1987) in the same volume.

through gender rather than through 'race' or ethnicity is telling. Whilst it would seem obvious enough that 'ethnomusicology is founded on difference' (Agawu 2003:152), for many decades scholars depended on essentialised notions of difference which served to obscure their constructed nature. Agawu has written at length about the constructed nature of difference in ethnomusicology and how this relates to issues of power (2003).

Any discussion of musical meaning clearly needs to position the agent(s) responsible for the creation of meaning. In relation to this, Averill usefully maps Nattiez's tripartite model of 'poesis', 'trace' and 'aesthesis' onto (a) the processes of musical creation, (b) the musical product itself and (c) reception/consumption, and considers these in relation to questions of power (1997:2–3). The separation of 'composerly intention from readerly interpretation' (ibid.:2) allows for a more nuanced understanding of how meanings are created in specific historical, social and economic contexts and how they may compete with one another. A number of the chapters presented here engage directly with the 'creative space of interpretive difference' (ibid.:3) arising from the dialectic between production and consumption, a space into which power easily slides. Note that in this tripartite model, only stages (a) and (c) involve direct human agency.[25] A number of the chapters focus on these two stages as sites of 'meaning creation' and deal with the complex interplay and tensions between meanings created by different actors (musicians, audiences, governments and so on) for different purposes, ideological or otherwise. Laura Lohman, for example, explores the ways in which Umm Kulthūm struggled to contain the potential meanings of her fundraising concerts at home (in Egypt) and concert tours abroad in the aftermath of the June 1967 war with Israel, when such meanings continually threatened to escape her control. Similarly, Spinetti discusses how prominent Tajik musician Dawlatmand Kholov has sought to create new meanings for the (originally) rural music traditions of southern Tajikistan by deploying discourses of 'authenticity' and 'classicising' the music both as a means of raising the prestige of south Tajik music, and specifically to challenge the historical authority of the northern *Shashmaqom* art music, strongly promoted during the period of Soviet rule as a 'national' music. Kholov thus invokes existing discourses and attendant power structures to accord to southern Tajik music the kind of cultural capital traditionally associated with that of the north. One can see, therefore, how musical sounds and styles (the music 'itself') come to embody or represent power relations – something which also features in the chapters on Egyptian *tilawa* and Iranian pop music – or even prefigure power relations yet to unfold.[26]

---

[25]   I use the term 'stage' as a convenience; in fact, the model implies a circular rather than linear trajectory.

[26]   In the words of Hebdige, 'The struggle between different discourses, different definitions and meanings within ideology is therefore always, at the same time, a struggle within signification: a struggle for possession of the sign which extends to even the most mundane areas of everyday life' (1979:17).

Whilst the tripartite model is useful in shifting the focus away from dominant musicological discourses which privilege stages (a) and (b) in the creation of meaning, there are some obvious lacunae. Where, for instance, would one position the state apparatus involved in shaping the social meanings of a particular music style? Such an apparatus may not necessarily be directly involved either in producing the music itself or consuming it; yet state policies and discourses often play a significant role in determining musical meanings. And how does the tripartite model account for the non-sounded meanings of music?

Axes of Difference: Gender, Religion, Nationhood

Difference is a central concept in this volume since much of the mapping of social power discussed lies along particular 'axes of difference', seen most obviously in a trinity of key, and often intersecting, areas: gender, religion and nationhood. Moreover, music provides an important means for the expression and negotiation of difference. Perhaps the most naturalised, and hence arguably the most powerful, of all social divisions is gender, which provides a particularly interesting area of focus because of the parallels with music mentioned above and the fact that both music and gender are heavily freighted ideologically in the Middle East. It is perhaps not surprising, then, that gender has emerged, somewhat unintentionally, as a sub-theme in the book. Where issues of power are invoked, it seems, gender relations are almost always implicated in some way, and this can be seen in many of the chapters presented here. Whether as a central focus of the chapter (DeBano and Shelemay on Iranian and Jewish musics respectively), one theme among several (Harris, Davis, Langlois) or more tangentially (Stokes, Lohman), gender clearly represents a highly significant site of power in the region. DeBano's discussion of the state-sponsored Jasmine Festival, a festival of women's music, clearly illustrates the ways in which gender intersects with the other main axes of difference, since the festival promotes a particular vision of the relationship between gender, religion and nationhood using the central figure of Fatemeh (daughter of the Prophet Mohammad and wife of the first *Shi'eh* Imam, Ali) to project an idealised image of womanhood and to reinforce gender norms and expectations within a religious-nationalist framework. In this context, Fatemeh iconically comes to embody the three central discourses of power in the region and serves as a 'gendered symbol of nation'.

Religion is another important locus of power where practices and discourses often depend on notions of difference, for example the relationship between sacred and secular (often mapped directly onto the tradition–modernity dualism) or differing interpretations or branches of Islam or Judaism (Frishkopf), as well as the relationship between 'centres' of religious power and the more peripheral and heterodox practices, including the Sufi and Maraboutic rituals discussed by Harris and Langlois respectively, and domestic religious rituals, particularly those pertaining to life-cycle celebrations as discussed by Shelemay for the Syrian

Jewish tradition. The prominent presence of women in the peripheral and the heterodox is noteworthy.

The themes of nationhood and broader issues of identity and belonging are central to several chapters. Such concepts are, of course, heavily reliant on discourses of difference and, as an important boundary marker and an emotive signifier of 'place', music regularly provides an arena for negotiating and playing out local, national, regional and even global identities. Considering the national, the chapters by Lohman and Stokes both document the role of music (and in the latter, film) in unifying the Egyptian nation. In the case of Umm Kulthūm, her music and persona served both to bring together a nation suffering the trauma of the 1967 defeat and to re-establish Egypt's pride and regional prestige. But Lohman also takes us beyond the national to consider Umm Kulthūm's music in the context of the larger Arab 'nation' which her concert tours allowed her to speak to, providing a 'performance of Arab unity'. Whilst Stokes focuses on mediating technologies, particularly the microphone, there are many parallels in his discussion of how such technologies were used both to unify the Egyptian nation and to promote a broader sense of Arab unity, but always emphasising the long-standing centrality of Egyptian culture within that. The tension between concepts of Arab unity on the one hand and national/local identities on the other is central to Frishkopf's discussion of recent challenges to Egyptian centrality with the increasing prominence in Egypt of Saudi-inflected Islamic practices and *tilawa* styles (as well as an orientation towards Saudi modes of public morality), in contrast with traditional Egyptian Sufi-inflected Islam. Here, contestation between national identities (Egyptian vs Saudi) and local interpretations of Islam (*Salafi* vs Sufi) are symbolically acted out through attempts to dominate public space through sound.

As Bohlman observes, music often acquires heightened power at moments of encounter (2002:14), both as a means of preserving existing boundaries and in the creation of new identities. In this context, changing discourses of national identity impact directly on music, for instance in determining which musical styles become claimed as the national patrimony and legitimised as symbols of nation; in this context, the need of newly independent nations to identify particular musical genres as 'national' is interesting. The question of what represents the nation engages so directly with issues of power that it often constitutes a site of, sometimes very intense, public contestation. Davis, for example, discusses changing discourses of nationalism in Tunisia from the 1930s to the present day. For many decades, the promotion of a nationalist agenda by the government served to elevate the art music of the *ma'lūf* to the status of a 'national' music, particularly through the work of the Rashidiyya Institute, and in contrast to more heterogeneous popular styles, including the *ughniyya* which was closely associated with Jewish musicians. Much of the discussion at this time revolved around notions of Tunisian vs non-Tunisian and many popular musicians were denigrated by the establishment for abandoning their 'own' music and adopting Egyptian and other musical styles. The fact that the *ma'lūf* also drew on Egyptian musical elements and used Egyptian and

European instruments did not prevent it from being presented as wholly Tunisian, in contrast to 'foreign' and 'corrupt' popular styles. Since the 1987 coup, the advent of more inclusive notions of Tunisian identity has prompted a return to and renewed interest in previously marginalised traditions such as the *ughniyya* which have gained more centrality within the national imaginary. Similarly, as Langlois discusses for Morocco, the art music *andalus* repertoire is widely accepted as a 'national treasure', partly because of its strong class associations and in spite of its minority listenership.

Clearly, notions of nationhood are forged in the context of a dialectic which is simultaneously inward-looking and outward-facing: a nation defines itself in terms of what it includes and what it excludes. This self–other dynamic looms large in several chapters, particularly in relation to the neo-/post-colonial encounter. Certainly, for many of the countries discussed here, discourses of nationhood have been strongly shaped by the experience of post-colonial nation building and the imperative to develop post-colonial national identities. The question of how nations deal with the colonial inheritance is not straightforward and one often finds an ambiguous, even conflicted, relationship with that inheritance, particularly since many of the cultural consequences of the colonial encounter remain deeply embedded locally. In Iran, for instance, discourses of national identity since the 1979 revolution have been shaped both by Islamic (*Shi'eh*) nationalism and by the strong historical consciousness of the pre-Islamic heritage, as well Iran's long-standing quasi-colonial relationship with the West (primarily Britain and the United States). The reaction against that relationship after 1979 was symptomatic of a country seeking to separate itself and establish an identity independent of its former colonial power. Despite this, many of the discourses and patterns of musical prestige established before 1979 continue to hold. As I discuss in my chapter, many young Iranians are today forging new identities which are increasingly outward-looking and cosmopolitan, thereby subtly challenging official discourses of national identity; and music offers a public forum for such challenges quite unlike any other. Similarly, for Tajikistan, developing a post-Soviet, post-civil war national identity has meant addressing both the country's relationship with its former colonial power and the internal dynamics of ethnic division.

The inherent tensions between belonging and affinity on the one hand, and demarcating the national from what doesn't belong on the other are expressed time and time again through dualistic pairings such as local–global, tradition–modernity, 'pure'/'authentic'–hybrid, and so on. Like all dualisms, these 'create longs chains of associations, virtuosic in their ready applicability, that exercise a strong and virtually subliminal influence on the ways we position and interpret groups of people, their behaviour, and their works' (Solie 1993:11), and are always deeply rooted in relations of power. Nation state politics in the region have tended to privilege and even naturalise 'mono-culturalism', often masking earlier pluralities. Thus, one regularly finds the first of each pairing above (local, tradition, 'pure', 'authentic') invoked in the name of nationhood and placed in direct contrast to the second of each pair. As a result, musics which self-consciously index modernity, hybridity and globality have often proved problematic for governments. Ironically, increasing global interconnectedness and the emergence of new transnational cultures leads to more plural identities which are arguably rooted in much older forms of identification than contemporary nation state discourses would concede. Thus, for instance, the more inclusive notions of national identity in Tunisia since 1987, discussed by Davis, are reflected in the revival of previously denigrated musical styles which, she argues, are in fact more 'authentic' in their eclecticism. Spinetti reports on the efforts to find ways of dealing with plurality in post-Soviet, post-civil war Tajikistan, a region which had a long history of cultural and linguistic diversity prior to the Soviet creation of the Central Asian republics. In the case of Tajikistan, one can see clearly how music is at times mobilised in the service of marking difference, and at others to negotiate and perhaps erase (or at least reduce) difference, as in the current period of national reconciliation; such a possibility is also mooted by Baily for Afghanistan.

Other axes of social difference which figure in the discussion include class (Langlois, DeBano), racial or ethnic alterity (Spinetti, Harris, Langlois), and notions of space, both physical – as in the urban–rural divide (Langlois) and the relationship between private and public domains (Langlois, DeBano) so culturally and religiously significant in this region – and metaphorical, as in concepts of centre and periphery. Another significant axis concerns religious and/or state policies in relation to the boundaries between legal and illegal cultural activities. In the case of music, such controls are strongly informed by the ambiguity of religious doctrine in this area, with the result that local religious and/or state authorities often take on the role of deciding on the legality of particular musical activities, or prohibiting music altogether (see Baily).

So much for the intersection of power and social difference; what about power and *musical* difference? This touches on a number of well-used binaries, including the amateur–professional divide (Davis, DeBano), in which the former traditionally marked a higher social status, but this is starting to change; mediated versus unmediated musics (Stokes, Frishkopf); controlled versus 'uncontrolled' emotional expression (Stokes, Langlois); choice of lyrical language, particularly in relation to discourses of linguistic purity, for instance in the use of 'standard' versus colloquial Arabic (Davis, Langlois); as well as musical categorisations which often place art music on one side and other styles (folk, popular and so on) on the other. The question of categories is particularly pertinent to the earlier discussion of nationhood because of the ways in which certain styles and genres become promoted as emblems of nation, and a number of examples have already been cited. In Tajikistan, from the 1920s, and in order to promote social cohesion in the newly formed Soviet states, the central authorities created emblems of national musical heritage. In the case of Tajikistan this was the *Shashmaqom* (which was historically a repertoire shared with the Uzbek-speaking populations of the region prior to Sovietisation). Significantly, as in the case of Tunisia and Morocco, it was a form of art music which was promoted as a symbol of national culture.

Clearly, classifications of any kind embody relative value and the cultural weight accorded to 'classicism' by Soviet ideology and the Tunisian cultural elite illustrate the clear connections between the relative status of musical styles and cultural capital, prestige and power. In Tajikistan, it is interesting to note that such classificatory hierarchies have persisted in post-Soviet discourses deployed in the creation of a new national culture. Thus, rather than challenge discourses which present art music as being of greater 'value' than other genres, Dawlatmand Kholov engages the same discourses and attempts to raise the prestige of *falak* by presenting it as a form of art music. Harris describes a similar situation in the Xinjiang Uyghur Autonomous Region of China, where government policies led to the canonisation of the Twelve Muqam repertoire as the national 'folk classical' (*khaliq kilassik*) music of the Uyghur people, and which is now 'commonly held up as the jewel in the crown of Uyghur national culture' and as a 'symbol of a long and civilised Uyghur culture'.

The Chapters in this Volume

Each of the eleven chapters in this volume presents a case study around a particular musician, issue or tradition. The individual contributions represent a range of scholarly and methodological approaches from the strongly ethnographic and contemporary to the more historical. The book is arranged loosely according to geography, starting in the geographical centre of the region with a trio of chapters on Egypt, after which the focus shifts to Central Asia. From there, we travel to the western end of the region for two chapters on North Africa before ending with two chapters on Iran and one on Jewish music.

The first two chapters, by Laura Lohman and Martin Stokes, focus on two of the most popular singers of Egyptian music in the twentieth century, the great Umm Kulthūm (1904–75) and film star and crooner 'Abd al-Halim Hafiz (1929–77), whose lives both spanned the central section of the century. In '"The Artist of the People in the Battle": Umm Kulthūm's Concerts for Egypt in Political Context', Lohman discusses Umm Kulthūm's fundraising concert campaign following Egypt's defeat in the June 1967 Six Day War, examining the ways in which Umm Kulthūm was obliged to make 'fundamental decisions about how to present herself as she sought to engage in and unite artistic and political endeavours after the war', particularly as the concert tours extended from a domestic to an international arena. Lohman examines the complex relationship between Umm Kulthūm's artistic work and her political message, particularly given her grass-roots appeal and her high profile non-musical activist work. Central to this was Umm Kulthūm's often ambiguous presentation of self, which fed into the media portrayal of her. Whilst she often insisted that she was 'just an artist' and sought to downplay suggestions that her music invoked direct political messages, her later, more politicised, concerts in Libya tell a different story. As Lohman documents, Umm Kulthūm's fundraising concerts played a pivotal role in projecting an image of unified Arab support for Egypt to the rest of the world, as well as offering the Egyptian people a collective public outlet through which to ameliorate the psychological trauma of the war and its aftermath. In other words, music served as a space in which listeners could become personally and symbolically empowered, a theme which emerges again and again in different contexts in the chapters of this volume.

With Martin Stokes' chapter, ''Abd al-Halim's Microphone', we remain in mid-twentieth-century Egypt but turn to a very different musical style, as Stokes explores the intersection of public expressions of emotion, nostalgia, excess and sentimentalism – something far removed from the musical world of Umm Kulthūm – and the role of the microphone in this. Specifically, Stokes explores the ways in which newly-amplified voices from the 1950s onwards created a 'techno-political complex [which] possessed unprecedented powers to control the social and political imagination, powers that appealed to the heart and the ear in new ways'. Stokes marks a contrast with (earlier) singers such as Umm Kulthūm and Mohammed 'Abd al-Wahhab who were much less intimately associated with the microphone and with technology in general. With the advent of such technology, the network of discourse around music's power to move is rendered highly complex: music's power should be used judiciously by musicians; to use music's power over listeners in the manner of emotional sentimentality is to exert a control over the audience and to somehow take music beyond the realm of artistry and *tarab*, in its relatively egalitarian listener–musician relationship. The discussion of emotional expression has a strong gender dimension, as Stokes discusses, particularly the fact that 'Abd al-Halim's amplified voice generated anxieties of a gendered nature, of emotionality out of control and in contrast to the predominantly male-gendered and more private environment of the *tarab* setting. A central question was how to control music's power of excess, particularly when unleashed, via the microphone, to a vulnerable female audience. Stokes prompts a long-overdue re-evaluation of the role of technology in the public expression of emotion. Quoting from Paul Théberge, he notes that microphones and amplification have become so naturalised in our musical culture that we often fail to interrogate the socio-political impact of such technologies. Stokes explores the complex ambivalence over 'Abd al-Halim's music, his use of technology and his sentimentalism, and how all of this relates to questions of power in the public domain.

The question of mediation and technology is also central to Chapter 3, 'Mediated Qur'anic Recitation and the Contestation of Islam in Contemporary Egypt', in which Michael Frishkopf explores the ways in which musical styles acquire meaning through difference, focusing specifically on the recent rise of a new form of Saudi-inflected Islam in Egypt and how this has impacted on styles of *tilawa*. Traditionally, there were two main *tilawa* styles in Egypt, known as *mujawwad* and *murattal*, but since the recent arrival in Egypt of cassettes of Saudi *tilawa* and also the adoption of Saudi style chanting by local Imams, there has been a discernable shift in the musical 'style sign' of local *tilawa* chant in order to maintain the semiotic distinction between styles. Whilst such style shifts are ostensibly linked to aesthetic preferences, Frishkopf illustrates through detailed analysis how particular musical styles, and the differences between them, have become freighted with ideological associations, particularly through processes of mediation and dissemination. In this, he draws heavily on ideas from structural linguistics and semiotics, particularly the work of Saussure and Peirce. Such shifts are also seen in the graphics accompanying commercial recordings. Moreover, style changes are playing a central role in local contestation over the control of Egyptian public space between 'traditional' Sufi-inflected Islam on the one hand and Saudi-style *Salafi* or New Islam, on the other, such that 'The individual decision to play a particular cassette tape in a public place, or to distribute copies, thus constitutes a social act of communication', often an ideological one promoting a particular view. As Frishkopf argues, the fact that music operates non-discursively renders it potentially more powerful a medium than the discursive, for conveying, promoting and negotiating changes in ideology. Music's non-discursiveness allows it to operate at a partially subliminal level and to present itself as part of the naturalised order of things, 'to fly "beneath the radar" of critical thinking', in the words of Frishkopf, and to contest without appearing to do so.

With Chapter 4, we travel to Central Asia for the first of three chapters on countries where musical practices and meanings have been significantly impacted by communist ideologies. In 'Music, Politics and Nation Building in Post-Soviet Tajikistan', Federico Spinetti explores the issues and debates surrounding the cultural representation of the Tajik nation, focusing on how official state policies have sought to define 'national' culture in an ethnically diverse country, from the early Soviet period through the political vacuum which followed the demise of the Soviet Union and the subsequent civil war (1991–97), and into the current period of national reconciliation. The ethnic tensions which led to the civil war were partly the result of earlier Soviet policies which had privileged certain ethnic-linguistic groups, primarily in the north of the country. In terms of cultural policy, this included promoting the repertoire of the *Shashmaqom* art music, closely associated with northern Tajik and Uzbek culture, to the status of a national music. Following the end of the civil war, there have been attempts to rebalance the hierarchies of power established during the Soviet period and to promote southern Tajik culture, including its music. Exploring the close connection between music and identity construction, Spinetti discusses the work of Dawlatmand Kholov, one of the best known musicians in Tajikistan, who has devoted himself to raising the prestige of southern Tajik music, partly by questioning the legitimacy of the *Shashmaqom*, to the extent of suggesting that it isn't really Tajik at all, but Uzbek, and by 'classicising' southern Tajik music styles. Spinetti thus shows how attempts to formulate a national music culture often involve intense contestation over which musics to include (and which to exclude), as well as the relative prestige of each. In the case of Tajikistan, such contestation revolves around discursive binaries of geography (north–south), cultural identity (Uzbek–Tajik) and musical style (classical–folk, 'learned'–popular).

Moving to neighbouring Afghanistan, John Baily's chapter also deals with an ethnically diverse country which experienced many years of communist rule and civil war, but where conflict was rooted primarily in differences of ideology and religion rather than in regional and ethnic allegiances. Starting in the 1970s, Baily charts the attempts by successive regimes to control musicians and music-making through various forms of censorship and prohibition, from the Daud Presidency (1973–78), the period of communist rule (1978–92) and the coalition period (1992–96) through to the Taliban (1996–2001) and post-Taliban periods. Islamic proscriptions on music-making have had a significant impact, seen in its most extreme form in the attempt by the Taliban to ban music entirely. Baily considers the doctrinal basis for such proscriptions, particularly as found in the Qur'an and the *hadith*. As Baily observes, 'Islamic cultures which are tolerant towards music are likely to be liberal in other respects … music is a sensitive indicator of a whole set of other values and attitudes'. In the immediate post-Taliban period, the presence of music came to symbolise the end of Taliban rule, but restrictions on music were quickly reinstated, partly because of the strength of traditional social mores and also because of the fragmented nature of governance where decisions made by one official body were often overruled by another. Baily cites the example of the state radio and television organisation which broadcast historical footage of two female singers on television, but which was subsequently condemned by Afghanistan's Supreme Court. As in other parts of the region, music in Afghanistan has become a medium for exercising social and political control, particularly in relation to gender behaviour. Such control is in part a response to, and an acknowledgement of, music's power. In the words of Baily, 'One ponders the mystery of what it is about music that makes it so powerful, and how that power might be harnessed for performances of reconciliation instead of conflict.'

In the third Central Asian chapter, 'National Traditions and Illegal Religious Activities amongst the Uyghurs', Rachel Harris discusses the intersection of political, spiritual and musical power among the Uyghur people of western China, focusing on a range of popular Islamic religious practices including shrine festivals, *sama* rituals held both at festivals and in (male) Sufi lodges, and the often very private gatherings of female *büwi* ritualists. Such heterodox practices occupy an ambiguous space, caught between government recognition of Islam as one of China's five 'systematised religions' on the one hand, and attempts to control 'illegal' religious activities on the other. The various practices described by Harris have generally been regarded with suspicion by local and central government, both because of their perceived 'disorderly' and 'backward' nature and, more recently, because of government concerns over potential links between such expressions of local identity and demands for Uyghur separatism, as well as the rise of Saudi-style Wahhabi fundamentalism in the region. The latter concern is somewhat ironic given the opposition of Wahhabism itself to Sufism and other heterodox practices. In fact, Sufi practices have faced opposition on two fronts: from the communist ideology of the government and also more locally from Uyghur nationalist intellectuals.

As well as addressing the tension between local religious power and central political power, the chapter also deals with questions of difference along a number of axes, including between local Uyghur 'ethnic' identity and the central Chinese state, between orthodox and heterodox Islamic practices, and (within the latter) between the relatively influential male Sufi lodges and the female *büwi* ritualists. The *büwi* find themselves doubly marginalised: first, on account of their exclusion from traditional male religious power structures, and second because their activities are regarded as lying somewhere between the categories of (illegal) 'feudal superstition' and the less problematic 'folk customs'. Harris' discussion pinpoints an interesting problematic: the relationship between local religious practices and the central communist state in a country where the sacred and secular are traditionally inseparable. And since music serves as a potent link between sacred and secular, it is perhaps not surprising that this problematic has been played out through the 'classical' repertoire of the Twelve Muqam, promoted by the Chinese authorities as a symbol of Uyghur culture, but which is also the repertoire of local Sufi music. As Harris documents, the process of creating a 'national' music out of the Twelve Muqam involved modifying certain aspects of it, particularly the poetry, in order to reduce the influence of religious elements.

With Chapters 7 and 8 we return to North Africa. In 'Jews, Women and the Power to be Heard: Charting the Early Tunisian *Ughniyya* to the Present Day', Ruth Davis traces changes in the social status of the Tunisian *ughniyya* in the context of changing discourses of nationalism. As discussed earlier, from the 1930s, in an attempt to forge a national music culture in the context of a strongly nationalist ideology, the art music repertoire of the *ma'lūf* was promoted, particularly by the newly-established Rashidiyya Institute, whilst popular musical styles such as the *ughniyya*, in which Jewish and female performers played a prominent role, were denigrated and marginalised. After independence in 1956, the *ma'lūf* officially gained the status of a national music and became an emblem of Tunisian musical identity. As Davis discusses, post-independence discourses presented the 1920s and '30s as a period of decline and decadence. However, the situation has changed significantly since 1987 as the emergence of more inclusive notions of Tunisian identity has been accompanied by a renewed interest in and revival of older musical styles whose eclecticism (in musical style, lyrical language and instruments), Davis argues, is in fact highly 'traditional', in contrast to the claims of 'purist' discourses. Davis discusses the work of El 'Azifet, an all-female amateur ensemble formed in 1992 by Amina Srarfi, which has played a leading role in the post-1987 revival of popular musical styles from the 1920s and '30s, but which also includes in its diverse repertoire music from the *ma'lūf*, now presented on the same stage as *ughniyya* and on an equal basis. Through their high-profile public performances, El 'Azifet position previously marginalised musical genres and performers (women) at the centre of Tunisian cultural space.

In Chapter 8, Tony Langlois explores the connection between musical genre, social position and expressive behaviour in Morocco, Algeria and Tunisia, focusing on three musical genres: the high art *andalus* repertoire found across North Africa, *g'nâwa* maraboutic rituals from Morocco, and Algerian *raï*. Langlois discusses the ways in which these genres map onto the fairly rigid social boundaries of gender, 'race' and class in the region. The high prestige *andalus* art music has traditionally been associated with the urban elite and benefited from state support in all three countries. In Morocco, *andalus* is presented as an inclusive symbol of national identity and many acknowledge it to be a 'national treasure', yet its strong class associations and popular perceptions of it as dull and antiquated mean that the music has a limited audience in comparison with more eclectic (and arguably socially inclusive) popular styles such as *raï*. Like other non-commercial art music genres, *andalus* has depended heavily on state support and in Algeria the questioning of *andalus*'s privileged status following the Islamic political 'turn' of the early 1990s led to a severe reduction in state funding and a decline in activity. Moving on to issues of gender and 'race', Langlois reports on his observations of *g'nâwa* rituals in Oujda, Morocco, arguing that such rituals serve to essentialise both physical and emotional difference and to reinforce racial and gender stereotypes, thereby perpetuating the marginalisation of the (generally low status) women who participate in them and the 'black' *g'nâwa* musicians who provide the music. Langlois contrasts the 'uncontrolled' physical and emotional expression in *g'nâwa* gatherings with the very controlled behavioural norms found at *andalus* performances. The third case example, *raï*, presents another traditionally marginalised genre with strong local associations, which in entering the 'world music' market has shed its peripherality, at least outside Algeria. Layered onto its earlier 'immoral' associations, the new associations of modernity, plurality and hybridity have continued to render *raï* problematic in the eyes of political Islam at home, provoking at times violent reactions. But with *raï*'s increasing popularity abroad, government attempts to control the music, and even prohibit it, during the 1990s proved unsuccessful. In contrast to *g'nâwa* and *andalus*, then, *raï* has managed to evade categorisation – and thereby control – which links it strongly to particular social groups. Langlois also considers the political implications of technological developments, particularly sound recording, which have enabled genres such as *raï* to transcend the traditionally strong boundaries separating public and private spheres and to enter spaces from which they would traditionally have been absent.

Chapters 9 and 10 focus on Iran. In 'Singing against Silence: Celebrating Women and Music at the Fourth Jasmine Festival', Wendy DeBano explores various aspects of women's musical performance in Iran, focusing on the annual Jasmine Festival and drawing on ethnographic work undertaken during the 2002 festival. A state-sponsored women-only event which began in 1999 and which is held annually on the birthday of Hazrat Fatemeh, the Jasmine Festival provides an interesting prism through which to explore issues of gender and music in Iran. The chapter begins by discussing the changing social position of both women and music since the 1979 Revolution, and the ways in which both have in various ways been 'peripherised' by official discourses. One of the central paradoxes of the post-1979 period is that despite attempts to restrict women's activities by certain government factions, women have become more socially active than ever. DeBano discusses various aspects of the Jasmine Festival, including the process by which musicians are invited to participate and how those selected have to tailor their image to meet the requirements of the Ministry of Culture and Islamic Guidance, as well as how the different 'actors' (musicians, organisers, audiences and so on) use the festival for their own purposes. As an all-female event, one of the most heated areas of debate centres on whether the festival represents a form of imposed gender segregation or a means of female empowerment. DeBano explores a range of views, from those who choose not to participate, either because of segregation or because the festival is sponsored by the state, to those who welcome the all-female nature of the festival and the opportunity to perform in a high-profile venue. As DeBano shows, the festival represents a site of intense struggle between the organisers and their attempts to reinforce state-defined gender norms and the musicians who seek to maintain control over their self-representation and to make their voices heard.

Staying in post-1997 Iran, my chapter focuses on the pop band Arian and specifically the ways in which the band's musical and lyrical discourses have been shaped by, and resonate with, the ideas of President Khatami's reform period (1997–2005). Emerging as a grassroots band on the wave of post-1997 liberalism, Arian has achieved phenomenal success in part because of its down-to-earth image and because its music touches on a wide range of contemporary issues with which many Iranians identify. I start by assessing the political and socio-cultural environment of the late 1990s, particularly the emergent youth culture and the growing civil society infrastructure in Iran. Among the reforms which impacted most directly on music, the legalisation of pop music after almost 20 years of prohibition was perhaps the most far-reaching, and in particular the shift from periphery to centre which transformed pop music from a symbol of Western cultural imperialism to an icon of post-1997 changes. Moving on to discuss Arian, I explore some of the reasons for the band's immense popularity, and how its music reflects some of the same concerns as the reform movement, including 'building a diverse civil space, responding to a growing youth culture and rethinking notions of national belonging in an increasingly global environment', seen for instance in the band's collective working methods, its musical eclecticism and the involvement of women musicians. The final section of the chapter focuses on two songs, '*Iran*' and '*Fardā*' ('Tomorrow') to illustrate some of the ways in which Arian explores, and at times subtly contests, a range of dominant discourses using the centuries-old technique of veiled comment. In the case of '*Iran*', the melding of a cosmopolitan consciousness with a strong sense of the local becomes a platform for presenting alternative visions of nationhood; '*Fardā*' offers a statement of youth enfranchisement. In this way, music facilities the expression of ideas which are still formulating in the public consciousness, or which can't be expressed elsewhere.

In the final chapter, 'The Power of Silent Voices: Women in the Syrian Jewish Musical Tradition', Kay Kaufman Shelemay discusses the hidden but often crucial role of women in traditions from which they are ostensibly absent, focusing on the case of the paraliturgical Jewish-Syrian *pizmon*, sung in Syrian Jewish communities worldwide. As Shelemay argues, the traditional ethnomusicological focus on performance events, often in the public domain, has tended to reinforce male-centric perspectives on music-making, obscuring the myriad ways in which, whilst they may be silent as performers, women participate 'behind the scenes' as teachers and transmitters of traditions; as organisers of life-cycle rituals and domestic events through which traditions are perpetuated, including the preparation of food without which such events could not happen; as repositories of musical memory and of oral histories of music; and so on. Through analysis of song texts and interviews with Syrian Jewish women, Shelemay uncovers the extent of women's 'muted presence' in the *pizmon* tradition, a repertoire strongly associated with men and performed for instance at circumcision ceremonies. The three *pizmon* texts which Shelemay discusses include both overt and more hidden references to women, generally in the context of their roles as wives and mothers and reaffirming existing gender behavioural norms. Shelemay considers the impact of religious ideology on women's music-making, particularly through the dictate known as *kol isha* which defines the female voice as sexually arousing and a distraction to men, and through traditional concepts of female modesty (*tsniut*). Whilst the impact of cultural and religious expectations are variously implemented within different communities, in general women's musical participation has been limited, particularly in the public domain. However, as Shelemay points out, women's absence from active participation does not necessarily mean that they are not involved in other ways. In the case of *pizmon*, Shelemay found many of her interviewees had a good knowledge of the songs, both from having accompanied their fathers to synagogue as young girls (prior to puberty) and because the melodies are largely derived from Arabic secular song, representing a centuries-long shared Judeo-Arabic tradition with which many women are familiar from their secular listening experiences. Elsewhere in this introduction, I have noted the close connection between music, memory and power; Shelemay highlights the important role which women play as repositories of musical memory, both of repertoire and of the stories which comprise the lifeblood of music's oral history. As noted, the scholarly focus on music in performance has tended to sideline the importance of understanding music as it lives in the memory and imagination.

An important issue raised by Shelemay concerns the position of the scholar *vis-à-vis* apparent asymmetries of power in the societies and musical traditions studied, in this case asymmetries of gender power. As Shelemay observes, it is all too easy for scholars to apply binary concepts of domination–submission or compliance–resistance, often using a Western liberalist yardstick. But is the 'unmasking' of what appear to be naturalised inequalities a scholarly conceit? Whilst Shelemay cites her own discomfort and that of other scholars with certain power structures within the Jewish tradition, she also recognises that the lived realities of her informants often transcend such binaries; for most, the acceptance of male and female domains as different but complementary is deep-rooted.

Notwithstanding the position of some Jewish feminists who have argued for change, few within the tradition studied by Shelemay have sought to challenge gender positioning. Above all, Shelemay enjoins us to question the assumption that active participation indexes power, and conversely that silence equates with exclusion and oppression, and to acknowledge the power of silence and quietness. As she observes, 'In some *public* contexts, the *absence* of musical activity appears to mark a woman's special power'; for other women, the choice of silence is a means of exercising power.

Silence, Voice and Agency

I'd like to draw this introduction to a close by pursuing a little further some of the issues raised concerning agency. As the chapters of this book testify, music is quixotic in its ability to serve both dominant power positions and ideologies and at the same time give voice to those disempowered by them. In the latter case, music's very presence can become a signifier of agency, something encountered repeatedly in the pages of this volume, whether in post-Taliban Afghanistan (Baily), in the 'resistance' songs of El 'Azifet (Davis), the performances of women musicians in Iran (DeBano), or the expressive outlet which *g'nâwa* rituals offer women in rural Morocco (Langlois). We know that music gives voice when nothing else can. Given that music's presence is so often taken to be an indicator of agency, it seems hardly surprising that its absence often comes to indicate the reverse. Many of the chapters presented here chart attempts by political, religious and other authorities to manipulate, control and even silence music. Indeed, perhaps the strongest statement and acknowledgement of music's power is that it invokes such intense reactions. And yet, whilst the ultimate curb on music's power is to silence it, such silences are rarely absolute. Significantly, in a volume about music, power and ideology, silence is a theme that emerges again and again and also appears (or is implied) in a number of chapter titles, particularly in relation to gender. Given that the semantic domain of music within which ethnomusicologists usually operate extends well beyond sound, the relationship between music and 'silence' is complex. Silence is not music's opposite, nor its absence; indeed, we know that silence is part of the very fabric of music. In a lecture series entitled *The Silence of Music* (2007), Bohlman points to the ways in which we experience 'musical meaning beyond sound' and how 'silence itself allows for a proliferation of meaning'. Considering the aesthetic dimensions of silence, Bohlman argues that making silence can be as much an act and a statement of agency as making music. Such ideas resonate strongly with the work of anthropologist Michael Herzfeld, who has written about (linguistic) silence as an active strategy rather than a passive imposition among women in rural Crete. Through what Herzfeld terms the 'poetics of silence', women claim agency by using silence discursively. Thus, 'Domestic behaviour can invert public appearances' (1991:90) and 'What appears to the outside's eye as an uncritical acceptance of hegemony becomes, from an internal perspective, the expression of defiance' (93). Like Shelemay, then, Herzfeld challenges the assumption that silence equals disempowerment, an assumption which he suggests can be attributed to the fact that 'Absences are harder to interpret than presences' (1991:81). Herzfeld describes the 'muted' ideologies (83) of female discourses, using terminology derived from Ardener (1975) and strongly recalling the 'muted presence' of the women described by Shelemay in a musical tradition which appears to exclude the female voice (both metaphorically and physically), but which turns out on closer inspection to be saturated by the presence of women. The fact that such presences have previously remained largely unremarked upon is significant and should alert us to the need to look beyond the well-worn binaries of domination and resistance, victimiser and victimised, voice and silence, which are simply too unwieldy to engage with the complexity of lived musical experiences where sound and silence co-exist and intertwine with one another. As Herzfeld observes, 'Absence and presence represent two kinds of power that cannot exist independently of each other, but of which, in a verbocentric world where all is presence, absence takes on the outwardly lower symbolic value' (1991:84–5). Like music, 'Silence both expresses and represses' (92), and as with music we need to understand what silence means in specific contexts. In the performance-centric world of ethnomusicology, silence as a discursive strategy and as a form of power has all but been ignored.

In conclusion, it is my hope that the case studies presented here will contribute to a greater understanding of the complex play of music in power and power in music in the Middle East, North Africa and Central Asia; and ultimately, to an understanding of what it is about music that enables it to permeate every area of human life, weaving together the social, political and aesthetic in ways which are at times overt, at others so subtle that nothing can match its power.

Chapter 1

'The Artist of the People in the Battle': Umm Kulthūm's Concerts for Egypt in Political Context

Laura Lohman

Introduction

Following Egypt's rapid defeat by Israel in the war of June 1967, the veteran Egyptian singer Umm Kulthūm launched an unprecedented fundraising campaign that contributed the equivalent of $2 million to the rebuilding of the armed forces and countered the psychological damage inflicted by the war.[1] Starting with fundraising activities and concerts in Egypt, Umm Kulthūm quickly took her concert campaign abroad. Because of Egypt's earlier attainment of a dominant regional position in the recording, radio and film industries and the wide distribution of Egyptian cultural products throughout the Middle East and North Africa, she had acquired a huge following outside Egypt and was, as a result, able to offer a series of highly successful international concerts that generated additional funds for the war effort.

Umm Kulthūm had long supported the Egyptian government following the 1952 revolution. She had recorded a series of patriotic anthems commemorating political and military events, one of which was adopted as the national anthem. Her concerts on the anniversaries of the revolution were attended by leading figures

---

[1]   Born in a small Egyptian village in 1904, Umm Kulthūm established herself as a singer in Cairo in the 1920s. Through recordings, radio and film, she became extremely popular in the 1930s and 1940s. Distinguished by her improvisatory skills and vocal stamina, she sustained her career and her popularity through the 1950s and 1960s despite the challenges presented by younger singers and listeners. See Danielson (1997). Like most Egyptians, the sexagenarian singer initially responded with shock to the 1967 war that had been set into motion in May by Soviet reports of an imminent Israeli attack on Syria. These reports prompted a fateful series of decisions by the President and military leadership of Egypt: positioning the army in Sinai, evacuating the United Nations Emergency Forces from their peace-keeping positions along the Egypt–Israeli border and blockading the Tiran Straits to Israeli shipping. The war began on the morning of 5 June as the Israeli air force wiped out its Egyptian counterpart in just three hours. By 11 June, Israel had defeated the Egyptian, Jordanian and Syrian forces and captured the Sinai peninsula, the Gaza strip, the West Bank and the Golan Heights. See Oren (2002) and Danielson (1997:184–6).

in the government. Nevertheless, her post-war campaign was unprecedented in both substance and scope. After her first fundraising concerts in Egypt, many organisations and prominent individuals outside Egypt invited her to sing abroad. In turn, the Egyptian government recognised and aided her efforts by conferring upon her a state award and giving her a diplomatic passport. 'The Artist of the People in the Battle', as she was soon dubbed, was forced to make fundamental decisions about how to present herself as she sought to engage in and unite artistic and political endeavours after the war. By tracing changes in Umm Kulthūm's public presentation of self and the Egyptian mass media's portrayal of her campaign through its domestic and international phases, this chapter explains why her campaign was so effective as a response to the war. It demonstrates precisely how Umm Kulthūm and the Egyptian media offered an empowering mechanism for individual Egyptians to respond to the psychological impact of the defeat both by creating opportunities for active involvement and by presenting a vital picture of broad, unified Arab support for Egypt. It explains why her campaign was so sustainable emotionally and financially, both as an international undertaking and in relation to the agendas of the Egyptian regime.

Initial Responses

Umm Kulthūm's public responses to the outcome of the war during June and July 1967 and their portrayal by the Egyptian media provided a rich context that shaped the efficacy and meaning of the fundraising concerts that began in August. Her initial public responses quickly distinguished her from other artists. One of her most lauded acts was the donation of £20,000 obtained from Kuwait in exchange for her performances and recordings.[2] In the midst of widespread discussion of the need to obtain hard foreign currency to replace lost canal and tourism revenues, this large and prompt donation, made just over a week after the shocking revelations of the war, distinguished Umm Kulthūm from other celebrities and prompted journalists to place her at the top of the 'honour roll' of stars who had made and collected donations for the war effort.[3] The 'impressive and unrivalled example' set by Umm Kulthūm left other artists open to chastisement by the press for their meagre donations of £E20 (equivalent to $46)[4] and the intensity and diversity of her continued activities further distinguished her from other celebrity artists.

---

[2]   'Umm Kulthūm Presented a Check for 20 Thousand Pounds Sterling', *al-Ahrām*, 20 June 1967:8; 'Word of Truth: Where Are 'Abd al-Wahhāb and Farīd al-Atrash?', *al-Kawākib*, 27 June 1967:12–13. In this chapter, '£' indicates pounds Sterling, whilst '£E' indicates Egyptian pounds.

[3]   Fawmīl Labīb, 'City Lights for the Sake of the Refugees and Victims', *al-Kawākib*, 25 July 1967:10–11.

[4]   Ṣāliḥ Jawdat, 'Three Stories', *al-Kawākib*, 27 June 1967:8; Muḥammad Jalāl, 'Question Mark', *al-Idhā'ah wa al-Tilīfizyūn*, 1 July 1967:24.

Journalists described the severe disruption of her notoriously regular schedule, calling her a 'dynamo' and likening her to 'a train running on more than one track'.[5] In July, she not only worked on new patriotic repertoire but also devoted herself to numerous non-musical projects.

Two of Umm Kulthūm's non-musical efforts during this month were particularly important for contextualising her subsequent fundraising concerts. Firstly, she broadcast public appeals using propagandist slogans. By early August, listeners accustomed to hearing one of her songs on the daily radio programme *With Umm Kulthūm* would instead hear her say, 'In America they say "Pay a dollar and we kill an Arab for you." We say, "Pay a piaster and we defend an Arab for you. For we are not bloodshedders, but we protect freedom and peace".'[6] Her messages reached an even wider audience as newspapers and magazines reproduced these slogans.[7] These messages distinguished Umm Kulthūm from her colleagues and, like her earlier donation of £20,000, were historically unprecedented. Whilst singers had long produced nationalistic songs as a means of rousing and channelling patriotic sentiment, none had ever stepped so far beyond the bounds of art to make verbal appeals in order to accomplish these goals. Particularly as described in the press, her decisions and initiative in broadcasting these appeals conveyed a sense of sincere personal commitment to the war effort.

Second, Umm Kulthūm utilised the existing infrastructure of women's organisations to mobilise public activism, focused on a small number of key issues. In early July, she convened a National Assembly of Egyptian Women (NAEW) comprised of representatives from numerous women's organisations and which, at its first meeting, identified four crucial agendas for responding to the war: thrift, hospital work, communication and the collection of donations.[8] During the remainder of July, she contributed conspicuously to the latter two by presenting donations collected by the NAEW and participating in its international

---

[5]　'Umm Kulthūm Travels to Saudi Arabia and Kuwait to Collect Donations', *al-Akhbār*, 22 July 1967 (*al-Ahrām* clippings file 'Umm Kulthūm'); Muḥammad Sa'd, 'Umm Kulthūm Says', *al-Idhā'ah wa al-Tilīfizyūn*, 29 July 1967:16–17. This chapter draws on evidence from a variety of periodicals published in Egypt and the Arab world. The leading daily Egyptian newspapers *al-Ahrām* and *al-Akhbār* each had a circulation of several hundred thousand, while that of the daily Egyptian newspaper *al-Jumhūriyyah* and the weekly magazines *al-Muṣawwar* and *Ākhir Sā'ah* were between 50,000 and 100,000. The weekly Egyptian magazines *al-Kawākib* and *al-Idhā'ah wa al-Tilīfizyūn*, as well as the Jordanian, Tunisian, Lebanese and Moroccan newspapers cited below, had smaller circulations in the tens of thousands.

[6]　Sakīnah al-Sādāt, 'Umm Kulthūm Calls All the Arab Citizens', *al-Muṣawwar*, 4 August 1967:34.

[7]　'Umm Kulthūm Travels to Saudi Arabia'.

[8]　Nuwāl al-Bīlī, 'What Did Umm Kulthūm Say in the National Assembly of Egyptian Women?', *Ākhir Sā'ah* 19 July 1967:26–7.

mailing campaign.[9] Her efforts on both fronts appeared to culminate less than one week before she was scheduled to give her first fundraising concert.[10] Under a headline announcing her collection of a second 16kg in donations of gold, the most widely circulated Egyptian newspaper detailed the NAEW's current propaganda project and her participation in it. Reproducing English and Arabic versions of a letter espousing the Arab perspective on Palestine, the article encouraged readers to request copies to distribute internationally in a massive mailing campaign and specifically cited the example set through Umm Kulthūm's production of 2,000 copies.[11] Previously criticised for distracting people from active involvement in current issues, Umm Kulthūm's convening of the NAEW created a means by which citizens could co-ordinate their efforts and address pressing economic, social and political needs (Danielson 1997:185).

Concerts in the Governorates

Two months after the conclusion of the war, Umm Kulthūm's fundraising concerts were set to begin in Egypt. In August 1967, she performed in the *marākiz* (administrative centres) of two governorates: Damanhūr and Alexandria. After beginning the international phase of her concert campaign in November, she continued the series of governorate concerts in al-Mansūrah in early February 1968. In each case, ticket proceeds were designated for the war effort. As Umm Kulthūm also constructed the concerts as occasions for the contribution of additional donations, both adults and children donated money, jewellery and gold, ranging from small trinkets to gold ingots. At the same time that these concerts raised funds for the war effort, they also constituted an empowering mechanism for popular responses to the war. The rapid defeat that followed misleading public assurances of military strength and readiness had precipitated a deep and widespread psychological crisis.[12] The concerts provided a cathartic outlet for public expression, and in particular the most basic and widely shared feeling: a desire to sustain the war. Through the concerts Umm Kulthūm enabled individuals to take action and to make a tangible contribution to their country as a therapeutic mode of responding to the psychological crisis generated by the defeat.

---

[9]   'Umm Kulthūm Travels to Saudi Arabia'.

[10]   Her Damanhūr concert was originally scheduled for 10 August but was postponed due to health reasons. 'Umm Kulthūm Postpones Concert to August 17', *al-Akhbār*, 9 August 1967:1.

[11]   Kamāl al-Malākh, 'For the Second Time Umm Kulthūm Presents 16kg of Gold', *al-Ahrām*, 4 August 1967:8.

[12]   On an individual level, this crisis was illustrated by many Egyptians' confessions of remaining in a daze for weeks following the defeat. See, for example, Farid (1994:103) and Hussayn 'Uthmān, 'National Stances of Umm Kulthūm', *al-Mansūrah*, February 1977:25 (*Dār al-Hilāl* clippings file 65).

In comparison with other fundraising efforts, the concerts in the governorates appeared to be an expression of the people. There were several reasons for this. Firstly, unlike the collections organised by the Ministry of Social Affairs or initiated by publishing houses and run under the Ministry's auspices, where musicians and actors were called upon to walk through Cairo neighbourhoods and to gather donations from merchants, these concerts were not arranged and implemented by government agencies or media organisations.[13] Umm Kulthūm's two-month track record of action in response to the war strengthened her image as an autonomous agent. Second, Umm Kulthūm shaped these concerts as an extension of the earlier work of established citizens' organisations and of her gathering together pre-existing organisations under the NAEW umbrella. The decision to make her concerts occasions for giving additional donations shaped them as a continuation of the collection work she had facilitated through the NAEW. More specifically, and in the same way that she had described the NAEW's collection work, she constructed her concerts as occasions on which everyone could contribute something, regardless of age or class.[14] Furthermore, the decision to perform in the *marākiz* of the governorates, rather than in Cairo, allowed country folk and city dwellers alike to gather and to participate in some way.[15] Effectively, such decisions cast her concerts as an integral and logical extension of citizens' prior efforts to raise funds and boost morale.

Third, Egyptians' readiness to contribute additional funds to the war effort demonstrated that they were motivated not simply by the opportunity to hear Umm Kulthūm perform, but by a desire to restart the war in order to reclaim both land and a sense of national dignity. Individuals purchased concert tickets for the designated price and immediately returned them to be resold in order to generate twice the funds.[16] Many generously donated personal items of monetary and sentimental value, such as wedding rings. Others presented for sale at auction items that would have had little monetary value outside of this fundraising context. In al-Mansūrah, for example, a child contributed a symbolic handful of local soil which was auctioned for £E3,000 ($6,900) ('Awad 1969:156–7). Local contributors' enthusiasm was then broadcast to a larger audience though newspaper and magazine coverage of the concerts, which emphasised individuals' generosity in bringing their money, jewellery and gold and in 'competing with one another' to

---

[13]   'With the Committee of Artists for the Collection of Gold', *al-Akhbār*, 19 July 1967:8; 'An Artistic Demonstration in Wikālat al-Balah', *al-Kawākib*, 1 August 1967:4–5; Farūq Abū Zayyid and Fāṭimah Ḥussayn, 'The Arab Artist', *al-Idhā'ah wa al-Tilīfizyūn* 5 August 1967:3–6.

[14]   al-Bīlī, 'What Did Umm Kulthūm Say', 26–7; 'Umm Kulthūm Travels to Saudi Arabia'.

[15]   Ṭāriq Fūdah, 'After 23 Years Umm Kulthūm Sings in Damanhūr', *Ākhir Sā'ah*, 23 August 1967:32.

[16]   Muḥammad Wajdī Qandīl, 'A Day with Umm Kulthūm Among the Landmarks of her Memories', *Ākhir Sā'ah*, 7 February 1968:36.

purchase tickets for £E100 ($230).[17] Finally, the format of Umm Kulthūm's concerts in the governorates permitted a communal, ritualised display of public sentiment. The chosen venues – large open air tent theatres and sports stadiums – allowed as many as 12,000 people to assemble.[18] The structure of the concerts enabled local support for the continuation of the war to be incorporated as an integral part of the performances, and such support was portrayed through the measurable form of the total funds generated by the governorate.[19] Moreover, the formal presentation of cheques to Umm Kulthūm and the display of gold donations during the concerts enabled those present to witness the entire governorate's generosity as manifest through both ticket sales and additional donations, the latter gathered in the days and weeks preceding each performance.

In fact, Umm Kulthūm's image as an autonomous, self-inspired agent obscured the ways in which her actions supported the regime's strategies and agendas. Whilst her concerts provided an empowering mechanism for the public, they also conferred authority to the regime as it struggled to deal with both international and domestic pressures to respond to and resolve the war. Since her fundraising work channelled funds to the treasury for the purpose of re-equipping the armed forces, as well as gathering people in demonstration of support for these forces, it reinforced the legitimacy of the state military – as opposed to an Egyptian people's army or Palestinian guerrilla groups – as the force to be entrusted with continuing the conflict. More specifically, her summer activities and concerts in the governorates lent support to three specific government strategies in an overarching agenda of redirecting popular sentiment (Hussein 1977:289, 299). Firstly, rather than promoting popular desire for direct participation in the fighting through the performance of patriotic songs or spoken appeals, she urged productivity and reinforced the regime's message that citizens' real place in the war was in the factory or field (that is, out of the war).[20] Second, she did not use her public statements to encourage open political debate in response to the war and the military's handling of it; rather, she directed people's attention to the basic duty of supporting the regime and its plans (Hussein 1977:290–91). Concert announcers further emphasised these two messages for theatre and radio audiences

---

[17] 'Umm Kulthūm, Artist of the People in the Battle', *al-Muṣawwar*, 25 August 1967:44–5.

[18] 'The Last Hour: Key to the City of Alexandria to Umm Kulthūm', *al-Jumhūriyyah*, 1 September 1967:6.

[19] 'Abd al-Tuwāb 'Abd al-Ḥayy, 'Umm Kulthūm in the First Concert in the Series of Concerts of One Million Pounds', *al-Kawākib*, 22 August 1967:4–5; Sakīnah al-Sādāt, 'One Million Pounds that Umm Kulthūm Collects from 24 Governorates', *al-Muṣawwar*, 8 September 1967:44; and Salāmah al-'Abbāssī, 'Umm Kulthūm in the Fourth Governorate for the Sake of the War Effort', *al-Jumhūriyyah*, 3 February 1968:1.

[20] Maḥmūd Sālim, 'From and To', *al-Idhā'ah wa al-Tilīfizyūn*, 1 July 1967:7; Farūq Ibrāhīm, 'When Umm Kulthūm Preached to the People', 20 December 1967:10; Hussein (1977:280, 299, 304).

by characterising Umm Kulthūm as 'a combative citizen and great fighter who fights with the masses for the sake of the battle for respect, land and the future'.[21] In this way, they portrayed Umm Kulthūm and the contributing public as active collaborators in the continuation of the war through the donation of funds. Third, by giving concerts in large pavilions outside Cairo rather than in confined city-centre theatres, the demonstrations that Umm Kulthūm amassed served to illustrate 'the people's unity', one of the government's central messages aimed at discouraging class-based protest (Hussein 1977:289). Through their proximity to smaller cities, villages, agricultural land and factories, her concerts drew a much wider variety of listeners than did her monthly Cairo concerts, a fact that was visually enhanced both on-site and in press coverage by the outdoor theatres' encouragement of more casual dress.

Fundamental to Umm Kulthūm's ability to give concerts which both served as an empowering mechanism for the people and simultaneously reinforced government priorities was the explicit and exceptional patriotic context that her earlier efforts in July had established. Her public statements and participation in the NAEW's propaganda campaign had included forceful language sufficient to draw people to participate and to take credence in her own motivations for collecting funds. As a result, she could sing romantic songs in the governorates while neither creating ambiguity about the purposes of the concerts – to raise funds and morale – nor dampening public enthusiasm with respect to the war. Constructing emotionally and financially efficacious concerts around her romantic repertory, she drew people to participate in ritualised demonstrations that did not violate the regime's strategies of redirecting popular sentiment. Her concerts did not enable or encourage people to challenge the existing military, political and social systems, as the February riots of 1968 were soon to do (Hussein 1977:292–6).[22] Instead, they offered people a means of responding to the psychological damage inflicted by the war that remained thoroughly within the limits of the regime's agendas.

---

[21]   Salāmah al-'Abbāssī, 'How Did al-Buhayrah Spend the Night of Its Life with the Star of the East?', *al-Jumhūriyyah*, 19 August 1967:6.

[22]   As a result, her efforts did not silence leftist critics dissatisfied with the regime and her support of it. In *Kalb al-Sitt* ('The Lady's Dog'), leftist poet Ahmad Fu'ad Najm used an incident from Umm Kulthūm's daily life to satirise the revolution's failure to effect sufficient social change: Umm Kulthūm's dog bit and injured a man passing her villa. A common person would have been prosecuted for this offence, yet the singer escaped prosecution because of her elite standing and political connections. Her singing itself was criticised for intoxicating listeners into a docile acceptance of government repression. One writer described her performances of long romantic songs as excrement of repressive regimes. While predicting that the masses were finally sobering up, he portrayed her songs about 'love and its torment' as 'the dross floating on the dung of Arab society under which miserable millions are awakening'. 'Attack on Umm Kulthūm', *Middle East News Agency*, 18 November 1967 (based on an article in *al-Dustūr*, 18 November 1967) (*al-Ahrām* clippings file 'Umm Kulthūm').

Paris Concerts, Contextualised for Egypt

After giving her first two governorate concerts in Alexandria and Damanhūr in late August 1967, Umm Kulthūm prepared for her autumn trip to Paris. Negotiations for her two concerts at the Olympia theatre in Paris had been completed more than eight months before the war. The agreement included an extraordinarily high compensation (£7,000 for each of the two performances in comparison with £3,000 paid to Maria Callas) and specific requests for luxury accommodation, among other demands.[23] As originally conceived, Umm Kulthūm's Paris concerts would have likely appeared, at least in part, to be a self-aggrandising effort to increase her fame and wealth on an international scale. Now, however, Umm Kulthūm directed her compensation to the war effort and conspicuously integrated this trip into her ongoing fundraising campaign. Both before and during her visit to Paris, she took several steps to clarify the meaning of her trip for the Egyptian public. For example, her collaboration with the Egyptian press prior to the trip contextualised her Paris concerts as a logical outgrowth of her domestic fundraising activities. She granted a lengthy interview to the weekly Egyptian magazine *al-Muṣawwar* which confirmed that the Paris concerts would benefit the war effort. Interestingly, this interview was published in the same magazine issue as one with the director of the Olympia theatre and readers therefore turned directly from his discussion of the forthcoming concerts to her commentary on the governorate concerts. Moreover, since she went on to clarify the NAEW's fundraising efforts, which included collecting donations and obtaining hard currency by selling products in duty-free shops and tourist areas, the pair of interviews cloaked the Paris concerts within the larger fundraising agendas of the assembly. At the same time, Umm Kulthūm's self-deprecatory stance, which saluted the many working women who participated in the assembly's activities and downplayed her own role, cast doubt on the possibility that self-serving motives might underlie the concerts.[24]

Prior to her Paris trip, Umm Kulthūm had collaborated with an Egyptian journalist to prepare a persuasive, sustained explanation of the goals of the NAEW and the resulting statement was carefully timed to appear whilst she was on tour.[25]

---

[23] These concerts were originally scheduled for the first week in October, but were later postponed until mid-November. 'Umm Kulthūm Sings in Paris for 14 Thousand Pounds Sterling in Compensation', *al-Ahrām*, 29 September 1966 (*al-Ahrām* clippings file 'Umm Kulthūm'); Duriyah 'Awnī, 'Eastern Jews Came to Listen to Umm Kulthūm', *al-Muṣawwar*, 24 November 1967:9; Muḥammad Salmāwī, personal communication, Cairo, 31 May 2003.

[24] Samīr 'Abd al-Majīd, 'Conversation with Umm Kulthūm', *al-Muṣawwar*, 22 September 1967:4–5, 47; Duriyah 'Awnī, 'How Did Paris Prepare to Receive Umm Kulthūm?', *al-Muṣawwar*, 22 September 1967:2–3.

[25] Muḥammad Wajdī Qandīl, 'Where Do Egyptian Women Stand on Their Homeland's Struggle?', *Ākhir Sāʻah* 15 November 1967:11; Muḥammad Wajdī Qandīl, personal communication, Cairo, 8 March 2003.

In this statement, she stressed the need for thrift and donations, citing simple means of saving money such as serving smaller portions of tea and coffee and urging readers to donate the hard currency saved to the state. Such a chronological linkage of her statement on the NAEW and her Paris concerts suggested that listeners at home could still work alongside her, even as she sang in Europe. Although they could not donate money and other possessions in person on the occasion of her Paris concerts, as they had in the governorates, the timing and content of her article showed readers that everyone could contribute to the national cause just as she was contributing her compensation and proceeds of photographs sold in Paris.[26] Such framing efforts signalled that, despite the tenuous connection between singing on a famed Parisian stage and donating small sums of money to the national treasury, an underlying unity of purpose linked the two enterprises. In her statement, Umm Kulthūm went on to explain the NAEW's distribution of thousands of letters expounding the Egyptian point of view with the aim of gaining support in Europe and America, thus linking her own trip with the NAEW's communication agenda.[27] In this way, the Paris trip seemed to exemplify her personal contribution to such an aim. The Egyptian press reported that 'all of Europe [was] talking about Egypt', and supported the claim by reproducing and quoting French newspaper articles and passing on the singer's confirmation that she had 'felt the love of people from all corners of the world for Egypt'.[28] Umm Kulthūm's own statements and those of journalists suggest that she had rallied not only the Arab diasporic community, but also Europeans, around the Egyptian cause.[29] The Egyptian press perpetuated the French press's dubbing of her concerts as 'an Arab political-artistic rally in Paris', bragged that the French considered her to be a political personality and portrayed her concerts as a grand effort in communication that raised the profile of Egypt's plight on an international stage.[30]

---

[26] 'Abd al-Nūr Khalīl, 'With Umm Kulthūm in Paris', *al-Kawākib*, 21 November 1967:8.

[27] Qandīl, 'Where Do Egyptian Women Stand', 11.

[28] Samīr Tawfīq and Farūq Ibrāhīm, 'All of France Talks About the Voice of Umm Kulthūm', *al-Akhbār*, 13 November 1967:3; 'Umm Kulthūm Today on Every Station and Every Airwave', *al-Akhbār*, 15 November 1967:6; 'French Broadcasting Stays up with Umm Kulthūm until Morning', *al-Jumhūriyyah*, 17 November 1967:3; 'Biggest Historical Event for Egyptian Art in Paris', *al-Akhbār*, 20 November 1967:3.

[29] 'A Light in the Darkness', *al-Kawākib*, 21 November 1967:3; 'Awnī, 'Eastern Jews', 9.

[30] Tawfīq and Ibrāhīm, 'All of France Talks', 3; 'Umm Kulthūm Opens Her Vocal Season Today from Paris', *al-Jumhūriyyah*, 15 November 1967:1, 3; 'The Voice of Umm Kulthūm Conquers Paris for the First Time', *Ākhir Sā'ah*, 15 November 1967: 51–3; 'Umm Kulthūm Returned to Cairo', *al*-Jumhūriyyah, 25 November 1967:12.

International Presentation and Programming

The international phase of Umm Kulthūm's concert campaign entailed new challenges in the way that she presented herself in public. Unlike her previous fundraising concerts for local audiences in Egypt which were framed by broadcasting nationalistic slogans, she was now offering concerts for a national military and political cause abroad for mixed audiences and contextualising the concerts largely through international press conferences. Once outside Egypt, she faced basic questions about her role and motivations: was she an artist or a politician? As we have seen, some saw her Paris concerts as a valuable opportunity to disseminate an Arab perspective on the war and to influence public opinion in Europe. Accordingly, they expected her to fashion her concerts as political demonstrations, programme songs from her patriotic repertory, and utilise her trip as an occasion for Arab propaganda.[31] Yet, both in her public presentation of self and in her concert programmes, Umm Kulthūm chose a different approach. She distanced herself and her art from politics, leaving listeners the interpretive space to voluntarily supply political motivations and readings for her performances. In Paris, Umm Kulthūm began to do this through her press statements. Whilst reporters wanted to denote her a political figure, she insisted that she was 'just an artist',[32] offering denials and cryptic responses to journalists who were eager to interpret the European leg of her campaign:

Daily Mail reporter:	Do you believe that your presence occurring now after the war between Israel and the Arabs gives it a political goal?
Umm Kulthūm:	We agreed on the visit before the war.
Daily Mail reporter:	In this situation your visit has a greater meaning.
Umm Kulthūm:	I hope so.[33]

This tight-lipped response is particularly striking when read against the press statement made just a few hours before leaving Cairo for Paris. There, she had boldly announced her intention to 'say to each European face to face that every centime, pence or cent they give to Israel is transformed into a bullet killing an Arab person'.[34] The sustainability of her international campaign and her viability as an artist working for a military and political cause were in fact predicated on an apolitical presentation of self: contextualised by her restrained responses, Umm

---

[31] 'The Voice of Umm Kulthūm', 51–2; 'Awnī, 'How Did Paris Prepare', 2; 'Attack on Umm Kulthūm'.

[32] 'Umm Kulthūm's Press Conference in Paris', *al-Jumhūriyyah*, 13 November 1967:3.

[33] Tawfīq and Ibrāhīm, 'All of France Talks', 3.

[34] 'Umm Kulthūm in France', *al-Akhbār*, 10 November 1968:1.

Kulthūm's successful Paris concerts prompted further invitations taking her to Morocco, Kuwait, Tunisia and Lebanon in just five months.[35]

In both Paris and the Arab world, Umm Kulthūm regularly framed her efforts as broadly patriotic rather than political in a narrow sense, and as representative of her compatriots rather than an isolated or extreme view. Thus she explained, 'I am a patriotic woman and I love my country. I am ready to make any sacrifice for the sake of the freedom of my country – the concern of all Egyptians.'[36] She repeatedly described her efforts simply as a citizen's duty.[37] Since articles from abroad were often quoted in the Egyptian press, and since concerts in one country were covered in the press of others, her concise patriotic language was particularly advantageous since it admitted multiple interpretations. Such statements extended to Egyptians a continued, personal confirmation that an underlying unity of purpose linked her efforts with theirs, a shared impulse to serve one's country and to make personal sacrifices in doing so, impulses which could be appreciated and sympathetically received by a broad spectrum of Arabs and Europeans. At the same time, however, for those Arabs who wanted to infer a strong political stance underscoring her activities, her statements could be read as a characteristically humble expression of that position.

Just as public statements made in one country often found their way into the press of several others, Umm Kulthūm's Paris and Arab world performances reached diverse theatre and radio audiences. Her theatre audiences in Paris, the Middle East and North Africa gathered Arabs from many nations, and those in Paris also included many French listeners. Radio broadcasts carried her concerts across national boundaries in the Middle East and North Africa and her Paris concerts were also broadcast across Europe. Responding to the challenge of offering fundraising concerts abroad for these mixed audiences, Umm Kulthūm adopted an approach to programming which, like her verbal strategies, allowed individual listeners the interpretive space within which to understand the significance of her trips.

Crucial to this was her rejection of several types of songs: just as she avoided propagandist language, Umm Kulthūm rejected patriotic songs and their explicitly political messages, as well as songs which might have been perceived as tools for evoking national pride. For example, she consistently refrained from performing songs associated through subject matter, authorship or commissioning with the

---

[35] 'Umm Kulthūm Received Invitation to Sing in Tunisia', *al-Jumhūriyyah*, 15 November 1967:3; Samīr Tawfīq, 'Umm Kulthūm Postpones her Return until Thursday in Order to Take an Egyptian Plane', *al-Akhbār*, 21 November 1967:5; Ibrāhīm Nuwār, 'A Conversation about Art, Politics, and Literature', *al-Jumhūriyyah*, 18 December 1967:9; Sufiyah Nāṣif, 'Umm Kulthūm Sings Four New Songs', *al-Muṣawwar*, 3 May 1968:60–61.

[36] 'Umm Kulthūm's Press Conference', 3.

[37] *al-Idhāʿah wa al-Tilfāzah* (Morocco), 3 March 1968, reprinted in al-Marīnī (1975:191); Samīr Tawfīq, 'Umm Kulthūm Holds Press Conference in Rabat', *al-Akhbār*, 9 March 1968: 4; Jacqueline Naḥās, 'She Collected 400 Thousand Pounds Until Now for the War Effort in Egypt', *al-Ḥayāt* (Beirut), 12 July 1968:9.

specific country in which she was singing.[38] Instead, she programmed items which would appeal to the widest spectrum of theatre and radio audiences: the staple romantic *qaṣā'id* (sing. *qaṣīdah*) and *ughniyyāt* that were central to the aesthetic of *ṭarab*, or ecstasy, in which audiences request improvisatory repetitions of key poetic lines with melodic ornamentation, rhythmic changes and emotive variations in vocal timbre. The consistency with which she performed these listeners' favourites contributed strongly to the success of her campaign. Although she avoided songs with explicitly political or nationalistic messages, Umm Kulthūm regularly programmed romantic *qaṣā'id* which enabled listeners to derive their own political interpretations. For example, '*al-Aṭlāl*', the most frequently performed of her staple *qaṣā'id* and *ughniyyāt* during her fundraising concerts, allowed listeners great leeway in interpreting the key line 'Give me my freedom, set free my hands'. The text could be read as a purely romantic expression, but at the same time (and more so than many of her patriotic songs) it admitted numerous political interpretations including a critique of repressive local regimes (colonial or otherwise) or of the occupation of local or distant lands (for example, Sinai or Palestine). Whilst it mentioned no specific oppressor, oppressed people or occupied land, when framed through broadly-worded patriotic statements in which her concerts were characterised as a duty to her country and her Arabness, the words of '*al-Aṭlāl*' provided an ideal vehicle for listeners to reflect on what was widely perceived to be a shared legacy of colonialism.[39] Thus, the song prompted a Tunisian in Paris to contemplate her 'Arab brothers', and Palestinians in particular, and led a listener in Tunisia to confess, amidst his uncontrollable tears, that 'Her romantic words remind me of the tragedy of our homeland with colonialism and my tragedy with colonialism.'[40]

Unity of Culture, Unity of Feeling

Umm Kulthūm's 1967–8 international concert campaign was simultaneously received in two distinct forms. Before international audiences, Umm Kulthūm distanced herself and her art from politics and indeed the very success of her campaign largely depended on this apolitical presentation of self. For a

---

[38]   Examples of these songs include '*Tūf wa Shūf*', '*Yā Dārnā Yā Dār*' and '*Hādhihi Laylatī*'. The avoidance of such songs stands in stark contrast to her usual attentiveness and compliance with local listeners' requests during her trips. She did not comply with the request of Sudanese listeners that she sing the *qaṣīdah* '*al-Sūdān*' in one of her concerts there. 'How Does Sudan Prepare to Welcome Umm Kulthūm and Listen to Her?', *al-Jumhūriyyah*, 19 December 1968:11.

[39]   Nāṣif, 'Four New Songs', 60–61.

[40]   Sakīnah Fu'ād, 'Umm Kulthūm in the Notebook of Five Broadcasters', *al-Idhā'ah wa al-Tilīfizyūn*, 29 June 1968:6 (*Dār al-Hilāl* clippings file 'Umm Kulthūm'); Sāmiyyah Ṣādiq, 'An Evening with Umm Kulthūm', Part 2, Egyptian Radio Archive, Reel N68421.

domestic audience, however, the Egyptian media capitalised on her statements, performances, and public actions to offer a multidimensional representation of her concert campaign as cultivating Arab unity and popular support for Egypt's impending military action. The continued emotional impact of the campaign in response to the psychological effects of the June 1967 defeat was founded on this representation through the Egyptian media.

The domestic image of Umm Kulthūm's international concerts foregrounded a very different emotional impact from that of the Tunisian listener described above. In contrast to the scene of a grown man sobbing uncontrollably in the midst of thousands of listeners, the singer and the Egyptian media created a positive image of a broad community of people united by culture and feeling, and amongst whom Egypt held a position of leadership. In order to understand how this image was formed, one needs to go beyond the idea of 'performance' as comprising the vocal renditions alone and embrace a broad conception which includes the contributions of Umm Kulthūm, her audiences and media agents, and which extends from the concert stage to the farthest newspaper, radio or television receiver. Such a perspective reveals how an uplifting performance of Arab unity was offered by the domestic media based on six interwoven components: Umm Kulthūm's press statements, her public performances off the concert platform, her programming practices, foreign listeners' statements to the Egyptian media, Egyptian press commentary and Egyptian broadcasting practices.

Umm Kulthūm's statements and public performances away from the concert stage fuelled the Egyptian print media's multidimensional portrayal of Arab cultural unity. A number of statements made abroad and reproduced in the Egyptian press drew attention to aspects of shared Arab culture, such as similarities between folk singing in Morocco, Kuwait and Egypt, as well as similarities between eating customs in the Sudanese wedding party which Umm Kulthūm attended and those in the Egyptian countryside.[41] Her trips conspicuously included the celebration of Muslim holidays observed across the region and her broader public performances on these occasions were reproduced in words and images in the domestic press. Thus Egyptians read of her celebrations of *'Īd al-Aḍḥā* with a needy Moroccan family and the Prophet's birth in Tunisia with the singing of *mawāwīl* and *madā'iḥ*.[42]

Umm Kulthūm's performances of songs set to lyrics by non-Egyptian poets also strengthened such an image of Arab cultural unity. Whilst she sang the *qaṣā'id* of non-Egyptian poets in her Arab world concerts, her programming did not capitalise on their potential to evoke local, national pride, as one might have expected.

---

[41]   Ṣalāḥ Darwīsh, 'Sudan Rebels against Its Traditions Because of Umm Kulthūm', *al-Jumhūriyyah*, 2 January 1969:12.

[42]   Ṣalāḥ Darwīsh, 'Six Hours of Anxiety and Fear over Umm Kulthūm's Plane', *al-Jumhūriyyah*, 22 March 1968:9; Fu'ād, 'Umm Kulthūm in the Notebook', 6; Sufiyah Nāṣif, 'Umm Kulthūm's Tears', *al-Hawā*, 15 June 1968 (*Dār al-Hilāl* clippings file 'Umm Kulthūm').

For example, the *qaṣīdah* of Lebanese poet George Jordaq, '*Hādhihi Laylatī*', was not performed during the concert campaign in Lebanon, but rather in Sudan, and the *qaṣīdah* of Sudanese poet al-Hādī Ādam, '*Aghadan Alqāk*', was performed in Abu Dhabi rather than in Sudan (Danielson 1997:186). Effectively, this programming strategy served to display the sharing of linguistic and literary culture by a larger Arab nation rather than focus on local national pride. At the same time, the fact that such non-Egyptian poets were heard across the Arab world, including Egypt, in the context of compositional and improvisational idioms cultivated by *Egyptian* composers served to emphasise Egypt's continuing position of cultural leadership within the larger Arab 'nation'. The publicised requests of Sudanese listeners to hear the latest addition to her repertory, '*Hādhihi Laylatī*', in the second Sudanese concert exemplified the widespread appreciation of Arab listeners for the music of Egyptian composers and performers. This was underscored by Umm Kulthūm's personal testimony that Arab listeners responded to her performances with the same feelings and the same verbal expressions regardless of where they lived or where she sang.[43]

For the Egyptian press, Umm Kulthūm's concerts provided a wealth of evidence of the vitality of this shared musical and linguistic culture and the widespread esteem of its Egyptian cultivators. Egyptian journalists portrayed Arab listeners' intense desire for these performances by describing and photographing enthusiastic audience response, reporting on the thousands of telegrams and letters sent to Umm Kulthūm by local fans and reproducing excerpts from individual letters and interviews. Thus, one journalist reported, 'A senior Kuwaiti police officer said to me, "It is not among your Egyptian rights to pride yourself on Umm Kulthūm alone – all of us take pride in her ... We consider her an object of pride of the entire Arab nation"'.[44] In the face of financial, military and political setbacks, the singer and the Egyptian print media responded with an uplifting demonstration of cultural vitality to take pride in when there seemed little else to be proud of. Together, they sought to show that this shared culture was thriving more than ever before, that the larger community invoked by the Kuwaiti police officer existed in part because of it and that Egypt continued to occupy a position of cultural leadership within it. Moreover, the Egyptian media portrayed Umm Kulthūm's concerts as a healing force that forged a strong community united by feeling, as well as by culture. Writers and broadcasters interviewed listeners from across the region and recorded their impressions and personal interpretations. Egyptian radio broadcast a prominent Tunisian's testimonial that Umm Kulthūm's concerts created strong emotional ties between the Tunisian and Egyptian people.[45] Journalists quoted

[43] Nāṣif, 'Four New Songs', 60–61; 'Afāf Yaḥyá, 'Open Conversation with the Lady of Arabic Song', *al-Akhbār*, 10 January 1968:2; Nuwār al-Dīn al-Zarārī, 'Umm Kulthūm Says "The Arab Listener Is One in Every Nation"', *al-Jumhūriyyah*, 10 March 1969:5.

[44] Nabīl 'Asamat, 'What Was it That Umm Kulthūm Did in Kuwait and the Arab Gulf with its People?', *al-Akhbār* 5 May 1968:8.

[45] Ṣādiq, 'An Evening with Umm Kulthūm'.

from Kuwaitis who observed that she was 'uniting the ranks' and strengthening the Arab nation and from a Tunisian who concluded 'She confirms our Arabness, our brotherhood and our one destiny.'[46] Some even quoted from the foreign press, for example a Moroccan newspaper journalist's observation that 'Umm Kulthūm became for the entire Arab people a source of moral strength in the days of the Setback.'[47] An Egyptian writer paraphrased the singer's statements to explain the significance of her trips, 'Umm Kulthūm performs her important, powerful role in this decisive journey of the Arab nation by uniting the hearts and gathering feelings toward one goal – victory. And this is the hope that Umm Kulthūm lives for the sake of, as she told me many times.'[48] For Egyptians, such hopes seemed to be confirmed as they read of the Sudanese greeting her as the 'Uniter of the Arabs' whose voice was a weapon.[49]

Egyptian journalists cast listeners' willingness to channel money to the treasury as a vote of confidence in Egypt's ability to fulfil their shared hopes in response to the war. Whilst foreign press coverage tended to downplay the contribution of funds to the Egyptian treasury or to emphasise financial contributions to local causes, the Egyptian press never failed to label concert funds as being intended 'for the war effort'.[50] Journalists at home soon dubbed the war effort an Arab one and their constant quantification of international support for Egypt's impending military action complemented the statements of individual listeners.[51]

Umm Kulthūm's public performances away from the concert platform also served to reinforce the portrayal of Arab unity. Particularly powerful in this respect was a performance which displayed deference to local culture whilst simultaneously underscoring such unity. During her tour of the Tunisian capital, she prayed in the historical *al-Zaytūnah* mosque, and she wore a *burnūs* (traditional long, hooded cloak) for the occasion (see Figure 1.1). Whilst Tunisian commentators noted these two nods to local history and culture, the Egyptian press more thoroughly articulated the import of the timing of Umm Kulthūm's actions by stressing to

[46]   Nabīl 'Asamat and Samīr Tawfīq, 'Before the Curtain Rose, Umm Kulthūm Agreed to Have the Concert Broadcast', *al-Akhbār*, 27 April 1968:13; 'Umm Kulthūm in Balbek', *al-Jumhūriyyah*, 18 July 1968:5.

[47]   Samīr Tawfīq, 'Biggest Arab Festivities', *al-Akhbār*, 6 March 1968:1.

[48]   Samīr Tawfīq, 'In the Third Night Umm Kulthūm Sang Rubā'iyyāt al-Khayyām', *al-Akhbār*, 14 March 1968:3.

[49]   Sufiyah Nāṣif, 'How Did Sudan Celebrate with Umm Kulthūm?', *al-Muṣawwar*, 3 January 1969:54–5; Muhammad Tabārak, 'Sudan Says to Umm Kulthūm: Your Voice is a Weapon', *Ākhir Sā'ah*, 1 January 1969:28.

[50]   'Oum Kalthoum: premier gala, cette nuit, au Palais des Sports à El Menzah', *Le presse de Tunisie*, 31 May 1968:6; 'Oum Kalthoum: Je suis ravie de visiter le Tunisie', *L'Action*, 31 May 1968:1.

[51]   'Asamat and Tawfīq, 'Before the Curtain Rose', 13; Nāṣif, 'Four New Songs', 60–61; Sufiyah Nāṣif, 'Umm Kulthūm Prays in the al-Zaytūnah Mosque', *al-Muṣawwar*, 14 June 1968:4.

readers that she was praying on the first anniversary of the outbreak of the June
War and by reporting that Umm Kulthūm was accompanied by the first lady of
Tunisia with whom she had cried during the afternoon prayer whilst remembering
those killed in action.[52] Umm Kulthūm thus used her high-profile escorts and the
shared ritual of prayer to create the ideal photo opportunity and to demonstrate
that Tunisians were not simply linked with Egyptians through a shared cultural
practice, but were also united in feeling. That such shared feelings extended
beyond the leadership was confirmed as the press further reported that many
Tunisians had commemorated the war with the singer through Qur'anic recitation
and a performance of religious *tawāshīh* (songs) and that the Friday sermons in
Tunisia would honour those killed in action during the hostility.[53]

Figure 1.1   Umm Kulthūm praying in the *al-Zaytūnah* mosque alongside
               Tunisian first lady Wasila Bourguiba (photograph courtesy Dār al-
               Hilāl).

---

[52]   Salāmah al-'Abbāsī, 'With Umm Kulthūm in Her Seventh Encounter', *al-
Jumhūriyyah*, 14 June 1968:3; 'First Lady Wasila Bourguiba Accompanies Umm Kulthūm
on a Tour of the Capital', *al-'Amal*, 6 June 1968:1.

[53]   'Abd al-Salām Dāwūd, 'Umm Kulthūm Prays in the Most Famous Mosque in
Tunisia', *al-Akhbār*, 7 June 1968:1; Nāṣif, 'al-Zaytūnah Mosque', 4.

This representation of broad Arab concern for Egypt as a means of ameliorating the psychological impact of the war at home was completed by the domestic broadcasting and commercial sales of recordings of Umm Kulthūm's concerts. The mass media that had earlier established the foundation for her successful trips by distributing and broadcasting her recordings and films to audiences across the region, now worked in reverse. Instead of sending out a home-grown cultural product for foreign consumption, Umm Kulthūm's reception by audiences abroad could be sent back home for Egyptian consumption through radio, recordings, film and television. And the complementary nature of broadcasting and print media made for a powerful representation of her concert campaign: broadcasting and recording's temporal unfolding of her performances and audience response, coloured by the layers of interpretation offered by the Egyptian print media, offered listeners and viewers a vicarious experience of her reception more powerful than that afforded by prose descriptions and still snapshots alone.

The release of the stereophonic recording of '*al-Aṭlāl*' from one of the Paris concerts during the 1969 war of attrition was a particularly important means for Egyptians to experience Umm Kulthūm's foreign reception.[54] The stereophonic technology highlighted the immediate and wildly enthusiastic audience response during the performance, which featured a telling, visceral exchange of 'ahs' between singer and audience after the climactic line 'Give me my freedom, set free my hands'.[55] Regardless of the various sentiments motivating the audience response, Egyptian listeners were encouraged by the domestic media and the immediate circumstances of the war of attrition to hear it as an expression of support by the larger Arab community for Egypt's reclamation of land by military force. The release of this recording thus allowed Egyptians personally to possess a powerful record of Arab cultural and emotional unity, one that Umm Kulthūm and the Egyptian media had cultivated and exposed through the concerts.

As represented through the print and broadcast media, as well as through commercial recordings, the response of the transnational community was crafted to have a significant impact on the Egyptian psyche. For example, one Egyptian journalist observed that Umm Kulthūm's concert campaign 'returned a part of the lost dignity',[56] and the singer herself reflected on the import of her fundraising trips, 'They were intended to clearly encourage co-operation among all Arabs and to

---

[54] 'The Ambassador of Arab Art Umm Kulthūm Listens to the Stereophonic Recording of 'al-Atlāl'', *al-Idhā'ah wa al-Tilīfizyūn*, 25 October 1969:26. Following limited engagements with Israeli forces in Sinai in the second half of 1968, the war of attrition was begun in March 1969 to enable Egyptian forces to cross the Suez Canal and re-occupy the Sinai peninsula. Portrayed in the Egyptian media as a continuation of the 1967 war, the war of attrition continued until the ceasefire established in August 1970.

[55] This response can still be heard on *al-Aṭlāl, Ḥaflah Kāmilah*, Ṣawt al-Qāhirah cassette tape 81190 (Kulthūm 1981).

[56] Aḥmad Ṣāliḥ, 'What Happened on Umm Kulthūm's Night in Balbek?', *Ākhir Sā'ah*, 22 July 1970: 28–30.

convert it into something tangible. I wanted to prove that we (Arabs) are together in the view of Israel and that we (Arabs) are together in facing military aggression.'[57] More specifically, in her hands and in those of the Egyptian media, the concert campaign was designed to prove to Egyptians themselves that they did not stand alone but were supported by Arabs united around them as they continued to face the domestic economic impact of the 1967 war and to prepare for the war of attrition.

Whilst promoting this uplifting image of Arab unity and countering the psychological crisis generated by the defeat, Umm Kulthūm's concert campaign and its representation in the Egyptian media continued to operate within and to reinforce the regime's strategies, just as her domestic concerts had done. The campaign directed attention to problems and solutions abroad rather than at home; the performance of Arab unity generated by the media focused on the support to be found in the broader Arab world and the continually promised military action against Israel. It diverted attention from persistent internal problems that predated and outlasted the defeat, and from the regime's reluctance to make necessary changes in the country's economic, political and social systems.[58] By reinforcing, rather than challenging, the priorities and agendas of the government, Umm Kulthūm's campaign and its representation in the domestic media during this international phase proved to be highly sustainable.

A New Strategy

Umm Kulthūm's carefully restrained and productively apolitical and ambiguous portrayal of herself and her concert campaign for international audiences provided the foundation of the domestic media's portrayal of Arab unity through to the beginning of 1969. By this time, Umm Kulthūm had constructed a series of six international trips in addition to numerous pending invitations, and had collected the equivalent of half a million Egyptian pounds through her foreign concerts alone. The success of this approach, and of the complex domestic representations that it enabled, is highlighted through contrast with the subsequent strategy of public presentation adopted for her next trip abroad. After an intensive year of touring that concluded with a trip to Sudan in December 1968 and January 1969, Umm Kulthūm travelled to Libya in March 1969. Invited to give two concerts in Tripoli and Benghazi to benefit the *Fatah* organisation, she again faced the challenges of performing for a political cause in an international setting, but this time decided to adopt a new, openly political strategy of public presentation.

---

[57]   Muḥammad Wajdī Qandīl, 'Umm Kulthūm and a Conversation about Politics', *Ākhir Sā'ah*, 14 May 1969: 40. Interpolations in original.

[58]   This reluctance is illustrated by the rejection of Nasser's proposal of a two-party system by members of the Arab Socialist Union's Supreme Executive Committee in August 1967 and the comparatively limited reforms introduced through the March 30th Programme following the riots of February 1968. See Farid (1994:81–9), Hussein (1977:300).

In contrast to her previous concerts outside Egypt, Umm Kulthūm permitted her Libyan performances to be explicitly and specifically contextualised as political events. She agreed to sing in tent theatres with walls and stages carrying *Fataḥ* mottos such as 'Peaceful solutions will only continue over our dead bodies'.[59] In this context, neither live audiences nor television viewers could divorce her vocal performances from their meaning and purpose, as symbolised through the visual image of the coat of arms of *al-'Āṣifah* (lit. 'storm', the militant wing of *Fataḥ*) which hung directly behind her head throughout (see Figure 1.2).[60]

Figure 1.2   Umm Kulthūm singing in Libya in front of the coat of arms of *al-'Āṣifah* (photograph courtesy of Farūq Ibrāhīm).

[59]   Rajā' al-Naqqāsh, 'Umm Kulthūm and the Freedom Fighters', *al-Muṣawwar*, 28 March 1969:36–7.
[60]   Muḥammad Wajdī Qandīl, 'Umm Kulthūm Enlists her Voice for the Freedom Fighters', *Ākhir Sā'ah*, 19 March 1969:59.

Her voice and its political meaning were recontextualised by the displayed slogans, 'Committed Arab art is one of the weapons of the revolution' and 'In the blaze of the armed Palestinian revolution a new Arab people is born'. Referred to as a weapon, just as it had been in Sudan, Umm Kulthūm's voice was now cast as a weapon in the hands of guerrillas fighting for Palestine rather than as one to be used in Egypt's struggle to reclaim its occupied land.

Once dubbed 'The Artist of the People in the Battle', Umm Kulthūm now ventured further into the realm of politics through her public presentation of self. She spoke more like a politician than an artist. Concise statements about 'patriotic duty' were replaced by numerous and extended press statements in support of *Fatah* and its cause. Whilst she had explained the significance of her earlier trips through general terms such as 'homeland' and 'victory', drawing on widespread anti-Israeli sentiment and admitting numerous interpretations, she now spoke about the liberation of occupied lands, mentioning Palestine in particular, and characterised the freedom fighters' work as 'the model path for the restoration of Arab Palestine'.[61] In agreeing to give concerts for the benefit of *Fatah* and in lending explicit verbal support to the organisation and its causes, Umm Kulthūm walked a fine line between the Egyptian regime's agreement to support *Fatah* within the framework of the Palestinian Liberation Organisation (to the mutual benefit of both *Fatah* and the regime) on the one hand, and its desire to make the Palestinian resistance movement appear to be a secondary military force in comparison with the Egyptian army in the eyes of the Egyptian and broader Arab public.[62] This shift of verbal and monetary support to *Fatah* as a single resistance organisation, rather than to the PLO as a whole, thus by-passed the delicate mutual conferral of power established between *Fatah* and the Egyptian regime as the latter facilitated the former's rise to power within the PLO. The focus of Umm Kulthūm's statements and the support generated through her Libyan concerts represented a clear prioritisation of the Palestinian cause: ticket proceeds designated for *Fatah* totalled £E150,000 ($345,000) whilst her compensation, designated for the war effort, totalled only £E26,000 ($59,800).[63] Listeners in the wider Arab world responded to this new prioritisation. A reader of the Jordanian newspaper *al-Dustūr*, for example, enthusiastically called her to perform in Jordan, that is, in front of Palestinians themselves and at the front line of Palestinian resistance.[64]

---

[61]   al-Zarārī, 'Umm Kulthūm Says'; Ṣalāḥ Darwīsh, 'Umm Kulthūm Announces in Benghazi: "The Work of the Freedom Fighter is the Model Path for the Restoration of Arab Palestine"', *al-Jumhūriyyah*, 20 March 1969:11.

[62]   See Cobban (1984:45–7, 204–5), Shemesh (1996:103–4) and Hussein (1977:319–20). Interestingly, Egyptians today offer widely divergent explanations for the motivations behind these concerts, ranging from a Libyan request that Umm Kulthūm support *Fatah*, which enraged the Egyptian leadership, to covert Egyptian orchestration of the concerts as a vehicle for displaying Egyptian support of *Fatah* in a forum safely removed from the Egyptian soil and people.

[63]   Qandīl, 'Umm Kulthūm Enlists Her Voice', 58–60.

[64]   Ṣalāḥ, 'Umm Kulthūm', *al-Dustūr*, 16 March 1969:2.

Conclusions

Umm Kulthūm's Libyan trip, explicitly and specifically serving *Fataḥ*, seemed to have brought an end to her international campaign: the next 15 months included no foreign concerts. Whilst a modest donation to *Fataḥ* was made at her Tanta concert in May 1969, her publicised plan for collecting a second £E1 million ($2.3 million) through concerts in the governorates and abroad, including the contribution of a significant portion of concert proceeds to Palestinian resistance organisations, was left unrealised.[65] Instead, she directed her attention to unambiguously domestic projects. She sang for the rescue of the Roman era Philae temple (in Aswan) from decades of water damage and also collected funds (outside of the highly public context of concerts) for refugees relocated from the war-torn Suez Canal cities. In other words, it seems that in contrast to the restrained and ambiguous way in which she had presented herself to international audiences during her earlier trips, the new explicitly political stance adopted for the Libyan concerts proved to be unsustainable.

Despite these shifts in political stance and presentation of self, Umm Kulthūm's fundraising concerts following the war of June 1967 had a significant impact on both the end of her career and her reception history. Whilst not silencing leftist intellectual critics who saw her as a too well-positioned conservative force whose long 'intoxicating' performances diverted the public's attention away from pressing social and political problems at home, her fundraising concerts effectively articulated a new phase in her career and redefined her contemporary relevance for Egyptian society. As well as strengthening her ties with listeners abroad who had previously heard her only through radio and recordings, Umm Kulthūm's concerts outside Egypt solidified her international renown, providing occasions for the conferral of a diplomatic passport and numerous awards from foreign states.

More than a quarter of a century after Umm Kulthūm's death in 1975, her fundraising concerts have not been forgotten. On the contrary, when acquainting tourists and foreign residents in Egypt with the singer, Egyptians are quick to mention her fundraising efforts after the war. From affluent university graduates to the working poor, from grandmothers who saw the singer in their lifetime and teenagers born after her death, Egyptians from radically different backgrounds cite these concerts in order to establish the singer's national historical importance, to characterise her international success and to evoke personal qualities of compassion, activism, generosity and charity. Now remembered more simply and uniformly as concerts to benefit *Egypt*, her fundraising efforts have become one of the most enduring legacies of her posthumous legend.

---

[65] Ṣalāḥ Darwīsh and Waṣfah al-Rīfī, 'Revenues of Umm Kulthūm's Concert Reached 284 Thousand Pounds', *al-Jumhūriyyah*, 10 May 1969:4; Ṣalāḥ Darwīsh, 'Umm Kulthūm Sings in the Provinces, London, Paris and Montreal', *al-Jumhūriyyah*, 17 May 1969:8; Ṣalāḥ Darwīsh, 'Three Monthly Concerts of Umm Kulthūm in the New Season', *al-Jumhūriyyah*, 26 June 1969:11.

Chapter 2
'Abd al-Halim's Microphone

Martin Stokes

Introduction

This chapter is a preliminary attempt at a cultural history of the microphone in Egypt. I focus on one particular singer: 'Abd al-Halim Hafiz, Nasserite crooner and film star, who was born in 1929 and died in 1977 to massive public mourning, and who lives an elusive afterlife in Egypt and other parts of the Arab world today. The microphone was central to 'Abd al-Halim's art and he is rarely depicted without it. It is a simple fact, but one easily overlooked, that microphones are an unremarkable and everyday part of musical life for almost everybody today. I hope to show, though, that they were far from unremarkable in Egypt in the middle years of the twentieth century; rather, they were keenly debated and profoundly implicated in musical changes, particularly, but not only, relating to the voice. I also hope to show how they were central to 'Abd al-Halim's identification as a sentimentalist, to his rapport with female audiences and to his political association with Gamal 'Abd al-Nasser.

The broader question of how close, quiet, emotional and intimate voices circulated around public spaces in the Middle East (and changed the very nature of that public space) was a matter of significant concern and cultural elaboration.[1] For these new voices – circulated by microphones – connected the world of entertainment with the world of revolutionary politics, connected romantic love with the power to command and coerce, connected the heart with the state. Individuals at the

---

[1]   The thinking for this chapter took place during a year's leave courtesy of the Howard Foundation and a residency in the Franke Institute at the University of Chicago. I am also indebted to Farouk Mustafa, Noha Aboulmagd-Forster, Hala al-Badri, Joel Gordon and Charles Hirschkind for some major insights. The chapter is based on reading and research, a significant amount of which was done in the American University of Cairo and in the Dar al-Kutub: I am grateful to the staff at both institutions for their patient help. I draw on more or less formal interviews with Ziyad al-Tawil, Zakariya Amir and Qadri Surur. Though this discussion is ethnographic in the broad sense of being about music in culture, it does not draw on systematic fieldwork. It is, however, deeply informed by more or less constant chat in Cairo, and the rather exacting learning process involved in negotiating one's way around the city and its dense musical life as I have gone about my library research. I am grateful to Ahmad Yamani and Mustafa Morsi and their friends and families for everything they taught me and for their companionship.

centre of this new techno-political complex[2] possessed unprecedented powers to control the social and political imagination, powers that appealed to the heart and the ear in new ways. As Charles Hirschkind suggests, this was a moment in which the Islamic arts of rhetoric (the *ilm al-balagha*), with their associated auditory disciplines, became aligned to the administrative practices of the modern Egyptian state. The moment passed, but it continues to reverberate, as I shall try to show with reference to contemporary 'Abd al-Halim nostalgia later in this chapter.[3]

A Voice in Pictures

There are a large number of pictures of 'Abd al-Halim still in circulation: photographs, drawings and cartoons.[4] 'Abd al-Halim was a product of the era of mass photo-journalism. His prominence in Egyptian society was as much visual as musical, and remains so today. He lived his life and died his lingering death (of bilharzia) in the company of photographers. Never before, or perhaps since, has an Egyptian face been quite so well known, in such intimate detail, and in the light of such varying moods and contexts, by quite so many people. The would-be biographer can learn a great deal from these pictures as a documentary source: about his working methods and manner of interacting with others, about technology, instruments, performance practice and audiences. One might also consider this proliferation of images as a cultural fact in its own right, demanding interpretation and comment. How might it have shaped Egyptian senses of who musicians were and what they did, and what their power over people was? And how does it shape the ways in which 'Abd al-Halim is remembered today?

The pictorial record is an assemblage of sub-genres, ranging from the iconographic, to the candid, to the documentary. Early pictures depict professional scenes and public events: 'Abd al-Halim performing at media events, conversing

---

2   Term and usage borrowed from Mitchell (2002) and Abu-Lughod (2004).

3   Charles Hirschkind's analysis of contemporary cassette-sermonising (2004) became an important point of reference to me midway through the writing of this chapter. Like Hirschkind, I am interested in grasping the auditory dynamics of the Nasserite moment, and their ongoing reverberations today. I am inclined to stress the links between Nasser and 'Abd al-Halim Hafiz, rather than Umm Kulthūm whose attitude to the microphone, as I shall explain, was markedly different. The irony of the contemporary situation in Egypt, as Hirschkind hints, is that the auditory disciplines of the Nasserite state are more effectively deployed by the Islamist opposition than the state itself.

4   For example, photographs can be found in abundance in the popular cultural journals of 'Abd al-Halim's time – *Akhir Sa'a*, *Ruz al-Yusuf*, *al-Kawakib* and *al-Idha'a* (formerly *al-Idha'a al-Misriyya*) – which are held in the national archive, the Dar al-Kutub, and other good libraries in Cairo such as that of the American University. The lively trade in film and music nostalgia means that copies can also be located at various bookstores in the Azbakiyya Gardens. Published biographies invariably contain many photographs. See al-Imrussi (1994), Hassaneyn (1995), Fakhouri (n.d.), al-Shorabji (2000).

with fellow stars, rehearsing in the studio or at work on a song with his composers and arrangers. Later in life we see more intimate pictures: 'Abd al-Halim unwinding and relaxing, strolling the streets of London or Paris, flirting with Suad Hosni or one of the many other women with whom he was romantically associated, sprawled out on a grassy hillside. Towards the end of his short life, we see another kind of photograph: sick, struggling to work from his bed, embracing close relatives and friends as the end drew nigh, and, finally, dying amongst wires and tubes in a London hospital. And there is yet another kind of picture: giving his last performances, a tormented and haggard figure, a study in lines of pain and concentration invariably converging on the microphone in front of him, oblivious to all else.

As well as these photographs, cartoons and line drawings are also ubiquitous. Here one senses first a figure that Egyptian audiences were rather slow to warm to, slightly narcissistic and arrogant, puffed up with pretensions, the jokes hinting that he was perhaps not quite as good looking as was generally portrayed (see Figure 2.1). Another genre of cartoons emerged later, when 'Abd al-Halim had become an established artist and figure of respect. Some of these are a quasi-cubist assemblage of lines and shapes, almost abstractly conveying the intensity of his final performances. The microphone is seldom absent when he is depicted singing. More often than not, these drawings are detailed renderings of photographs in which the labour of the pencil communicates an intimate respect and affection.

'Abd al-Halim's tomb, in Cairo's City of the Dead (south of the citadel), is a complex site of remembrance, and full of pictures. Here, interestingly, microphones are conspicuously absent. Walking through the door, the visitor is greeted by a small display of photographs showing the young 'Abd al-Halim, for the most part simply gazing at the photographer and concentrating on the process of being photographed. Moving towards the tomb (one of two in the complex, the other being the unmarked grave of 'Abd al-Halim's sister), there are two large line drawings rendered in pencil on a white wall (see Figure 2.2), both of the older 'Abd al-Halim, the artist. He stares out into the middle distance, his face thoughtful and his lips closed. There is no microphone in front of him: it is as though singing was the business of life, with its struggles and pains. Here, 'Abd al-Halim is quiet and at rest. The absence of microphones here would seem to be as deliberate, studied and meaningful as its ubiquity elsewhere.

Other singers were depicted with microphones, of course. 'Abd al-Halim's main predecessors and rivals early in life, Umm Kulthūm and Mohammed 'Abd al-Wahhab used microphones and indeed, these are on display in their respective museums in Cairo. However, both learned their vocal art in the pre-microphone era and in the highly valued context of Qur'anic recitation. Umm Kulthūm, with her powerful voice, eschewed microphones. When she sang, even later in life, she kept the microphone at some distance from her, focusing and projecting her voice on the audience beyond. Cartoons show microphones either quaking with fear or somehow engulfed by her. 'Abd al-Wahhab, by contrast, knew how to use microphones, and adapted his vocal art with great suppleness.

Figure 2.1   'The Artistes at the Elections', *Ruz al-Yusuf*, no. 1421, 1957:42.
             From top to bottom: Umm Kulthūm (who won't do anything
             without Riyadh al-Sunbati); Mohammed 'Abd al-Wahhab (who
             absentmindedly wanders out of the studio to 'give voice' – i.e.
             to vote – to the huge irritation of the other musicians); 'Abd al-
             Halim Hafiz (who refuses to vote, but 'will only give voice to the
             microphone!!'). (Reprinted courtesy of *Ruz al-Yusuf*.)

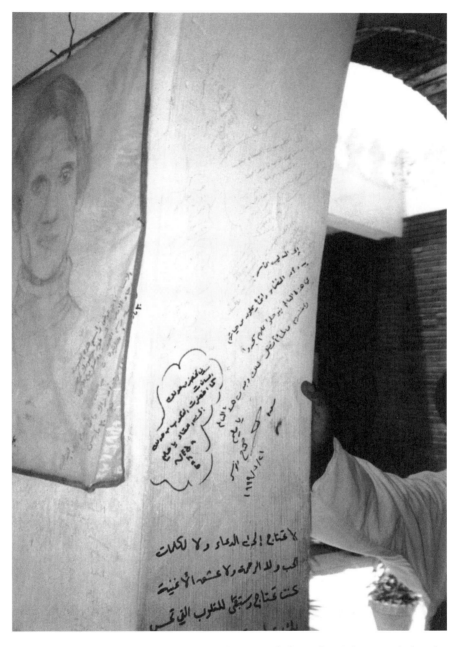

Figure 2.2   Drawings at 'Abd al-Halim's tomb in Cairo (photograph by the author).

He is remembered, though, for other things: his composition, and his training in traditional milieus that provided him with a voice that could, if required, hold its sway without amplification. Microphones do not figure prominently in the visual iconography associated with him. Indeed, they are often puzzlingly absent.[5]

This was not the case with 'Abd al-Halim. He largely abandoned his instrumental skills, at least in public, and did not compose.[6] He had only his voice, which may have been 'sensitive' (a positive quality), but which was also weak and incapable of operating without a microphone.[7] 'Abd al-Halim's intimate association with technology not only compromised him, in the view of many, but even made him a little uncanny, as though he himself were part machine. His nickname, 'the tape recorder', is still remembered by those associated with him. Ziyad al-Tawil, the son of one of 'Abd al-Halim's principal composers, Kamal al-Tawil, for example, passed on to me his father's reminiscences about their conservatory days in Alexandria.[8] 'Abd al-Halim, he recalls, was known even then as 'the recorder'. He could remember every tune he heard, and remind people of a song he had heard only once after a whole year. A joke he would play at the conservatory would be to sing what he would claim to be 'the latest song by Mohammed 'Abd al-Wahhab' and impress students with one actually by the young Kamal al-Tawil. The joke depends on the recognition of al-Tawil's credentials as a composer at such a young age, but also on knowledge of 'Abd al-Halim's machine-like memory: speedy, precise and efficient, a little unusual even in this society in which a capacious memory is a common and prized skill.

What microphones did 'Abd al-Halim use? Information is thin on the ground and hard to come by. However, the pictorial record is useful. One of the earliest pictures of 'Abd al-Halim singing, probably from the very early 1950s, is a mine of

---

[5] Cartoons of Umm Kulthūm rarely show her with a microphone. One in *Ruz al-Yusuf* (no. 1564, 9 March 1955:42) shows a microphone quaking with a mixture of fear and adoration, saying 'sing to me a little', a line from one of her songs. Another, with no caption, shows a microphone wedged between her breasts. A contemporary cartoon of Mohammed 'Abd al-Wahhab shows him lost in his own melancholy, with his trademark thick glasses and *oud*, and with children clambering over him. There is no microphone.

[6] 'Abd al-Halim trained as an orchestral oboe player, something which figures briefly in films such as *Delilah* (1956). *Delilah* makes the most of his instrumental skills – we see him as pianist, oboist and *oud* player, and he bears the role, here and elsewhere, of musical professional with some plausibility. Less and less of his instrumental musical skills figured in films from this point on though. (*Delilah*, 1956, dir. Muhammad Karim, Cairo: Gamal Elleissi Films.)

[7] An extensive and often contradictory vocabulary has been used to describe 'Abd al-Halim's voice, both in his lifetime and since. His voice was routinely described as 'delicate', *murhaf al-hiss* (*murhaf* indicating both a thinness and a precision), and also as possessing a certain clarity and simplicity of expression (*jila'*). The voice possessed subtlety (*diqqa*), but also a capacity to dazzle and astound (*khatf*). These terms are taken from many in Hassaneyn's two books on 'Abd al-Halim (1995 and n.d.).

[8] Interview, 10/12/03.

information.[9] It shows a small *takht* chamber ensemble, with Mohammed Mougi (his other main composer) on *oud* and Ahmet Fuad Hassan (leader of the *Firqa al-Masiyya*, the 'Diamond Ensemble') on *qanun*, crowded onto a small stage. The ornate backcloth suggests that the photograph may have been taken outside; much else in the picture suggests a rather modest gig and a singer very much at the beginning of his career. The ensemble is not amplified and 'Abd al-Halim has placed important people immediately around him – the leader of the ensemble on his right, a cello player on his left and Mougi, the composer, behind him – to help him keep the performance together. 'Abd al-Halim himself is using some version of the Western Electric 618, or 630A 'Eight Ball', moving coil microphone that had been in common use in the American music industry since the 1930s, replacing noisy carbon microphones and mechanically unreliable condensers. The Western Electric 618 was a 'moving coil' microphone, where the vibrations of the internal coil relative to a magnet in the microphone varies a current and produces an audio signal. It had the major advantage over its competitors, chiefly carbon and early condenser microphones, of being small, mechanically reliable and not requiring its own power supply; carbon microphones and condensers quickly disappeared from the market.[10]

However, ribbon microphone technology was also making an impact in Egypt. 'Ribbons', so called because of a two inch long ribbon moving inside a magnetic field, were highly sensitive, with a wide frequency response, and were directional, thus eliminating unwanted sound from the sides. Chief amongst the ribbon microphones of the period was the RCA 44A, a permanent magnet bi-directional microphone with a wide frequency response and a significant reduction in reverb and the pick-up of unwanted sounds. And it was this microphone that made crooning possible. Well-established stars such as Mohammed 'Abd al-Wahhab and Umm Kulthūm used them on stage and at the radio stations, in their different ways, and these are the kinds of microphone on display in their museums.[11] My guess is that well-equipped recording studios, such as Misr Studios, where many of the film soundtracks of the day were produced, made extensive use of the RCA 44A, and that when one listens to the 'Abd al-Halim movie soundtracks of the mid- to late 1950s, this is what one

---

[9]   This early archive picture published in *al-Kawakib* shows 'Abd al-Halim's home village and probably the first shot of him singing in public (*al-Kawakib*, no. 1704, 28 March 1984:28–33).

[10]   See Jim Webb's useful website on microphones of this period (*Twelve Microphones That Changed History*, <http://vintageking.com/site/files/12mics.htm>, accessed 12/08/08).

[11]   Umm Kulthūm and 'Abd al-Wahhab's use of the microphone was distinct. Umm Kulthūm often sang, particularly in concerts, as though there were no microphones present, projecting her voice outwards to a live, co-present audience. 'Abd al-Wahhab, also the possessor of a powerful voice, would, by contrast, tend to focus it on the microphone in front of him.

is listening to.[12] By the early 1960s, the photographic evidence is more extensive and memories are more reliable. Smaller uni-directional microphones, developed by Western Electric, RCA, Shure and others, made a rapid impact. Developments in ribbon technology enabled the leap to a single directional focus and microphones (such as the Western Electric 639A and B) that could be switched from single to omni-directional use enjoyed brief popularity. Shure's Unidyne model appears to have been widely used in Egypt and there are photographs of 'Abd al-Halim performing with this model, or something closely resembling it.

The most significant shift, however, seems to have followed the introduction of German and Austrian microphones later in the 1960s, particularly those manufactured by Neumann and AKG.[13] Both of these were extensively used by Telefunken, which cornered the global market in state-of-the-art sound recording systems in the 1960s and '70s. In 1964, the Egyptian State Broadcasting Corporation opened 'Studio 46', a showpiece of ultra-modern recording technology both symbolising and facilitating Nasser's use of mass media to animate Arab nationalism and to assert Egypt's pre-eminence within it. Composer Baligh Hamdi played an important role in setting up the studio. Hamdi was already working closely with 'Abd al-Halim and Studio 46 was, accordingly, where 'Abd al-Halim made many of his recordings in the last decade of his life. The studio had a staff of 150, directed by Selim Sahab, and included sound recording engineers such as Mustafa Sherif Galal and Zakariya Amir. The state attended lavishly to their professional development.[14] A 24-track Telefunken console was installed, with AKG microphones. This generation of German and Austrian microphones were small and could be held by hand, thanks to smaller capacitors and a standardised tube specially designed to minimise resonance and noise. They were also versatile (featuring both cardoid and omni-directional options). High frequency boosts enabled a good response when the microphone was used far from the sound source, which made them useful for orchestral recordings. But great efforts and ingenuity were evidently expended on making the new Neumann and AKG microphones as good as the old RCA 44A for close-up work.[15] For connoisseurs and technophiles, the AKG C-12 and its close relatives, the ELAM 250 and 251, continue to be counted amongst the best microphones ever made. They are fondly recalled by Egyptian sound recording engineers, such as Zakariya Amir, in their accounts of those days.

---

[12]   Misr Studios was the state-run studio, established in 1935 on Pyramids Road in Cairo with the funding of Talat Harb. See Vitalis (2000) for a critical historical discussion.

[13]   Zakariya Amir, interview with author (9/3/2003), Zamalek, Cairo. It is worth noting here that Frank Sinatra famously used the Neumann U47, marketed by Telefunkun, and known in the trade as the 'Telly'. These were introduced in America in the 1940s and were ubiquitous by the 1950s.

[14]   Zakariya was sent to pursue his studies at newly built studios in England, France and Greece (in the latter case, the EMI studios in Athens).

[15]   See Webb, *Twelve Microphones That Changed History*, for further technical details on the Neumann microphones.

It is easy to see how the AKG microphone adapted to 'Abd al-Halim's art, and he to it. Now that both chorus and solo functions could be picked up, recorded and amplified, large ensembles were possible. A distinct orchestral sound emerged, characterised by the large string chorus on the one hand, and solo instrumental voices set against and in relation to it on the other. Political pressures, both subtle and overt, encouraged the development of a musical style bringing together large forces and big names.[16] This was a musical vision of size, power, coordination, planning and discipline. Strings and percussion could be multiplied. Playing in unison, the effect was breathtaking. Simple passages of harmony and counterpoint made for striking contrasts; longer songs broke down into sections contrasting in instrumentation, *maqam*, meter and ensemble relationships. Voices could nuance words in a much more localised way. Bringing out the meaning of texts no longer had to rely solely on *maqam* or the handling of *qafla*s (cadential patterns), but on the precise shading of a word or phrase. Literary ambitions – already high – could be developed further. By the end of his life, 'Abd al-Halim was laying claim to the major works of leading modernist poets, such as Nizzar Qabbani. This was music with which to assert Egyptian leadership, not only in the Arab, but within the entire non-aligned world. The music of this period continues to be extremely influential across the entire region and one can plausibly argue that it was made possible by, and would not have happened without, the AKG microphone.

Ambivalent Sentimentalists

Why, then, the ambivalence? For ambivalence there certainly was and still is. Microphones are held to be a mixed blessing. Zakariya Amir, sound recording engineer in Studio 46 and today at the Cairo Opera, feels that with microphones, musicians' ability to 'play together' is compromised. 'Feeling' and 'quality' are lost. The habits of contemporary popular singers, relating to the sounds around them through headsets rather than with their own ears, as it were, is in his view a 'disaster'. A gentle question on my part probed to see whether he felt that 'Abd al-Halim was in any way responsible for, or somehow implicated in, the process, as seemed to be implied by much of what he was saying. The question prompted a slightly awkward silence in an otherwise chatty and comfortable interview. Zakariya's father was a well-known Western classical woodwind player and Zakariya discovered Arab classical music for himself at a later age, which may account for some of his purist reflexes. But his ambivalence is a more general phenomenon. 'Abd al-Halim is regularly included in the list of 'greats' that any Cairo taxi driver will instantly invoke the moment one declares an interest in Middle Eastern music. And yet he has not (yet) become a monument, as is literally the case with Umm Kulthūm and Mohammed 'Abd al-Wahhab. One will not see

---

[16]   See Danielson (1997:161–6) and Castelo-Branco (2001) for authoritative discussions of the cultural politics of the 1950s and '60s.

statues of him around Cairo or come across streets named after him. The first documentary film is only now being made. There are no museums dedicated to his memory. Though consistently listed as one of the 'greats', with whose death an entire era passed, his legacy today is ambiguous and contested.

This ambivalence, I would argue, is intimately connected to his use of the microphone. There are three related areas in which I would like to explore this assertion: first, the ways in which he was identified as a sentimentalist; second, his problematic connection with female audiences; and third, his close association with Gamal 'Abd al-Nasser. I will take these in turn. The public emotionality expressed and shaped in romantic cinema comedies and their songs is adjectivally qualified in Arabic as *'atifiyya*, a word appropriately translated as 'sentimental'. The term does not sit well with either Mohammed 'Abd al-Wahhab or Umm Kulthūm; for many, indeed, it is almost scandalously inappropriate. However, the term was consistently used to describe 'Abd al-Halim. Implicitly, it contrasts with *tarab*, the traditional Arab art of vocal enchantment (Racy 2003). *Tarab* demands, from both musicians and audiences, an extensive knowledge of musical traditions, genres and repertoire. It also demands a knowledge of *maqam* (modal structures) and the practices of *taqasim* (modal improvisation). It demands, above all, a thorough acquaintance with the unwritten rules of the *jalsa*, intimate performance occasions characterised by sustained interaction between musicians and their musically sophisticated audiences. As Racy shows, *tarab* has never systematically been deemed antithetical to modernity, and in fact adapted itself well to the concert hall and recording studio. Umm Kulthūm and Mohammed 'Abd al-Wahhab were mistress and master of *tarab*, but not sentimentalism. The notion, as I have suggested, is faintly insulting.

'Abd al-Halim, on the other hand, was a sentimentalist whose ability to 'do' *tarab* was, in the view of many, questionable. In contrast with Umm Kulthūm and 'Abd al-Wahhab, who developed as singers within traditional religious contexts and before concert audiences, his skills were honed in the media industry. Here, the traditional virtues of *tarab*, the respectful and knowledgeable interactions between vocalist, instrumentalists and the audience in performance, had no place. 'Abd al-Halim was capable of leaving audiences cold. Indeed, in some celebratory accounts today, much is made of his battling on, despite hostile audiences who only gradually learned to appreciate what he was up to.[17] He would rehearse for weeks before the beginning of the concert season in the spring (which coincided with the popular Shamm-i Nessim

----

[17]   For example, Nizar Homsi, in the brief (English and Arabic) biography that accompanies all of the EMI CD re-releases of many of 'Abd al-Halim's classics (see Hafez 1983), has this to say of his 1953 debut:

'The place was the al-Andalus Garden Theater Hall in Cairo; the time was 11 p.m.; the occasion was the celebration of the 1st anniversary of the July 23rd Revolution. That night the participating singers were Farid al-Attrach, Shadya, Mohammad Fawzi, 'Abd Aziz Mahmoud, Karim Mahmoud ... and others.

An historic broadcast had just taken place; the declaration announcing the abolition of the monarchy in Egypt and the creation of a republic. One hour later that great legend of the

holiday), his rehearsals famously exacting and disciplined. Pictures show 'Abd al-Halim at work, often looking harassed and exhausted, microphone, incidentally, always at hand. His contemporaries, however, remember him as the organising and disciplining force on these occasions, driving the composers, arrangers and ensemble members assembled either at his house or in specially rented rooms in the Sheraton Hotel. He also assumed a high degree of control over the editing (*intaj*) process, working directly with Zakariya Amir, for example, for up to four days on a single recording. Little was left to chance or to the moment of performance itself. This was a voice shaped by the abstracted and authoritarian work disciplines of the recording studio. 'Sentimentality', then, is to be understood not simply in terms of the presence or absence of a certain kind of emotionality, but in terms of specific social relations and processes of musical production.

The critique of sentimentalism in this context is, in a broad sense, political. On the one hand, there is *tarab*: represented as a democratic art, in which everyone listens to everyone else and everybody contributes equally in their particular way. The audience participates (encouraging the singer and musicians by their commentary and expressions of appreciation). The singer carries the text, and thus assumes a leadership role, but this is always understood to be qualified and tempered by the other musicians. On the other hand, there is sentimentalism: produced by a division of labour in which audiences have no voice, give and take between musicians is not possible and the singer assumes an authoritarian and undemocratic role. There is a strong sense of this in a contemporary cartoon showing the responses of the three dominant singers of the day to the elections for the presidency of the musicians' union, a powerful job dominated in subsequent years by Umm Kulthūm (see Figure 2.1). Umm Kulthūm is shown saying that she is going to do nothing until Riyadh al-Sunbati turns up. 'Abd al-Wahhab is shown walking away from a group of musicians probably waiting to record something. He is going to 'give voice' he says, but not in the sense of singing with them; he is going to leave them all hanging around whilst he goes to 'give voice' by voting. Finally 'Abd al-Halim is shown hectoring a musicians' union official who is shaking with frustration and irritation. 'Abd al-Halim will 'only give his voice to the microphone!!' ('*Ana ma addish sawti illa fi al-mikrofon!!*'). His self-absorbed and authoritarian habits were being lampooned as early as 1957.

Egyptian theatre, Yousif Wahba, appeared on the stage, and, in his wonderfully distinctive voice, introduced the audience to a new singer – 'Abdel Halim Hafez.

'Abdel Halim began to sing 'Safeini Marah was Jafeini Marrah' ... a composition by Mohamed El Mougy. Finishing the first passage of the song 'Abdel Halim noticed there was no reaction from the audience; no applause. He began to feel confused. His memory went back to that evening when he stood before an audience in Alexandria and they had pelted him with tomatoes, finding his voice not to their liking. He began to feel that his career as a singer was ending before it had started. Nonetheless, he continued. He sang through to the last verse. Suddenly there was uproar. Unending clapping and cries of admiration were heard all around him. He had found acceptance at last ....'

The figure of the crooner and his microphone elicited anxieties of a gendered nature as well. 'Abd al-Halim's appeal to 'women and the young' (al-Imrussi 1994:291) was a routine topic of journalistic comment, usually sarcastic. An early hint of this is to be found in a cartoon published in *Ruz al-Yusuf* in 1955, the year in which 'Abd al-Halim's first three films were released (see Figure 2.3). Gamal Kamil's cartoon is one of a series of humorous and cleverly drawn street scenes, character types and modern situations, which appeared weekly in *Ruz al-Yusuf*, an important forum for arts criticism in Egypt since the 1920s. The cartoon shows a composite figure, perhaps more Farid al-Attrash than 'Abd al-Halim, but with clear elements of both. We see only him and not the orchestra. He sings, eyes closed, into a microphone held at a rakish, Sinatra-esque angle. The microphone has been carefully observed by the cartoonist: with its horizontal grill, it looks rather like a Shure Unidyne, a ribbon microphone developed in the 1940s rather specifically for concert and public address work.

Figure 2.3   'The People ... and Songs', cartoon by Gamal Kamil, *Ruz al-Yusuf*, no. 1792, 1958:58. (Reprinted courtesy of *Ruz al-Yusuf*.)

The singer in the cartoon is performing to a large audience in a concert hall or movie theatre. One sees women in various stages of distress and tearfulness. They are, for the most part, young and fashionably dressed. A more conservatively dressed matron sobs mournfully just to the singer's left, allowing the artist to suggest both that gender is the unifying factor, but that within this broad category, age and generational distinctions also matter. Two younger women are in tears and hardly seem able to look at the singer. One, further to the left, with slightly more glamorous garb and coiffure, however, looks him boldly in the eye, hand on cheek, a gesture faintly reminiscent of women screaming at Sinatra, or possibly, even at this early date, Elvis.[18] One woman in the second row has fainted and is being revived by her husband with a handkerchief or piece of paper. The men in this picture are also important. The crooner, here and elsewhere, was satirised for his effect on and control over women. Gamal Kamil's cartoon, however, cleverly draws men into this social satire: men watching the women watching the crooner. One man, closest to us, looks at the singer with withering contempt. Another, in the middle, looks on impassively, the husband, I would guess, of the older sobbing woman. On the far left, another seems to be leaning over and staring at the women with a slightly aggressive expression on his face. In the second row, the bald man is entirely absorbed in reviving his wife. He looks worried. In the corner is another, possibly the usher or attendant. He has seen this all before, and is calmly going about his business.

If cartoons *satirise*, then 'Abd al-Halim's musical films of the period *dramatise* these gendered concerns about mass-mediated voices and public emotions. Many of his films tell a story about musicianship and stardom throwing a love affair into crisis, leaving 'Abd al-Halim isolated on the concert stage and the female lead sobbing at home in front of a television or radio.[19] *Maw'id Gharam* ('Appointment with Love') was made in 1956 and directed by Henry Barakat, co-starring Rushdi Abaza, Imad Hamdi, Zohra al-Ala and Fatin Hamama. With the exception of Hamdi, whose time as a silver-screen heart-throb was drawing to a close, the team of actors, directors, lyricists, composers and arrangers who made *Maw'id Gharam* at Masr Studios worked with 'Abd al-Halim throughout his career. It serves well, then, to illustrate a typical 'Abd al-Halim film. In *Maw'id Gharam*, a meeting with Nawal, a serious young journalist (played by Hamama), transforms the freewheeling life of genial playboy Samir ('Abd al-Halim) into that of a serious, socially-committed

---

[18]   On the presence of Hollywood films in Cairo in these years, see Vitalis (2000) whose account suggests that Sinatra would most likely have been familiar to Cairene movie-goers in the 1950s.

[19]   One might distinguish between films that portray musicianship, such as *Maw'id Gharam* ('Appointment with Love'), *Lahn al-Wafa* ('Song of Farewell', 1955), *Ma'budet al-Jamahir* ('Diva', 1967), and so on, and romantic films in which music is not explicitly part of the dramatic action, such as *al-Wisada al-Khalia* ('The Vacant Pillow', 1957) or *Abi Fawq al-Shajjara* ('Dad's Up a Tree', 1969). The distinction is not perfect: films in which music is part of the diegesis contain non-diegetic musical scenes in which 'Abd al-Halim sings not as a musician. However, all of the films which might be included in this category make a forceful link between musicianship and citizenly virtue. In no circumstances is the occupation of the (true) musician portrayed as being shameful. (*Maw'id Gharam*, 1956, dir. Henry Bareket, Cairo: Gamal Elleissi Films; *Lahn al-Wafa*, 1955, dir. Ibrahim Amareh, Cairo: Gamal Elleissi Films; *Ma'budet al-Jamahir*, 1963, dir. Hilmi Halim, Cairo: Gamal Elleissi Films; *al-Wisada al-Khalia*, 1957, dir. Salah Abu Yusef, Cairo: Gamal Elleisi Films; *Abi Fawq al-Shajjara*, 1969, dir. Hussein Kamal, Cairo: Gamal Elleisi Films.)

musician. Nawal conceals a mystery illness from Samir, which confines her to a
wheelchair at precisely the moment Samir leaves Cairo for Beirut to pursue the
musical career she has pushed him into. The stiffly upright 'Dr Kamal' steps onto
the scene, caring for and eventually falling in love with Nawal in Samir's absence.
The song, '*Beyni wa Beynak Eh?*' ('What is There Between Us?'),[20] performed
before a smart set in the al-Andalus gardens, propels Samir to fame and introduces
a sequence of scenes in which all of the major plot complications are introduced.
The next song, '*Law Kunti Yawm Ansak*'[21] ('If The Day Were to Come When I
Forget You'), marks a moment of crisis: we see Samir singing on stage in Beirut,
a lonely figure at the microphone in front of a vast orchestra. The song '*Law Kunti
Yawm Ansak*' is by turns melodramatic and extravagant, unsettled in mood and
affect, lasting a full eight minutes, an eternity even by the leisurely standards of
Egyptian musical cinema. Nawal listens to him on the radio in her Cairo apartment,
weeping bitterly. The camera relentlessly moves in on the solitary figure of Nawal,
immobilised in her wheelchair, finally coming to rest on a teardrop forming in her
eye. There is a happy ending, of course. Dr Kamal effects a reconciliation of the
lovers and a cure for Nawal's illness, literally stepping out of the picture in the
final scene in the airport. But it is the moment of crisis, the meandering songs
and the dark night of the soul that continue to absorb Egyptian viewers, and that
dominate Egyptian written discussions.[22]

Scenes in 'Abd al-Halim films echo and recapitulate one another. In his
penultimate film, *Ma'budet al-Jamahir* ('Diva', 1967), directed by Hilmi Rafleh,
Shadia plays the diva whose career is on the point of taking a downward turn when
she meets and strikes up an unlikely friendship with 'Abd al-Halim, an aspiring
actor. His career as a musician takes off as hers founders. He rockets to fame
with '*Gabbar*' ('Oppression')[23] and we see ever-growing audiences, newspapers
rolling and, finally, a globe spinning in the background to show that 'Abd al-
Halim has, over the course of a few short months, 'gone global'. As in *Maw'id
Gharam*, another song quickly follows: '*Lastu Qalbi*' ('Not My Heart'),[24] also by
Mougi and also long-winded and multi-sectional, see-saws between melancholic
introspection and rhetorical excess. Shadia is at home watching the performance
on television, surrounded by half-empty bottles of whiskey. She stubs her cigarette
out despairingly as the final cadence sounds, tears running down her face. Both
Fatin Hamama and Shadia are shown trapped in their homes, absorbed in their
own melancholy, cut off from meaningful and productive emotional exchange
with others.

Films and cartoons such as these articulate obvious male anxieties of the
time. Outside the controlling protocols of *tarab* performance, music now seemed

---

[20]   Lyrics by Mamoun al-Shinnawy; music by Kamal al-Tawil.

[21]   Lyrics by Mamoun al-Shinnawy; music by Mohammed Mougi.

[22]   See, for example, Hassaneyn (1995:40).

[23]   Lyrics by Hassan al-Sayyid; music by Mohammed Mougi.

[24]   Lyrics by Kamal al-Shinawi; music by Mohammed 'Abd al-Wahhab.

– thanks to the microphone and the technology to be associated with it – to be circulating in ways that were simultaneously interiorised and elusive, but also highly public. Who would now be able to control the effects of such emotional exhortations, to follow your heart's desire, to disregard the stares of the world? Bourgeois women's 'freedom' in new kinds of domestic spaces and new kinds of consumer economies (for example, in Muhendisin, the city quarter built for the country's emerging technocratic elite) could be celebrated with a relatively easy mind. After all, they provided means of control, as well as empowerment. But mass media – the idea of a direct line, as it were, between microphone and radio loudspeaker – unsettled the picture. What insidious work might a song or a film do, lodged out of sight and accountability in a woman's mind and in the privacy of her own home? Or, more to the point, in *anybody's* mind? Better to acknowledge the pleasures, but hobble their potential social and political claims by deeming them 'women's stuff', a minor and locatable art. This, one might argue, is a significant part of the gendered work being done by both the films, and the broader social conversation about the figure of the crooner in Egypt at the time.

Finally, anxieties about the microphone had an obvious political dimension. Gamal 'Abd al-Nasser swept to power in the wake of the Officer's movement of 1952. Nasser's grasp of the power of mass media is well known (see Danielson 1997), and he had an exquisitely honed sense of what could be achieved by the amplified voice in a society attuned to the traditional arts of Islamic rhetoric and audition, the *ilm al-balagha* (Hirschkind 2004:133). His was a quiet voice, as many contemporaries remember it, one that wasn't particularly capable of shouting or filling a large space unaided. It was also a nuanced voice, one that relied greatly for its rhetorical effect on subtle changes of intensity, inflection and emotional charge. Whether in large crowds, or listening to radio broadcasts or recordings, Egyptians responded to a voice that persuaded because it was intimate and proximate. He set a tone, quite literally, to which subsequent leaders were obliged to respond, whether to distance themselves from, or to align themselves with his legacy.

The techno-political issues surrounding microphone use in political oratory continue to reverberate.[25] As many readers of this volume will be aware, Nasser's successor, Anwar Sadat, slowly but emphatically distanced himself from the Nasserite political legacy, making peace with Israel and dismantling the command economy. Though rioting ensued when he abolished bread subsidies, he was able to cajole and coerce a large part of Egyptian society as a result of oil wealth and migrant remittances from the Gulf. The intelligentsia, on the other hand, initiated violent polemics that continue to this day around three ideological polarities: Islam, socialism and neoliberalism. In turn, Hosni Mubarak, Sadat's

---

[25]   As Hirschkind suggests, in his thought-provoking account of the politics of audition in contemporary Egyptian cassette sermons, Nasser was replaced by leaders for whom the ear became 'morally and epistemologically untrustworthy' (2004:145), allowing the Islamist opposition in Egypt to capitalise, in a later generation, on political techniques which Nasser – the secularist and socialist – had cultivated and prolonged.

successor, was saddled with the legacy of Sadat's reforms, but in the context of diminished oil revenues and migrant remittances, as well as growing support for the Palestinian *intifada*. Whilst a return to Nasserite social radicalism and defiance of the international order was politically impossible, much could be made of a more limited *cultural* recuperation.

If Nasserite imagery can only be evoked cautiously as a point of political reference at the current moment (see Gordon 2000), 'Abd al-Halim is an acceptable surrogate, and 'Abd al-Halim nostalgia has been prominent. In 1999, Egyptian radio launched a new programme, the *Idha'a al-Aghani*, almost exclusively devoted to the state-promoted repertories of the 1950s and '60s. Celebrations of the anniversary of 'Abd al-Halim's death gained momentum in the late 1990s, with rather sober articles in the heavyweight daily newspapers. His political repertory, taken off the airwaves after the Camp David talks (in 1979) reappeared, in recorded, broadcast and concert form. A flurry of books underlined his new public prominence.[26] The half-century anniversary of the Revolution on 23 July 2002 culminated with a sound and light show over the Nile in downtown Cairo, with 'Abd al-Halim's nationalist anthem, '*Sura Sura*' booming over the public address system.[27] Long delayed plans to make a biopic about 'Abd al-Halim are now underway[28] and 'Abd al-Halim films continue to be shown on television. Through 'Abd al-Halim, the state clearly believes that it can have its Nasserite cake and eat it: it can enjoy the nostalgia without entangling itself in the politics.

Politics and nostalgia, however, are not so easily disentangled and separated. Ambivalence continues to hover over 'Abd al-Halim, even as the official recuperation and appropriation of his art is underway. The revolutionary overtones of the films cannot be easily ignored. These are tales of young love prevailing despite the will of the old order and the tired patriarchs who preside over it, of wit, humour and charm overcoming the adversity of fate, stories that now seem to brim with the anti-colonial, nationalist and revolutionary sentiments of their day: uncomfortable tales to tell in Mubarak's Egypt. The still insistent claim that

---

[26] Biographies from these years include al-Imrussi (1994), Hassaneyn (1995), Fakhouri (n.d.), al-Shorabji (2000).

[27] Like many of his nationalist anthems, '*Sura Sura*' (1967) was set to words by colloquial poet Salah Jahim, with music by Kamal al-Tawil (who also worked closely on 'Abd al-Halim's film projects). See Hassaneyn (1995:118–25) for further discussion of this song in the context of his later nationalist anthems.

[28] The film was being made at the time of writing and, interestingly, stars Ahmad Zaki who played both Nasser and Sadat in nationalist biopics of the 1990s (see Gordon 2000). Zaki died during the making of the 'Abd al-Halim biopic and shots of his own funeral apparently feature as that of 'Abd al-Halim in the film. For an interesting and thoughtful discussion on what has happened to stardom in Egypt in the intervening years, with specific reference to 'Abd al-Halim and Ahmad Zaki, see Ala' Khaled, 'Bayn al-'Andalib wa al-Fata al-Asmar: Iradat al-Muti', *Akhbar al-Adab*, 1 May 2005, no. 616, <www.akhbarelyom.org. eg/adab/issues/616/0103.html> (accessed 11/12/06).

'Abd al-Halim's films are 'for women' betokens a more contemporary political anxiety, and an effort to put them out of harm's way. Their aggressively modern sexual politics are a more obvious issue. In the contemporary climate of extreme conservatism, 'Abd al-Halim's last film, *Abi Fawq al-Shajjara* ('Dad's Up a Tree', also known as 'the film of a thousand kisses', 1969), still has the power to shock, not only with its kissing and even today uncomfortable-to-behold beachwear, but as a rendering of Ihsan 'Abd al-Quddus's deeply disturbing account of father and son competing for the affections of a prostitute (see also Gordon 2002:126).

If we are to understand 'Abd al-Halim's voice as a site of ambivalence, anxiety and contest over the last 50 years, we must understand its central and constitutive relationship with the microphone. The point is worth emphasising and considering in a broad context. As Théberge has noted:

> The fundamental importance of the microphone in popular music is underscored, ironically, by the degree to which it has become 'naturalized' and its effect rendered invisible. Whether considering the 1930s notion of 'high fidelity' or the 'unplugged' phenomenon of the 1980s, engineers and critics alike have tended to reinforce the idea that microphones are essentially reproductive technologies, that they are, by design, transparent in their operation. However, such aesthetic discourses only serve to efface the profound impact that microphones have on people's experience of popular music. (2003:246–7)

It is hard to disagree with Théberge's claim. The profound impact that microphones have on people's experience of popular music has indeed been effaced by memories that are inclined either to forget or to trivialise technological issues, in Egypt, as elsewhere. What, then, do we gain, by resuscitating these issues, by searching for their traces in the historical record, by forcing people's memories and discursive habits against the grain? In the first instance, one comes across surprisingly rich veins of commentary on singers and their microphones, perhaps 'effaced' by the dominant aesthetic discourses, but by no means absent. Consider Bing Crosby and Frank Sinatra, whose use of the microphone was a topic of much contemporary and retrospective discussion in America,[29] usage critiqued, or celebrated, or nuanced with distinctions and discriminations. Crosby crooned, but Sinatra, in the view of some, could play the range, from crooning to full-blooded *bel canto*.[30] He turned the microphone into a sophisticated stage prop. At times it was a prosthetic, physical support for a thin and sickly body; at others, a dancing partner, playfully swirled and twirled. He could play with distance, colouring a line by moving his body toward, or away from, the microphone. In the 1950s,

---

[29]   On Crosby, see McCracken (2001); on Sinatra, see particularly Petkov (1995) and Shaw (1995).

[30]   It is worth noting that Sinatra was a product of the revolution in microphone technology that shaped 'Abd al-Halim's vocal art. On Sinatra's use of the 'Telly' see footnote 13.

microphones signified. And people knew that they did, even though the dominant aesthetic discourse consistently stressed their essentially 'reproductive' roles, as Théberge suggests.[31] In Egypt, I would argue that microphones were rather less transparent, less 'effaced'. One can, today, relatively easily access times, places and people for whom the microphone was an issue, for whom it was instantly associated with forms of coercion and persuasion that were, and remain, extremely problematic.

Concluding Remarks

Three points might be made in conclusion. Ubiquitous pictures of 'Abd al-Halim singing into a microphone, and visual jokes and puns relying on the presence of microphones suggest a complex current of commentary on voices, bodies, sounds and spaces in the period. And questions. Do the microphones suggest physical impairment and prosthesis – something subtracted at the same time as added? Do they suggest confinement, even as they imply new kinds of circulation and ubiquity? How might these suggestions of bodily lack and technological enhancement connect with the overthrowing of the old order and the embrace of a revolutionary future? Do they betoken confidence, or anxiety? And what are the gendered implications? 'Abd al-Halim sobs quietly into his microphone in Beirut, whilst Fatin Hamama sobs in her wheelchair in her apartment in Cairo. Is their confinement to be equated, or distinguished? Who has got the worst deal here? What are the implications in terms of class, power and social stratification? Are the powerful now to be characterised by their quietness and intimacy, the powerless by their noisiness? Are the new 'acoustics of national publicity', to borrow Currid's phrase (2000:147), subtly more divisive than those of the old order? And do 'Abd al-Halim's films mitigate these issues or draw attention to them? What lines of critical inquiry into the politics of this highly significant and still resonant moment might they still enable? What kinds of public might gather and shape themselves around these inquiries?[32]

Secondly, these questions about the microphone add a nuance to the well-trodden Andersonian picture of nationalism and the public sphere. Or, more accurately, add a nuance to a nuance. Walter Armbrust, in his well-known study of films in the formation of Egyptian modernity (1996), points out that allowance and

---

[31]   In Sinatra's case, the microphone was insistently portrayed as enhancing the 'natural' qualities of a natural voice. Note, for example, Shaw singing Sinatra's praises, 'In truth, the microphone permits a more natural manner of singing, because the vocal output is more consistent with everyday speech. And rather than aiding weak and flawed voices, it reveals flaws in an almost unforgiving fashion! The microphone is to natural singing what the motion-picture camera is to natural acting …' (1995:26).

[32]   I have Hansen's (1991) analysis of the formation of counter publics around early twentieth-century Hollywood film in mind particularly.

adjustment has to be made for societies in which literacy was not widespread and where habits of newspaper and novel reading were not deeply entrenched amongst the middle classes, as in Egypt. Film shaped modern Egypt, he suggests, and did so in rather particular ways, specifically in its production of what he describes as a 'split vernacular'. The language of Egyptian film unified the nation, but did so in ways that also lodged nagging tensions into the very heart of Egyptian, and by extension, Arab modernity, between the language of the streets, the language of audio-visual mass media and the language of the written word. The role of the microphone in shaping political process and the formation of public spheres at this juncture deserves careful consideration, as nuances of linguistic register attained enormous power and significance.

Thirdly, and finally, the figure of the sentimentalist with his microphone elicits nostalgia, in Egypt, as elsewhere. His was the voice that – in the conventional critique – ushered in the end of the golden age of modernism, its opening out into the morass of mass culture, and the restriction of the modernist project to ever smaller and ever more circumscribed cultural spaces. We thus constantly return to early twentieth-century modernism and turn away from the supposed moment of decline with embarrassment. The case of 'Abd al-Halim Hafiz, with his collaborations with the major artistic and literary figures of his day, suggests we draw these lines too quickly; specifically those that separate twentieth-century modernism from sentimentalism. There is much more going on here, and many more connections, than we are inclined to think.

Chapter 3

Mediated Qur'anic Recitation and the Contestation of Islam in Contemporary Egypt

Michael Frishkopf

Overview[1]

Islam in Egypt today is contested across a broad media spectrum from recorded sermons, films, television and radio programmes to newspapers, pamphlets and books. Print, recorded and broadcast media facilitate an ongoing ideological debate about Islam – its nature and its normative social role – featuring a wide variety of discursive positions.[2] What is the role of Qur'anic recitation (generally known as *tilawa*) within this debate?

Public *tilawa* is one of Islam's most essential and universal practices, deeply rooted in Islamic tradition and deeply felt by its practitioners (Nelson 2001). Can public *tilawa* participate in ideological struggles to define Islam? Certainly, Qur'anic recitation is immensely moving for Muslims. And yet, *prima facie*, one might expect the answer to be 'no', because the Qur'an's linguistic content is fixed and its recitation highly regulated. Nevertheless, *tilawa* allows significant scope for variation and stylistic variety. In the past, such divergence resulted from localised chains of transmission, shaped by contrastive contexts and did not typically convey widely significant ideological positions. However, over the past century the mass media has generally facilitated the formation and circulation of more broadly recognisable and influential *tilawa* styles within a more autonomous

[1] This chapter extends the seminal work of Kristina Nelson. In the postscript to the new edition of her book, *The Art of Reciting the Qur'an* (2001), Nelson comments on the rise of a Saudi style since the first edition appeared in 1985. This is precisely the period I am attempting, in part, to document here. My sincere thanks to Kristina Nelson, for her groundbreaking study and insightful comments on an earlier draft, to Wael 'Abd al-Fattah, Usama Dinasuri, Iman Mersal and Dr Ali Abu Shadi, for their critical insights and feedback, to staff at *al-Musannafat al-Fanniyya*, SonoCairo and the Islamic Research Academy of al-Azhar University, and to numerous Egyptians (reciters and others) with whom I've conducted countless informal discussions. This research was supported by generous grants from the American Research Center in Egypt (2003–4) and from the Social Sciences and Humanities Research Council of Canada (2004–6).

[2] Multiple discourses have been documented in recent years by a wide range of scholars including Kepel (1993), Gaffney (1994), Abed-Kotob (1995), Ibrahim (1996), Johansen (1996), Abdo (2000) and Wickham (2002).

sonic field. In this chapter, I aim to show how the cassette medium, embedded in the historical circumstances of its emergence in Egypt, has recently enabled a new ideological distinction between 'Egyptian' and 'Saudi' *tilawa* styles.[3] By means of this distinction, the latter powerfully represents, and promotes, influential reformist-revivalist Islamic ideology within contemporary Egyptian society.

Introduction to *Tilawa* in Contemporary Egypt[4]

For Muslims, the Qur'an is Divine Revelation (*wahy*), the fixed Speech of God (*kalam Allah*) as revealed in the Arabic language to the Prophet Muhammad, starting around the year 610 CE and continuing until the Prophet's death in 632 CE. Following the dominant *Ash'ari* creed, most Egyptian Muslims accept the Speech of God as a Divine Attribute, hence uncreated and eternal with God Himself. The Qur'an is inextricably attached to its recitation as solo vocal performance. Muslims rarely read the Qur'an without reciting it and the experience of the Divine text is therefore primarily auditory (Nelson 2001:xiv, Nasr 1995:57). The injunction to recite is explicit in both Qur'an and Sunna.[5] The word 'Qur'an' itself implies 'recitation' (Rahman 1979:30). God revealed (some say 'recited') the Qur'an to the archangel Gabril. Gabril subsequently recited it to Muhammad, who recited it to his Companions (*sahaba*), and so on in a continuous chain to the present. The Prophet said that Gabril taught him the Qur'an in seven '*ahruf*' (dialectical variants) in order to be intelligible to different Arab tribes (Tirmidhi 2000: no. 2867). Phonetic variation, perhaps stemming from the multiple *ahruf*, allowed different schools of recitation to emerge and eventually ten principal variant 'readings' (*qira'at*) were fixed, each associated with a particular teacher, plus sub-variants (*riwayat*)

---

[3]   Since the 1990s, other phonogram formats have emerged, including CD, CD-ROM (a single CD can contain the entire Qur'an plus commentaries) and video. Internet downloads are increasingly common, especially as Internet cafés proliferate, and Islamic satellite television channels (such as *Iqra'*) have greatly expanded synchronous bandwidth for Qur'anic recitation. But cassettes remain central, due to the ubiquity of playback equipment, low cost and the importance of asynchronous channels, as discussed below.

[4]   A number of studies of Qur'anic recitation have been published in English, the most comprehensive being that by Nelson (2001), which likewise focuses on contemporary Egypt. See also Pacholczyk (1970), al-Faruqi (1987a, 1987b) and Rasmussen (2001).

[5]   Sunna constitutes the customs of the Prophet Muhammad as passed down through reports (*Hadith*) about his speech and behaviour. The most reliable *Hadith* collections (including those of Muslim, Bukhari, Tirmidhi, Ibn Majah, Darimi and Ibn Hanbal cited here) are known as '*sahih*' ('true'). The first revealed verse (Qur'an 96:1) begins with the command '*iqra*' ('recite!') (Lings 1983:43–4; Bukhari 2000: no. 3 [note that *Hadith* citations in his chapter employ the al-Alamiah Enumeration]). The Qur'an itself clearly states (in 73:4) '*rattil al-Qur'ana tartilan*' ('chant the Qur'an in measure') (Pickthall 1953), and from the Prophet's Sunna, 'He is not one of us who does not chant the Qur'an' (Bukhari 2000: no. 6973).

associated with their students. In Egypt, the principal reading is presently *Hafs 'an 'Asim*: the *riwaya* of Hafs bin Sulayman (d. 796) from the *qira'a* of his father-in-law, 'Asim of Kufa (d. 745) (Sa'id 1975:69). Since the manner of the Prophet's recitation carried the force of Divine authority, it was codified as *ahkam al-tajwid*: the fixed 'rules' governing correct recitation of the Qur'an. A large component of *tajwid* concerns phonetics, including proper articulation of each letter and rules for their assimilation (*idgham*), emphasis (*tafkhim*) and de-emphasis (*tarqiq*). Other topics include regulation of the length of the *madd* (long vowels), handling the *waqf* (pause) and *ibda'* (resumption) and the relative speed of recitation (from *tahqiq* to *hadr*) (see 'Abd al-Fattah 2001, Nelson 2001).

Despite the importance of recitation and oral transmission, a written tradition also developed in parallel with the oral one. With the Prophet's approval, some of his literate companions recorded Qur'anic verses in Arabic script and after his death the first textual recension (*mushaf*[6]) was carefully prepared by the first Caliph Abu Bakr (r.632–34 CE). By the time of the third Caliph, 'Uthman (r.644–55 CE), a number of written versions existed (stemming partly from the multiple *ahruf*) and disputes arose over various Qur'anic passages, thus undermining the unity of the *Umma* (Muslim community). Soon after 650,[7] 'Uthman responded by fixing a second authoritative recension and having all other versions burnt (Sa'id 1975:19ff.). This 'Uthmani recension has remained the only authoritative *mushaf*; augmented with diacritical marks (points and vowels), the text corresponds to a particular *qira'a*. The *mushaf* comprises 114 *suras* (chapters), each divided into a number of *ayas* (verses) and arranged approximately in order of decreasing length (the opening *sura* excepted). Independently, the *mushaf* is divided into 30 roughly equal units (*ajza'* [sing. *juz'*]) to facilitate orderly monthly recitation, especially during Ramadan.

What then is fixed and what is variable in *tilawa*? Fixity is an important property of most sacred objects, for the sacred – presumably – does not change. *Tilawa* is fixed, to a large extent, by three discursive sources: the written text (*mushaf*), its phonological 'readings' (*qira'at*) and its rules of recitation (*ahkam al-tajwid*). In the analysis which follows, I define a *variable* as an association of each *tilawa* performance (or each moment in each performance, for time-dependent variables) with a value along a dimension, qualitative or quantitative. Once a *mushaf* passage has been selected for recitation, the range of its possible sonic realisations is sharply limited by *qira'at* and *tajwid*. Yet certain variables, each corresponding to a particular sonic, textual or pragmatic dimension (Bussman 1996:374), nevertheless remain free (within limits). By means of variation along these dimensions, different yet equally acceptable recitations of the same passage in the same *qira'a* may be distinguished. Over time, with the accumulation (inherent

---

6   Pronounced '*mus-haf*' ('sh' is not a digraph).

7   R. Paret (2006), 'Kira'a', in P. Bearman, Th. Bianquis, C.E. Bosworth, E. van Donzel and W.P. Heinrichs (eds), *Encyclopaedia of Islam* (web edition), Brill Online, University of Alberta, <www.brillonline.nl.login.ezproxy.library.ualberta.ca/subscriber/entry?entry=islam_SIM-4383> (accessed 12/12/06).

in oral traditions) of sonic communications through historically-conditioned social networks, such variability enables contrastive *tilawa* styles to emerge.

Given a particular passage and *qira'a*, recitational variation is non-discursive: it does not alter the linguistic text of *tilawa* (Bussman 1996:13, 479). Many free variables capture paralinguistic dimensions of recitation, often with continuous (for instance, pitch, duration, loudness) or complex (for instance, timbre) values, and typically time-dependent, as opposed to the discrete-sequential phonological variables of linguistic discourse.[8] Being non-discursive, such variables also resist discursive description or specification (indeed, the difficulty of specifying continuous time-varying features is one reason they have not been fixed by *ahkam al-tajwid*) and tend to remain out of awareness. Rather, their significance is primarily expressive and affective, selectively emphasising and colouring but never altering the cognitive meaning of a Qur'anic passage. At the same time, their provision for spontaneous, situational expressivity enables great affective power.

Table 3.1 summarises some of the variable aspects of *tilawa*, including sonic and textual variables (under the reciter's direct control), together with others relating to the social context of recitation and the social positions of participants. A fourth set of variables is applicable for commercially recorded *tilawa*.

Table 3.1   The principal free variables defining public *tilawa* style (variables in italics). Media variables apply to recorded *tilawa* only. While the number of variables is arbitrary, this particular set defines a 38-dimensional vector space, within which styles can be represented as distinctive regions.

1. Sonic Variables	
1.1 Timbral	1.1.1 Vocal *timbre*
	1.1.2 Emotional *expression* (as judged by Egyptian reciters and listeners)
1.2 Tonal	1.2.1 *Ambitus* (width of tonal range)
	1.2.2 *Tessitura* (centre of tonal range)
	1.2.3 *Mode* preference[9]
	1.2.4 Extent of modal *modulation*
	1.2.5 *Melodicity* (melodic complexity, development, ornament)

---

8   While at the phonetic level discourse is also continuous, at the phonological level continuities are aggregated into a discrete set of phonemes; discourse (as the term is used in the field of linguistics) comprises a sequence drawn from this set.

9   A mode is a tonal structure comprising a pitch set carrying additional structures, including tonal functions (tonic, dominant, leading tone) and melodic tendencies. In Arabic, mode is known as *maqam* and the same modes are used in secular music and *tilawa*. Commonly used *tilawa* modes include *Bayyati* (D, E half-flat, F, G, A, B half-flat, C) and *Rast* (C, D, E half-flat, F, G, A, B half-flat).

1.3 Temporal	1.3.1 Use of interphrasal *pause*
	1.3.2 *Tone rate*[10]
	1.3.3 *Rhythm*
1.4 Dynamic	1.4.1 *Dynamic level* (*sirran* or *jahran*, plus amplification level)
	1.4.2 *Dynamic range*
	1.4.3 Use of *accent* (stress)

2. Textual Variables	
2.1 Setting	2.1.1 *Melisma* (average number of tones per syllable)
	2.1.2 *Word painting* (*taswir al-ma'na*)[11]
2.2 Text pacing	2.2.1 *Repetition* (of textual segments)
	2.2.2 Average *syllable duration*
	2.2.3 *Syllable duration variation* (standard deviation)
2.3 Text selection	2.3.1 Selection of *textual passage*[12]
	2.3.2 *Textual boundaries* of selection[13]
	2.3.3 Inclusion of *du'a'*, or not[14]
2.4 Phonetics	2.4.1 *Regional accent*[15]
	2.4.2 *Qira'a*

3. Pragmatic Variables	
3.1 Context	3.1 *Occasion* (for example, obligatory prayer, listening *majlis*, study session, *maytam*, studio recording)
3.2 Status	3.2 Reciter's *social position* (status, specialisations, professionalism)
3.3 Presentation	3.3 Reciter's *personal image* (dress, comportment)
3.4 Audience	3.4.1 *Attendance*
	3.4.2 *Listener behaviour*

---

[10]   Tones per second (tps). In a monophonic vocal context, I take a 'tone' to be a maximal temporal interval exhibiting approximately constant pitch and bounded by an adjacent pair of syllabic attack points (which would, if transcribed, correspond to a 'note'). Thus the set of tone boundaries comprises the union of (1) syllable onsets and (2) moments of pitch change.

[11]   For example, raising the tonal level to describe Paradise, or matching *maqam* to textual mood.

[12]   Although the *mushaf* is fixed, the particular passage recited is variable; its selection may be influenced by contextual factors, personal preference, or in order to express a particular message through the Qur'anic medium.

[13]   In theory, the reciter may begin and end with any verse. However, boundaries are most typically determined either by *sura* or *juz'* boundaries, especially on recordings.

[14]   During certain prayers (especially dawn and Ramadan *tarawih* prayers), the reciter may append a concluding *du'a'* (supplicative prayer) to his recitation.

[15]   The careful phonetic specifications of *tajwid* manuals do not preclude a certain degree of variability, enabling regional Arabic accents to recognisably emerge.

4. Recorded Media Variables	
4.1 Medium	4.1 *Medium* (for example, cassette, CD, CD-ROM)
4.2 Sound effects	4.2 Artificial *reverb*
4.3 Cover graphics	4.3.1 *Cover text*
	4.3.2 *Cover fonts*
	4.3.3 *Cover images*
	4.3.4 *Cover art*
4.4 Production	4.4.1 *Producer name*
	4.4.2 *Producer specialisation*
4.5 Distribution	4.5 Primary *retail location* (for example, sold from cassette shop, stationery shop, newspaper kiosk, street display)
4.6 Use	4.6 *Use* (for example, pedagogy, background sound)

In Egypt, the reciter is generally called *qari'*, though in the context of congregational prayer he may be the *imam* (prayer leader) or (on Friday) *khatib* (preacher).[16] The teacher of recitation and professional reciter specialist is called *muqri'*. Recitation itself is called *qira'a* ('reading'), *tajwid* ('improving') and *tartil* ('chanting'). Besides their more general meanings, however, each of the latter two terms is also associated with a style of recitation, whose name is derived from the same linguistic root. These recitational styles are called *mujawwad* (derived, like *tajwid*, from the Arabic root j-w-d), and *murattal* (derived, like *tartil*, from r-t-l). These styles, corresponding to distinctive regions of the 'free variable' space defined above, developed in response to social and media forces of mid-twentieth-century Egypt. *Mujawwad* (or *tajwid*) is a slow-paced, melodically elaborate style, designed for the listener's contemplation and requiring great skill from the reciter, who is a highly accomplished (usually professional) specialist. *Murattal* (or *tartil*) is a faster, less melodic style used for individual devotions and study, as well as obligatory prayer.[17] The world-wide influence of the Egyptian *tilawa* tradition has rendered the *mujawwad–murattal* contrast globally significant.

The experience of recitation is never merely a matter of the cognitive apprehension of Qur'anic text and meaning. Rather, it is pre-eminently emotional.[18] Emotional power is stirred both by meanings of the fixed Divine text and by the

---

[16]   The following summary of *tilawa* practice is based primarily on my own participant-observations and conversations in Egypt, supplemented by secondary sources (Sa'id 1975, Daoud 1997a, Nelson 2001).

[17]   *Tajwid* may also refer to the rules governing recitation (see below) and *qira'a* applies to any act of reading, not just Qur'anic recitation. As such, the most general term denoting all Qur'anic recitation (no more and no less) is *tilawa*.

[18]   The Prophet himself offered advice concerning the appropriate emotions, both experiential and behavioural, associated with Qur'anic recitation, stating in a *hadith*, 'indeed the Qur'an was revealed with sadness [*huzn*], so if you recite it weep, and if you can't weep then feign weeping' ('*in al-Qur'ana nazala bil-huzni, fa idha qara'tumuhu fabku wa in lam tabku fa tabaaku*') (Ibn Majah 2000: no. 1327). Sufis in particular ascribe great emotional power to recitation (Ghazali 1901:733ff.).

sonic substrate created by the reciter (partly in response to those meanings). As the Prophet said, 'Beautify the Qur'an with your voices, for the beautiful voice increases the Qur'an in beauty' (Darimi 2000: no. 3365). The reciter's personal expression of affective response is sonically communicated through free variables in the domains of timbre, dynamics, accent, timing and pitch.

Recitation may be performed privately or publicly. Quiet private recitation (*sirran*) not intended to be heard by others, occurs in individual prayer, in certain *rak'as*[19] of congregational prayer (*salat al-jama'a*) and for individual study and devotions. It is never *mujawwad*. By contrast, public recitation, intended to be heard by others (*jahran*), may be performed *mujawwad* or *murattal*. The Prophet himself exhorted public recitation, stating 'I like to hear [Qur'an] recited by someone other than me' (Bukhari 2000: no. 4661), indicating that both reciter and listener receive spiritual rewards (Ibn Hanbal 2000: no. 8138). Public recitation is most constrained during the first two *rak'as* of dawn, sunset, night and Friday congregational prayers. Here, where there is neither time nor inclination (nor, often, ability) for *mujawwad* and where responsorial behaviour is precluded, the *imam* or *khatib* recites *murattal*. Memorials (*maytam, arba'in, dhikra*)[20] allow considerable flexibility for professional *mujawwad* recitations, as does the *tilawa* listening session (*majlis*), performed in the mosque before or after prayer (especially before dawn and Friday noon congregational prayers), and on religious holidays. Again, the reciter is usually a *mujawwad* professional. Additionally, listeners can respond, expressing spiritual-aesthetic feeling at the *qafla* (melodic-textual cadence) with cries of '*Allah!*' or '*Ya Salam!*' which stir the reciter to greater expressive heights in a feedback process closely resembling the *tarab* (musical ecstasy) aesthetic of traditional Arab music (Racy 2003). These exclamations stimulate highly affective states, including profound sadness (*huzn, shajan*) and mystical or musical ecstasy (*wajd, tarab*), the latter highly controversial. Such sessions have often attracted listeners for aesthetic as well as spiritual reasons. Finally, recorded recitations (of any of the above types) allows the listener maximal contextual freedom.[21]

The relationship between *tilawa* and music is complex, one manifestation of what Nelson calls the '*sama*' polemic' (2001:32ff.), related to a long-standing Islamic debate over the admissibility of music generally (Roy Choudhury 1957, Farmer 1957). Whereas music and singing were widely practised throughout

---

[19] Each prayer is composed of between two and four *rak'as*; each *rak'a* includes Qur'anic recitation, followed by a bow and two prostrations. The *imam* recites Qur'an publicly during the first two *rak'as* of dawn, sunset, night and Friday congregational prayers. Recitation in other *rak'as* is private.

[20] Memorial recitations are generally held outdoors after evening prayers, in a colourful *suwan* (tent) where guests can be received, and are loudly amplified. The *maytam* occurs immediately after burial, the *arba'in* after 40 days and the *dhikra sanawiyya* annually thereafter. Egyptian intellectuals and Islamic reformists alike deem the *arba'in* a pre-Islamic Pharaonic survival; the latter also condemn it.

[21] See Nelson for a more detailed summary of recitation contexts (2001:xxiii–xxviii).

Islamic societies, normative religious discourse – drawing primarily on *Hadith* – counterposed a Sufi point of view (that under the right conditions music supports spirituality [for example, Ghazali 1901]) with a more puritanical one (that music, at best, is a distraction from God; at worst, an incitation to sinfulness [for example, Dunya 1938]).[22] Unsurprisingly, the 'polemic' intensifies concerning application of music to recitation of the sacred text itself. For Muslims, *tilawa* is not singing, just as the Qur'an is not poetry. Textually and theologically, the distinction is obvious: the Qur'an is unique; its inimitability (*i'jaz*) Divine. Sonically and pragmatically, the distinction is more ambiguous. But, unlike song, *tilawa* contains neither poetic nor musical meters; it is performed as an improvised vocal solo, unaccompanied by instruments, and is sonically marked by *ahkam al-tajwid*.

Yet public recitation is always pitched, exhibiting the tonal logic, and sometimes the complexity, of music. Further, in pre-mass media Egypt a broad region of overlap between musical and religious sonic-social practices prevailed. Public recitation draws upon musical resources, especially the modal system of *maqamat*. Traditionally, *tilawa* and singing were often performed at the same events, even by the same performers. Up until the early twentieth century, *tilawa* experts such as Shaykh Ali Mahmud (1878–1949) and Shaykh Muhammad Rif'at (1882–1950) also sang *qasidas* and *muwashshahat* (elevated art music genres) (Tawfiq 199x:16, 19, 67),[23] and the *kuttab* (Qur'an school) provided vocal training for the greatest singers, including Umm Kulthūm and Muhammad 'Abd al-Wahhab (Tawfiq 199x:31, Danielson 1990, 1997), at least through the first third of the twentieth century.

Undoubtedly, 'free variables' have always enabled the differentiation of discernable *tilawa* styles, but until modern times such styles could only crystallise and propagate through face-to-face interaction and thus must have remained both numerous and relatively localised, or at least of limited influence. The advent of broadcast and recording technology in the twentieth century, however, has catalysed a new quasi-independent symbolic field of recitations, and a new dimension of symbolic difference within that field. Despite some early reservations,[24] uptake of *tilawa* into the mass media system – starting with phonogram discs in the early twentieth century (Racy 1976:33–4, 1977), followed by radio in the 1920s – was

---

[22]   Thus in one *hadith*, the Prophet allows girls to sing for the *'Id* (Muslim 2000: no. 1479); in another, the devil is told that his voice is *mizmar* (a wind instrument) (Qalamuni 2000:109).

[23]   Where precise dates of publication are not known, but where the decade is known, the latter is indicated (for example, 199x) in preference to n.d.

[24]   For instance, the concern that *tilawa* recordings might be played in inappropriate contexts was articulated. Shaykh Muhammad Rif'at consulted with Islamic legal experts before his first radio broadcast in 1934, and was always reluctant to record (lest an impure person touch a phonograph disc) (Tawfiq 199x:66–7). Shaykh Muhammad Salama, who began reciting in 1910, only became convinced of the legality of radio broadcasts in 1948 (Sa'dani 1996:41).

rapid. In 1934, Radio Egypt (*al-Idha'a al-Misriyya*) was launched (ERTU 2004:47) with melodious recitations by Shaykh Rif'at (Rizk 2004, Tawfiq 199x:66) and *tilawa* was aired frequently thereafter. Radio set ownership expanded significantly in Egypt during the 1950s (Starkey 1998:424), and in 1964 the government added a new station called Radio Qur'an (*Idha'at al-Qur'an al-Karim*), specialising in *tilawa* and other Islamic programming (ERTU 2004:47). Egyptian Television (*al-Tilifizyun al-Misri*, founded 1960) soon featured religious programming as well. With direct access to radio archives, the state-owned recording company, SonoCairo (*Sawt al-Qahira*, founded 1964), became Egypt's largest phonodisc producer, offering a wide range of popular music and producing most of the great reciters, including Shaykh Mustafa Isma'il (1905–78), Shaykh 'Abd al-Basit 'Abd al-Samad (1927–88), Shaykh Mahmud Khalil al-Husari (1917–80) and many others, for world-wide export.

What was the impact of mass media on the form and meaning of recitational styles? First, the mediaisation and concomitant commercialisation of audio production (together with the decline of the *kuttab*) induced an unprecedented bifurcation between religious and secular vocal forms, since the commercial value of the latter increasingly profited from a fashionable sexiness unacceptable within the religious domain (though socially acceptable outside it).[25] Singers no longer trained their voices in *tilawa* and Qur'an reciters gradually withdrew from other vocal specialisations. The sonic-social separation of *tilawa* and singing ultimately enabled the former to emerge as an independent expressive field within which disparate Islamic ideologies could potentially be expressed (though that potential was not yet realised). Moreover, mass media – facilitating broad dissemination, repeatability and context-independence – enabled the crystallisation of widely-recognised sonic styles, which therefore attained broader social significance and communicative potential.

In exploring this significance and potential, it is useful to analyse content diversity and concentration of production, and to distinguish between synchronous and asynchronous channels of mass media distribution. Synchronous broadcast media (for example, radio and television) enforce simultaneity on producer and consumer, while asynchronous 'product' media (LP, cassette, CD) do not. The latter thus enable greater user control and repeatability (particularly if user-recordable), and typically offer more diversity as well. Discrete and tangible media products also tend to reify sonic styles through synecdochic relations to them. Asynchronous media therefore enable a more flexible symbolic language of social communication, by which style can be embedded into quotidian discourse at a 'grass-roots' level through local playback operations.

Until the late 1990s, synchronous Egyptian mass media, monopolised by the state, featured relatively low diversity and high concentration, for both ideological

---

25 In the 1930s, radio authorities declared the voice of the female reciter to be '*'awra*' ('shameful') and forbid its broadcast (Daoud 1997a:82); ironically, female singers (including the greatest stars of popular music) were not affected by this ruling.

and economic reasons. Such media therefore represented a coercive form of top-down communication. Until the 1970s, production of asynchronous mass media (LPs) likewise featured low diversity and strong centralisation, due to the high cost of manufacturing equipment and state dominance. Furthermore, the social impact of any diversity was limited by the costliness of playback equipment. *Tilawa* diversity was also constrained by the fact that al-Azhar-trained reciters enjoyed the greatest prestige and therefore provided the ideal models for Qur'anic recitation, both within Egypt and abroad. These factors precluded the development of a *system* of *tilawa* styles adapting in dialectical relation to the social conditions of their production and consumption, in which consumers' playback preferences could constitute utterances in a non-discursive communicative language of style. During this period one main public mediated style – Egyptian *mujawwad* – dominated.

Two related seismic changes of the mid-1970s enabled an asynchronous, decentralised mass media system to emerge in Egypt for the first time: the advent of inexpensive cassette technology and the development of a free market capitalist economy. With the subsequent growth of new Islamic trends in the 1980s came the crystallisation of an additional *tilawa* style and the ideologisation of the entire *tilawa* style system. This development will be extensively analysed below.

A Semiotic Theory of Style Differentiation and Communication

Whereas simple signs (for example, representational photographs) may represent absolutely, *tilawa* style signs are abstract, bearing no autonomous relation to the non-*tilawa* world.[26] As Saussure argued for language, sonic style signs *mean* only relatively, insofar as they, and their meanings, are differentiated from one another.[27] However, sonic style signs and linguistic signs are fundamentally different. While the linguistic system is large and complex, its constituent signs (morphemes) are simple, lacking much internal complexity. By contrast, the sonic style system is simple, while its constituent signs (styles) are complex, providing affective potential. In performance, the affective immediacy of the sonic style sign naturalises its own meaning (see Langer 1957). Speaking of language, Saussure argued that 'the terms *arbitrary* and *differential* designate two correlative properties' (1986:116). However the complexity of the abstract (hence differential) style sign enables it to mean in non-arbitrary (iconic, indexical) ways, while its abstraction implies that even non-arbitrary meanings arise only

---

[26]   A note on terminology: Saussure's sign comprises the pair signal/signification (Saussure 1986:67) while Peirce's is a triple representamen/semiotic object/interpretant (Merrell 2001:28). For the moment I will conflate object and interpretant with signification as *meaning*, while signal and representamen will be my *sign*.

[27]   'A linguistic system is a series of phonetic differences matched with a series of conceptual differences' (Saussure 1986:118).

in relation to other such style signs. That is, the system of style signs exhibits both Saussurian and Peircean properties in that it comprises a set of meaningful differences, which may be non-arbitrarily related to meaning.

The total possible meaning of a style sign (in a social space) is the aggregation of such meanings over all active differences in which the sign participates (within that space). By 'active difference' I mean those semiotic contrasts which are socially realised – through cognitive or practical juxtaposition – by agents sharing the social space. By 'semiotic value' I mean a potential meaning for a particular sign user in a particular social space. Then the set of all such semiotic values comprises the value space for a particular sign. I claim that in a social-semiotic system (S), the meaning of one sign relative to another is simply the difference between their respective semiotic values: that is, the aggregated difference in potential meanings.[28] Symbolically, one may write the total meaning (M) of s in S as a sum of differences: $M(s, S) = \sum \{v(s) - v(s')\}$ where s is a sign, $v(s)$ is its set of associated semiotic values and the sum $\sum$ ranges over all signs s' such that (s, s') constitutes an active difference in S. Note that a semiotic value w in $v(s)$ is cancelled by its recurrence in $v(s')$, but may be highlighted by another sign s'' when $v(s'')$ does not contain w. We will encounter concrete examples of this phenomenon later on.

Likewise, ideology is always embedded in a system of differences, since one ideology exists only in oppositional relation to others. When aligned with ideological differences, total meaning is ideological: semiotic differences are ideologised and the semiotic system is ideologically activated. In this case, semiotic differences may both express and promote ideological differences with which they are aligned. The mass media serve not only to differentiate ideologically active style signs, but also (subsequently) to empower them.

My claim is that with the advent of asynchronous mass media (and particularly cassettes) and associated political, economic and social changes, the space of Egyptian *tilawa* styles has been ideologically activated and has begun not only to express Islamic ideologies, but also to promote them (non-discursively) through social communication of stylistic preference, concretised in acts of cassette selection. Embedded in activities of cassette production, retail, purchase and playback is a style-selection operation which is also ideological. The dissemination of the selection itself thus constitutes an ideological message and a statement of position.

In the discussion which follows, I contrast a pair of semiotic differences within the evolving semiotic system of *tilawa* styles in Egypt. The first is the non-ideological difference between *murattal* and *mujawwad* styles, as found in the traditional binary style system prevailing up until the 1970s. The second is the contemporary difference between Egyptian *mujawwad* and the 'Saudi' style of

---

[28]   In fact, meaning will vary according to the perspective of the agent, who constructs a particular meaning through a process of selection and emphasis for which the system can never entirely account. More accurately, then, meaning is a *weighted* set of differences, where weights represent these selections and emphases.

public recitation (see Hassan 1999, Nelson 2001:236). The latter style entered the Egyptian soundspace in the late 1970s, at a time when the cultural, technological and economic conditions for the ideologisation of *tilawa* style (bifurcation of Egyptian soundspace; decentralised, free-market economy; asynchronous media) were already in place.

I aim to show how a distinctive 'Saudi' style of Qur'anic recitation, by accumulating a distinctive set of meanings within the symbolic system of *tilawa* styles, becomes ideologically activated, powerfully promoting a set of discursive positions collectively comprising a reformist-revivalist Islamic ideology prevalent in Egyptian society today. This ideology, sometimes termed the 'New Islam' (*al-Islam al-Jadid*), opposes the traditional mystical-aesthetic values of Egyptian Islamic practice. In turn, the appearance of this newly-ideologised Saudi style sign has induced the counter-ideologisation of traditional Egyptian *mujawwad* recitation, transforming it into an oppositional style sign evoking traditional Egyptian-Islamic values.

The Traditional Binary Style System

Table 3.2 sets out the differences between Egyptian *mujawwad* and *murattal* style signs in the pre-cassette era.

Table 3.2   Differences between *mujawwad* and *murattal* style signs in the *pre-cassette* era (variables with identical values across the two style signs are omitted). This analysis is rooted in interpretive fieldwork in Cairo; in particular, the concept of 'expression' is based on general consensus among Egyptian listeners.

Free Variable	Mujawwad	Murattal
1.1.1 *Timbre*	More tense	More relaxed
1.1.2 *Expression*	More expressive	Less expressive
1.2.1 *Ambitus*	Wide	Narrow
1.2.2 *Tessitura*	Lower	Higher
1.2.4 *Modulation*	Extensive	Little
1.2.5 *Melodicity*	Elaborate, developmental	Low
1.3.1 *Pause*	Lengthy, following cadence (*qafla*)	Little
1.4.1 *Dynamic level*	High (amplified)	Low
1.4.2 *Dynamic range*	Wide	Narrow
1.4.3 *Accent*	More	Less
2.1.1 *Melisma*	Extensive	Little
2.1.2 *Word painting*	Some	None
2.2.1 *Repetition*	Much	None
2.2.2 *Syllable duration*	Long	Short
2.2.3 *Syllable duration variation*	Higher	Lower

2.3.1 *Textual passage*	Some preference for narratives[29]	No preference
3.1 *Occasion*	*Majlis, maytam*	Prayer, study
3.2 *Social position*	Professional specialist – *muqri'*	Any
3.3 *Personal image*	Traditional reciter image	Any
3.4.1 *Attendance*	Many (public setting)	Variable (private or public)
3.4.2 *Listener behaviour*	Feedback	No feedback
4.1 *Medium*	Phonograph records	Rarely mediated[30]

In order to contrast *mujawwad* and *murattal*, it is helpful to control variables by comparing recordings of the same Qur'anic passage by a single reciter. Thus I present below a transcription and analysis of recordings by Shaykh Mustafa Isma'il (1978) (1999), reciting a single passage in both styles (see Examples 3.1 and 3.2, and Tables 3.3 and 3.4).[31] This passage, from Surat Yusuf (Qur'an 12:4[32]), contains 43 syllables and can be transliterated as follows: *idh-qaa-la-yuu-su-fu-li-a-bii-hi-yaa-a-ba-ti-in-ni-ra-ay-tu-a-ha-da-'a-sha-ra-kaw-ka-ban-wash-sham-sa-wal-qa-ma-ra-ra-ay-tu-hum-liy-saa-ji-diin.*[33]

Transcriptions are prepared using a graph: a continuous-time, relative-pitch system resembling standard staff notation. The horizontal axis represents time, marked in seconds, while the vertical axis represents pitch, on a 6-line quasi treble staff (the top line is F5; the bottom line is C4). The melody is indicated by a heavy horizontal line. Small vertical tick marks along this line appear at the start and end of tones (constant syllable-pitch units).[34]

---

[29]   Many Egyptians express some preference for listening to narrative Qur'anic passages in the *mujawwad* style, especially the dramatic story of the Prophet Yusuf (Joseph), though this preference is neither universal nor absolute.

[30]   Shaykh al-Husari was the first to record the complete Qur'anic text in *murattal* style (*al-mushaf al-murattal*) on LP in the early 1960s (see Sa'id 1975), and his version remains authoritative. However, this recording was innovative and exceptional: from the early twentieth century until the 1980s *tilawa* recordings centred on *mujawwad* performance.

[31]   The same passage will be used for analysis of the Saudi style (see Example 3.3, below).

[32]   'When Joseph said to his father: Oh my father! Lo! I saw in a dream eleven planets and the sun and the moon, I saw them prostrating themselves unto me' (Pickthall 1953:12:4).

[33]   Arabic syllables are generally of two types, short (CV) and long (CVV or CVC), and frequently cross word boundaries. Here, a dash marks syllable boundaries, long vowels are doubled, and the consonant *hamza* (glottal stop, typically marked ') is not notated when initiating a syllable.

[34]   Thus three successive syllables sung on a single pitch will be represented as a heavy vertical line divided into three segments; conversely, a single syllable may be sung on three pitches (melisma).

In the *mujawwad* recording, 12:4 is recited in three breath phrases (with intervening pauses filled by audience response) for a total duration of 93 seconds. The first segment begins with 'idh-qaa-la', ending on 'kaw-ka-ban'; the second begins at 'in-ni-ra-ay-tu', completing the verse. Only the third breath phrase, presenting the entire verse without pause, is transcribed in Example 3.1. This kind of repetition is typical of the *mujawwad* style. Tables 3.3 and 3.4 compare specific variables in the two styles.

Example 3.1 Segment from recitation of Qur'an 12:4 by Shaykh Mustafa Isma'il in the *mujawwad* style (Isma'il 1978). The *maqam* is *Bayyati* on D4 (E4, second line from bottom, is half-flat); absolute pitch is *Bayyati* on D3 (an octave below); the horizontal axis indicates seconds. The text runs as follows (syllables are separated by one or more dashes and asterisks; the latter indicate melismatic tones on the preceding syllable): *idh-qaa-*-la-yuu-su-fu-li-a-bii-*-*-*-hi-yaa-*-a-ba-ti-*-in-*-ni-ra-ay-*-tu-a-ha-da-'a-sha-*-ra-kaw-*-*-*-ka-*-ban-*-*-wash-*-*-sham-*-*-sa-wal-*-qa-*-ma-*-ra-*-ra-ay-*-tu-hum-*-*-liy-*-saa-*-*-*-ji-*-*-diin-*-*-*-*-*-*-.*

Example 3.2 Recitation of Qur'an 12:4 by Shaykh Mustafa Isma'il in the *murattal* style (Isma'il 1999). The *maqam* shown is again *Bayyati* on D4; absolute pitch is *Bayyati* on G3. Again, dashes separate syllables and asterisks denote melismas. Text: *idh-qaa-la-yuu-su-fu-li-a-bii-hi-yaa-a-ba-ti-in-ni-ra-ay-*-tu-a-ha-da-'a-sha-ra-kaw-ka-ban-wash-sham-sa-wal-*-qa-ma-ra-ra-ay-tu-hum-liy-saa-ji-diin.*

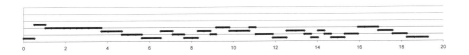

Table 3.3   Differences between *mujawwad* and *murattal* recitations of Qur'an 12:4 as performed by Shaykh Mustafa Isma'il. Note that not all differences listed below are visible in the notations.

Free Variable	*Mujawwad*	*Murattal*
1.1.1 *Timbre*	More tense	More relaxed
1.1.2 *Expression*	More expressive	Less expressive
1.2.1 *Ambitus*	Wide ambitus (7th)	Narrower ambitus (5th)
1.2.2 *Tessitura*	Lower tessitura	Higher tessitura
1.2.5 *Melodicity*	Melodically elaborate	Melodically simple
1.4.2 *Dynamic range*	Wide	Narrow
2.1.1 *Melisma*	Much (1.884)	Negligible (1.047)
2.2.2 *Syllable duration*	Longer (average 0.74 seconds)	Shorter (average 0.45 seconds)
2.2.3 *Syllable duration variation*	Higher (56% of average)	Lower (40% of average)
3.1 *Occasion*	Live recording (*majlis*)	Studio recording

Table 3.4   Differences between *mujawwad* and *murattal* recitations by Shaykh Mustafa Isma'il, considering the same recordings analysed above, now in the context of a longer sequence of verses.

Free Variable	*Mujawwad*	*Murattal*
1.2.4 *Modulation*	Frequent and elaborate modulations	Few and simple modulations
1.2.5 *Melodicity*	High: extended melodic development, climaxing at periodic cadences (*qaflas*)	Low
1.3.1 *Pause*	Long pauses between phrases	None
2.2.1 *Repetition*	Much repetition	No textual repetition
3.4.1 *Attendance*	Many	None
3.4.2 *Listener behaviour*	Ecstatic listener responses during pauses	None (studio)

These contrasts along multiple sonic, textual and pragmatic dimensions enable the differentiation of two style signs, implying contrastive meanings stemming primarily from contrasts in the contexts and purposes which shaped them. *Murattal* is shaped by its uses – among all Muslims – for practice and memorisation, personal devotions, and obligatory prayer (*salah*), all contexts requiring a relatively rapid and simple recitational style. *Mujawwad*, by contrast, is used by trained reciters in public listening ceremonies less constrained by either ritual or pedagogical requirements. Here, recitational complexity can flourish, and this fact has demanded a specialisation and professionalisation in which success is equated with the ability to move the listener using musical and expressive techniques, while remaining faithful to *mushaf*, *qira'at*, and *ahkam al-tajwid*.

The meaning of *mujawwad* relative to *murattal* may then be 'computed' with reference to the semiotic values of each, as shown in Table 3.5.

Table 3.5   Some partial meanings (third column) of *mujawwad* relative to *murattal*, computed as differences between semiotic values. Until the advent of Saudi style, these differences were related to contextual contrasts, but not consistently ideologised.

Semiotic values		Differences
Egyptian *mujawwad*	**Egyptian *murattal***	**Partial meaning of *mujawwad* with respect to *murattal* within Egyptian social space**
More musical	Less musical	Music, song, artistry
Tarab aesthetic and behaviour	No *tarab*	*Tarab*
Highly expressive	Less expression	Expressivity
More sonic	More textual	Non-discursive experience
Artistic elaboration of text	Functional performance of text	Artistic form (over function)
Public	Private	Performance
Tilawa professional	General; non-specialised	Professional specialisation
Participation as listener	Participation as performer	Contemplation
Egyptian contexts and reciters	Egyptian contexts and reciters	–
Traditional Egyptian Islam	Traditional Egyptian Islam	–

Despite this differentiation, the meanings of *mujawwad* and *murattal* never consistently attained ideological significance because they were derived primarily from the contexts within which they were performed. As late as 1978, Kristina Nelson found little evidence of *murattal* in the media (2001:xxiii). Even after mediation of the *murattal* style, the same public performers (for example, Shaykhs Mahmud al-Husari, Mustafa Isma'il, 'Abd al-Basit 'Abd al-Samad) recorded *tilawa* in both *mujawwad* and *murattal* styles. Thus *tilawa* styles could not even be consistently associated with particular individuals, much less with any ideological positions.

The Emergence of a Third Style Sign in Egypt: Historical Forces and Trajectories

A reconfiguration of the binary Egyptian *tilawa* style system was effected by three forces starting in the mid-1970s: the technological impact of a new mass medium (audio cassettes) enabling widespread asynchronous communications, the economic impact of laissez-faire capitalism and the influence of Saudi Islamic culture. The incursion of a new Saudi *tilawa* style into the binary Egyptian *tilawa* style system generated a new set of active differences, transforming the meanings of all three styles. In particular, those meanings now acquired an ideological cast not formerly present. It is important to trace the historical process of this transformation, because that history is embedded in their ideological power.

Having escaped the ravages of Crusaders and Mongols, Egypt has continuously remained a principal political, economic, religious and cultural centre throughout Islamic history, largely due to its large population, fertile land and geographical centrality. Cairo has the oldest and most important Islamic university in the world, al-Azhar (founded 972), drawing an international student population. Here, for centuries, reciters trained and disseminated Egyptian *tilawa* styles globally. While Islam's sacred geographical centres – the *ka'ba* at Mecca and the Prophet's mosque at Medina – are located in the Arabian Hijaz, Egypt was politically, economically, educationally and culturally dominant.[35] During the twentieth century, that dominance was magnified as Egypt became the first Muslim country to develop significant media production capabilities. Early mass media (phonodisc and radio) must have consolidated an Egyptian *tilawa* style through the suppression of local variation, while powerfully projecting a small number of reciter-stars to worldwide proportions. Egyptians' sense of their own global importance is captured by their oft-repeated saying, 'The Qur'an was revealed in the Hijaz, copied in Istanbul and recited in Egypt' (Sayyid 2003:24).

Throughout the Mamluk and Ottoman periods (1250–1798) and into the early twentieth century, mainstream Islam in Egypt was thoroughly permeated by Sufi mysticism, for which aesthetic expression and experience (musical, poetic, calligraphic, architectural) constitute both sign and means of spiritual development.[36] The broad overlap between musical and religious domains, as exemplified by chanted religious poetry – *inshad dini* (Frishkopf 2002) – and musical *tilawa* in the *mujawwad* style, as well as the thriving of Sufi orders and rituals among all strata of the population, characterised traditional Egyptian Islam for at least seven centuries. However, the twentieth century witnessed the development of new reformist-revivalist trends in Egypt, trends which increasingly drew close to the Islamic practices of Arabia.

Ever since the eighteenth century, Arabia has featured a different kind of Islamic piety, inspired by the Arabian revivalist-reformer Muhammad ibn 'Abd al-Wahhab (1703–92), and sharply contrasting with the traditional Sufi-inflected

---

[35]   From early Mamluk times (thirteenth century) until 1962, Egyptian superiority was symbolised by a splendid annual gift to Mecca: the *Ka'ba*'s magnificent hangings (*kiswa*), carried in an opulent procession (the *mahmal*) replete with music and ritual, and symbolising political protection over the holy places. The gifting of the *kiswa* was interrupted in the early nineteenth century and again from 1926–37 due to conflicts with the Wahhabi *ikhwan* who considered it a heresy (*bid'a*) (Fr. Buhl [2009], 'Maḥmal', in P. Bearman, Th. Bianquis, C.E. Bosworth, E. van Donzel and W.P. Heinrichs [eds], *Encyclopaedia of Islam* [2nd edition], Brill Online, University of Alberta, <http://www.brillonline.nl.login.ezproxy. library.ualberta.ca/subscriber/entry?entry=islam_SIM-4789>, accessed 24/03/09). In the early nineteenth century, Egyptian ruler Muhammad 'Ali (r.1805–48) conquered most of Arabia, withdrawing only in 1840 (Vassiliev 2000:140ff.).

[36]   See Heyworth-Dunne (1939:10), Lane (1973:244), de Jong (1978), Fernandes (1988), Taylor (1989), Winter (1992) and Shoshan (1993).

Islam prevalent in Egypt. Rooted in the conservative Hanbali legal school, and influenced by reformist writings of theologian Ibn Taymiyya (1263–1328), 'Abd al-Wahhab advocated a return to pure *tawhid* (monotheism), as established in the Qur'an and Sunna, and an unmediated relationship with God. 'Abd al-Wahhab's followers[37] advocated strict application of *Shari'a* (Islamic law), purging medieval accretions they viewed as *shirk* (idolatry) and *bid'a* (heretical 'innovation'), including saint and Prophet veneration, shrines, concepts and rituals of intercession, musical ceremonies and other popular beliefs and practices especially common among Sufis. The Wahhabi movement acquired political power due to an alliance concluded with the Sa'ud family of al-Diriya in 1744 and which formed the basis for the modern Saudi Arabian state, established by 'Abd al-'Aziz Al Sa'ud (Ibn Saud) during the first third of the twentieth century (Vassiliev 2000:235ff.).

Egyptian reform and revival (*islah wa tajdid*) movements, generally critical of Sufi beliefs and practices, coalesced starting with a group of nineteenth-century thinkers known as the '*Salafiyya*', due to their emphasis on *al-salaf al-salih* ('pious ancestors') of the Prophet's community as an enduring ideal for Muslim societies.[38] From the early twentieth century, such movements began to change the character of mainstream Egyptian Islam, without, however, dislodging Sufism entirely. Diverse reform-revival organisations (most importantly, the Muslim Brothers, *al-Ikhwan al-Muslimun*[39]) shared a number of characteristics: the revival of Islamic principles as grounded in direct readings of Qur'an, Sunna and early Islamic society; the rejection of 'heretical innovation' (*bid'a*), including Sufi or musical ritual, perceived as counter to those principles; reform through *ijtihad* (reasoning) so as to incorporate economic and technological aspects of modernity; focus on the unmediated relation between worshiper and God as idealised on the Day of Judgment; transnational pan-Islamism and *da'wa* (missionising); and socio-political engagement. Within Egyptian reformist discourse, music and aesthetic experience is widely condemned as *haram* (forbidden) and the historic connections between Islam and aesthetic expression are generally severed. Historically and ideologically, Egyptian reformist movements find their spiritual *élan* both in Arabia and in Wahhabism. The spiritual movement at the heart of the social one is a break with received Islamic tradition via a dual 'return' to Arabia: a *temporal* return to Islamic historical origins (in seventh-century Mecca and Medina) and hence to 'true' Islam, but equally a *spatial* return to these sacred

---

[37]   The term 'Wahhabi', widely used in both English and Arabic, is usually pejorative; followers prefer the name *muwahhidun*, 'unitarians'. However, for want of alternatives clearly identifying this religious trend, 'Wahhabi' and 'Wahhabism' (Ar. *Wahhabiyya*) are nevertheless used here.

[38]   Such thinkers included Jamal al-Din al-Afghani (1839–97), Muhammad 'Abdu (1845–1905) and Rashid Rida (1865–1935).

[39]   Founded in 1928 by Hasan al-Banna (1906–49) (Mitchell 1969).

sites as ritualised in the annual *hajj* (pilgrimage).[40] Furthermore, Egyptian Islamic reformism found common ground with Wahhabi ideas. Rashid Rida, for example, commended Wahhabism in several of his writings (Vassiliev 2000:292).

Following independence in 1952, Egypt's leading Islamic and media role was consolidated and empowered, regionally by President Gamal Abdel Nasser's pan-Arabism, and internally by statist-socialist policies of centralisation. The new state monopolised religious institutions (for example, al-Azhar University) and broadcast media, and seized key industries (Roussillon 1998:345) including primary audio media producer Misrphon, known from 1962 as SonoCairo (*Sawt al-Qahira*) (Frishkopf n.d.). Media concentration and expansion entailed the unprecedented amplification of Egyptian media stars – actors, singers and reciters – throughout the Arab and Islamic worlds. At the same time, limitations on imports and foreign investments as well as restrictions on exit visas, inhibited foreign cultural influences. Nasser also repressed the Muslim Brothers and other reformist-revivalist pan-Islamic currents, some of whose members sought refuge in Saudi Arabia where they were welcomed, taking up positions as teachers and influencing the development of Wahhabi thought.[41] These conditions sustained a relatively closed system of Egyptian public *tilawa*, centred on the prevailing *mujawwad* style as epitomised by its most famous exponents and dominating the wider Islamic world.

But Egypt's cultural-religious centrality and closure was shaken by its June 1967 military losses to Israel. Many Egyptians attributed defeat at the hands of a sectarian state to insufficient religiosity, and a national turn to faith for solace and solutions ensued, swelling the ranks of reformist-revivalist Islamic organisations Nasser had tried to suppress (see Toth 2003:548). Soon after Nasser's death in 1970, President Sadat reversed Nasser's socialist course, guiding Egypt instead towards both capitalism and Islam. Expelling Soviet advisors (in 1972), he forged new political and economic links with the United States and Saudi Arabia and loosened restrictions on Egyptian emigration (Ayubi 1983:442, LaTowsky 1984:12).

The crucial turning point came on 6 October 1973 (the 10th of Ramadan and Jewish Yom Kippur), when Egyptian forces succeeded in crossing the Suez canal, overcoming Israeli defences in an operation code-named '*Badr*'. The success of what became known as 'the crossing' was deliberately freighted with reference to the early days of Islamic history, the period of greatest concern to Islamic

---

[40] This 'return' contrasts sharply with traditional Sufi-inflected Islam in Egypt, closely associated with mysticism, a profusion of local sacred places (saint shrines), the aestheticisation of spiritual life, and esteem for the continuous, cumulative oral Islamic tradition.

[41] Esther Peskes and W. Ende (2009), 'Wahhābiyya', in P. Bearman, Th. Bianquis, C.E. Bosworth, E. van Donzel and W.P. Heinrichs (eds), *Encyclopaedia of Islam* (2nd edition), Brill Online, University of Alberta, <http://www.brillonline.nl.login.ezproxy. library.ualberta.ca/subscriber/entry?entry=islam_SIM-4789>, (accessed 24/03/09). The Saudi government generally sympathised with the Brothers (Vassiliev 2000:292).

revivalists.[42] As a military hero, Sadat could now initiate another 'crossing'. As detailed in his 'October Document', the *infitah* (economic 'opening') aimed primarily to stimulate state and private sectors by attracting financial and technical aid from Arab and Western sources (Aulas 1982:7, Waterbury 1983:416ff.). New laws now opened Egypt to foreign imports and free market capitalism, as well as foreign ideas (Roussillon 1998:361).

The 'opening' and 'crossing' of Egyptian society was not only westward towards capitalism and Western culture, but also eastward towards Saudi Arabia. Sadat feared the left, whether Nasserist or Communist. In order to counter its return, he allowed *Salafi* movements, formerly persecuted, to proliferate (Ayubi 1980:491–2, Roussillon 1998:370) and a number of Muslim Brothers forced into Saudi exile under Nasser were allowed to return (Ayubi 1980:488). Sadat promoted Islamic revivalists such as the renowned Egyptian Shaykh Sha'rawi (1911–98), who returned to Egypt in the mid-1970s (after teaching at King 'Abd al-'Aziz University in Jeddah, Saudi Arabia) to host an Islamic programme on Egyptian television, *Nur 'Ala Nur* (Lazarus-Yafeh 1983:284). Sadat also reformed the constitution to declare S*hari'a* the primary source of law. Nasser had continually strained Egypt–Saudi relations, assisting the Yemeni revolution against Saudi-supported royalists. Sadat repaired Egypt's relations with the Saudi kingdom[43] (whose support helped enable his pro-Western policy of *infitah*) and the self-styled 'believer president' continued to burnish his Arab-Islamic-hero image as a source of legitimation (Ayubi 1980:488, Roussillon 1998:348–9, Vassiliev 2000:400).

Meanwhile, the 1970s witnessed the ideological rise of Saudi Arabia as a world-wide political player and Islamic power, underscoring connections between Islam and petro-dollars (Ayubi 1980:482). In 1973, retaliating against Western support for Israel, Arab oil producers cut production and Saudi Arabia suspended petroleum shipments to the United States. The price of oil tripled overnight, and producers – especially Saudi Arabia – enjoyed a dramatic increase in revenues and global influence (Vassiliev 2000:401). King Faisal (r.1964–75) exploited post-1973 windfalls to develop his country, a policy followed by King Khaled (r.1975–82). Many Muslims, Egyptians included, interpreted this new wealth and power as a Divine vindication of Saudi-style piety.

Saudi Arabia's newfound wealth and global power modernised Wahhabism, which subsequently drew closer to Egypt's more progressive, and burgeoning, *Salafi* trends. Through the early twentieth century, many Wahhabis had applied a strict concept of *bid'a*, often rejecting even technological 'innovations' such as

---

[42]   In Ramadan of the year 624 CE, the Prophet Muhammad first overcame his Meccan enemies at the Battle of Badr. This victory confirmed the early Muslims' faith. Nearly 1,500 years later, Sadat's reputation was boosted through these religious-historical parallels.

[43]   Sadat referred to Saudi King Faisal as 'Commander of the Faithful', the classical expression of caliphal power (*amir al-mu'minin*) (Waterbury 1983:416).

electricity.[44] From the mid-twentieth century, however, mainstream Wahhabi views were tempered – and empowered – by oil wealth (and concomitant close relations to Western powers), as well as by interactions with Egyptian Salafism. Such 'neo-Wahhabism' embraces modern technology, capitalism and consumerism and, buoyed by oil, has become extremely powerful worldwide.[45] In particular, Saudi Arabia has financed many Islamic groups and social projects in Egypt (Ayubi 1980:491).

During the same period (1970s), Egypt was seized by economic turbulence. Free market capitalism enabled some to accumulate vast wealth, but both inflation and unemployment soared, the public sector declined and foreign investments failed to materialise. Government employees on non-indexed salaries were especially impoverished. In 1979, a separate peace with Israel triggered Arab ostracism of Egypt and erased hoped-for investments from the Gulf states. What saved many Egyptian families were remittances from migrant labour, primarily in Iraq, Kuwait and Saudi Arabia. With Saudi development had come a huge demand for immigrant Arabic-speaking labour and from the late 1970s Egyptian workers migrated to Saudi Arabia in droves, often illegally and under the pretext of performing pilgrimage.[46] There, sometimes accompanied by their families, they observed at first-hand Saudi luxury, together with the neo-Wahhabi creed. For many such workers, the combination of material and spiritual wealth found in the 'holy land' was compelling. Acculturating to the Saudi lifestyle, they came to view Egypt as comparatively poor, both economically and religiously. Far from contradicting religiosity, conspicuous consumption validated the Saudi model as the just reward for uncompromising conformity to Islamic principles: Wahhabi religious ideals were sanctified by Saudi oil.

---

[44] For example, Saudi *'ulama* (religious scholars) resisted Ibn Saud's introduction of radio and telegraph. In June 1930, an assembly of Saudi *'ulama* protested against the teaching of technical drawing and geography, ostensibly because the former paved the way to artistic portraiture while the latter taught that the earth is round (Vassiliev 2000:290, 292).

[45] Esther Peskes and W. Ende (2009), 'Wahhābiyya', in P. Bearman, Th. Bianquis, C.E. Bosworth, E. van Donzel and W.P. Heinrichs (eds), *Encyclopaedia of Islam* (2nd edition), Brill Online, University of Alberta, <http://www.brillonline.nl.login.ezproxy. library.ualberta.ca/subscriber/entry?entry=islam_SIM-4789>, (accessed 24/03/09).

[46] In 1975–76, the number of Egyptian school teachers seconded to Arab countries exceeded 20,000. For four or five years' service in Saudi or Kuwait, the teacher could earn more than a lifetime of Egyptian wages (Ayubi 1983:438). One study of rural migration observed that between 1975 and 1980, Saudi was the preferred destination. After 1980, Iraq was favoured (due to labour shortages caused by the Iran–Iraq war) while Saudi remained popular (Nada 1991:27). In 1976, migrant labour comprised 4.7 per cent of Egypt's total labour force (Aulas 1982:9); there were hundreds of thousands of Egyptians working in Saudi Arabia in the late 1970s (Vassiliev 2000:428). Some scholars estimate that 10 to 15 per cent of the labour force was abroad in 1984. See Ayubi (1983:434–5, 438–9), LaTowksy (1984), Toth (1994:43–4), Kandil (1999).

Many scholars have noted the economic consequences of Egyptian labour migration.[47] Fewer have noted its socio-cultural implications. However, the Saudi influence on Egyptian culture during this period was increasingly direct. As the oil economies cooled after 1986, most workers returned to Egypt, bringing with them new wealth and new ideas (Toth 1994:39). The most visible (and audible) signs of this wealth were electronic media devices, especially televisions and cassette players (Nada 1991:42, Roussillon 1998:364), as well as new small businesses, new construction, and the urban sprawl which sprang up to accommodate it all. The return of migrant workers also brought a Saudi Islam that dovetailed easily with the ideologically-related Egyptian *Salafiyya*. But the new *infitah* bourgeoisie (Infitah 1986), infused with Saudi-Islamic wealth, values and practices, extended far beyond the boundaries of more organised *Salafi* movements. Thus, along with the economic remittance came a *cultural* remittance, forming in Egypt a reflected image of that distinctive complex of Saudi culture – wealth, consumerism and Wahhabi Islam – encapsulated in the alliance between royalty (Al Sa'ud) and the Wahhabiyya.

Powerful influences from both east and west greatly weakened Egypt's former cultural and religious centrality. With traditional ideologies substantially discredited, a new mainstream source of Egyptian Islamic discursive authority split from Egypt-centric, Sufi-inflected traditional Islam (represented as late as 1978 by the al-Azhar rector, Shaykh 'Abd al-Halim Mahmud) towards a more pan-Islamic revivalism-reformism, centred upon the neo-Wahhabi petro-capitalism of Saudi Arabia. Pejoratively, some Egyptian critics dub this mixture 'petro-Islam' (*al-Islam al-nafti*), 'Saudization' (*sa'wada*) or 'Gulfification' (*khalwaga*). Others refer to it more neutrally as the New Islam (*al-Islam al-Gadid*), in contradistinction to the more traditional Egyptian Islam, with its mystical and aesthetic sensibilities.

The Egyptian New Islam is capitalist and consumerist (albeit in Islamised forms, as seen for example in Islamic banking) more than socially activist, reflecting Saudi and *infitah* values mixed with Egyptian Islamist emphasis on private ownership (Abed-Kotob 1995:327, Roussillon 1998:392). Further, this new wave of bourgeois Islamisation is not on the whole politically engaged, or even self-conscious as a social movement: it is a 'class in itself' rather than a 'class for itself' (to reuse a Marxist trope) and profoundly conservative, not only due to religious strictures, but because its material interests lie in maintaining political stability. Though often replete with political discourse on unassailable Islamic issues (Palestine, Kashmir, Chechnya), the New Islam refrains from overly-public challenges to local authority (Morsy 1988:360, Zubaida 1992:9), focusing on a personal piety of salvation (for example, the obligation to veil, to pray) more than politics. The New Islam is thus an amorphous socio-cultural trend in Egypt, generally subsuming non-violent organised political-social movements (such as the Muslim Brothers), but so much broader as to not be characterised

---

[47]   See Ayubi (1983:447), LaTowsky (1984), Kandil and Metwally (1990), Nada (1991), Toth (1994), Kandil (1999).

by them. Following the forceful suppression of militant Egyptian Muslim groups (for example, *al-Jama'a al-Islamiyya*) in the mid 1990s, it has become clear that the New Islam enjoys extremely broad public support, even among political and cultural elites. Beyond its core of *Salafis* and ex-Saudi workers, New Islamic symbols and practices are diffused through social networks defined by family, friends and workplace relationships. Observation suggests that the mass media, especially asynchronous media such as cassette tapes and pamphlets, have also played a key role in this process.

It is no coincidence that the 'cassette revolution' (Castelo-Branco 1987) accompanied the political, economic and social upheavals of the 1970s. Sadat's *infitah* enabled both the import of technology (cassette recorders, duplicators, players and blank cassettes), and the accumulation of capital to pay for it. Phonodisc production and consumption had been relatively expensive, requiring significant capital investments and costly playback equipment, and hence enjoyed a limited market. New *infitah*-era wealth, remittances and free market consumerism precipitated both the formation of private sector cassette production companies and a much broader distribution of cassette players. By the mid 1980s, 'boombox' cassette recorder-players were nearly universal throughout Egypt, supporting the rapid development of a private sector audio cassette industry. A mass 'cassette culture' (Manuel 1993) – including both musical and religious content – escalated.[48]

In the context of *infitah*, the 'cassette revolution' constituted a seismic transformation of Egyptian mass media space from predominantly state-centralised synchronous (radio, television, cinema) towards relatively unregulated, private sector, decentralised, asynchronous (cassette), thus localising control at the level of the social agent. Producing (or selecting and playing) a cassette tape in public now became an act of social communication open to nearly anyone. While state regulatory mechanisms, requiring pre-publication authorisation from the Censor for Artistic Works (*al-Raqaba 'Ala al-Musannafat al-Fanniyya*, for music) and al-Azhar's Islamic Research Academy (for Islamic tapes), enabled some control, in practice only flagrant violations of religious, moral and political codes have been rejected, especially from the 1990s onwards,[49] and 'underground' production

---

[48] For instance, SonoCairo's total production in 1970 was 995,763 phonodiscs (LPs and 45 rpm discs); at this time there was little private sector competition. By 1985, SonoCairo's cassette production had reached 1,922,140. In 1995 (by which time SonoCairo no longer dominated the market) it was 2,072,418 (Egyptian Ministry of Information 1999:182). These figures neglect the simultaneous dramatic expansion of the private sector during this period, though for various reasons its output is difficult to estimate precisely.

[49] Conversation with Dr Ali Abu Shadi, former head of the Censor for Artistic Works (2004).

flourished (Khalafallah 1982).[50] Government control of recorded media has thus shifted from active stylistic production to a more limited filtering function.

All these developments set the stage for a double foreign colonisation of Egypt's sonic media space (comprising primarily musical and Islamic recordings) from west and east. By the late 1970s, recorded music was awash with the sounds of Western rock, pop and jazz. A few years later, Islamic cassettes – recorded sermons, lectures and *tilawa* – proliferated, much of it exhibiting a New Islamic-Saudi direction, including recognisable Saudi *tilawa* styles. Such cassette tapes (and later CDs, CD-ROMs and videos) not only introduced foreign ideas, but also amplified and disseminated them throughout Egyptian society.

By the 1990s, whole Cairo neighbourhoods bore the symbolic imprint of New Islamic values and practices, particularly in Nasr City, and, on a humbler economic scale, Faisal Street (aptly named for the eponymous Saudi King). While these symbols do not always necessarily derive from Saudi Arabia, they are often perceived as such. Their rapid reproduction both expresses the New Islam and provides a communicative mechanism for the diffusion of its ideologies. Women veil, often in the Saudi style, yet elegantly so. Men may sport Saudi-style dress (Ayubi 1980:494). Local sacred spaces, especially the shrines of saints, are eschewed as *bid'a*, as is Sufi ritual generally. The Ramadan *tarawih* prayer is extended, resembling Meccan practice. Traditional Egyptian rituals are rejected, including memorials (depriving the *mujawwad* reciter of his main income) and the newborn's seventh-day feast (*subu'*), which is replaced by the Saudi-style *'aqiqa*. New business enterprises typically reflect the Saudi-Islamic values of their entrepreneurs, in products (women's veils), names (such as 'Hajj and 'Umra Market') or Qur'anic signage (for example, 2:172: 'O ye who believe! Eat of the good things that We have provided for you' on a sandwich shop; 37:107 on a butcher's shop; 76:21 on a café, and so on) (see Figure 3.1).

More pertinent to the present discussion are Islamic media production companies founded in Egypt in the mid-1980s and 1990s. Capitalising on the Islamic trends, these companies reproduce and distribute sounds, images and texts signifying the New Islam (Gharib 2001:5–8). Even their names – *al-Risala*, *al-Nur*, *Taqwa* and *Harf* are four examples – imply reformism.[51] Such companies do not traffic in music or Sufi cassettes. Formerly *tilawa* recordings were produced by general audio production companies (such as SonoCairo) whose catalogues also included music and songs. Producing music and *tilawa* under one roof summarised the historically close relation between the two fields. In the New

---

[50]   The Reciters' Union and Egyptian Radio also censor *tilawa* recordings (thanks to Kristina Nelson for this information).

[51]   '*Risala*' ('message') connotes both the Qur'an and missionising; '*nur*' ('light') symbolises God (Qur'an 24:35); 'taqwa' means 'purity'; '*harf*' ('letter') connotes a Qur'anic reading, but also implies literalism.

Islam, that relation does not hold.[52] These companies specialise in Islamic vocal genres, including *tilawa*, *du'a'*, *anashid*[53] (without music), *khutab* (sermons) and *durus diniyya* (religious lectures). Their *tilawa* catalogues feature Saudi reciters and de-emphasise the *mujawwad* style of traditional Egyptian Islam.[54]

Figure 3.1   The Faisal Street branch of *El-Tawheed & El-Nour* ('Monotheism & Light'), a phenomenally successful chain of Egyptian department stores, selling a wide variety of household goods and garments, especially conservative women's clothing (visible in the upper two display windows), at cut-rate prices, all wrapped in Islamic garb. The brightly illuminated glass storefront, brimming with wares, clearly symbolises the consumerist-capitalist New Islam of Egyptian *Sa'wada*, to which it caters. Besides the religious name, short Qur'anic verses and Islamic sayings, displayed on external signage, colours (green for Islam, white for purity) and the goods themselves convey an ethos of religious conservatism. (Photograph by the author.)

---

[52]   It should be noted that the unprecedented disconnection between the social field of music and the New Islam in Egypt does not mean that Muslims refuse music in its entirety, but rather that the two fields are separated in practice.

[53]   Islamic hymns, also called *inshad*. New Islamic discourse prefers the term '*anashid*', perhaps since '*inshad*' is associated with traditional Islamic and Sufi performance.

[54]   Thus, in 2003, *al-Risala*'s catalogue contained 12 reciters: nine Saudis, one Kuwaiti and two Egyptians (one of whom is the Saudi-oriented Shaykh Muhammad Gabril).

Through these companies, and increasingly through mainstream audio producers as well, the distinctive sound of Saudi-style recitation (a sound closely associated with the New Islam) has been widely disseminated in Egypt, supplying, and extending, a growing New Islamic market.[55]

What is this Saudi style of public *tilawa*? Though often labelled '*murattal*', Saudi style should not be confused with traditional Egyptian *murattal*. According to a prevailing Saudi view, Egyptian contexts for *mujawwad* (the *maytam* or the mosque *majlis*) are *bid'a* and *tilawa* professionalism is frowned upon. Rather, live public *tilawa* occurs primarily in congregational prayer (*salat al-jama'a*), where the reciter is the *imam* (prayer leader). Even on studio-recorded cassettes, Saudi *tilawa* retains the meaning of prayer because such recordings feature the same imam-reciters and styles. During Ramadan, the longest such recitations occur during *tarawih*, most importantly at the sacred mosques of Mecca and Medina, culminating in a lengthy melodic *du'a'*. These recitations are broadcast and released on cassette and CD.

Certain sonic contrasts between Saudi and traditional Egyptian styles directly support theological interpretations, while others present arbitrary semiotic differences, aligning with theological ones through usage. The Wahhabi philosophy prevailing in Saudi Arabia attenuates melodic elaboration and *tarab*-like repetition characteristic of traditional Egyptian *mujawwad*: by contrast, Saudi recitation is rapid, melodically simple and direct. At the same time, Saudi recitation tends to be more melismatic and is perceived as more emotionally expressive than Egyptian *murattal*, deploying a plaintive, beseeching timbre iconic of supplicatory prayer (*du'a'*).[56] The *tarawih du'a'* is primarily an emotional appeal to God for salvation on the Day of Judgment, and it invokes an enormous upswelling of weeping. To a large extent this supplicatory ethos characterises Saudi *tilawa* generally. While the reciter doesn't actually weep, his voice is typically tinged with remorse far more than that of his Egyptian counterpart – such is the widespread Egyptian perception.[57] The sound of Saudi recitation is shaped by the acoustics of its most common live venues – the enormous sacred mosques at Mecca and Medina.

---

[55]   In 1999, even SonoCairo, which had always championed the traditional Egyptian reciters, released recordings of Saudi Shaykhs al-Sudays and al-Sharim.

[56]   This timbre frequently contrasts with the actual meaning of the text; unlike Egyptian *mujawwad*, the Saudi style is not concerned with *taswir al-ma'na* (word painting, sonically 'depicting the meaning'), but rather with expression of the reciter's response to that meaning.

[57]   In Egypt, there is also a misconception – promoted by detractors – that Saudi reciters actually weep while reciting, a practice criticised as distorting the Qur'anic message and as *ibtizaz* ('extortion' of emotion). I have never heard such weeping and I suspect that such accusations have resulted from the confusion of *tilawa* with *du'a'* (with which *tarawih* prayer concludes and which is often featured on Saudi tapes). At the same time, a few Egyptian reciters, notably Shaykh Muhammad Siddiq al-Minshawi, are also prized for a 'weeping voice'.

Reverberating in their cavernous spaces, the reciter's voice becomes an index of the mosques themselves, sounding sacred space. Saudi-style recitation also indexes *salah* (often the context of recordings), the Muslim's fundamental daily obligation, as well as the Saudi Arabian linguistic accent.

These indexical and iconic sonic features of Saudi style, in stark contrast to Egyptian style, express a direct relation to God – affectively coloured with fear, awe, sorrow, repentance and hope of forgiveness – and are strongly linked to Arabia. Through them, Saudi style points to the New Islam with its literalist, anti-intercessionist, Arabia-centric and eschatological emphases. Other sonic contrasts to Egyptian style, including a higher tessitura and a preference for *maqam Rast* (rather than *Bayyati*), cannot be interpreted as indices or icons, and are not directly susceptible to theological interpretation. Resulting from vicissitudes of local oral tradition, such sonic features become arbitrarily associated to the New Islam through usage.

Pragmatic differences also support this semantic contrast of Saudi and Egyptian styles. Public Saudi reciters differ sharply from their traditional Egyptian counterparts in social status and role. The traditional public Egyptian reciter is perceived as a professional performer, an artist specialised in *tilawa* and (formerly, at least) religious song, admired for his vocal artistry and ability to produce *tarab*, close to the world of Egyptian music and far from Islamic politics. Thus Shaykh Muhammad Rif'at has been described as a natural musician who played the *'ud* and enjoyed Western classical music. Likewise, Shaykh Mustafa Isma'il loved music; the popular belief that he even played the piano, though false, is also telling (Khalil and Hafiz 1984:1703, Tawfiq 199x:19).[58]

The Saudi reciter, by contrast, typically rejects recitation as a profession, adopting instead the status of Islamic prayer leader, preacher, missionary (*da'i*), teacher or scholar, with no connection to music, except occasionally to condemn it. Moreover, through sermons and teachings, Saudi reciters may promote religio-political positions. Reciters such as Shaykhs 'Ali 'Abd al-Rahman al-Hudhayfi and 'Abd al-Rahman Sudays are widely known as *imams* (at Medina and Mecca respectively) and for polemical sermons drawing them into global media debates. One of Sudays' sermons, for example, incurred an angry editorial retort from Fox News[59] and his invitation to a Florida Islamic conference stirred protests charging him with anti-Semitism.[60] Al-Hudhayfi has been taken to task for a political sermon, widely distributed on the Internet, in which he reportedly stated 'I am

---

[58] Shaykh Mustafa's piano playing is a myth stemming from the fact that an interview in his home showed the piano. Thanks to Kristina Nelson for clarifying this matter with Shaykh Mustafa himself.

[59] John Gibson (2002), 'Saudi Arabia: Time to Draw a Line in the Sand (Foxnews. com)', <www.foxnews.com/story/0,2933,54437,00.html> (accessed 11/2003).

[60] Susan Jacobson (2003), 'Islamic Conference Speaker Draws Wrath', <www.orlandosentinel.com/news/local/osceola/orl-locsaudivisit03120303dec03,1,3864465.story> (accessed 3/12/2003).

warning America to stop interfering in the affairs of our region'.[61] Shaykh Ahmad al-'Ajmi is well known for leading *tarawih* prayers in large Saudi mosques, as well as through cassette recordings and broadcasts on radio and television. He is also a preacher, urging reciters to 'call forth visions of the Day of Judgment' in their recitations and warning:

> If you recite for anything other than God – for impermanent worldly things, reputation or fame – then God will hold you accountable, and will ask you: for what did you recite? And you answer: I recited it for you. And He responds: you recited so that it might be said that you are a reciter, and indeed it was said. And then He throws you into the Fire. And you will be among the first to burn in the Fire.[62]

These Saudi reciters are public discursive actors, for whom *tilawa* represents a particularly affective, and effective, form of Islamic outreach (*da'wa*) and education (*tarbiya*) (Mahfuz and al-Zahrani 2002:30).

Live Saudi-style recitation is restricted to mosque prayers. However dissemination is effected through broadcasts and cassette recordings, particularly those recorded during *tarawih* in the mosques of Mecca and Medina as well as in studios, which enjoy broad popularity throughout the Gulf states. Many Saudi reciters decline remuneration for such recordings, thus facilitating rapid diffusion, since their cassettes can be sold for only slightly more than the cost of blank tape. Following the new Saudi influence, there is a broad receptivity to such cassettes in Egypt and over the last ten years they have flooded the Egyptian market, displacing recordings of the traditional reciters.

Studio recordings of Saudi reciters sold in Egypt are frequently enhanced by artificial reverb, indexing the enormous Masjid al-Haram in Mecca. Cassettes also index *tarawih* prayers by deploying the *juz'* (nightly Qur'anic portion during Ramadan) rather than the *sura* as the textual unit, and by appending the concluding *du'a'*.[63] Graphics are also significant. Just as music cassette covers generally feature the singer, traditional Egyptian *tilawa* cassette covers always featured a photograph of the reciter as artist, clad in traditional clothing and framed with traditional medieval arabesques. In contrast, and in keeping with Wahhabi bans on portraying the human form, the reciter's photograph does not

---

[61]   Reported in Shaykh 'Ali 'Abd al-Rahman al-Hudhayfi (1998), 'Historic Khutbah of Imaam of Masjid-un-Nabawiy Sheikh Ali Abdur Rahmaan Hudhayfi', <www.islamworld.net/historic_khutbah.htm> (accessed 12/2006).

[62]   Ahmad al-'Ajmi (2006), <www.alajmy.com/> (accessed 10/2006), translation by Michael Frishkopf. Shaykh al-'Ajmi's website also contains sermons, including a diatribe against singing, and political discourse on current events.

[63]   Cassettes containing the Qur'an's final *juz'* (*juz' 'amma*) are particularly popular.

appear on Saudi-style tapes or on other New Islamic media.[64] Instead, symbols, bold contemporary graphics and a preference for smooth-edged fonts and bright colours over traditional calligraphy and arabesques, suggest a simple, direct, yet contemporary Islam centred on the Qur'an, Mecca and Medina, a graphical style – evoking the New Islam – which I call 'Islamic Modern' (see Figure 3.2).

In the contemporary Egyptian soundspace, the traditional *mujawwad* reciter retains an important social role in the widely-celebrated *maytam* and is still heard in mosques.[65] However, in the more widely influential phonogram media, and increasingly even on the radio, the Saudi style now dominates. Its popularity has transformed channels of distribution. While a range of *tilawa* styles is still available in larger cassette shops, smaller kiosks and Islamic bookstores often emphasise *murattal* and Saudi styles. More informally, New Islamic media are sold from sidewalk stands alongside revivalist literature, and even by itinerant street vendors. New distribution channels may be a response to a new and broader audience; they may also result from the trend (as in production) towards separating religious from musical material.

The transfer of Saudi style to Egypt induces an important semiotic transformation. In Saudi Arabia, Saudi style blends seamlessly with the broader social fabric, and thus may not appear as overtly communicative or even recognisable as a coherent style sign. In Egypt, however, the symbolic coherence of Saudi style emerges from its stark contrast to the traditional Egyptian styles against which it is juxtaposed. Taken out of context, Saudi style points unambiguously to Saudi Arabia and the New Islam. As a reaction, traditional Egyptian Islamic practices have also acquired new ideological meanings. In particular, the meanings of both Saudi and *mujawwad tilawa* styles have shifted dramatically since being juxtaposed in a single social system. Self-consciously adopted, public broadcast of the new style sign (via cassette players) becomes an *ideologically* charged communicative act, serving as a proclamation of faith which *opposes* the traditionally prevailing social norms, a non-discursive form of New Islamic proselytisation. All this is to be expected, since social juxtaposition of contrasting styles produces new active differences. It remains to examine these differences in greater detail (see Table 3.6).

---

[64] Capitalising on the increased popularity of *murattal* in the wake of Saudi influence, SonoCairo has re-released the *murattal* tapes of Shaykh Mustafa Isma'il (Isma'il 1999), Shaykh 'Abd al-Basit 'Abd al-Samad and others in new packaging. Significantly, whereas the original tapes featured a photograph of the reciter, the new ones do not. I spoke with the SonoCairo engineer who designs many of their album covers and he confirmed that the reason for this change is the preponderance of '*Sunniyyin*' ('fundamentalists') drawn to *murattal* who consider such images to be *haram*.

[65] Celebrations of *arba'in* and *dhikra* have abated somewhat.

Table 3.6   The ternary style sign system – principal differences between the Saudi style and the traditional public Egyptian styles, *mujawwad* and *murattal*, as *recorded* (on cassette tapes).

Free variable	Saudi	*Mujawwad*	*Murattal*
1.1.1 *Timbre*	Most tense, nasal	Moderate tension	Most relaxed
1.1.2 *Expression*	Plaintive, awe-filled (*huzn, shajan*)	Mixture of *huzn* and *tarab* (ecstasy)	Least affective
1.2.1 *Ambitus*	Intermediate range	Widest range	Narrowest range
1.2.2 *Tessitura*	Highest	Lower	Middle
1.2.3 *Mode preference*	Focus on *Rast*	Focus on *Bayyati*	Focus on *Bayyati*
1.2.4 *Modulation*	Little	Much	Little
1.2.5 *Melodicity*	Low	Great	Lowest
1.3.1 *Pause*	Few; short	Many; long	Few; short
1.3.2 *Tone rate*	Highest	Lowest	Lower
1.4.1 *Dynamic level*	High	Medium	Low
1.4.2 *Dynamic range*	Narrow	Wide	Narrow
1.4.3 *Accent*	Highest	Moderate	Low
2.1.1 *Melisma*	Less melisma	Most melisma	Least melisma
2.1.2 *Word painting*	None	Some	None
2.2.1 *Repetition*	None	Much	None
2.2.2 *Syllable duration*	Shortest	Longest	Short
2.2.3 *Syllable duration variation*	High	High	Low
2.3.1 *Textual passage*	No preference	Some preference for narratives	No preference
2.3.2 *Textual boundaries*	*Juz'* and *Sura*	*Sura*	*Sura*
2.3.3 *Du'a'*	Yes	No	No
2.4.1 *Regional accent*	Saudi accent[66]	Egyptian accent	Egyptian accent
3.1 *Occasion* (primary)	Prayer, especially *tarawih* (live or recordings), studio (recordings)	*Maytam* and mosque *majlis* (live, recordings)	Prayer (live), studio (recordings)
3.2 *Social position*	*Imam*, preacher, missionary, scholar	Performer, artist, *shaykh*	Performer, artist, *shaykh*
3.3 *Personal image*	Saudi style *shaykh*	Azhari *shaykh*	Azhari *shaykh*
3.4.1 *Attendance*	Congregation or none	Audience	Congregation or none
3.4.2 *Listener behaviour*	None or weeping (especially at *du'a'*)	Ecstatic feedback	None

---

[66]   This Saudi linguistic accent (sometimes pejoratively called 'Beduin' in Egypt) is easily recognised by Egyptians. One Egyptian expert even explained to me that the Saudis, in order to promote their reciters abroad, called for Egyptian *muqri*s to teach them, for otherwise their recitations would be incomprehensible to non-Saudis.

4.1 *Medium*	Cassette, CD, CD-ROM (latest technology)	Cassette	Cassette
4.2 *Reverb*	Often added in studio	None	None
4.3.1 *Cover text*	Name of textual segment central	Name of reciter central (as 'artist')	Name of reciter central (as 'artist')
4.3.2 *Cover fonts*	Straight, modernist	Traditional calligraphy	Traditional calligraphy
4.3.3 *Cover images*	Qur'an and holy places in Hijaz central; no photograph of reciter	Reciter's photograph central	Reciter's photograph central
4.3.4 *Cover art*	'Islamic modern'	Traditional Islamic ornament (arabesques)	Traditional Islamic ornament (arabesques)
4.4.1 *Producer name*	Islamic	General	General
4.4.2 *Producer specialisation*	Islamic (Qur'an, *du'a'*, *khutba*, *anashid*)	General	General
4.5 *Retail location*	Outside music stores	Music cassette shops	Music cassette shops

New Meanings for *Tilawa* Styles

The influence of Saudi *tilawa* in Egypt not only produced a new style sign carrying new meanings, it also transformed the meaning of *mujawwad* itself. This impact is unsurprising once it is understood that all meaning (arbitrary or not) is a function of active differences within a semiotic system operating in a social space. Introducing a new sign into that system may increase the number of active differences for all signs in the system. The particular historical conditions under which the Saudi style entered Egypt freighted it with semiotic values (related to Saudi Arabia) not associated with traditional *mujawwad*. In juxtaposition, the Saudi style consequently came actively to signify the New Islam. Conversely, the principal public Egyptian style (*mujawwad*) also acquired an ideological cast, for this juxtaposition simultaneously served to highlight *mujawwad*'s formerly tacit connection to Egypt's national heritage and traditional Egyptian Islam: more liberal, less politicised, more Sufi and more tolerant of aesthetic expression. In Egypt, the principal semiotic opposition is now the difference between the Saudi style and Egyptian *mujawwad*. These ideas are illustrated in Table 3.7. In the ternary system, Egyptian *murattal* becomes a mediating style, pragmatically connected to the old Egyptian school and sonically connected to the Saudi one, whose meaning is observer-dependent. For exponents of the Egyptian tradition, *murattal* carries many of the meanings of *mujawwad*; for exponents of the New Islam, *murattal* is associated with the Saudi styles.

Table 3.7   Some partial meanings of Saudi style relative to *mujawwad*, and *vice versa*, in Egyptian social space. Again, meaning appears as the sum of differences (third column). Unlike the *mujawwad/murattal* distinction, the *mujawwad*/Saudi one has become ideological (compare with Table 3.5 above).

Semiotic values		Differences
Saudi	***Mujawwad***	**Partial meaning of Saudi style with respect to *mujawwad* style, within Egyptian social space**
Anti-musical	Musical	*Shari'a*, beauty of pure Islam (music as *haram*)
Saudi Arabia	Egypt	Holy sites (Mecca, Medina)
Saudi economy	Egyptian economy	Oil wealth
Congregational prayer (especially *tarawih*)	*Maytam, dhikra*	*Shari'a*, mosques, worship, anti-*bid'a*
Islamic expression, evoking Judgement Day	Beauty of expression	*Shari'a*; fear, contrition and repentance
Affective response to text	Melodic elaboration of text	Power of text itself
Qur'an centred	Performer centred	Transcendence of Qur'an
New Islamism	Traditional Egyptian Islam	*Infitah, sa'wada* and New Islam in Egypt
Political discourse from reciter	Apolitical reciter	Politicised, activist Islam
Narrow aesthetic range, straightness	Arabesques, wide aesthetic range	Wahhabiyya, representing Islam's 'straight path' ('*al-sirat al-mustaqim*', Qur'an 1:6)

Semiotic values		Differences
Mujawwad	**Saudi**	**Partial meaning of *mujawwad* style with respect to Saudi style, within Egyptian social space**
Musical	Anti-musical	Music and song
Tarab aesthetic and behaviour	No *tarab*	*Tarab*
Spiritual beauty of expression	Fear of Judgment Day	Spirituality of worldly beauty
Melodic elaboration of text	Affective response to text	Power of reciter
Performer centred	Qur'an centred	Performer as artist
More interpretive, circuitous	More literal, direct	Sufism, traditionalism, arabesque
Specialised *tilawa* professional	Non-professional *tilawa* specialist	Professionalism, profit
Shrine-mosques	*Haramayn* (Mecca, Medina)	Saint veneration, traditional localised Egyptian Islam
Egyptian reciters	Saudi reciters	Egyptian heritage (*turath*)
Traditional Egyptian society	New Islam, *infitah and sa'wada*	Pre-*infitah* Egypt
Egyptian secular state	Saudi religious state	Liberalism

Examples

Sonic Differences

In order to illustrate the differences embedded in the ternary sign system, it is helpful to compare instances of all three styles as disseminated through the Egyptian media. In contrast to the examples of traditional Egyptian *murattal* and *mujawwad* presented earlier (Examples 3.1 and 3.2), therefore, Example 3.3 presents a transcription of the same passage (Qur'an 12:4) performed by the Saudi Shaykh Ahmad al-'Ajmi. (Differences in the ternary sign system are presented in Table 3.8.)

Compared with Shaykh Mustafa Isma'il's *murattal*, Shaykh Ahmad al-'Ajmi's performance is extremely rapid. Expression is conveyed by timbre, melisma and high syllable length variation, yet none of this detracts from the forward momentum of a simple melodic line. Melodic speed and lack of ornamentation combined with vocal purity and a 'child-like' tessitura suggest New Islamic emphases: unmediated directness (the 'straight path') and spiritual innocence. Aside from such iconicity is the indexical connection to Saudi Islam via recitation by a famous Saudi *imam* and *da'i*, regarded (in Egypt at least) as representing the Wahhabiyya and the Holy Places (*Haramayn*) of Mecca and Medina, in a Saudi accent. These places are further emphasised by artificial studio reverb, an icon of the real acoustical reverberations caused by (hence indexing) the vast spaces enclosed by the *Haramayn*. Finally, other differences such as the Saudi preference for *Rast*, as compared with the Egyptian preference for *Bayyati*, serve as differential 'hooks' on which to hang arbitrary meanings supported by (non-arbitrary) iconic and indexical factors.

Example 3.3   Recitation of Qur'an 12:4 by the Saudi, Shaykh Ahmad al-'Ajmi ('Ajmi 1996a, 1996b). The *maqam* is *Rast* on C4 (E4, second line from the bottom, is half-flat); absolute pitch is *Rast* on A3 (a minor 3rd below); the horizontal axis indicates seconds. Dashes separate syllables and asterisks denote melismas. Text: *idh-qaa-la-yuu-su-fu-li-a-bii-hi-yaa-*-*-*-*-*-*-*-*-*-a-ba-ti-*-in-*-*-*-*-*-*-ni-ra-ay-tu-a-ha-da-'a-sha-ra-kaw-*-ka-ban-wash-sham-sa-wal-qa-ma-ra-ra-ay-tu-hum-*-liy-saa-ji-diin.*

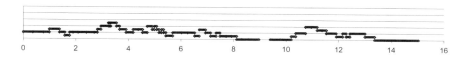

Table 3.8   Differences among Saudi, *mujawwad* and *murattal* style recitations of Qur'an 12:4, as based on recordings partly notated in Examples 3.3, 3.1 and 3.2 respectively. Note that not all differences listed above are visible in the notations.

	Saudi style	*Mujawwad* style	*Murattal* style
1.1.1 *Timbre*	Most tense, nasal	Moderate tension	Most relaxed
1.1.2 *Expression*	High	Moderate	Least
1.2.1 *Ambitus*	Intermediate	Widest	Narrowest
1.2.2 *Tessitura*	Highest	Lower	Higher
1.2.3 *Mode preference*	*Rast*	*Bayyati*	*Bayyati*
1.2.4 *Modulation*	Little	Much	Little
1.2.5 *Melodicity*	Intermediate	High	Lowest
1.3.1 *Pause*	Few; short	Many; long	Few; short
1.3.2 *Tone rate*	Highest (4.0 tps)	Lower (2.4 tps)	Lower (2.3 tps)
1.4.2 *Dynamic range*	Narrow	Wide	Narrow
2.1.1 *Melisma*	Some (1.419)	Most (1.884)	Negligible (1.047)
2.2.1 *Repetition*	None	Much	None
2.2.2 *Syllable duration*	Shortest (average 0.34 seconds)	Longest (average 0.74 seconds)	Short (average 0.45 seconds)
2.2.3 *Syllable duration variation*	Highest (81% of average)	Higher (56% of average)	Lowest (40% of Average)
3.1 *Occasion*	Studio recording	Live recording	Studio recording
3.4.2 *Listener behaviour*	None or weeping (especially at *du'a'*)	Ecstatic feedback	None
4.2 *Reverb*	Medium	None	None

Visual Differences

Graphics are key to symbolic power and are a universal aspect of phonogram-mediated *tilawa*. Since traditional Egyptian *murattal* and *mujawwad* do not differ in this respect, I contrast instances of Saudi and Egyptian style cassette covers in Figure 3.2 (Sa'idi 1999, Hudhayfi 1995).[67] The cover on the left, featuring the reciter wearing traditional Azhari garb, conveys Egyptian Islamic traditionalism. Here, the *performer* is central, featured as 'artist' just as a secular singer (*mutrib*) would be. His name is rendered in elaborate calligraphy, full of decorative lines and frills inessential to the underlying letters, like an ornamented melody. The effect is completed with a busy arabesque carpet-like background. These features establish a link between *mujawwad* recitation and other traditional Islamic arts. The name of the production company (*Sout el-Tarab*, 'The Sound of *Tarab*'),

[67]   While they may carry Saudi sound and meanings, it should be noted that most 'Saudi' style cassettes sold in Egypt are produced there as well. As such, although these graphics are associated with the Saudi sound in the Egyptian imagination, they may not be Saudi in origin and in fact are applied to new releases of Egyptian reciters as well.

which also produces Sufi and music cassettes, underscores the connection between *tilawa*, music and mysticism.

By contrast, the image on the right – a clear instance of Islamic Modern style – evokes the New Islam. In the centre, a radiant Qur'an illuminates the night sky, implying cosmic, even apocalyptic, significance. Plain white script foregrounds the names of the *suras*. Arching overhead, in dark letters set aglow by the Qur'an's brilliant light, is the name of the reciter, Shaykh 'Ali 'Abd al-Rahim al-Hudhayfi. Egyptian Muslims will instantly recognise the green dome of the Prophet's mosque in Medina. Much smaller letters just above introduce al-Hudhayfi as the reciter of that mosque, but his image is absent (as per Wahhabi prohibitions). Font design, simple and direct, eschews traditional elaborations and the use of colour, line and light appears 'modern', connecting Revelation to the present. The image thus summarises the New Islam by emphasising the central place of the Qur'an and the Prophet in the modern world, simultaneously subordinating the reciter.

Figure 3.2   Qur'anic recitation cassette covers produced in Egypt. The cover on the left (Sa'idi 1999), centred on the reciter, Shaykh Mahmud Abu al-Wafa al-Sa'idi, is typical of traditional Egyptian *tilawa* tapes. That on the right (Hudhayfi 1995) is an instance of 'Islamic modern', typical of Saudi-style tapes. *Sura* names (Yusuf and al-Ra'd), cosmic imagery and a representation of the Prophet's mosque in Medina, rendered in brightly coloured modern graphics, are foregrounded. This 'Islamic modern' visual style preponderates across New Islamic media productions such as pamphlets and recorded sermons.

The production company, *Mu'assasa al-Risala li al-Intaj wa al-Tawzi' al-Islami* ('The Message Foundation for Islamic Production and Distribution'), specialises in New Islamic media and their publicity literature explicitly underscores the harmonious fusion of private enterprise and *da'wa* (Gharib 2001).

Discursive Representations

If *tilawa* style has acquired significant non-discursive ideological power in Egypt, then one might expect that power to be acknowledged in ideological discourse. Indeed, a sign of the ideological power of a non-discursive channel is its occasional eruption into oral and written language. In Egypt, there are two primary discursive positions concerning the three styles. Firstly, there is a pro-*murattal* (Saudi or Egyptian) position, which is pan-Islamic, Arabia-centric and anti-*mujawwad*. Written sources taking this position comprise New Islamic literature (for example, Murad 199x) seeking to reform many Egyptian practices. The second position is anti-Saudi, pro-*mujawwad* and pro-Egyptian. Written sources adopting this position include those championing the Egyptian Arabo-Islamic heritage (*al-turath al-masri*) (for example, see Qadi 1999) and secularist writings (see various in Daoud 1997a). Both types cherish the Egyptian aesthetic heritage and condemn newer '*Salafi*' trends.[68]

Many sources adopting the first position point to exhortations to *tartil* in the Qur'an (73:4) and Sunna (Husari 196x:20, Murad 199x:111) while criticising music and *tarab* in recitation for distorting the Book of God (Husari 196x:21–5, Sa'id 1975:116–17), distracting from contemplation (Shalabi 1997:57–8, 60, Murad 199x:153–4, 'Abd al-Fattah 2001:83) or venal profiteering (Hilawi 1984?:80, Jaris 199x:21, 'Abd al-Fattah 2001:83). The complexities of *mujawwad* are implicitly critiqued for introducing professional mediators into recitation (Sa'id 1975: 81, 82–3, 111–15, 117) and memorial recitations are condemned (Murad 199x:153–4). The artless but sincere voice is preferred to a musically trained one (Husari 196x:15, Murad 199x:154). A well-known *hadith* stating that non-Arabian melodies are dissolute[69] is invoked and the pure, simple voices of desert nomads (Arabians) are praised (Shalabi 1997:62–3).

In contrast, the second position celebrates *mujawwad* as an instance of Egyptian greatness, demonstrating the beauty and joy of spirituality (Fadl 1997:110). *Tajwid* is regarded as a spiritual art that produced great reciter-artists, many of whom were also great musicians (Khalil and Hafiz 1984:6–10, 161, 170, 174). A number of books purporting to speak of reciters in general implicitly take a nationalist

---

[68]   A third position, which promotes the precision of *murattal* while explicitly denouncing its more emotional (weeping) manifestations as displayed in the Saudi style, is occasionally enunciated as well (Murad 199x:154).

[69]   Jalal al-Din 'Abd al-Rahman al-Suyuti (2003), 'al-Itqan fi 'ulum al-Qur'an' ('Mastery of Qur'anic Sciences'), <www.alwaraq.com/>, p. 142 (accessed 08/03).

position by documenting the Egyptian *tilawa* tradition only (Bulk 1992?, Qadi 1999, Daoud 1997a, Hamam 2000, Sayyid 2003). Saudi reciters are 'Beduin' in a pejorative sense. For example, Daoud describes the 'torture' of listening to 'Beduin' reciters: their Arabic is incomprehensible, their recitations unbeautiful (1997b:34). According to this position, beauty is spiritual while constant weeping is sanctimonious and inappropriate, obscuring Qur'anic meanings. As Fadl observes, 'You will be surprised to find [Saudi reciters] weeping during *ayat* talking of … Paradise, instead of their hearts dancing with happiness and longing' (1997:109). The 'terrible wave' of *Salafiyya* is a corruption of 'our religious tolerance', sacrificing the inner beauty of religion for the sake of outward appearances (1997:107–10).[70] One of the most strident polemics occurs in an article by Ahmad Yusuf entitled 'The Dissonance[71] of Shaykh al-Hudhayfi'. After emphasising the historical relation between music and *tilawa*, the author goes so far as to actually accuse the Saudi reciters of destroying Egyptian music:

> Suddenly Arab music in Egypt went up in smoke … it didn't occur to us that the true cause … is the spread of *tilawa* in the manner of the Saudi Shaykh al-Hudhayfi or, more precisely, the spread of false Salafiyya trends coming from the petroleum countries, which planted in the sentiments of a broad section of the population this deformed idea: that 'legal' *tilawa* … is that which is free from any tinge of beauty, and which denies completely the relation between the Qur'an and music, to the extent that he who tries to establish such a relation is near to be accused of committing a great sin … The Egyptian people … know by natural intelligence the musicality of Qur'anic rhetoric … and so produced many generations of great reciters who established all of Arabic music via *tilawa*. (Yusuf 1997:70–74, translation by Michael Frishkopf)

Conclusions

Through broad dissemination, the mass media promote the development of widely-recognised sonic styles. The decentralisation of an asynchronous media system, diversifying content and localising control of both production and playback, facilitates the development of a system of contrastive non-discursive style signs circulating as ordinary discourse, moving closer to the real social conditions of their production and consumption. Unlike television and radio, asynchronous media enable the 'end user' to become a 'broadcaster' by freely disseminating style within a local audio sphere, or by circulating recorded media. The individual decision to play a particular cassette tape in a public place, or to distribute copies,

---

[70] Notably, Fadl exempts Shaykhs Sudays and Hudhayfi from his censure, claiming that they are closer to the Egyptian tradition. One suspects, however, that their great popularity in Egypt compelled him to exempt them.

[71] The Arabic is '*nashaz*', a word also used to describe poor musical performances.

thus constitutes a social act of communication, sometimes an ideological one. As I have argued in this chapter, such an utterance implicitly disseminates and advocates a sonic style together with its attendant meanings. Sonic style signs accumulate broader social meanings (even entire ideologies) both as a function of active differences within the synchronic social system (following a Saussurean logic) and of diachronic socio-historical trajectories along which they accrue iconic and indexical meanings (following a Peircean one). Rhetorically, dissemination of stylistic meaning is rendered 'sensible' through the affective charge of sonic experience, the 'presentational' (Langer 1957) quality of style (instantiated in performance) that naturalises meaning. 'I feel it to be true', one says, and no further justification is necessary. Thus the act of stylistic playback simultaneously conveys messages of personal conviction ('I feel that …') and persuasion ('you should feel that …'). Such messages are all the more powerful for being non-discursive, for ideological positions are then diffused under cover of taste preferences. A non-discursive sign cannot easily be represented, or opposed, in discourse.

Twentieth-century mediation enabled widespread dissemination of a dominant public *tilawa* style (*mujawwad*) in Egypt. The commercial evolution of music media precipitated the extrusion, from what was once a continuous music-*tilawa* field, of a quasi-autonomous field of *tilawa* practice that, divorced from music, could accommodate a greater stylistic range. However, as long as the media remained centralised under state control, one main public *tilawa* style continued to dominate in practice. Then, out of the radical economic, political, social and technological transformations of post-1973 Egypt, two non-discursive *tilawa* style-signs – *mujawwad* and Saudi – emerged, freighted with broadly distinctive ideological meanings. As the Saudi style has become associated with the New Islam (transnational, *Salafi*, consumerist and capitalist), the traditional *mujawwad* style has (reactively) become ideologised as well, coming to signify traditional Egyptian Islam and Egyptian cultural heritage. Installed in thousands of shops, restaurants, markets and taxis, each cassette audio system radiates an ideologically-charged, non-discursive, invisible audio sphere through which Egyptians are constantly passing. In selecting and playing a *tilawa* style, the controller of playback equipment (the message 'sender') is, consciously or not, cryptically disseminating a powerfully affective, non-discursive Islamic sensibility to a localised 'public' (the message 'receivers'), broadcasting an ethos without calling cognitive attention to its associated worldview (Geertz 1973a).

For the religious discourse of sermons and print media demands cognitive attention, and thus triggers the critical faculties which enable the individual to filter, for instance, New Islamic discourse clashing with entrenched beliefs (attacks on music, Sufism or saint veneration, for example). But for Muslims, affective *tilawa* (correctly performed according to *mushaf*, *qira'at* and *tajwid*) is nearly impossible to reject. If the non-discursive meanings of *tilawa* styles are inarticulate, their transformative powers are all the greater for their emotional impact. Operating outside the realm of verbal discourse, the power of Qur'anic recitation is well-nigh incontestable, crypto-rhetorical, since it presents no logical challenge for the critical faculties to take up, but simply presents the *feeling* of certainty, deftly bypassing the gatekeepers of the self. For the dissemination of New Islamic meanings, then, the act of blaring Saudi-style *tilawa* via cassettes in a public place is far more effective than preaching in the mosque or distributing pamphlets on a street-corner – and less politically dangerous.

The same considerations apply to media gatekeepers of the state. Though asynchronous media production has become increasingly privatised, theoretically the state retains the right to 'filter' cassette productions. However, such censorship relies upon discursively-defined criteria, resting primarily on text. Songs are banned by the state's Censor for Artistic Works only when *lyrics* tread on sensitive ground (mainly politics, religion or sex), not for sonic-stylistic reasons.[72] Likewise, *tilawa* cassettes are banned – by al-Azhar or Egyptian Radio – only for violations of discursive principles of recitation (as fixed by *mushaf, qira'a* and *tajwid*).[73] To ban a 'sound' there is neither will nor way. Yet arrayed in a semiotic system, non-discursive *tilawa* styles can become ideologically powerful, compensating with affective persuasiveness what they lack in referential specificity. Such styles carry a covert – even subversive – ideological force, all the more powerful for not being explicitly recognised as such.

In this connection I will cite a single anecdote. In 641 CE the Arab general 'Amr ibn al-'As 'opened' Christian Egypt to Islam, establishing the Arab city of Fustat and building the first mosque in Africa. Often rebuilt over the centuries (see Creswell 1969:58–9, 131, 149–51), over the last 15 years this now enormous mosque, adjacent to Coptic Cairo, has served as a principal centre for the New Islam in Cairo.[74] In 1995, state authorities finally evicted the mosque's outspoken *Salafi* preacher, Dr 'Abd al-Sabur Shahin. However, his *protégé*, the *imam*, reciter and *da'i* Shaykh Muhammad Gabril (principal Egyptian exponent of the Saudi style[75]) was permitted to remain, a stylistic beacon of the New Islam. Dr Shahin has himself testified that the mosque's attendance grew largely on the strength of Gabril's voice (Hassan 1999). Today, the congregation for Shaykh Muhammad's Ramadan *tarawih* prayers exceeds half a million, and his *tilawa* recordings are widely distributed by various companies. Even state-owned SonoCairo, historically charged with promoting the traditional Egyptian musical and Islamic heritage, published Gabril (starting in 1990) and (in 1999) two Saudi reciters as well (Shaykhs Sudays and Sharim) (SonoCairo 199x:47ff.). Here is a vivid illustration

---

[72]   Conversation with Dr Ali Abu Shadi, former head of the Censor for Artistic Works (2004).

[73]   Conversation at al-Azhar Islamic Research Academy, Cairo (1995).

[74]   Perhaps because this capacious mosque contains no saint's shrine, resembles the *Masjid al-Haram* of Mecca and symbolises the strength of the early Islamic community.

[75]   Besides similar sonic and pragmatic features, Gabril's Saudi credentials include winning the world Qur'an recitation competition in Mecca in 1986, the first Egyptian ever to do so (Hamam 1996:39–41).

of how Egyptian authorities, far from being able (or even willing) to oppose non-discursive content clashing with traditional Egyptian values, finally embrace it.

Today, the cities of Egypt are increasingly filled with local audio broadcasts of cassette-mediated Saudi-style recitations, a phenomenon both expressing and propelling the waves of Egyptian Muslims moving towards a more Saudi-inflected, New Islamist viewpoint. But this movement is also supported by other symbols of the New Islam, including tracts and sermons. The particular significance of the non-discursive sonic style sign disseminated through asynchronous media inheres in its affective power, its ability to fly 'beneath the radar' of critical thinking, while circulating throughout the social system as ordinary discourse, via localised acts of broadcast and distribution. The implications of these attributes are profound. Just as 'receivers' absorb affective ideological messages without necessarily recognising them as such, equally 'senders' may disseminate them without necessarily intending to do so. As 'receiver' in turn becomes 'sender', potent ideological meanings rapidly circulate throughout the social system, largely independent of the conscious, discursive intentions of its social agents. Recognition of this phenomenon is critical, not only as a means of understanding contemporary struggles to define Islam in Egypt, but for the study of music and power more generally.

Chapter 4

Music, Politics and Nation Building in Post-Soviet Tajikistan[1]

Federico Spinetti

Introduction

Largely ignored by the outside world, the political history of Tajikistan (Figure 4.1) has recently been characterised by extremely grave events. A ferocious civil war (1991–97) has severely destabilised this small former Soviet republic and has tragically affected the lives of its people. Given the regional and ethnic dimensions of the Tajik conflict and the legacy of an almost century-old Soviet policy on 'nationalities', issues of national identity and social cohesion are paramount to contemporary Tajik political, cultural and social realities. This chapter addresses the interplay of identities embedded within different musical traditions in Tajikistan and suggests ways in which this interplay may be related to broader political and ideological issues. In particular, I am interested in the processes of nation-building initiated by the Soviet regime and redefined in the political climate of the post-Soviet era, and which have profoundly affected the ways in which music is socially organised, performed, evaluated and used to construct identity. Politics and music would seem to be connected in particularly powerful ways in twentieth-century Central Asia, where more than 80 years of displacement and shifting cultural boundaries have served to redefine the role of music in identity formation. The introduction of 'national culture' as a concept, and the deployment of strategies to realise it, have generated the fundamental concepts around which official discourses and public attitudes towards music have crystallised.

In this chapter, I will explore aspects of the relationship between music and social determination, a notion which (drawing on the work of Raymond Williams) I take as referencing the 'pressures and limits' that inform a wider social terrain (Williams 1977:83–9, Turino 1990:399, 407). The perspective adopted here is based on the

[1]   This chapter owes much to a PhD research project supported by the University of London (Ouseley Memorial Studentship and Central Research Fund), by the Art and Humanities Research Council and by the School of Oriental and African Studies, University of London (Additional Fieldwork Award). I undertook fieldwork in Tajikistan between November 2002 and October 2003, mainly in the capital Dushanbe and in the southern region of Kulob. I would like to thank Professor Owen Wright for his comments on drafts of this chapter.

argument (informing much contemporary ethnomusicology) that musical practices are integrally embedded in the conceptual and material forces which inform specific social settings and that music may also play a central role in articulating social patterns of representation and action.[2] I am specifically interested in connecting music to the construction and deployment of hegemonic values and practices in the Gramscian sense. In particular, Gramsci has elaborated a theory on the validity of ideologies, according to which cultural representations are viewed as practical understandings that make sense of and establish specific concrete relationships. These relationships are of central importance in the organisation of society, their solidity, effectiveness and diffusion being *the* conditions for establishing a certain social order and in elaborating and consolidating ways of thinking and behaving which are inextricably interwoven with the exercise of power (Gramsci 2001:868–9, 1234–5, 1250, 1411–16, 1569–70). The discussion which follows will focus on aspects of official policy and ideological developments in relation to music, as well as outlining a chronological trajectory and pinpointing major changes and reformulations in the representation of national identity through music.

Figure 4.1   Map of Tajikistan showing the main regions.

---

2   See in particular Attali (1985:4–6, 19), Turino (1993), Stokes (1994b) and Frith (1996).

In an article on music professionalism in Bulgaria, Donna Buchanan refers to the writings of Václav Havel and Michel Foucault in order to illustrate how truth is 'a fluid and relativistic concept, is culturally structured and socially validated' (1995:383). Anthropology and social theory have been increasingly informed by the notion that norms of conduct and worldviews are cultural constructs, arguing against essentialist approaches to representations of self and the world (Hall 1996:1–4). In focusing on the connection between music and identity construction in Tajikistan, I explore the possibility that changing perceptions of identity in music are part of a shifting paradigm of representation and of a 'fight for objectivity' (Gramsci 2001:1411–16).

The Soviet Period

Nation Building

Tajikistan was formed in 1924 with the constitution of the Autonomous Province of Tajikistan within the boundaries of the Uzbek Soviet Socialist Republic. In 1929, the Autonomous Province acquired the status of a Republic and the Soviet Socialist Republic of Tajikistan was born, its territory covering the eastern lands of what had been the Emirate of Bukhara prior to Soviet intervention (Fragner 1994:22). The creation of Tajikistan was part of the political and territorial strategy usually referred to as Soviet nationality policy. The complex of economic, administrative and political motivations from which this policy arose is the subject of much scholarly debate, and my intention here is to sketch only a few significant points. In the first place, the emergence of 'nations' was regarded as a transitional process between feudalism and modern industrialised society, a condition necessary to unite people on the path towards proletarian consciousness (Levin 1984:75–9). This ideological foundation was paralleled by the logistic necessity of establishing well-defined social and territorial groupings where Soviet institutions and power structures could take root. In Central Asia, Uzbekistan and Tajikistan represented a splitting of the bi-lingual region of Transoxiana where Uzbeks and Tajiks had co-existed for centuries. As such, not only were the Soviet authorities responsible for creating a separation between peoples who had previously shared a cultural history, but through the promotion of two national languages there emerged a new opposition between Turkic and Persian cultures (Rosen 1973:69, During 1998a:103–8, Levin 1996:47–9).

An important factor in the Soviet partition of Central Asia was the perceived need to combat Pan-Turkist ideas which had spread in the region under the influence of the Young Turks. In particular, the advocacy of cultural reformism and modernisation which characterised the movement known as Jadidism was often allied to the Pan-Turkist nationalistic ideal of a politically unified 'Greater Turkistan' much disapproved of by the Soviets. The establishment of the Uzbek S.S.R. was partly a response to Pan-Turkist political goals. However, while certainly frustrating the idea of a 'Greater Turkistan', this response ultimately and paradoxically fostered a territorially delimited reformulation of Pan-Turkist ideas through eradicating cultural pluralism and establishing a nation founded on a Turkic language and cultural heritage (Fragner 1994:21). This had important implications for the birth of Tajikistan. Although no Tajik national consciousness had evolved before Soviet nationality policy was imposed, the process of 'Uzbekization' promoted prior to the establishment of the Tajik Republic encouraged many Persian-speaking intellectuals to resist attempts to efface Persian cultural components in the region and led to the formulation of ideas on 'ethnicity' and 'nation' which had never existed before (Chvyr 1993:246–50). Thus, the idea of a Tajik nation and of a Tajik state emerged in the 1920s and was eventually backed by Moscow, not least with the purpose of halting possible problems of destabilisation within Uzbekistan on the part of the Tajik population in the south, which was isolated from the bi-lingual cultural environment of Bukhara and Samarqand.

The Soviet formulation of 'nationality' strongly emphasised concepts of linguistic and territorial unity (Fragner 1994:22). Great importance was attached to the assertion of distinctive national cultural heritages that could serve to differentiate between nationalities and provide them with internal cohesion (Naby 1973:110, Jahangiri 1998:14, During 1998a:34). For the new Central Asian states, this meant a reformulation of both history and cultural traditions in national terms. For example, Tamerlan was re-invented as the founder of the 'Uzbek nation', while Tajiks claimed a Samanid legacy, re-interpreting this dynasty as the first 'Tajik empire' (Rosen 1973:69).[3] Whilst journals and newspapers were the main vehicles by which intellectuals became involved in this construction of 'Tajikness', projects launched by the Nazorat-i Ma'orif (Commissariat of Education) were also important, as was the influential Sadriddin Aini (1878–1954), an early promoter of Tajik culture and the acknowledged father of modern Tajik literature. These activities focused mainly on language, the cornerstone of Soviet nationality policy. For example, projects such as the *nowsozī va budyodkorī-i zabon-i tojikī* ('renovation and establishment of the Tajik language'), initiated in the 1920s, aimed to standardise the Tajik language and to re-evaluate and promote classical Persian literature as a Tajik national heritage. These were the first assertions of a Tajik national identity.[4]

The particular way in which Tajikistan was created inevitably marked its future development. The sudden creation of a nation with no historically-rooted national consciousness created tensions between the building of a unified national

---

[3]   The Samanids ruled over Khorasan and Transoxiana between 875 and 999 CE. They were munificent patrons of the arts and contributed significantly to the development of centres such as Nishapur, Bukhara and Samarqand, as well as supporting eminent Persian poets such as Rudaki and Ferdowsi. On the Samanids, see Frye (1975) and Bosworth (1995), among others.

[4]   Aini's *Namunai Adabiyyoti Tojik* ('A Sample of Tajik Literature'), published in Moscow in 1926, was particularly significant.

community on the one hand and long-standing regional and clan allegiances on the other.[5] Such unresolved tensions are still very much evident today and have been a major factor in the degeneration of political debate into armed conflict in recent times. On the whole, however, regional cleavages have not led to a questioning of the very concept of nation itself. Rather they have taken the form of disputes over supremacy within the nation state and who is truly entitled to represent it. This illustrates the extent to which the nationalist ideology planted by the Soviets, although corroded from within, has ultimately proved to be an extremely persuasive force.

Policy on Music

Soviet cultural policy on the arts resulted in several major interventions which entailed both the promotion of traditional art forms and a concurrent effort to bring them closer to European models in accordance with an evolutionary concept of artistic development. This was paralleled by a fostering of purely European art forms. A pervasive institutionalisation of education and realisation was introduced for all literary, visual and performing arts through a close network of unions (*ittifoq*), societies (*jam'iyat*) and houses of culture (*khona-i madaniyat*), over which direct control was exercised by state bureaucracy and the Communist Party apparatus (Naby 1973:112, Djumaev 1993:43–6).[6] Central to Soviet cultural policy was the creation of national artistic monuments and the promotion of national cultural heritages. In both Uzbekistan and Tajikistan, this was achieved by elevating the art music tradition of the Bukharan *Shashmaqom* to the status of national emblem. This large repertoire of vocal and instrumental pieces ordered into suite-like sequences is a clear manifestation of cultural and musical symbiosis developed over centuries by both Uzbeks and Tajiks (with the crucial contribution of local Jews) in the bi-lingual environment of pre-Soviet Bukhara. In the Soviet era, however, the *Shashmaqom* was subjected to a process of cultural separation based on language and devised to honour the newly formed national units. Beginning in

---

[5]   In general, Tajiks attach great importance to regional identity. In particular, a basic distinction between north and south is further articulated along more localised regional units such as Khujand, Gharm, Kulob, Hisor, Badakhshon, Darwoz and so on. The names of regional groups deriving from such areas (Khujandi, Gharmi and so on) designate membership of specific local communities rather than simple geographical origins. Aspects of regional differentiation may include linguistic features, cultural practices, clothing, food and, not least, music. Regional identity, intersecting with sub-regional (district, village) and family (*awlod*) clan loyalties, was crucial to the articulation of political alliances during the Soviet period and especially in the context of the civil war. For further discussion on this issue, see Chvyr (1993:250–57), Jawad and Tadjbakhsh (1995:13) and Roy (2000, in particular 13–15).

[6]   For useful comparison with official policies in socialist Eastern European countries see Rice (1994:174–86) and Slobin (1996:2–3).

the 1920s, when Abdurauf Fitrat (Minister of Education in the Bukharan People's Republic which preceded the Uzbek S.S.R.) ordered that the original Tajik texts be omitted from the publication of the *Shashmaqom*, this process culminated with the creation of two distinct versions of the repertoire which were published in the respective national languages between the 1950s and 1970s (Djumaev 1993:45–7, Levin 1993:55–6). As a result, there also arose protracted disputes over cultural ownership of the *Shashmaqom* which paralleled debates over the cities of Bukhara and Samarqand, placed within Uzbekistan's borders according to Soviet territorial policy but long regarded by Tajiks as the lost centres of their civilisation.

Both 'national demarcation' and 'modernisation' of traditional music in Central Asia are well documented in the scholarly literature.[7] However, I would like to revisit briefly some salient features of these processes and assess their particular relevance to Tajikistan. The situation of the *Shashmaqom* has one main peculiarity: the repertoire belonged, and continues to be confined to, a specific geo-cultural region, the north (particularly the cities of Khujand and Panjakent), whose artistic expressions are closely related to those of Bukhara and Samarqand in Uzbekistan and whose population is largely bi-lingual in Uzbek and Tajik. What had been the musical and literary monument of Persian civilisation in Central Asia, largely shared with the Turkic-speaking population in a cultural and social symbiosis, became with partition the expression of a minority culture in the context of Soviet Tajikistan (During 1993a:39). Nevertheless, this music continued to enjoy high prestige because of the cultural and political supremacy held within the executive and key state institutions by intellectual elites and bureaucrats from the northern region of Khujand during most of the Soviet period. This distribution of power has profoundly informed official cultural policy and promotion of the arts, and has crucially entailed the attribution of the highest status to the *Shashmaqom* in line with discourses emphasising the centrality of the cultural power of Bukhara and Samarqand in the history of Persian/Tajik civilisation in Central Asia. It may be suggested that Soviet cultural ideology succeeded in forging a truth according to which Tajik music possesses both a classical tradition (*klassikī*) and a popular one (*khalqī*), the former consisting of the *Shashmaqom*, the latter comprising the various distinctive musical styles of south Tajikistan together with the musical forms of the north outside the *Shashmaqom*. Although purportedly valid for the entire Tajik population, the hierarchy of prestige and artistic value associated with this polarity between learned and popular traditions created what it was arguably designed to conceal: a hierarchy between regional musical cultures, most notably between north and south. As a result, the choice of the *Shashmaqom* as a Tajik national emblem (receiving most of the state's financial support for traditional music and much media visibility) meant that a large part of the population – that living in the centre and south of the country – came to view its own musical culture

---

[7]   See Naby (1973), Levin (1979, 1996:46–51, 89–93, 111–15), Kosacheva (1990) and During (1993a:35–41, 1998a:91–115).

as partially marginalised from official sponsorship, thus possibly facilitating the emergence of contrasting regionally-based sentiments about music.

In local terminology, the music traditions of central, southern and south-eastern Tajikistan (also shared by the Tajik population of northern Afghanistan) are most frequently known as 'mountain music' (*kuhistonī*). Such a term encompasses and foregrounds the affinity of a number of regional traditions, although the distinctiveness of each of these is also emphasised locally.[8] On the whole, Tajik mountain music differs in many respects from the traditions of the north, including aspects of instrumentation, vocal technique and modal structure, as well as melodic and rhythmic configuration.[9] Whereas the *Shashmaqom* is the expression of an urban culture, south Tajik music has its roots in rural society. The *falak* (lit. 'firmament, destiny') genre is the most widespread style in south Tajikistan and is dominant among non-professional singers and musicians in rural areas.[10] Its texts consist of popular quatrains of unknown authorship which are typically linked to expressions of desolation, unrequited love or suffering at being remote from home.[11] The musical vocabulary of *falak* is also strongly associated with sentiments of grief and longing. The two main performance styles of *falak* are the unmeasured solo-voice style and the measured, accompanied *falak*.[12] Additionally,

---

[8]   Within Tajik mountain music, the traditions of the Pamir (in the Badakhshon region) have highly typical traits, including characteristic performance genres such as *maddoh* ('song of praise') and *dargilik* ('song of longing'), as well as distinctive rhythms and instruments. Notable are the use of Pamiri lutes such as *rubob*, *tanbur* and *setor*, and the absence of the *dumbra*, the most widespread lute in other mountainous areas of Tajikistan. On Pamiri music in Tajik Badakhshon, see Karomatov and Nurdzhanov (1978–86), During (1993b), van den Berg and van Belle (1997), Koen (2003a, 2003b, 2005), O'Connell (2004), van den Berg (2004).

[9]   Typical instruments of south Tajik music include the *dumbra* (also called *dutorcha* or *dutor-i mayda*, a small, fretless two-stringed long-necked lute), the *ghijak* (spiked fiddle with metal resonator), the *tablak* (single-headed, goblet-shaped drum) and the *tūtūk* (small fipple flute). The most characteristic lutes of the north, such as the plucked *tanbur*, the bowed *tanbur* (*sato*) and the large fretted *dutor* are virtually absent, while *doyra* (frame drum) and *nay* (transverse flute) are used in all Tajik music traditions. Major distinctive features of south Tajik modes are the frequent occurrence of minor second (between the first and second degrees of the scale) and augmented second (between the second and third degrees) intervals and the considerable use of chromaticism. As for rhythms, the predilection for metres of five- and seven- time units is characteristic of south Tajik music. See During (1998b), Feldman (1992:240–41), Slobin and Djumaev (2001:14–15).

[10]   On *falak* see Ayubi (1989), Temurzoda (1990) and, in connection with Badakhshon, van den Berg (2004:145, 350–56). With reference to Afghanistan, see Slobin (1970, 1976:124–5, 204–10) and Sakata (1983:53–7, 156–68).

[11]   See Shahrani (1973) for English translations of a number of *falak* songs in the context of Afghanistan.

[12]   The solo-voice *falak* is generally called *falak-i dashtī* (or, in the context of Badakhshon, *be parvo falak*). The accompanied *falak* is either simply called '*falak*', or is

the repertoire of south Tajik singers (*hofiz*) includes settings of verses by classical Persian poets such as Rumi, Hafez and Bedil or contemporary Tajik poets such as Loyiq Sherali; the songs are usually named after the poetic genres employed (for example, *ghazal*, *marsiya*, *na't*, *mukhammas*). It is not unusual for these songs to be combined in groups of three or four, a practice that often involves changes of pitch material (mode and melody, for example) and rhythmic configuration (including metre). Indeed, this combined-song form, together with dance songs, has become central to the repertoire of professional singers and constitutes the core of *khalqī* music as developed during the Soviet period.

During the Soviet period, the promotion of national emblems was accompanied by a considerable redefinition of performance, whether for urban art traditions or for rural ones. The ideal of Europeanisation fostered by the Soviet authorities entailed the introduction of large ensembles, harmonisation of monophonic tunes and the adjustment of instruments to fit tempered tuning and the different registers required for symphony orchestras.[13] In Uzbekistan and Tajikistan, large *Shashmaqom* ensembles, folk orchestras and choirs were created within state-supported broadcasting institutions (radio, and later television) which played an important role in disseminating the new 'modernised' idioms. As mentioned above, there was also a reformulation of musical education and European structures and methods gradually replaced or complemented the traditional oral one-to-one transmission of musical knowledge. There also emerged at this time a new institutionalised music professionalism. As such, *khalqī* music is a professional popular genre which has been predominantly cultivated within state institutions and urban circuits of music making, reworking and expanding traditional forms on the basis of the musical resources encountered in those settings. In contrast, the genre of *falak*, although undoubtedly used as a source of inspiration by a number of professional musicians and composers of *khalqī* music, has continued to be cultivated mainly by non-professional or semi-professional performers in rural contexts. *Falak* has therefore remained largely unaffected by the development of urban professionalism. A notable exception is the singer and musician Odina Hoshimov (1937–94) from the southern region of Kulob, who from the 1960s performed *falak*s professionally in ensemble arrangements and within an institutional framework. During his lifetime, Hoshimov achieved great renown and is still regarded as the undisputed master of *falak* singing.[14]

---

named according to distinct performance styles (*ravya*, lit. 'path'): in the region of Kulob, for instance, musicians may differentiate between *falak-i ravona* ('walking *falak*'), *falak-i zina ba zina* ('step-by-step *falak*'), and so on. In addition, unmeasured *falak*s may be performed on a solo instrument, usually *dumbra*, *ghijak* or *nay-tūtūk*, and may be called *navo-i falak* ('melody of *falak*') or *nola* ('cry').

[13]   See Levin (1979:154–5, 1984:44–60, 1996:45–51, 111–15) and During (1998a:91–101).

[14]   For a biography of Odina Hoshimov see Jalilzoda (1985); see Tabarov (1988) for a discussion of his art and Yorov (1988) for an interview with him.

Insofar as it implies a north/south divide, the *Shashmaqom/khalqī* polarity was instrumental in achieving a two-fold hegemonic objective: on the one hand, different musical traditions were brought together under the 'umbrella' of Tajik national music (classical and popular), thus responding to the Soviet imperative to create unitary national communities; on the other, its inherently hierarchical structure reflected the distribution of power within Tajikistan itself, and in particular the political supremacy of the northern elites. The official Soviet representation of Tajik music may thus be interpreted as having the requisites of a truly hegemonic discourse in the terms delineated by Antonio Gramsci.[15] As well as articulating a set of ideas consistent with the material organisation of Soviet power structures, it also succeeded in gaining wide *consent* and acquiring the status of truth among the population regardless of regional affiliation, thus helping to consolidate those very power structures.

Indicative of this consent is the fact that many of these ideas still hold in contemporary Tajikistan, despite the upheavals that followed the end of the Soviet Union. In effect, such representations encouraged regionalist and political readings of music that contrasted with the unitary, albeit hierarchical, representation of Tajik music constructed by Soviet national ideology. In particular, whilst the Soviets had promoted the *Shashmaqom* for the whole country, underplaying both the regional and political implications of such a choice, the *Shashmaqom* came increasingly to be regarded by south Tajiks as the emblem of a different regional culture and of a political oligarchy. At the same time, the concepts of 'classical' and 'popular' have become so rooted as a result of Soviet hegemony that they continue to be part of a meaningful classificatory terminology today, even among those who associate them with specific regions or classes rather than with the nation as a whole.

Furthermore, the upheavals of the early post-Soviet era had the effect, particularly in official circuits of music-making, of reversing the north/south power relationship (in line with changes in the political sphere), resulting in attempts to counter the supremacy of the *Shashmaqom* by 'classicising' south Tajik traditions. The legacy of Soviet hegemony can best be illustrated by the fact that, firstly, models of 'classicism' have been drawn by and large from the *Shashmaqom*, and second, imbalance was perpetuated as an integral structural feature of official approaches to music in the early post-Soviet period, as evidenced by the aspirations of the post-Soviet government to yet another unitary, monolithic representation of national culture.

---

[15] On the concept of hegemony as an integral junction of conceptual formations and material practices, see Gramsci (2001:1091, 1265–7, 1589–97). On the necessity of a wide social consent for hegemonic processes to be realised, see Gramsci (2001:914–15, 1330–32, 1515–22) and Turino (1993:10–11).

Post-Soviet Tajikistan

From the Beginning

In order to interpret music in Tajikistan after independence (1991) it is necessary to take account of cultural changes which began two decades earlier. During the 1970s, revivalist tendencies which focused on the idea of an 'authentic' Tajik culture gradually emerged. In broad terms, their claims (which were far from homogeneous) laid considerable emphasis on Islam as a significant element of Tajik identity and the consequent necessity of an Islamic renaissance in the country,[16] at the same time insisting on the Persian/Iranian cultural legacy in contrast to the Turkic heritage of other parts of Central Asia, as well as exalting the rural life-style as an emblem of Tajik culture.

The spread of revivalist ideas was indicative of the failure in Tajikistan of the Soviet project of convergence (*sblizhenie*) and merging (*sliianie*) with Russian culture (Rosen 1973:62, Dudoignon 1998:54), based on the idea that Soviet nationalities ought to be linked by 'brotherhood' in order to develop socialist solidarity (Fragner 1994:25, Naby 1973:120). The underlying assumption was that the various nationalities would gradually adopt the dominant Union-wide culture of Russia and that this would lead them towards 'progressive' goals and 'modernity' (Levin 1984:90–91). In Tajikistan, a number of factors frustrated this process of 'Russification' (Rosen 1973:65, Niyazi 1993:268), including profound differences in standards of living between Russian colonists and the majority of the population, the low degree of country-to-town migration and the fundamentally rural character of Tajik society. Furthermore, as will be discussed below, the persistence of traditional life styles and social networks of unofficial religious affiliations and clan loyalties (Chvyr 1993:252–8, Niyazi 1993:274) were actually preserved and reinforced by the Soviet authorities as a tool for political stability through the administrative practice called 'localism'. More generally, the idea of nation planted by the Soviets became the framework and programmatic foundation for forces that were bound to clash with Union-wide cohesion (Balzer 1994:85). The stress on national culture with clear nationalistic overtones, which began in the 1980s, was thus a product of an unresolved tension in Soviet policies between the nationality demarcation project, and the ideal of inter-nations collaboration and workers' internationalism (Rosen 1973:71).[17] Thus, it may be argued that the revivalist trends are better understood as emerging out of the contradictions of the

---

[16]   The thinking of Indian Muslim poet Muhammad Iqbal (1877–1938) has had considerable influence on ideas about Islamic renaissance in Tajikistan. An anthology of his works was first published in Tajikistan in 1978 (Dudoignon 1998:56, 65).

[17]   In the wake of Turino (2000:13–14, following Gellner and others), I define nationalism as a political and cultural movement that both seeks to establish a direct and exclusive relationship between nation and legitimate political sovereignty over a territory, and promotes a cultural heritage labelled 'national'.

nationality policy and as cultural relocations profoundly affected by the pressures of Soviet ideology, rather than as claims for a return to pre-Soviet cultural and social life or a response to anti-Soviet sentiment (Fragner 2001:20–21).

Among the arts, cultural revivalism first made its appearance in literature. The works of many Tajik poets and novelists of the 1970s and 1980s revolved around a re-imagination of the distant past of the Tajik people. Zoroastrianism, the role of the Samanids in Central Asian history, as well as that of the Sogdians,[18] were all accorded unprecedented emphasis in discourses about the Tajik nation and its civilisation. This was seen, for example, in the celebrated novel *Riwoyat-i Sughdī* ('*Sogdian Tale*', published 1977) by Sotim Ulughzoda (1911–97) (Dudoignon 1998:54). Also significant in this respect was the immense popularity of the book *Tojikon* ('*The Tajiks*'), a history of the Tajik people written by Bobojon Ghafurov (1909–77), historian and long-term First Secretary of the Tajik Communist Party.[19] During the 1980s, cultural revivalism was championed by the poets Bozor Sobir (b.1938) and Loyiq Sherali (1941–2000), and the idea of *vatan* ('homeland') gained widespread currency in the literary arts thanks to works such as *Bevatan* ('*Without a Homeland*'), a play by Sulton Safar (b.1935), or the poem *Vatan* by Gulrukhsor (b.1947), both published in 1971 in the journal of the Union of Writers of Tajikistan, *Sado-i Sharq* (Rosen 1973:71). At the same time, there was a counter-current, at least at official levels, with some importance attached during the 1970s to toning down cultural boundaries between Uzbekistan and Tajikistan.[20]

In the domain of music, official promulgations of 'friendship' between the two republics forged the idea of an Uzbek-Tajik or Tajik-Uzbek *Shashmaqom*, and seemed to reflect an orientation towards reassembling a musical tradition which had been artificially split for decades (Levin 1993:56, 1996:47). In fact, this policy was to be revealed as a last-gasp effort by Soviet cultural strategists to reassert international collaboration and to stem growing nationalistic discourses, but which ultimately proved futile. Tajik nationalism perpetuated the theme of distinction from Uzbekistan, and debates around cultural ownership of the *Shashmaqom* increasingly divided academic and cultural discourse during the 1980s (Djumaev 1993:49). At the same time, there was an emerging trend towards identifying south Tajikistan as the cradle of nationhood at the expense of the bi-cultural northern regions. This entailed dismissing the *Shashmaqom* as an Uzbek tradition in order to give south Tajik music the dignity of a proper national art. In particular, because of its emblematic rural character (a much emphasised theme in 'revived' Tajik culture and traditional life), *falak* acquired a central position within the embryonic reconstruction of a 'pure'

---

[18]   The Sogdian civilisation developed in pre-Islamic Transoxiana from the seventh century BCE to the eighth century CE (see Dresden 1983, Marshak and Negmatov 1996).

[19]   Ghafurov's work was first published in Russian (Moscow, 1972). The Tajik version which became so popular in Tajikistan was published in two volumes in 1983 and 1985 respectively.

[20]   As reported by Levin (1979:153). See also Naby (1973:120).

Tajik culture[21] and was increasingly represented as the ancient and original art form of the Tajik people with its roots stretching back to pre-Islamic times.[22] I have encountered a clear perception on the part of a number of individuals that *falak* had attracted official disfavour for years, but that from the mid-1980s it started to receive unprecedented attention within national broadcasting and at festivals. Official hostility is commonly understood by my informants as relating to the specific association of *falak* with religious sentiment (since it addresses destiny or God) and with feelings of sorrow, both of which may have been regarded as incompatible with 'progressive art'.[23] Official opposition is also explicitly understood as being linked to the regionally-based imbalance of political and cultural influence. Whilst I do not have sufficient data to examine the nature and extent of possible official restrictions in greater detail (it seems that there was no overt censorship as such), I believe that the perception of changing trends within official policies is of major significance: the re-emergence of *falak* from long-term official neglect announced the strength of new social and political forces in the making.

Perhaps the most representative contemporary exponent of *falak* is Dawlatmand Kholov (b.1950) from the southern region of Kulob, one of the most appreciated artists in Tajikistan today. Kholov's music draws from Tajik mountain traditions and his compositions are inspired by a variety of regional sources within south Tajikistan, which he combines and reworks. He has striven over the years to raise the prestige of south Tajik musical traditions, and thanks to his immense popularity and activity within the media, he has long been perceived as the champion of the perspective which identifies in south Tajik music the only authentic Tajik tradition. In 1989, he founded the Falak Ensemble, based in the town of Kulob, with a view to creating staged performances – primarily involving a repertoire rooted in Kulobi folklore – that would provide *falak* with a nationwide profile.[24]

---

[21]   The growing interest in *falak* is exemplified by the unprecedented number of articles which were published in the late 1980s and early 1990s in the periodical *Adabiyot va San'at*, organ of the Union of Writers of Tajikistan and prominent cultural forum. See, among others, Rajab (1990), Temurzoda (1991), Fathulloev (1991), Salim (1993).

[22]   Claims regarding the antiquity of *falak* have been made, for instance, by the eminent singer Dawlatmand Kholov and by Ubaydullo Rajabov, former actor turned artistic director and choreographer who, at the time of writing, was Director of Tajik State Radio and Television. In an interview which I held with Rajabov in December 2002, he emphasised the link between *falak* and religious sentiment, and claimed that this link dates back to before the time of the Arab conquest (eighth century CE) when the *gatha*s of Zardusht (Zoroaster) were sung. Similar arguments are discussed in Temurzoda (1989) and Shakarmamadov (1990).

[23]   On Soviet-driven ideological restrictions and controls on musical topics, see Naby (1973:120), Kosacheva (1990:19) and During (1998a:34), among others. For a comparison with socialist Bulgaria, see Rice (1994:171–2).

[24]   The Falak Ensemble was the first group of its kind, the second being that which Kholov was to create some twelve years later in the capital Dushanbe (see below). On the Falak Ensemble in Kulob, see also two interviews with Kholov in Ghoib (1989) and Muhmammadi (1991).

The music drama, *Sawt-i Falak* ('*The Voice of Falak*'), which was performed by the Falak Ensemble under the artistic direction of Dawlatmand Kholov and Ubaydullo Rajabov and presented in Kulob and Dushanbe in theatres and concert halls, displayed an interaction of dramatic elements and musical genres with a powerful emblematic value. Its simple plot, set in a rural scenario, centres on life-cycle rites and portrayals of traditional occupations such as herding and textile-making, and provides a framework for the performance of various styles of Tajik mountain music, especially those related to the traditions of Kulob.[25] While being a completely Soviet-style choreographic narrative of co-operative rural bliss, the representation of Tajik society as constructed by *Sawt-i Falak* emphasises the lifestyle and music of the mountain valleys as core elements of Tajik cultural heritage.[26]

According to Dawlatmand Kholov, the *Shashmaqom* is a wholly Uzbek, Turkic (*turkī*, *turkestonī*) or Mongol (*mughul*) tradition.[27] A few excerpts from an interview which I held with him in May 2001 (in London) may serve to illustrate his views on cultural ownership of *Shashmaqom* and *falak* in Tajikistan, and of the relationship between them:

> F.S.: What kind of music do you play?
> D.K.: My style of music is mainly in the field of national music, national folklore. I sing classical songs and folklore. But I want to expand it. I also mix folklore with other traditions.
> F.S.: What do you mean by 'other traditions'?
> D.K.: My music is pure. I don't mix *Shashmaqom* with it. I value the keeping of our particular folklore. I want to mix it as much as possible with modern music and use folklore with symphony orchestras …
> F.S.: What about *falak*?
> D.K.: *Falak* is our old national music, a style of singing of the people who work on the land. Also the *Shashmaqom* comes from *falak* … The *Shashmaqom* played in Tajikistan has many Uzbek and Turkic [*turkestonī*] elements. *Falak* is our national opera. The opera of every nation is the oldest one that is played in the folklore of that nation.[28]

---

[25] The debut of the Falak Ensemble (April 1990) is reviewed and described in detail in Ghoib (1990). I was first able to watch a recording of *Sawt-i Falak* in 2001 on a video cassette kindly provided by Ms Masoumeh Torfeh. During my fieldwork I also had occasion to appreciate the continuing recognition which *Sawt-i Falak* has attained over the years. The play remains popular with musicians and audiences alike and recordings are still broadcast on Tajik national television.

[26] Musical dramas or comedies such as *Sawt-i Falak* are art forms introduced by Soviet cultural programmes and which have become extremely popular in Tajikistan (see Naby 1973:114). They do have local antecedents, such as the dramatic plays and folk scenarios traditionally enacted in rural mountainous areas (see Slobin and Djumaev 2001:15).

[27] See During (1998b:4), as well as related issues in During (1993a:39, 1998a:156–7).

[28] Interview conducted in Tajik Persian with the invaluable help of Ms Masoumeh Torfeh. Translation by the current author.

In this interview Kholov not only touches upon the *Shashmaqom*/south Tajik music divide in terms of identity perception, but also highlights aspects of musical practice and understanding which have been central both to the ways in which he has approached that divide and to his commitment to formalise and raise the status of south Tajik traditions. For instance, the ways in which Kholov understands the term 'classical' (*klassik* or *klassikī*) in relation to south Tajik songs is significant. Whilst the term is used in a south Tajik context to refer to verses from classical Persian poetry (*she'rhoi klassikī*), the notion of 'Tajik classical music' is generally reserved for the *Shashmaqom* and is not commonly used to designate a distinct tradition of art music within south Tajikistan. In contrast, Kholov uses the term *surudho-i klassikī* ('classical songs') to underline specific features of performance style and modal complex which characterise part of his repertoire.[29] For Kholov, south Tajik 'classical songs' belong to an art music tradition which he regards as both distinct from the *Shashmaqom* and as having a specific identity with respect to south Tajik *folklor* (including *falak*), whence it originated. On a number of occasions he has remarked that 'classical songs' are characterised by being *orom* ('calm, placid') or *mu'tadil* ('moderate, sombre'). In this respect it should be noted that an important aspect of Kholov's re-working of southern traditions has entailed a predilection for performances in a grave, slow-paced manner, thereby adopting a feature commonly associated with classical traditions in Tajikistan, and specifically with the *Shashmaqom*. In addition to his classicising performance style, Kholov has taken a significant step further by setting out a formal classification of south Tajik modes. His terminology takes as its model, and reflects in part, that of the classical *maqom*s (for example, *dast-i du* or *dugoh*, *dast-i se* or *segoh*, and so on), while also invoking the authority of a wider Middle Eastern theoretical tradition by claiming that the core of 'classical' south Tajik music derives from a 12-mode system (*duvozdah maqom*).[30] According to this reading, south Tajik music would be related to a classical tradition older than the *Shashmaqom*, something which would account for the affinities between Tajik music and the music of Khorasan, Afghanistan and Kashmir. For Kholov, then, 'classical' acquires a precise reference to a modal complex with international ramifications and an ancient pedigree.

Kholov's approach to southern traditions, while building upon a number of traditional concepts, results in their reformulation. It is common practice within south Tajik musical culture to distinguish between songs employing classical

---

[29]   The following discussion draws substantially on additional interviews with Kholov undertaken in December 2002 and March 2003.

[30]   By referring to the *duvozdah maqom* Kholov recaptures a well-established theme in Tajik musical historiography, where the 12-mode system has generally been discussed in connection with the genealogy of the *Shashmaqom* (see for example Rahimov 1986, Rajabov 1989; such connections were first discussed by the Uzbek scholar Ish'aq Rajabov, see Slobin and Djumaev 2001). Kholov reinterprets the issue by relating the *duvozdah maqom* to south Tajik music and, further, by claiming that both the *duvozdah maqom* and the *Shashmaqom* derive ultimately from *falak* (see below).

poetry (*she'r-i klassikī*) and those using folk poetry of anonymous authorship (*she'r-i khalqī*), between professional popular music (*musiqī-i khalqī, musiqī-i kasbī*) and grassroots musical genres such as *falak* (*folklor*), between the notion of original composition (*ejodiyot*) by a composer of traditional music (*bastakor*) and the repertoire of folk melodic or structural formulas (*ohangho-i khalqī*, among which the various types of *falak* are located). These distinctions, however, have rarely resulted in the formulation of a notion of 'classical' as opposed to folk or popular music; thus, the historical absence of a division between 'high' and 'popular' idioms still obtains in south Tajik music. What is remarkable about Kholov's views is that he reinterprets the roles of classical poetry, professionalism and original compositions precisely in order to forge such an idea, which is further emphasised by the importance which he confers upon a particular performance style and a theoretical modal complex.

In drawing upon the combined symbolic authority of performance style, modal theory and poetic genre, Kholov's model of classicism reveals a primary indebtedness to the *Shashmaqom*. At the same time, this model is used to reposition and legitimise south Tajik music in the frame of national musical symbols, and specifically to question the very authority of the *Shashmaqom* by elevating south Tajik music to the same rank.[31] This process is additionally carried out through a re-imagining of Tajik musical history. As the interview above highlights, Kholov accords a pivotal role to *falak*. Whilst *falak* (and more generally all the genres that belong to *folklor*) is not included in his notion of south Tajik classical songs, it has an important symbolic function in validating the authority of southern traditions, for 'the totality of melodies of Tajik music has taken life from the genre *falak*' ('*tamom-i ohangho-i musiqī-i tojikī az zhanr-i falak eh'yo gardidaand*'.[32] Thus, in Kholov's worldview a primeval form of *falak*, which he calls *falak-i aslī* ('original *falak*'), was already established by the seventh or eighth centuries CE and flourished thereafter, particularly in the

---

[31]   On the 'classicisation' of south Tajik traditions see During (1993a:39, 1998a:156–7) who has argued that this process has sometimes brought south Tajik modal structures closer to those of the classical traditions of the north. He has also observed that such 'classicising' orientations are far from new, since they had already emerged with earlier masters such as Akasharif Juraev (1896–1966). I would further suggest that other south Tajik musicians, such as Zafar Nozimov (b.1940), Odina Hoshimov (1937–94) and Faizali Hasanov (b.1948), may be included as examples of those involved in 'classicisation'. These masters have been receptive to northern classical aesthetics and have occasionally included compositions in their repertoires which are inspired by classical idioms. However, it can be argued that their 'classicisation' differs in important respects from that of Dawlatmand Kholov, particularly in terms of intention and ideology. Hasanov, for instance, whilst discussing some of his compositions in the classical style rejected any regionalist reading of Tajik music and stressed that the *Shashmaqom* stands as the classical heritage for all Tajiks (Interview, summer 2003). The motivations behind Hasanov's classicisation thus fall within the framework of Soviet-style national ideology, the prestige and the hegemonic influence of the *Shashmaqom* being as resilient as the unitary representation of Tajik national music.

[32]   Interview, March 2003.

popular traditions of the Samanid Empire. According to Kholov, *falak* has provided the basis for the development of musical complexes in a wide Central Asian and Middle Eastern area, including the *Shashmaqom* and, most importantly, the older *duvozdah maqom* set, which he claims to be the direct offspring of *falak* ('*asosash dar zamina-i falak*').[33] *Falak* is accordingly defined by Kholov as the 'father and pillar of Tajik music' ('*padar va shohsutun-i musiqī-i tojik*'[34]).

Finally, as seen in the earlier interview, Kholov is particularly interested in combining traditional and symphonic musics. In accordance with now well-embedded aesthetic dispositions, he makes arrangements for Soviet-style ensemble or uses other composers' arrangements for orchestra and choir with a view to enhancing the prestige of traditional music. This modernising attitude coexists with an apparently opposite interest: that of recapturing the roots of local traditions in the face of the perceived devaluation they have been subjected to as a result of Russian interference. Accordingly, Kholov foregrounds features such as microtonal intervals and the occasional use of non-tempered intonation, as well as individual or small ensemble performance as identity markers of Tajik national culture. His 'nativist' approach, however, does not undermine the prestige he continues to confer on orchestral arrangements and other European-derived performance features.

The techniques adopted by Kholov in reworking south Tajik music, while laying emphasis on idiosyncratic features of the south Tajik musical vocabulary, illustrate the pervasive influence of the aesthetic paradigms promoted by official Soviet policies with their twin endorsements of Europeanisation and of the *Shashmaqom* as the most prestigious form of Tajik music. Indeed, it is precisely because of the enduring strength of this legacy that Kholov is able to use it as a means of reversing the hierarchy of musical practices fostered by Soviet policies. It is worth noting in this respect that whilst Kholov's music is receptive both to Tajik classical and European musics, his ideological position has the effect of challenging the authority of the former but not of the latter, thus prolonging the hegemonic influence of Soviet-derived modernist ideology.

Although one rarely finds the prestige of the *Shashmaqom* subverted as radically as Kholov has done (especially in matters of terminology), the emerging discourses representing the nation and its cultural monuments have certainly shifted the hub of Tajik culture from the north to the south. This new formulation has gained purchase on popular perceptions and also held sway in official policy during the tragic events of the civil war and its immediate aftermath.

Civil War and Regional Loyalties

At the end of the 1980s, in the climate of *perestroika*, the first two reformist parties were established: the nationalist Rastokhez (in 1989) and the Democratic Party (in 1990). Both grew out of academic institutions and the cultural intelligentsia,

---

[33]   Interview, December 2002.
[34]   Interview, March 2003.

and stood in opposition to the communist regime. They were joined, in an alliance that considerably enlarged the opposition support base, by the Islamic Rebirth Party of Tajikistan (IRPT, created 1990). The latter quickly abandoned the idea of an Islamic republic in favour of an agreement with its political partners on emphasising Islam as integral to Tajik national identity and society (Dudoignon 1998:66–8, Niyazi 1993:273). A further member of the opposition alliance was the La'li Badakhshon ('The Ruby of Badakhshon') Party, which represented the Isma'ili population of the south-east. In 1993, the alliance took on the name of United Tajik Opposition (UTO).

With the collapse of the Soviet Union in 1991, political ideology and cultural life in Tajikistan (as in other former Soviet republics) was increasingly informed by nationalistic discourses. Suddenly faced with an independence bequeathed more than sought after, both the regime and the newly emerged opposition parties responded to the necessity of securing social and political cohesion by attempting to reinforce national identity, and cultural revivalism thus came high on the agenda. However, the nationalistic rhetoric shared by all of the parties was profoundly at odds with the regional rivalries which underpinned specific alliances. The debate between the Communist Party and the UTO, which rapidly escalated into military confrontation, apart from issues such as democratisation, economic transformation by way of introducing a free-market economy, freedom of religious expression, and so on, involved power disputes between political elites which were tightly linked to regional loyalties. Political representatives from all factions sought support from regional and clan chiefs, the most authoritative figures in rural communities. A major factor in this was the legacy of a Soviet administrative practice whereby such loyalties were incorporated in the allocation of administrative positions in the hope of ensuring stability through preserving local hierarchies. In the context of Tajikistan, this practice (known as 'regionalism' or 'localism'; Tajik: *mahallgaroyī* or *mahallchigī*, Russian; *mestnichestvo*) served to link local community loyalties to political life.[35] The highest government and Party ranks, as well as key posts in culture and propaganda agencies, were secured by groups from the northern region of Leninobod (Khujand), which also had a monopoly on state commercial enterprises and industry. Most Party officials and bureaucrats were recruited from the region of Kulob (in the south), the trading system was in the hands of groups from the Gharm region (south) and the security forces had been recruited from among the Isma'ili Pamiris (from Badakhshon) since the 1970s. Given the extent to which regional loyalties are traditionally rooted in Tajik rural society, it seems unlikely that the Soviet system merely inherited long-standing regional rivalries and appeased them in order to maintain control. Rather, by actively engaging in the distribution of power, Soviet politics exacerbated differences between sections of a population that had never been united by a sense of common national belonging or by any form of autonomous political cohesion. Such loyalties thus acquired unprecedented political significance during the Soviet period. In particular,

---

[35]   On regionalism in Tajikistan, see footnote 5 and Dudoignon (1998:57–70).

the Khujand-dominated executives, whilst trying to balance different regional interests, kept central power to themselves, thus generating widespread discontent among other regional groups.[36]

The civil war erupted in 1991, dragging the whole country into inter-regional confrontations and inter-clan violence. The main conflict occurred between the coalition of Kulobis and Khujandis, still operating within the shell of the Communist Party (and also backed by factions from Hisor and by local Uzbeks), and the coalition of Gharmis and Pamiris, the bulwark of the opposition. The most ferocious fighting involved factions from the centre and south of the country, namely Kulobis against Gharmis and Pamiris. At the same time, it should be noted that the central objective of all contending forces was to attain political leadership and destroy the traditional supremacy of Khujand in the north. Crucially, this held true for the faction from Kulob which, whilst being allied with Khujand, in fact superseded its leadership within the Party in the course of the war. Power within state agencies and the Communist Party shifted from officials of Khujand to those of Kulob as early as 1994 when the Kulobi Emomali Rakhmonov took office as President. From that moment onward, clan and regional loyalty to the President marked power allocation. The scale of the conflict called for United Nations intervention, and in 1992 a peace-building mission was mandated to Tajikistan in collaboration with the Organisation for Security and Cooperation in Europe. In 1994, the Inter-Tajik Talks began and, after lengthy negotiations, led to the General Agreement on the Establishment of Peace and National Accord in 1997 (Brenninkmeijer 1998:180–98, Nourzhanov 2000:161). The winning force in the war was the Communist Party which could count on the allegiance of large parts of the army, in addition to well-equipped unofficial militia squadrons and support from Russia. In the government of national reconciliation which was established following the end of the conflict in 1997, 30 per cent of executive posts were assigned to the parties of the UTO. The rest were allocated to Kulobis, with only a scant representation of Khujandis.[37]

Loss of power on the part of the northern elites had immediate consequences as far as cultural policy is concerned. During and directly after the war, as a result of the allied front from Kulob wresting political and cultural supremacy from the north, the *Shashmaqom* encountered official disfavour to the point of being

---

[36]   Additionally, regional disputes significantly intensified as a result of large-scale forced migrations which, since the 1950s, have dislocated people from various parts of south Tajikistan to the cotton plantations in the south-west. Pre-existing regional loyalties survived the migrations and even crystallised in the context of competing *kolkhozes* (collective farms). In particular, the rural areas surrounding the city of Qurghonteppa became the site of fierce confrontation between Gharmi, Pamiri and Kulobi clans. See Roy (2000, in particular x–xi, 85–100).

[37]   For further details on the Tajik Civil War, see in particular Niyazi (1993), Jawad and Tadjbakhsh (1995), Brenninkmeijer (1998), Dudoignon (1998) and Nurdzhanov (2000).

apparently left altogether to Uzbekistan.[38] It may be suggested, however, that the decline of the *Shashmaqom*, whilst partly attributable to the influence of the newly established Kulobi-dominated executive, was also significantly linked to the general south-oriented trajectory of Tajik nationalism. In the post-war period, when the profound political and social divisions of the south were laid bare, the increasing support given to south Tajik music as a national emblem forefronted the possibility that unity could be found in cultural and artistic domains. However, especially after the rifts exacerbated by the war, any cultural cohesion in the south was bound to be more of a process of construction undertaken by the state, which needed to identify an effective tool for implementing the re-building of the nation. This process is a major aspect of contemporary cultural policy, including the policy on music, as will be illustrated below.

Towards National Reconciliation?

In the post-war period, official cultural policy in Tajikistan has reflected a preoccupation with enacting the political compromise embraced by regional elites which brought about the resolution of the civil conflict. In terms of its approach to music, the post-Soviet government has sought to balance the diverse cultural components of the country. In particular, recent official manoeuvres seem to be oriented towards rehabilitating and circumventing the exclusion of the *Shashmaqom* from public cultural life and, concurrently, towards promoting the construction of music monuments able to represent the south as a whole.

Dushanbe maintains to date a number of state organisations inherited from the Soviet period which still operate as major centres of music education, production and dissemination. Among these are the State Philharmonia (an organisation affiliated to the Ministry of Culture which finances and supervises a number of state ensembles), the Institute of Arts Named After Mirzo Tursunzoda, the Theatre of Opera and Ballet Named After Saddriddin Ayni and Tajik State Radio and Television. The state-sponsored music and dance ensembles hosted by these institutions still play a central role in nationwide broadcasting and at official events, although their position has been profoundly affected by the disastrous economic conditions of state cultural bodies after the collapse of the Soviet system and the civil war, and they have also undergone significant transformations in the face of the emerging importance of unofficial circuits of music making in post-Soviet Tajikistan.[39] A number of contemporary state ensembles in the domain of traditional music date back to the Soviet period, including the folk music

---

[38] See During (1993a:39, 1998a:156, 1998b:4). The precarious situation of the *Shashmaqom* during this period is exemplified by the almost complete absence, between 1992 and 1997, of articles on the *Shashmaqom* in the periodical *Adabiyot va San'at*.

[39] See Spinetti (2005).

ensembles Ganjina and Daryo, and the dance troupes Zebo and Jahonoro.[40] But the activity of these groups decreased during the 1990s, and priority in official policy is now being given to promoting the Shashmaqom State Ensemble[41] and the newly formed Falak Ensemble. Both resident at Tajik State Radio and Television, these are currently the most prestigious ensembles of traditional music. They share the highest reputation as authoritative exponents of national music and are intended to distinguish between, and yet give equal importance to, northern and southern musical traditions, in contrast both with the hierarchy upheld during the Soviet period and its opposite during the years of warfare.

I suggest that these recent trends are consistent with the climate of national reconciliation fostered by the Tajik government. President Emomali Rahmonov's regime, whilst undoubtedly relying on the prominence of groups from Kulob in political and institutional life, also endeavours to ensure a balanced distribution of power among regional political elites, assigning prominent governmental posts to all regional factions. In particular, the government has reacted to the growing dissatisfaction of the north at being politically (and culturally) marginalised after the rise to power of the Kulobis (which resulted in demonstrations and riots in 1996 and which also fuelled secessionist discourses) by granting a certain political weight to the north and by appointing a Khujandi to the post of Prime Minister. Similarly, the cultural exclusion of the north from representations of the Tajik nation is now being appreciably reduced. Although there is a widespread perception that the *Shashmaqom* was far more visible in Soviet times, the recent support given to this music is notable. The Shashmaqom State Ensemble appears frequently in official concerts and within the media and is extensively involved in educational activities. Television programmes reiterate the association of the *Shashmaqom* with the artistic splendours and the history of the 'Tajik' cities of Bukhara and Samarqand. Alongside the alleged personal appreciation of the *Shashmaqom* by President Rahmonov (which given his almost absolute authority could well be a sufficient factor), I believe that the rehabilitation of the northern traditions is intimately related to the politics of conciliation. It is noteworthy that many people from Kulob (amongst whom my research was mainly conducted) not only identify the *Shashmaqom* in terms of regional belonging, but often and immediately associate its current public visibility to political discourse. It is also indicative that views on cultural belonging (such as those of Dawlatmand Kholov) that represent the *Shashmaqom* as being alien to the 'genuine' Tajik national heritage are nowadays discouraged by the official establishment; there is a clear perception that such views are being suppressed and Kholov has been personally invited not to insist openly on

---

[40]   Ganjina and Daryo were both founded in the late 1980s and were intended to encompass both northern and southern popular (*khalqī*) and folklore (*folklor*) traditions. On the Ensemble Ganjina, see Rajabi (1986) and Rahimov (1987).

[41]   Which has resumed performance in official settings after the disbanding, during the civil war, of the historic Ensemble of Maqom Masters Named After Fazluddin Shahobov (*Ansambl-i Ustodon-i Maqom ba nom-i Fazluddin Shahobov*), founded in 1961.

his opinions about Tajik musical culture. When I asked him about the reasons, he gave a very neat reply: 'That is because the country is tired of war.'

Another major element of contemporary cultural policy concerns attempts to develop a unitary representation of the musical traditions of the south through the establishment of the Falak Ensemble. The combination of various local mountain traditions within the repertoire of a single ensemble is not a novelty in Tajikistan, but after the war this certainly received unprecedented emphasis as a tool for nation rebuilding. Whilst the discussion so far might have suggested a picture of southern Tajikistan as a cultural whole, the events of the civil war have highlighted its political and social fragmentation. Southern cultural and musical traditions, while undoubtedly exhibiting a high degree of affinity, are variously perceived by local people who often give prominence to aspects of differentiation. The dialectic of unity and local demarcation is paramount within current policy on south Tajik music, and I would like to explore this issue in connection with the Falak Ensemble.

The Falak Ensemble was established in 2002 (after a presidential decree in November 2001), under the auspices of Tajik State Radio and Television in Dushanbe and with the artistic direction of Dawlatmand Kholov and Rahmondust Qurboniyon, a long-standing collaborator of the late celebrated master Odina Hoshimov.[42] This ensemble marks a significant step forward in the promotion of *falak* which began with the group of the same name founded by Kholov some twelve years earlier in Kulob (discussed above). With the new ensemble, Kholov has been entrusted by the authorities to continue his initiative with central support, and has been able to involve artists beyond the sphere of Kulob, thus attaining a degree of universality which answers fully to his understanding of mountain music as a cultural whole. Indeed, the distinguishing trait of the Dushanbe ensemble is that it includes musicians and, especially, singers, from diverse parts of the south who are particularly skilful in their local idioms. The Falak Ensemble consists of some thirty female and male singers, musicians and dancers. Whilst the majority of musicians and dancers are from the region of Kulob, the singers come from a variety of regions including Badakhshon, Gharm, Kulob, Varzob and Zarafshon. Against a backdrop of Soviet-style, standardised arrangements in a concert format for a large set of traditional instruments, the repertoire of the ensemble emphasises local performance inflections, and especially singing styles, which remain easily recognisable, whilst at the same time bringing together the distinctive traits of various local styles in a powerful emblematic contiguity.

---

[42]   Thanks to the intervention of Kholov, I was given permission to conduct research at the headquarters of Tajik State Radio and Television in Dushanbe, and this gave me the opportunity to attend rehearsals, recording activities and public performances of the Falak Ensemble over a period of four months (November 2002 – February 2003). Much of the information in the following paragraphs derives from direct observation or from interviews with musicians from the ensemble. I also discuss issues of which I became aware not through formal interviews but as they were debated informally amongst ensemble members on a day-to-day basis.

A particularly clear example is provided by the *Syuita-i Surudho-i Mardumī* ('Suite of Songs of the People'), one of the main pieces of the ensemble's repertoire, which weaves together seven songs of diverse regional origin in a chain which entails changes in rhythm and vocal and melodic styles. The sequence consists of a *falak-i dashtī* from Kulob, an accompanied *falak* from Badakhshon, a dance song from Zarafshon, a dance song from Gharm, a *ghazal* and dance song from Kulob, and a dance song from Hisor. This suite has been forged *ex novo* in the context of the Falak Ensemble and has no antecedents or parallels in traditional practice. I contend that the performances of the Falak Ensemble, as represented by the *Syuita-i Surudho-i Mardumī*, embody a cultural policy oriented towards the construction of musical monuments of cohesion for the regional cultures torn apart during the civil war, thus constituting a form of nation (re-)building within which it becomes as important to emphasise local identities as to bring them together and state their affinities.

Although the performances of the Falak Ensemble are by no means confined to the *falak* genre, it is in fact this genre (which is paramount in south Tajik rural society) that is being proposed as a conceptual focus. Central to the official policy supporting the Falak Ensemble is an argument about the oneness of the *falak* and its potential for becoming the unifying badge of cultural reconstruction of the south. In this context, Dawlatmand Kholov's theory of the *falak* as the ultimate foundation of Tajik music acquires particular significance, and has certainly contributed to his attaining a position of leadership in contemporary official circles. In his hands, the notion of *falak* moves away from its traditional identification with one or more related musical genres and closer to an underlying principle whence a whole constellation of musical forms are believed to have originated. Although Kholov's views on the cultural ownership of the *Shashmaqom* do not enjoy official backing, the inclusiveness of his reading of *falak* has nevertheless attained symbolic value and his commitment to assemble diverse regional expressions under a single banner has become a mission that fully meets the aspirations of current official trends. Private opinions within the Falak Ensemble, which emerged from interviews and during informal discussions amongst musicians, are particularly revealing of the dynamics of unity and differentiation which lie at the heart of this process. Some musicians and singers insisted on the uniqueness of their performance style and held fast to markers of their regional identity, showing a certain dissatisfaction with what they perceived to be a homogenising process;[43] others foregrounded the affinities linking south Tajik idioms, stressing that 'despite accents (*lahja*) the *falak* is one'.[44]

By including the music of Zarafshon within the spectrum of the ensemble's repertoire, a case is being made that the *falak* is also part of the musical culture of a

---

[43]   In particular, Panjshanbe Jorubov (singer from Badakhshon) and Sa'dullo Niyozov (singer and *dumbra* player from Varzob) expressed this idea at various times during informal conversation with myself and other members of the ensemble.

[44]   Interview with Kulobi singer and *ghijak* player, Nosir (January 2003).

region which lies on the fringes of northern Tajikistan. Significantly, this involves an attempt to extend the geo-cultural area for which the *falak* may function as a representative of cultural affiliation, something which represents a significant break with traditional perceptions. The Zarafshon mountains and valleys are the natural barrier separating northern and southern Tajikistan. In fact, there is no musical style in Zarafshon called *falak*,[45] and indeed the vocal techniques and general types of melodic contour heard in Zarafshoni music bear little resemblance to any form of *falak* found in the south. Nevertheless, Zarafshoni music has been enlisted as one of the regional styles performed by the Falak Ensemble. In particular, song forms from Zarafshon performed *a cappella* (traditionally called *ruboī* or, in the case of wedding songs, *naqsh*[46]) are being (mis)represented as variants of the solo-voice *falak* (*falak-i dashtī*). In the sequence of different styles of *falak-i dashtī* which make up another typical performance by the Falak Ensemble (and which featured at the opening of a number of stage performances in 2003), a solo *ruboī* from Zarafshon is sung alongside *falaks* from Kulob and Badakhshon. Examples 4.1–4.3 present transcriptions of the three solo-voice pieces in question, performed by Muhammadvali Hasanov (Kulob), Panjshanbe Jorubov (Badakhshon) and Ruziboy Idiyev (Zarafshon).[47]

Example 4.1 displays a number of characteristic structural and stylistic features of the Kulob tradition. The melody centres around three main pitches a semitone apart – a, b♭ and c♭ – with occasional occurrences of c♯ and g♯ (and a g♮ at the end). A distinctive descending melodic movement – from c♭ to b♭ to a – occurs repeatedly over extended syllables, returning again to b♭. This, together with the quasi-syllabic treatment of the text are characteristic features of the solo *falak* of Kulob. Rapid trills (*farshliyak*) are particularly valued as markers of aesthetic quality. Example 4.2 (from Badakhshon) shows a number of similarities to Example 4.1, including the narrow range, the melodic intervals used, the melodic contour, as well as other aspects of performance style including ornamented trills and extended syllables. Specific to the Badakhshoni style are the emphasised yodels and the final downward slides. The *ruboī* from Zarafshon, on the other hand, contrasts with Examples 4.1 and 4.2 in a number of ways, including the phrasing structure, the overall melodic movement, which develops over a full octave and which is strictly diatonic, the timbre and the ornamentation; there are no trills, but instead the singer uses glissandi (shown in Example 4.3 using slurs).[48] Table 4.1 presents a comparison of some of the musical characteristics of Examples 4.1–4.3.

---

[45]   I am grateful to Professor Jean During for bringing this point to my attention.

[46]   For a discussion of *naqsh*, see Levin (1996:218–27).

[47]   The pieces transcribed were recorded by the author in 2003. Recording sessions were held separately with each performer in the premises of Tajik State Radio and Television.

[48]   In this context I use the term 'diatonic' to refer to a collection of intervals made of whole tones and semitones, and 'chromatic' to refer to one featuring a series of contiguous semitones.

Example 4.1   Transcription of a *falak* from Kulob (*falak-i dashtī*), performed by
Muhammadvali Hasanov (actual pitch: a"=b').

Text:[49]

> *Afsūs ki dar ayn-i javonī murdem*
> *Dar bolin-i marg-i notavonī murdem*
> *Guftem namurem umra barem zi miyona*
> *Nokom budem ajal purarmon murdem*

> Alas, in the season of youth we died
> On a deathbed of helplessness we died
> We said 'we will not die until we use up our whole lifetime'
> We hoped in vain, full of regret we died.[50]

---

[49]   Additional syllables in the sung text (as transcribed under the music staves) are
typical of *falak* singing style, especially at the beginning and end of each poetic line. They
are also used, but less extensively, in Zarafshoni singing.

[50]   Translations of song texts by the author.

Example 4.2   Transcription of a *falak* from Badakhshon (*be parvo falak*) performed by Panjshanbe Jorubov (actual pitch: a''=g').[51]

Text:

> *Dunyo guzaronest ciho memonad*
> *Yak nom-i khush-i mo-u shumo memonad*
> *Tukhm-i abadī agar bikorem ba zamin*
> *Neki-u badī judo judo memonad*

> The world passes away, what will remain?
> For you and me, one good name will remain
> If we sow the seed of eternity in the earth
> Good and bad separated will remain.

---

[51]   A note on the transcriptions: since there is no notion of absolute pitch in Tajik music, all three examples are notated with a'' as the tonal centre in order to facilitate comparison. Each stave presents a single phrase, which in performance is followed by a prolonged rest. The individual phrases are numbered according to the line of the quatrain being sung. The numberings 2/2a and 4/4a are used when poetic lines are split over two phrases or repeated in full using different melodic material. Since the performances are unmeasured, the time values notated should be understood as approximate. The same applies to pitches, particularly in Examples 4.1 and 4.2 where actual pitches are often slightly flatter or sharper

Example 4.3 Transcription of a *ruboī* from Zarafshon, performed by Ruziboy
Idiyev (actual pitch: a"= a").

Text:

> *Boshad ki falak ba kom-i inson boshad*
> *Har mushkiliye baroyash oson boshad*
> *Yak pora-i non-i gandumī az Mascho*
> *Yak kosa-i ob az Zarafshun boshad*
>
> May the destiny fulfil people's wishes
> May every obstacle be easy for them
> May a piece of bread be from Mascho[52]
> May a cup of water be from Zarafshon.

than notated. Note in particular that the second and third degrees above the tonal centre in
Example 4.1 are consistently sharper than notated. Ascending bowed slurs indicate rapid
slides into the pitch from below, while descending lines indicate slower, downward slides.
Crossed notes represent a yodelling effect obtained by a sudden leap to an indistinct high
pitch. Ornamentation was transcribed by slowing the recordings to half speed; the resulting
level of detail clearly highlights the differences in ornamentation between Examples 4.1
and 4.2 on the one hand, and Example 4.3 on the other.

[52]   An area in the upper Zarafshon valley.

Table 4.1   Comparison of some of the musical characteristics of Examples 4.1–4.3.

	Kulob	**Badakhshon**	**Zarafshon**
Range	g to d♭ (diminished fifth)	g♯ to c♭ (diminished fourth)	a to b' (major ninth)
Pitch-class collection	Predominantly chromatic	chromatic	diatonic
Main melodic movement	c♭ to b♭ to a b♭ to c♭ to a to b♭	c♭ to b♭ to a c♭ to b♭ (a to b♭)	a" to e' e' to a" a' to e'
Ornaments	trills; long drawn-out melismas	trills; long drawn-out melismas	glissandi; moderate melismas

At various times, I explored issues related to Zarafshoni music with Dawlatmand Kholov. In one interview, he suggested that since Zarafshoni people are mountain dwellers, then obviously their music should be regarded as *kuhistonī* ('of the mountains', that is south Tajik music) and should accordingly be expected to include forms of *falak*. Similarly, the Director of Tajik State Radio and Television, Ubaydullo Rajabov, explicitly referred to the *naqsh* as being an alternative name for the *falak*, and he traced on a map of Tajikistan the upper borders of south Tajik musical culture ('*falak* culture', '*madaniyat-i falak*', as he put it) just north of the Zarafshon mountain range (Interview, December 2002). The emblematic significance assigned to *falak* thus entails an expansion of the very notion of the cultural area of south Tajikistan, and the inclusion of Zarafshoni music therein. The extent to which this perspective differs from a more traditional approach is highlighted by the fact that a number of musicians in the Falak Ensemble, among those from 'truly' southern regions, were not comfortable with the inclusion of Zarafshoni music in a south Tajik repertoire. They considered Zarafshoni music as alien ('*begona*') to southern traditions and called it *Leninobodī* or *Khujandī* music, thereby assigning it explicitly to the north. Interestingly, the kind of encompassing value attributed to the *falak* in the context of this ensemble's music seems able to go beyond the level of an artificial construction of cultural strategy, and to exert pressures capable of influencing traditional perceptions. For example, the singer from Zarafshon in the Falak Ensemble, Ruziboy Idiyev, has on several occasions expressed the view that his vocal style, even if not named *falak* in his homeland (*vatan*), is in fact a form of *falak* with a distinctive regional accent (*lahja*).[53]

---

[53]   For example, this view was expressed in an interview with the current author in February 2003. The question of the relationship between contemporary official representations of *falak* and traditional perceptions in Zarafshon would require a separate discussion and further ethnographic detail. Here, my example points to the type of discourse which Idiyev felt he should accommodate in the context of the Falak Ensemble; as a testimony of Idiyev's genuine beliefs, his comments should be treated with some caution.

Conclusion

As Soviet socialist hegemony has withdrawn from Tajikistan and as the power distribution which it promoted has begun to vacillate, the profound social and political contradictions fuelled by that hegemony have rapidly surfaced and escalated into open conflict. In the domain of cultural representation, Soviet 'truths' about the Tajik nation and its cultural heritage have been undermined and exposed to open discussion. Nevertheless, in the debate over identities and the reformulation of power relations, the idea of the nation continues to maintain an authoritative position, albeit disputed or proposed as a means to 'paper over the cracks'. Current official positions seem to be concerned with salvaging national sentiment and identifying effective tools for implementing national cohesion in both political and cultural domains. The possibility that music might function as a tool for reconciliation and play a role in re-enforcing national identity in Tajikistan certainly appears to be a central aspect of cultural policies. In the continuing unstable climate of national reconciliation, a pivotal question is whether such policies will continue to be driven by attempts to reinstate Soviet-style dichotomies and hierarchies, or whether they will be perceptibly oriented towards new ways of dealing with cultural pluralism.

Chapter 5

Music and Censorship in Afghanistan, 1973–2003

John Baily

Introduction

This chapter traces the complicated narrative of the censorship of music over a 30-year period in Afghanistan, principally in the cities of Kabul and Herat.[1] It takes us from the relatively calm period of Mohammad Daud's presidency (1973–78) when an informal muted censorship was certainly in operation, via the strict controls of the Rabbani Coalition, the complete ban on music imposed by the Taliban, to the varying degrees of censorship in post-Taliban Afghanistan.

Music has probably been censored from time immemorial in the region known today as Afghanistan. In a country with no democratic tradition and no laws guaranteeing freedom of speech, often ruled by despots and autocrats, there can be little doubt that singers of the past guarded their tongues in an effort not to give offence to those in power. When radio broadcasting from Kabul began in earnest in the late 1940s, the single radio station was run by the Ministry for Information and Culture which exercised tight control over what was broadcast. We can call this censorship, though censorship usually involves restrictions on the performance of certain kinds of music or the gagging of particular individuals whose views are

---

[1] My information derives from many years of direct contact with Afghan music and musicians, starting with two years of ethnomusicological fieldwork in the 1970s in the provincial city of Herat. This was followed by three months research for a film about Afghan refugee musicians in Peshawar (Pakistan) in 1985, further visits to Islamabad and Peshawar in 1991 and 1992, to Herat in 1994, Mashhad (Iran) in 1998, Fremont (California) in 1999, and Peshawar and Fremont again in 2000. After the fall of the Taliban I spent a month in Kabul in October and November 2002. Apart from my own observations and interviews with Afghans I have relied heavily on newspaper reports published in the UK and Pakistan. I have also drawn extensively on the film *Breaking the Silence: Music in Afghanistan* (2002, documentary film, 58 mins, dir. Simon Broughton, John Baily, consultant, screened BBC4, 11 March 2002, London: Songlines Films) which was shot in Kabul and Peshawar in January 2002 shortly after the departure of the Taliban from most parts of Afghanistan. I was consultant for this film and my Freemuse report provided much of the narrative. I thank Marie Korpe and the Danish Human Rights Organisation Freemuse, which she directs, for commissioning a report on the censorship of music in Afghanistan (Baily 2001) which led to my rethinking the whole issue.

judged inimical by those in positions of control, and should be distinguished from
what might be regarded as the normal proprieties of the culture concerned. When a
political group like the Taliban imposes a ban on all forms of what they categorise
as 'music', we encounter censorship of a completely different order, for now it is
music itself which is banned for reasons of religious fundamentalism. Contrary
to popular belief, this is not a specifically Islamic issue: Christianity too has had
its problems with music and certain sects such as the Quakers were in the past
staunchly opposed to the sounds of musical instruments, while ready to use the
unaccompanied voice in the service of God.[2] Other religions, such as Judaism and
Buddhism, also have clear rules about the appropriateness of music.

Music has been a sensitive issue within Islam from its inception.[3] Although the
Holy Qur'ran does not include any explicit statements about music, a number of
suras (Qur'anic verses) have been variously interpreted as either sanctioning or
condemning music. The *hadith* (the sayings and actions of The Prophet Mohammad
according to his Companions) are also ambiguous. Two often cited *hadith* suggest
that music was sanctioned by the Prophet:

> On the day of *Bu'ath*, 'Āyisha was enjoying a song of some Ansār girls in the
> presence of the Prophet who was lying on his bed. Abū Bakr on entering the
> room rebuked them for playing the instruments of Shaitān in the house of the
> Prophet … The Prophet remonstrated the protest; He said, 'don't disturb them'
> … 'Give her up, oh Abū Bakr. This is the day of *'Id.*' After this the Prophet
> took rest. But 'Āyisha winked her eyes and they departed. (Roy Choudhury
> 1957:67–8)

> Once an Abyssinian musician appeared in presence [sic] of the Prophet on the
> occasion of *'Id*. The Prophet asked 'Āyisha if she liked to enjoy music. On
> 'Āyisha giving assent, the Abyssinian was called in. The place of performance
> was the Prophet's own house. The mosque of the Prophet was adjacent to his
> house. The courtyard of the house of the Prophet and that of his mosque was
> the same. In fact, the performance took place in a sacred place – *hareem*. The
> Abyssinian acrobat sang and danced and 'Āyisha enjoyed it for a pretty length
> of time. (ibid. 69)

There is, however, endless scope for the interpretation and reinterpretation of
such traditions. For example, these two *hadith* principally relate to singing, and

---

[2]   A useful summary of the attitudes of The Society of Friends to music can be found
in Scholes (1995:853–4). Somewhat similar restrictions on secular music were applied by
Presbyterians on the islands of Lewis and Skye in Scotland, with the argument that music
leads to dancing and dancing leads to fornication (Dr Peter Cooke, personal communication,
2004).

[3]   See Farmer (1929), Robson (1938) and Roy Choudhury (1957) for summaries of
the debate.

singing in itself is not usually regarded as 'music' within Islamic culture. The instrument(s) played in the first *hadith* above is presumably the frame drum (*daff* or *daireh*) which is strongly associated with women in much of the Islamic Middle East (Doubleday 1999). It is sometimes argued that because the frame drum is sanctioned according to this *hadith*, other instruments are also lawful; others dispute this claim. The frame drum, a very simple instrument in terms of its construction, is a special case and is the one instrument not banned by the Taliban. Thus the permissibility of music is a grey area, and therefore – to be on the safe side – best avoided altogether. Islamic cultures which are tolerant towards music are likely to be liberal in other respects, and music is a sensitive indicator of a whole set of other values and attitudes.

Herat and Kabul in the 1970s

In 1973, Mohammad Daud staged a *coup d'etat* in which he seized power from his cousin (and brother-in-law), King Zahir. The King was out of the country at the time and the coup resulted in comparatively little bloodshed, but it was this action which paved the way for the communist takeover in 1978. The five years of Daud's presidency were characterised by relative stability but the tightening of state control over the media was immediate. The free press was closed down, as were privately owned theatres.[4] During this period, my wife, Veronica Doubleday, and I lived and carried out extensive fieldwork for two years in the city of Herat (Baily 1988, Doubleday 1988). We observed and participated in a rich 'life of music' which embraced a number of contrasts: city and village, professional and amateur, men and women, adults and children, solo and ensemble, sacred and secular.

The most important occasion for music making was the wedding, with separate parties for men and women. In the city, a band of male musicians, singing and playing instruments such as the *'armonia* (Indian harmonium), *rubab*, *dutar* and tabla drums would perform a programme lasting between six and eight hours. This would include serious *ghazals*, popular songs from the radio, a few local Herati songs, music for solo and group dancing and music for comedy routines. The women's wedding party, in an adjoining courtyard in the same or a neighbour's house, would be entertained by one of Herat's groups of professional women musicians, singing and playing *'armonia*, tabla and *daireh*. Their engagement would last for 24 hours, starting at six in the evening, with a few hours' break for sleep at the house where the women's party was taking place and continuing the next day until 6pm. Music was also played at the birth of a son or daughter, and to celebrate male circumcision.

The Herat theatre, run by the local office of the Ministry for Information and Culture, had its own troupe of actors, playwrights, directors and musicians, who presented nightly dramas and concerts of music throughout most of the year.

---

[4]   A brief account of Daud's presidency can be found in Hyman (1984:63–71).

In the spring, over a period of 40 days, there were regular country fairs, with tented tea-houses and small bands of musicians. The month of fasting, *Ramazan*, was particularly rich in musical performance, with half a dozen restaurants and cafés offering nightly performances, often with bands of musicians from Kabul hired for the month. And there were private music parties of many kinds, whether women's gatherings in the build-up to the big wedding celebrations, dinner parties, after-dinner parties, and get-togethers of music enthusiasts for the sake of having fun. The most obvious illicit music was *bacheh bazi* (lit. 'boy play'), the performance of a transvestite dancing boy, wearing ankle bells, padded breasts and make-up. Dancing-boy parties were prohibited by the authorities in Herat and were likely to be raided by the police, the dancer and his accompanists arrested and fined or sent to prison for a short term.

Musical life in Kabul, in contrast, was much more sophisticated. In the old city, there was a large musicians' quarter (the *Kucheh Kharabat*) with many hereditary musician families, some of them descendants of court musicians from the Indian subcontinent brought to Kabul in the 1860s. They were familiar with the genres of Hindustani music and conversant with Indian music theory and notions of *raga* (melodic mode) and *tala* (metric cycle), and had a rich musical vocabulary. In due course, these musicians created a type of vocal art music which was distinctly Afghan in style: the Kabuli *ghazal*. The *Kharabat* was also a place for musical training. Many musicians ran private music schools, in which they taught youngsters from within the *Kharabat* through an apprenticeship system, as well as instructing amateur students from outside the musicians' quarter.

The main feature of musical life in Kabul was the radio station, opened in 1940, which came to occupy a central position in the musical life of the country, with a strong emphasis on broadcasting music. It employed many musicians, who played in a number of different orchestras. Afghan popular music originated in response to the need to create a style suitable for radio broadcasting. The regional music of mixed Pashtun-Tajik areas near Kabul (such as Parwan) provided the models on which the new popular music broadcast by the radio station was based, bringing together Dari (Afghan Persian) or Pashto texts, the Pashtun musical style and Hindustani theory and terminology. The development of Afghan popular music took place with the assistance of the above-mentioned descendants of Indian court musicians, whose knowledge of Indian music theory and terminology and high standards of performance were important for organising small ensembles and large orchestras at the radio station. They played a key role in training musicians, both professionals and amateurs.

Many new songs in the popular style were created by composers and musicians working at the radio station. Others were originally regional folk songs performed in the popular style. In this way many of the folk songs of Afghanistan were given a new lease of life by radio broadcasting. There was also an input from the Indian and Pakistani films regularly shown in cinemas, and from the popular musics of neighbouring countries such as Iran and Tajikistan. Listening to radio broadcasts from Kabul was an important part of daily life for many people in provincial urban centres like Herat, bringing them up to date with the latest popular songs, which were then incorporated into local repertoires. The government saw radio as a way to inform the population about its policies and development programmes. Radio music placed its listeners in that modern world of which the government aspired to be part. Western popular music (generally called *jaz*) enjoyed a certain degree of exposure on Radio Afghanistan. Amongst students in Kabul there was certainly a following for music of this kind, and there were various rock bands amongst the younger generation of the Westernised elite (Western instruments were relatively expensive and therefore only available to an affluent minority).

Another aspect of the modern world impacting on music in Afghanistan at this time was the audio cassette. In Kabul, companies such as the Music Center recorded many famous singers and instrumentalists in sophisticated studios equipped with recording technology imported from Europe. Cities such as Herat also had a cassette industry, but here local artistes were recorded on inferior equipment: their cassettes were reproduced by endless copying of the master and sold, with no printed labels, in specialist shops in the bazaars.

The level of music making during this period (1940s to 1970s) is indicative of a modernising and somewhat liberal society, most clearly manifest in the way that many originally amateur musicians joined the ranks of the professionals. The most notable was Ahmad Zahir, the 'Afghan Elvis', whose father, Dr Zahir, was for a short period Prime Minister. Ahmad Zahir represented the most Westernised form of Afghan music during the 1970s: he played the electric organ and was accompanied by musicians playing instruments such as trumpet, electric guitar and trap drum set. A number of women, mostly from educated middle-class families, were also enabled to become radio stars. Perhaps the most remarkable was Farida Mahwash, who in 1975 was awarded the title of *ustad* by the Afghan government. The question of music and religion in Herat in the 1970s has been discussed at length in Baily (1988). While there continued to be reservations about music as a profession (and hereditary musicians had in general a low social standing), religious censure of music was seen by many to be a thing of the past, 'Who thinks about such things today?' was how one of my principal informants put it.

In the late 1970s, I commissioned a written opinion from Sheikh Ibrahim Munir, an Iraqi theologian who was teaching Arabic at Herat's Theological College for a year. He made the following points. Firstly, several of the *hadith* may be cited to show that the Prophet sanctioned performances of music on a number of occasions. Second, intentionality and the uses to which music is put are of crucial importance. When music is well-intentioned, either for worshipping God or simply for recreation, it is not unlawful. However, when music is used in a wrong way and its performance occurs in mixed parties of men and women, or is associated with unlawful sexual intercourse or with drinking alcohol, it is unlawful. This opinion was later read to Abdul Wahab Saljuki, Herat's great *'alem* (theological scholar) of the time, who signed it after appending 'When music possesses the above conditions it is lawful, there is no fault in listening to music or playing music. Its teaching is also lawful' (Baily 1988:148).

The *Jihad* Period (1978–92)

In April 1978, Nur Mohammad Taraki staged a coup against President Daud and a communist government came to power for the first time in Afghanistan. For the next 14 years the seven main Mujahideen parties based in Pakistan and Iran engaged in *jihad* ('holy war') against a succession of communist governments and their Soviet backers. A civil war started and many people fled to Pakistan and Iran which in due course became host to several million Afghan refugees, most of them living in squalid refugee camps. Detailed research has yet to be conducted on music in Afghanistan during this period. The succession of communist governments supported music, which they saw as indicative of the type of secular society they believed they had established. The television network already planned in President Daud's time came into being soon after the coup, with a central television station in Kabul followed by local stations in some provincial cities. Television was a powerful way through which to present music to the general public. The television studios had the latest equipment and created extravagant and imaginative sets for the new music programmes. Local radio stations were also established and controlled by the Ministry for Information and Culture which exercised tight control over what was broadcast, and music was certainly used for propaganda purposes. Some singers were ready to perform in praise of the new regime; others were not and went into exile. It was not a simple choice, especially given the flexibility and corruptibility of government agencies. Exile posed a whole set of uncertainties, but so did life in communist Afghanistan.

Raja Anwar's remarkable book, *The Tragedy of Afghanistan*, provides a number of valuable insights into the role of music in the early days of communist rule. He describes how in 1979 Taraki obtained a *fatwa* (religious injunction) from a sympathetic religious establishment 'which declared that *jihad* against religious reactionaries who followed in the footsteps of the *Akhwan ul-Muslimi* [the fundamentalist Muslim Brotherhood of Egypt] had full religious sanction' (1989:150). In other words, the communist government declared a holy war against those who had declared holy war upon it. He continues:

> The official media were also directed to use the *fatwa* to attack the Mullahs and their campaign. On TV (whose transmissions did not go beyond Kabul), it was made the basis of skits, songs and plays. One chorus broadcast regularly by both TV and radio had the refrain:
>> *Lannat bar tu aye Akhwan-ul-Shaitan*
>> (May the curse of God be upon you, you brothers of Satan) (ibid.)

In this text, the *Akhwan ul-Muslimi* (Muslim Brotherhood) has been transformed into *Akhwan ul-Shaitan* (the Brotherhood of Satan).

Concerts were held in support of the Taraki regime. Anwar describes one memorable performance:

On the evening of 14 September [1979], a concert of Afghan folk music was in progress on the lawns of Afghan Music, an academy next to the Indonesian embassy and barely a kilometre away from the presidential palace. Such evenings were regularly organised by the Khalq [communist] government to propagate Party programmes and achievements. As was customary, the stage was profusely decorated with large photographs of the 'great leader'. Popular artists, including Qamar Gul, Gul Zaman, Bakhat Zarmina, Master Fazal Ghani, Ahmed Wali and Hangama, were busy singing the praises of the Revolution and the Party. The well-known comic, Haji Kamran, who was acting as master of ceremonies, was dutifully leading the crowd into chants of 'Long Live Taraki' and 'Long Live Amin' whenever a new performer appeared on stage. At about 6.30 p.m., when the concert was at its climax, tanks from the 4th Armoured Corps moved into the city, taking positions in front of important buildings and occupying major squares. The rumble of the tanks on the roads so unnerved the organizers of the concert and the artists that they ran away helter-skelter, leaving even their musical instruments behind. (ibid. 172)

Hafizullah Amin's coup to depose President Taraki had just begun. Two of Amin's supporters, Taroon and Nawab, who were killed in the coup, were later commemorated and 'special songs were commissioned for radio and TV extolling their "great deeds"' (ibid. 171).

It seems that popular music in Kabul continued the gradual process of Westernisation manifest in Kabul's rock groups and the music of Ahmad Zahir. For example, the *International Herald Tribune* for 6 June 1986 ran an article about one private engagement party in Kabul:

There was disco dancing, an ear-splitting band, proud parents and the nervous young couple – all the elements of an engagement party anywhere in the world. Then there were a few extras: the armed soldiers at the entrance to the gloomy hotel, the slick band leader singing 'Our Heroic Party', and the portrait of Afghanistan's president, Babrak Karmal, gazing over the crowded ballroom … At the party for Roya and Kamran, the future student bride and groom, Kabul's young men eagerly went through their disco paces – with other young men. Although they have long given up the Moslem custom of covering up their eyes and legs, the women stayed in a corner by themselves, swaying to the deafening music. 'Yes, this is quite modern, it is not an arranged marriage', shouted the bride-to-be's father, Colonel Nur Ahmad, over the din. 'Nowadays, young people meet first and then consult their parents about marriage', said the Colonel, who said he taught military subjects at Kabul University … [The] lead singer of the band at the engagement party said his five-piece group was booked for functions like this most nights. Besides Western music and tunes from Indian movies, the band's repertoire includes patriotic songs about the Communist Party and against the counterrevolutionaries, as Kabul calls the Moslem rebels. 'I always try to topple the counterrevolutionaries in my poems and songs', the singer told government officials acting as interpreters for visiting foreign journalists. (Heneghan 1986:2)

Amongst exiles in Iran and Pakistan, conditions were very different. In Iran, there was strict censorship of music from the time of the 1979 Revolution; in Pakistan, things were rather more complicated. As well as a great diversity of regional musics, Pakistan has a film music industry and shares the classical traditions of North India. Most Afghan refugees in Pakistan lived in camps not far from the border with Afghanistan, and these camps were connected to the various Mujahideen parties and were under the control of mullahs. When I went to Peshawar in 1985 to make a film about Afghan music in time of war[5] I found that the religious authorities had banned any kind of music in the camps, not only live performance and audio cassettes, but even listening to music on the radio. One reason given was that most of the people living in these miserable conditions had lost family members in the war and were in a perpetual state of mourning, thus making the playing of any kind of music inappropriate. The roots of the Taliban movement lie in these camps.

For a variety of reasons many Afghan refugees chose to live outside the camps. This included a number of refugee musicians who wanted to continue with their normal occupation. I met a number of them in Peshawar in 1985. These musicians were mainly Pashto speakers and had become integrated into the Pakistani musician community, which was also Pashto speaking. Their main source of income came from playing at Pakistani (rather than Afghan) wedding parties, and they travelled long distances to make a living. In the wedding context they would provide the usual love songs in Pashto that were considered appropriate for such festivities, rather than political songs. The Afghan style of Pashtun music enjoyed a considerable vogue in Pakistan because it was considered to be rather more sophisticated and informed by art music than the Pakistani variety.

During my 1985 visit, I attended an Afghan wedding party in a poor suburb of Peshawar where many refugees were living. The musicians were well known and usually well paid, but here were performing for no payment as an act of charity. As usual, they had microphones and a PA system. A few minutes after the music started there was a loud banging on the door of the courtyard where the wedding was taking place, and two mullahs were admitted. I was recording the music at the time and caught the following exchange on tape:

> Mullah: We have come as refugees from Afghanistan, we left everything behind but we should not leave behind our honour and customs. Don't play that thing because God and the Prophet will be offended. You play these things on happy occasions like weddings and circumcisions but it's not right to play here, we've come as refugees and if other people hear us [they'll say] it's just not right to

---

[5]   *Amir: An Afghan Refugee Musician's Life in Peshawar, Pakistan*, 1985, documentary film (52 mins) with accompanying study guide, dir. John Baily, London: Royal Anthropological Institute.

hear such merry making. Turn it down! Because other people may be offended and your party may turn sour. I can tell you this thing is forbidden because it is *sorud* [music]. ... If you play too loud the whole neighbourhood will stay up late and they will miss their [morning] prayers. And then God will ask you on Judgement Day why were you playing that game, and so putting the whole community to such inconvenience?

Singer: The best thing would have been if you had discussed this amongst yourselves before inviting me. I am a radio and television singer, wherever I go this thing goes with me.

Mullah: Alright, we understand it is a happy occasion, we're not going to stop you but cut the speakers off completely.

Singer: Okay.

Mullah: ... although God and the Prophet have forbidden this thing.

Singer: Well, Sir, it is the custom.

Mullah: Any wedding that has got you in it is not going to be a good wedding because the angels are not going to come and visit. Cut the speakers!

Musician: Haji Sahib, it's finished, it's the end, the subject is dead, and we are going to start our concert. These people you refer to are our neighbours, they are not strangers, what are you talking about? ... And if you feel like that about it, you go along to the radio station and the television station and tell them to stop playing music ...

In the end, the wedding continued, but with the sound system switched off. The mullahs had their way. This incident illustrates several themes in the censorship of music by Afghans: firstly, the direct interference by mullahs in the performance of music; second, the idea that music is inappropriate implicitly (though not stated outright here) because people are in a state of mourning; third, that listening to music will cause people to neglect their prayers; and finally, tension over the matter of amplification.

At this time, Peshawar had a thriving cassette industry and many cassettes of Mujahideen songs were recorded by Afghan musicians. Whilst little research has been carried out on this subject, we do know that some of the songs were long epics recounting the exploits of particular Mujahideen groups and their military campaigns. It seems that many of these recordings were bought by Mujahideen fighters and taken to Afghanistan for entertainment purposes. One such cassette in my possession contains a 40-minute epic about a particular Mujahideen group operating in the north of Afghanistan. At one point the singer declaims:

> It was in the dark of night when the Mujahideen were fighting
> It was difficult to tell between friend and foe
> In the morning it was time for the third attack
> *Allah o Akbar* [God is Great] could be heard amongst the bombardment
> [Instrumental section]

> The Mujahideen advanced into the district
> And they were happy for the blood they shed in martyrdom
> When they made their third attack on the town.

Following the line describing the Mujahideen advance into the district, there is a prolonged interlude in which imitations of gunfire are played on the tabla drums. Sometimes the sounds of genuine gunfire, presumably recorded at the scene of a battle, were mixed into the music in the studio. A former member of the Mujahideen interviewed in *Breaking the Silence* explained the importance of such recordings to the men engaged in the fighting:

> Although it was a holy war, we still listened to music. We were not narrow minded. Music was our entertainment. Here is an example of what we used to listen to [turns on tape recorder]. There was the sound of weapons firing. These tapes calmed us down when we were fighting. When we sat with our friends, this was our entertainment.[6]

Pashtun (female) singer Naghma described the rivalry between the Mujahideen and the government over the support of singers:

> During the Communist times I was singing on television. I was in danger from people who objected to me singing. They were the Mujahideen of Islam. They wanted me to sing for them and not appear in public. On one side the Communists wanted me to sing for them, and the Mujahideen wanted me on their side. Several times people tried to shoot me when I performed. Many times I was told to stop singing for the Communists. My husband and I had threats and our lives were in danger. But I continued to perform and one night when I was out they killed my sister in error because she looked like me.[7]

According to Anwar, this was part of a broader campaign against 'un-Islamic' practices:

> Fundamentalist rebels are not only the major enemies of the Soviets, but also of music, education, art and literature which they consider interventions of the devil. Musicians like Fazal Ghani and Khan Qarra Baghi and the well-known TV woman presenter Saima Akbar were all killed by the rebels after 1980. Dr Mohammed Usman, the only Afghan novelist of note, survived through sheer luck after an attack. It can be safely said that the rebels have launched a crusade against modern knowledge. (1989:241)

---

[6]   *Breaking the Silence*, 14'30" (time from the first frame of the film). Quotations are taken from the English subtitles.

[7]   *Breaking the Silence*, 16'37".

The Coalition Period (1992–96)

The Soviet Army withdrew from Afghanistan in 1990 and the communist government they left in Kabul fell to the Mujahideen in 1992, effectively ending the *jihad*. In this period, after the communists and before the Taliban, Afghanistan was ruled by a weak government comprised of opposing Mujahideen factions under President Rabbani, leader of a predominantly Tajik Mujahideen party, the *Jamiat-e Islami*. But for the inhabitants of Kabul, the war was not over. They were now subjected to a bewildering series of alliances battling for control of the city. Up until 1992, Kabul had survived the war more or less intact, but now with long-distance rocketing by one faction or another much of Kabul was reduced to rubble. Most of the casualties were civilians and many musicians and their families who had remained in the city now left because the musicians' quarter was frequently hit by stray rockets.

Under UN auspices, I visited Herat for seven weeks in 1994 in the middle of this period of instability. Herat was controlled by Ismail Khan, a Rabbani supporter and a highly successful Mujahideen commander during the *jihad*. He was known for his commitment to social programmes during the war and had given strong support for education (for girls as well as boys) in areas of western Afghanistan under Mujahideen control. Herat under Ismail Khan was a city in a state of deep austerity, although the economy was booming with the return of wealthy businessmen from exile in Iran. Senior religious figures had an important say in how the city was run, and an 'Office for the Propagation of Virtue and the Prevention of Vice' was established. Various edicts affecting the day to day lives of ordinary people were issued. For example, Heratis were keen pigeon fanciers and many men kept pigeon lofts on the roofs of their houses in the old city and would fly their flocks of birds as a hobby, catching them again with large nets. This activity was banned, on the grounds that it could lead to men spying into the courtyards of their neighbours' houses and observing their womenfolk unveiled. When the ban was announced on local television the point was emphasised by several pigeons having their necks wrung in front of the camera: a warning of what would happen to the birds of anyone apprehended indulging in this illicit sport. Likewise, there was a ban on flying kites from the rooftops in case young men were on the lookout for girls.

There were severe restrictions on music at this time. Professional musicians had to apply for a licence which specified that they could only perform songs in praise of the Mujahideen or songs with texts drawn from the mystical Sufi poetry of the region. This effectively meant that a great deal of other music, such as love songs and music for dancing, could not be performed. The licence also stipulated that musicians must play without amplification, an idea we already encountered in Peshawar in 1985. Music could be performed by male musicians at private parties indoors, but professional women musicians were forbidden to perform and several were briefly imprisoned for transgressing this regulation. Whilst male musicians were technically allowed to play at wedding parties, often in such cases agents of the Office for the Propagation of Virtue and the Prevention of Vice would arrive to break up the party. They would confiscate instruments, which were usually returned to the musicians some days later on payment of a fine or a bribe. Veronica Doubleday, who visited Herat in March 1994, reported just such an incident when a band of musicians was playing at a country fair held in the grounds of a Sufi shrine. The performance was stopped and the instruments confiscated (they were recovered the next day). On occasion, however, musicians were called upon by the local administration to play (without payment) at official receptions for honoured guests, such as a delegation from Iran. Professional musicians could hardly make a living from performing music. They depended on the generosity of their long-standing patrons, often from the wealthy business/merchant class, who would pay them to play at private parties or simply give them handouts in order to help them.

There was very little music on local radio or television during this period. Due to technical problems and shortages of fuel to power the generator, broadcasting time was in any case severely curtailed to about one hour in the morning and an hour in the evening. Occasionally, a musical item would be transmitted. If a song was broadcast on television, one did not see the performers on screen, but a vase of flowers was shown instead; and names of performers were not announced on radio or television. It is clear that the religious lobby was exercising tight control over music, but not in anything like as severe a form as the Taliban were to display when they took Herat in 1995. The *dutar* maker had re-opened his business in one of the main streets and had resumed the making and repair of musical instruments; a *rubab* maker was also active. The audio cassette business continued, with a number of shops in the bazaars of Herat selling cassettes, some of Herati musicians. Ironically, early in 1995, three well-known Herati musicians were issued with passports by the authorities to travel to Paris to play at an important concert in the Théâtre de la Ville, and to record a CD for OCORA (part of Radio France).[8] They were accompanied by a translator-manager who organised their travel to Europe and back to Herat.

The censorship of music in Kabul at this time was less severe than in Herat. President Rabbani tried to set up an Office for the Propagation of Virtue and the Prevention of Vice, but certain members of the government such as Ahmad Shah Masud did not support such strong measures to control the populace. In the dying days of the Rabbani period, before the fall of Kabul to the Taliban, Gulbuddin Hekmatyar was appointed Prime Minister in a new coalition government. He was the Pashtun leader of one of the most extreme Mujahideen parties and his forces had subjected Kabul to a deadly rain of rockets for months. He lost no time in closing Kabul's cinemas and banning music on radio and television. A report in the Pakistani newspaper *The Muslim* for 15 July 1996 quoted from a government spokesman:

---

[8]   *Afghanistan. Rubāb et Dutār. Ustād Mohammad Rahim Khushnavaz et Gada Mohammad*, recorded under the direction of John Baily by OCORA (Radio France), Paris (OCORA C560080, 1995).

No music or musical instruments should be heard on radio or television … Any sort of music being played on air was illegal because it has a negative effect on peoples' [sic] psyches. (author unknown)

At the time, Abdul Hafiz Mansoor, head of the state press agency, Bakhtar, commented:

The government of President Burhanuddin Rabbani tried to shut down cinemas and ban music when it came to power four years ago, but it proved to be an unrealistic ideal which only lasted a few weeks … It's difficult and potentially dangerous to take away a few simple pleasures from people who live in a ruined city with no electricity, [or] running water and which comes under constant rocket attack. (ibid.)

The Taliban Period (1996–2001)

When the Taliban took control of Kabul in 1996, they imposed an extreme form of music censorship, including banning the making, owning and playing of all types of musical instrument other than the frame drum. The concept of 'music' in Afghanistan (as in some other parts of the world) is intimately bound up with musical instruments and thus a ban on music means a ban on musical instruments. Unaccompanied singing does not, according to this definition, constitute music.

A number of decrees were published by the Taliban, including the following concerning music:

To prevent music … In shops, hotels, vehicles and rickshaws cassettes and music are prohibited … If any music cassette found in a shop, the shopkeeper should be imprisoned and the shop locked. If five people guarantee, the shop should be opened [sic] and the criminal released later. If cassette found in the vehicle, the vehicle and the driver will be imprisoned. If five people guarantee, the vehicle will be released and the criminal released later.

To prevent music and dances in wedding parties. In the case of violation, the head of the family will be arrested and punished. (Rashid 2000:218–19)

The disembodied audio-cassette, tape waving in the breeze, became the icon of Taliban rule. Musical instruments were destroyed and hung from trees in mock execution or burned in public in sports stadia. For example, the local Herati newspaper *Itafaq-e Islam* for 10 December 1998 announced that Herat's Office for the Propagation of Virtue and Prevention of Vice had seized a number of unlawful instruments and goods, which were set on fire and destroyed in Herat's stadium. The newspaper cited the following *hadith* to justify this action, 'Those who listen to music and songs in this world, will on the Day of Judgement have molten lead poured into their ears.'[9] The list of destroyed goods was reported as follows: 14 truck-loads of hashish plants; seven colour televisions; ten VCRs; four small and large cassette players; 3,500 video cassettes; 5,500 unworthy photographs; 95 statues (toy figurines); 50 plastic dolls; ten musical instruments and accessories (such as instrument cases).

The one musical instrument that was excepted from this ban was the frame drum, which in any case is not regarded as a musical instrument in the full sense of the word (Baily 1996:169–70). It is mainly played by women to accompany their domestic singing and dancing and also has important religious significance, its use having been sanctioned on one occasion by the Prophet Mohammad, as recounted above. The frame drum continued to be sold in the bazaar in Kabul, although its use was highly circumscribed. The many instruments kept at Radio Afghanistan were destroyed, though curiously several pianos survived. The Chishti *khanaqah* in Kabul's *Sang Taroshi*, an important place for Sufi musical gatherings and much patronised by Kabul's musicians, also had its instruments destroyed.

During the Taliban period, no music was broadcast by the radio station in Kabul, renamed Radio Sharia, which mainly broadcast news and religious programmes. Women had no role as broadcasters. The large tape archive, including 5,000 hours of music, survived. In the early days of Taliban rule a number of tapes of Indian film music and Iranian popular music were offered by the archive's staff as constituting the music collection, and these recordings were destroyed, but the main body of the archive remained on the shelves.[10] The Taliban established their own collection of recordings of speeches, sermons and chants (*tarana*s). The television station's video archive also survived. Whilst the Taliban made no use of film, video or television, considering representations of animate beings sinful, they did not destroy the television equipment in the studios, possibly thinking that it might have its use one day for broadcasting religious programmes.

Those musicians who remained in Afghanistan had to find other ways to make a living. Ahmad Rashid Mashinai,[11] a *sarinda* (bowed lute) player, became a butcher, 'They stopped the music and destroyed my instruments. I needed another job so I had to become a butcher. I've been working here for five years. I had to feed my family'.[12] While the Taliban banned all forms of what they perceived to be 'music', they allowed various types of unaccompanied religious singing, and created a new genre, the Taliban *tarana* (lit. 'song'/'chant'). The texts of these songs were usually in Pashto (but also used other languages of Afghanistan such

---

[9]   This *hadith* is found in the writings of the sixteenth-century jurist Ibn Hajar Haytami of Egypt (d.1567 CE). I am grateful to Katherine Brown for this information. The *hadith* seems to have had common currency in Pakistan but is not generally accepted as authentic.

[10]   Information from a visit which I made to the archive in October 2002.

[11]   Called 'The Machine' (*Mashinai*) because of his ability to learn very quickly by ear, like a tape machine (tape recorder).

[12]   *Breaking the Silence*, 2'22".

as Dari and Uzbek) and made frequent reference to the Taliban, their commitment to Islam, their readiness to sacrifice themselves for their country and their martyrs (*shahid*) who had died for the cause. Recorded *tarana*s made substantial use of electronic effects such as delay and reverberation, much favoured in the secular music of this part of the world. *Tarana*s in Pashto used the melodic modes of Pashtun regional music (such as *Pari* and *Kesturi*), were strongly rhythmic and frequently used the two-part song structure typical of the region. In other words, these songs were like Pashtun folk music, but with new texts and no musical instruments and therefore 'not music'.

Some musicians who stayed in Kabul were forced to sing these *tarana*s. Aziz Ghaznawi, a well-known singer of popular songs (and today in charge of musicians at the radio station) described his experience:

> After two years a big-shot Taliban minister sent for me. He said, 'Why don't you sing? Don't you like our regime?' 'That's not true', I protested, afraid they would kill me. 'No-one invited me to sing', I said. 'What if I ask you now?', he replied. 'Of course I will sing', I said. He handed me the text:
>   'When the conquering sun rises
>   It brings light to the darkness.'
> I went home and showed it to my wife. 'If I sing, I betray my principles. If not, I must flee the country.' I have a family of fifteen. My mother had just died, and I had no money to flee. My wife said, 'You've no choice. You've got to sing.'[13]

And so he did:

> 'The evil night has gone
> The morning sun has risen
> Thanks to you fighters peace has come
> The river will kiss your feet a hundred times.'[14]

Even the broadcast *tarana* could have other meanings. Nairiz, another radio singer who stayed in Kabul under the Taliban, explained:

> I was put in charge of 'songs without music'. They wanted to hear me sing, so I chose one that went:
>   'Remember the poor are protected by God
>   One day He will answer their cries
>   And their oppressors will be punished.'
> The Taliban liked the song but didn't understand its meaning. They were proud Pashto speakers, but I sang in Farsi and the song was a big hit.[15]

---

[13] *Breaking the Silence*, 32'24".
[14] *Breaking the Silence*, 32'24".
[15] *Breaking the Silence*, 34'24".

Not all singers were so unwilling to record for the Taliban. In Peshawar in 2000 I met a musician who had recently returned from Kabul, where he had gone to record some unaccompanied *na'ts* (songs in praise of Prophet Mohammad) for Radio Sharia.

Punishments for playing music or being caught with cassettes varied greatly, from confiscation of the goods and a warning, to severe beatings and imprisonment. Despite these measures, there was a great deal of clandestine music making and listening to music. Western journalists loved to report how their drivers would play cassettes in their vehicles, then substitute a Taliban *tarana* when they came to a check-point. In Herat, a strongly anti-Taliban city, BBC correspondent Kate Clark was surprised to find that taxi drivers drove about the city playing music cassettes rather freely. Instruments were hidden behind false walls or buried in the ground. Many houses in the cities have a basement area which is used in the summer against the heat; such rooms lent themselves readily for underground music sessions. Although the frame drum was the one instrument not proscribed, women were very careful about their traditional music sessions. According to one young lady, 'Kabul and the whole country was like a prison for women. It was not a happy place. Every family knew the Taliban were watching. We would only risk playing if we were 100 per cent sure it was safe. Look-outs were posted to watch for Taliban coming. Then we'd silence our music and hide our tambourines (*daireh*s)'.[16]

The best documented example of resistance to the Taliban comes not from the field of music, but from the film *Titanic*. In November 2000, Kate Clark reported that while cinema, television and video were all banned in Afghanistan, this film was undergoing an extraordinary surge of popularity. Everybody in Kabul seemed, somehow, to have seen it, in some cases many times. Even the Taliban seemed to know all about it. According to a joke current at the time, a mullah giving his Friday sermon to a crowded audience warned listeners that they were committing many sins. He told them, 'I know you are listening to music, you're hiring video players, you're watching films. You should be careful. You're all going to be damned and drown just like the people in the Titanic film!' Leonardo DiCaprio's haircut, known as the 'Titanic haircut', became very popular in Kabul and many barbers were punished for styling it. Clothes, rice and motor oil were all were sold with the Titanic logo. Expensive wedding cakes were baked in the shape of the Titanic, and the most extravagant added the iceberg as a supplement. The bazaar which had recently appeared in the bed of the dried up Kabul River was dubbed 'Titanic Bazaar'. Various reasons could be suggested for the popularity of the film but it is surely relevant that the love story is in the classic Leyla and Majnun or Yusuf and Zulaikha mould.[17]

---

[16]   *Breaking the Silence*, 31'46".

[17]   Perhaps at a deeper level, the ship was a symbol of an Afghanistan founding on the iceberg of civil war; or perhaps the Afghans saw *Titanic* as a symbol of the Taliban, seemingly impregnable, but in the event unsound. VHS copies of *Titanic* were probably

The Taliban never succeeded in gaining control of the whole country. The province of Badakhshan in northeast Afghanistan, a mountainous and remote region, was one such Taliban-free zone. Although the area was not under Taliban control, however, severe restrictions on music and dance were imposed by local mullahs and Mujahideen commanders. Bruce Koepke carried out research in the town of Ishkashim in 1998 on what he calls 'non-religious practices of performative human actions' (Koepke 2000:93). Despite the restrictions, Koepke was witness to one solo male dance event, held in the guest room of the residence of a local Isma'ili community leader. After the small band had played for two hours, the community leader exchanged a glance with one of the musicians who then got up to dance. From Koepke's description, the dance sounds very similar to that performed in turn by young men at wedding parties back in the 1970s. When the first dancer had finished, the leader of the band performed a dance which was more in the style of a dancing boy, with effeminate and somewhat erotic gestures. After wiggling his shoulders, the dancer 'slowly lowered his body by gradually squatting to the floor, and eventually kneeling in front of an audience member' (Koepke 2000:104), a gesture typical of erotic dance. Koepke's interpretation of this is of great interest:

> It seems that the dances were [performed] on this occasion as an opportunity for the Isma'ili leader to reinstate himself as the official authority in the Ishkashim region. In his own home, he was able to condone a performance that was otherwise prohibited. By organizing a private social event, he demonstrated his authority, hiring musicians from the lower stratum of society who then performed much-loved music and dance for his guests. (ibid. 104–5)[18]

Many of Afghanistan's professional musicians had already gone into exile before the Taliban conquered most of the country. Poorly educated hereditary musicians from cities such as Kabul, Mazar, Herat, Kandahar and Jalalabad, generally went to neighbouring countries such as Pakistan and Iran. In *Breaking the Silence*, *delruba* (bowed lute) player Amruddin describes movingly how he tried to take his instrument with him to Peshawar:

> When the Taliban took Mazar-e Sharif, I had a shop with instruments from both East and West. When the Taliban came we buried some and burned some, we got rid of them all. I kept just one *delruba*. It belonged to my father and was very dear to me. I wanted to keep it till I died. But on the way to Herat there

---

imported from Pakistan or Iran, dubbed in Urdu or Farsi. There is no suggestion that the film was favoured simply because it was made in the West.

[18]   The population of Ishkashim is largely Isma'ili, a sect within the main body of Shiah Islam. Koepke does not explain the circumstances that led to this un-named community leader needing to (re)assert his authority within the community, using music as a means of self-empowerment.

were many check-points. At first no-one noticed my *delruba*. I had removed the strings and stripped it to the bare wood. But in Herat a local boy recognised what it was. He smashed it to pieces against the car. I don't mind the other things but that *delruba* meant a lot to me.[19]

In exile, many of Kabul's musicians from the *Kucheh Kharabat* (the musicians' quarter in the old city) set up business premises in Khalil House, a modern apartment block in University Road, Peshawar. About 30 music groups were located in this one building and we may suppose that there was an element of self-protection in this huddling together in a potentially hostile environment. The musicians did not live in the building, but each room became the 'office' of a group. Here prospective patrons would come to visit, to negotiate and hire bands, usually for wedding parties. Nearby, there were shops selling everything needed for a wedding such as wedding dresses and accessories, as well as banqueting rooms where large receptions could be held, with separate parties for men and women. Some musicians also ran their own 'music schools'; indeed, Khalil House was a hothouse of musical activity with a great deal of teaching and practice going on, as well as informal music sessions where young musicians competed to show off their virtuosity and technical skills.

Music in the Post-Taliban Period

During the war of 2001 that led to the defeat of the Taliban, spontaneous outbursts of music greeted the liberation of the towns and cities. Music in Afghanistan has always been associated with joyous occasions, such as wedding festivities and the country fairs held over a period of 40 days in the spring. For most people, the end of Taliban control was the occasion for rejoicing and for music making, whether by playing cassettes loudly in the streets or by playing musical instruments. The very sound of music became a symbol, even a signal, of freedom. Once music was heard coming from a local radio station, people knew that the Taliban had lost control over their area. The sound of music heralded a return to (comparative) normality, for the chronic absence of music is symptomatic of a dysfunctional society.

The mood of euphoria felt in many parts of the country was short-lived. At the time of writing (2003), the situation in Afghanistan was in many ways a reversion to the immediate pre-Taliban period, with the Northern Alliance the successor to the Rabbani Coalition, and Hekmatyar in alliance with remnants of the Taliban and other extreme fundamentalists. Strong censorship of music continued. In Kabul, there was a complete ban on women singing on state-run radio and television, and on the stage or concert platform. Women could announce, read the news, recite poetry and act in plays, but they could not sing. This ban was the subject of intense argument within the radio and television organisations, which are under

---

[19]   *Breaking the Silence*, 25'10".

the control of the Ministry for Information and Culture. The explanation offered for the ban was that to do otherwise would give the government's fundamentalist enemies an easy excuse to stir up trouble. In the case of television, a further reason given was that there were no competent women singers left in Kabul, and the tapes in the video archive (dating mainly from the communist period) showed women wearing clothes that would now be considered too revealing. This excuse obviously did not apply to women singing on radio. A third reason – that it would place the women in danger of attack – could not be accepted either, since most of the music broadcast is from the archive. This same reason was offered to explain why women were not allowed to sing at a concert celebrating the 70th anniversary of the BBC World Service in January 2003.

If there is some censorship of music in Kabul, protected and patrolled by the International Security Assistance Force (ISAF), outside the capital much tighter restrictions are imposed by local fundamentalist commanders. The lengthy Human Rights Watch report *'Killing You is a Very Easy Thing For Us': Human Rights Abuses in Southeast Afghanistan*, published in July 2003, catalogues a string of abuses, including attacks on musicians in areas close to Kabul. Paghman, located in the foothills of the Hindu Kush and once a resort, has a particularly poor record under the governorship of Zabit Musa, a prominent member of the powerful *Ittehad-e Islami* party. In a village near Paghman, two musicians were killed when hand-grenades were thrown at a wedding party. Whilst it is not certain that this attack was specifically anti-music in motivation, it seems likely. One of the musicians, a well-known and respected *doholak* (drum) player, Abdul Paghmani, might well have been deliberately targeted. A resident of Paghman described a visit by Zabit Musa and his gunmen to the local bazaar:

> I was there – I saw the whole thing. It was morning … He had three or four soldiers with him. When he got to the bazaar, he went towards some shopkeepers who were listening to tape recorders, to music, and he grabbed them and pulled them out of their shops. He yelled at them: 'Why do you listen to this music and with the volume so high?' A shopkeeper said, 'Well, it is not the time of the Taliban. It is our right to listen to music!' But the governor got angry and he said, 'Well, the Taliban is not here, but Islam is here. Shariat is here. We have fought for Islam – this fight was for Islam. We are mujahid. We are Islam. We did jihad to uphold the flags of Islam.' And then he took them out of their shops and started beating them with his own hands. He beat up two people himself, along with his troops, slapping them, kicking them. And the others were beaten just by the soldiers. Then they closed the shops, locked them. Many people were there. It was not the first time these sorts of things had happened. (Human Rights Watch 2003:65)

Another example comes from a wedding in Lachikhel, a village in Paghman district, when soldiers came at midnight to break up a wedding party:

> They beat up the musicians, who had come from Kabul. They made them lie
> down, and put their noses on the ground, and swear that they would not come back
> to Paghman to play music. Then they destroyed their instruments. (ibid. 66)

A young man who had been dancing was taken off to the governor's house and
was allegedly raped. The soldiers started to beat the guests, who were detained at
the house throughout the night. In the morning, Zabit Musa arrived and reportedly
ordered the younger men to be released, but chose to berate and beat the older men
with 'long beards':

> He made them stand in a line, and he walked down the line, looking at each in the
> face. He would look at them like he was deciding, and then he would start slapping
> them in the face. And as he slapped them, he would say things like, 'Be ashamed
> of your acts! Look at your beard! At your age, how old you are! You should be
> ashamed!' And so as he beat them, he insulted them with bitter words. (ibid.)

In these circumstances music becomes a potent symbol of local power. As a young
farmer noted in Paghman:

> The majority of the people hate the governor, and his meanness, and his people.
> They are hypocrites. They have weddings! They have music at their weddings!
> But they prosecute us for having the same. Well, perhaps we disagree about
> whether Islam allows music at a wedding, but look: *they* have music. If the
> gunmen have music, why can't we? (ibid. 66)

Not surprisingly, musicians from Kabul have become very wary about where they
will go to play and for whom; they have to feel adequately protected. Such precise
information as that provided by Human Rights Watch for southeast Afghanistan is
not available for other parts of the country, but it is clear that the situation varies
greatly from place to place. Ironically, the one city where women were able to
perform on local radio and television was Kandahar, formerly a Taliban stronghold,
the reason being that the Governor of Kandahar was a great music lover.

   On 12 January 2004, a few days after the ratification of the new constitution for
Afghanistan by a Loya Jirga (National Assembly), Kabul TV (the state television
station) broadcast old video footage of female singers Parasto and Salma (Reuters,
13 January 2004). Explaining the reasons for this dramatic break with the recent
past, Information and Culture Minister Sayed Makdoom Raheen told Reuters, 'We
are endeavouring to perform our artistic works regardless of the issue of sex.'
However, the action provoked an immediate backlash from the Supreme Court.
Deputy Chief Justice Fazl Ahmad Manawi told Reuters on 13 January 2004 that
the Supreme Court was 'opposed to women singing and dancing as a whole' and
added 'This is totally against the decisions of the Supreme Court and it has to be
stopped' (reported in *Saudi Gazette*, 16 January 2004 [author unknown], story
attributed to Reuters). On 23 January, the press agency AFP reported that Ismail

Khan, the Governor of Herat, supported the Supreme Court's judgement and had banned the sale of audio and videotapes featuring women singers in Herat. Despite these statements, however, the radio and television have persisted with the new policy (Graham 2004:34).

Conclusions

What can we conclude from this narrative of music censorship in Afghanistan? It is a complicated situation of which the most interesting aspect is not so much the nervousness about music from a religious point of view, but the ways in which music is used in relation to power. It is a general fact of musical life that the rank of a ruler is measured in part by the music he can command. For several centuries, rival European courts were involved in intense competition to attract the best composers and performers (Hogwood 1977). In nineteenth-century India, many Maharajas and other princely figures were stripped of their political power by the British Raj and consequently 'Rulers and nobles no longer permitted to fight wars often squandered their incomes instead on their courts, including the musical establishments. There was an explosive development of Hindustani classical music and much rivalry and exchange among the many princely music centers' (Powers 1979:23). Some of John Blacking's early writings on Venda music make similar points about communal music and political power. Blacking argued that 'the music a man can command or forbid is a measure of his status' (1965:36). Whenever a ruler holds a *domba* initiation (which lasts for several months), other forms of communal music in his area are banned. Blacking also gives a graphic account of how a chief's attempt to install a new headman of his choice was defeated when the present incumbent was able to attract a larger group of men to perform the reed-pipe music *tshikona* (ibid. 38). Many other examples of this kind of phenomenon are to be found in the present volume.

At various points in the foregoing narrative we see that music is the focus for the exercise of political power. During the *jihad* period, the Mujahideen ban music in the refugee camps, but use it for their own entertainment in the war zone. In Herat, musicians are under extreme pressure, but are occasionally summoned by the local authorities to entertain visiting dignitaries or sent abroad as cultural ambassadors. In Badakhshan, a local commander displays his authority by organising an evening of music in his house, with a display of 'naughty dancing'. In Paghman, people complain that the gunmen have music for themselves but prevent others from having access to it. After the passing of a new constitution, the Afghan Government reinstates women singers on state television; the Supreme Court tries to intervene in order to reinstate the ban, but is unsuccessful. Not only do we see (yet again) how sensitive an indicator of broader social and cultural processes music is, but how fiercely control over music is contested. One ponders the mystery of what it is about music that makes it so powerful, and how that power might be harnessed for performances of reconciliation instead of conflict.

Chapter 6
National Traditions and Illegal Religious Activities amongst the Uyghurs

Rachel Harris

Introduction

The aim of this chapter is not to provide a systematic study of ritual music in Uyghur culture, but rather to highlight some of the many complex ways in which music plays at the nexus of political and spiritual power in the northwesternmost region of the People's Republic of China, the Xinjiang Uyghur Autonomous Region. The Uyghurs are speakers of a Turkic language and followers of Sunni Islam of a type strongly influenced by Sufism. They are the most numerous of the peoples of this desert and mountainous region which borders on the Central Asian states of Kazakhstan and Kyrgyzistan. Culturally, in their musical and religious practices, they are closely related to the other Central Asian peoples. The traditional musical and ritual practices of the Uyghurs are historically entwined with the play of political power. Sufi orders have historically wielded considerable political power in the successive khanates which ruled the region, and the musical forms associated with Sufi rituals are inextricably interlinked with the repertoires now classified as 'folk' or 'classical'.

During the twentieth century these ritual practices have been periodically disrupted by politics, especially during the war-torn 1940s and during the Cultural Revolution period of the 1960s–70s. In recent years, alongside many aspects of life, they have been affected by new tensions in the region following the establishment of the independent Central Asian states in 1991, the rise of orthodox or fundamentalist forms of Islam across the region, and responses by the Chinese state to fears of Uyghur separatist activity. Whilst small numbers of Uyghurs are known to be participating in the terrorist organisations active in the Central Asian states (Rashid 2002:204, Gladney 2004:389–92), the Chinese state response has been widely criticised as disproportionate to the actual threat (Becquelin 2004, Millward 2004). These responses have included the introduction of measures of control and coercion amongst the broad Uyghur population, involving mass education campaigns of a type rarely seen since the Cultural Revolution, and anti-'illegal religious activities' campaigns which have impacted on a wide range of popular religious and musical practices which are far removed from fundamentalist Islam.

This chapter discusses the cultural and musical expression of both organised Sufism and a range of popular Islamic practices amongst the Uyghurs. It highlights the links between music in these ritual contexts and the 'classical' Uyghur *muqam* traditions, and it juxtaposes recent attempts to control and suppress the former with ongoing state support for such musical forms as folklore: decontextualised, revised and re-presented in the performances of the state-sponsored song-and-dance troupes.

Shrine Festivals

As is commonly found across Islamic Central Asia, the Uyghurs practise pilgrimage to the tombs or shrines (*mazar*) of saints which are scattered around the deserts and towns of Xinjiang (see Figure 6.1). These shrines are sites of pilgrimage in part because they are believed to have the power to cure infertility and disease, and avert disasters, natural or other. Pilgrimage also serves as an assertion of religious faith. A few of the major shrines hold big annual festivals to honour the saint and mourn his death. This practice of pilgrimage and holding festivals at the tombs of saints is widespread across Central Asia, Afghanistan, India and Pakistan (Bennigsen and Wimbush 1985, Djumaev 2002).

In Xinjiang such shrines are numerous. In the course of several years' fieldwork the Uyghur ethnologist Rahilä Dawut documented the existence of over two hundred around the region (Dawuti 2001).[1] The most widespread, and those which attract the greatest number of worshippers are the tombs of kings and transmitters of Islam, and martyrs (*shehit*) killed in battle against the Buddhist kingdoms of Xinjiang. Also numerous are the tombs of leaders of Sufi orders (*silsila*), whose cults are more localised. More widely known are the tombs of the Khoja rulers of Kashgar.[2] The tombs of philosophers and writers have in the past been important sites of pilgrimage for students of Islamic schools. Other sites of pilgrimage are the tombs of craftsmen, which are thought to be efficacious in healing specific diseases such as skin complaints. Many tombs are sites of pilgrimage for women, especially those who seek a child.

Ildikó Bellér-Hann stresses the 'deeply Islamic nature' of such popular religious practices amongst the Uyghurs whilst also recognising their syncretic nature, integrating Sufi traditions with Buddhist and other pre-Islamic ritual practices (2001a:10). For contemporary Uyghurs the practice of pilgrimage is a powerful force, especially for the poorer peasants of southern Xinjiang who come to the tomb sites every year in their thousands, treading and re-treading the pathways which criss-cross the Taklimakan desert, often virtually impassable for modern vehicles. If the new roads and railways of Xinjiang may be seen as new pathways of power, bringing new development and new immigrants, opening

---

[1]　'Dawuti' is the Chinese transliteration of the Uyghur name 'Dawut', given thus since this book is published in Chinese.

[2]　A Naqshbandi Sufi dynasty which ruled the southern part of this region from 1679 to 1756.

up and marking out the territory, clearly displayed on the printed maps of the region, then these sacred tombs and the paths between them serve to map out an alternative, sacred landscape which is marked only in the minds of the Uyghur pilgrims, one very different from the printed maps of Xinjiang and imbued with a different kind of power.[3]

Scenes from the Ordam

The Ordam, Xinjiang's largest shrine festival, is held deep in the Taklimakan desert near Kashgar at the tomb of the eleventh-century martyr Ali Arslan Khan of the Qarakhan (the region's first Muslim kingdom), who died in battle during the 50-years' war against the neighbouring Buddhist kingdom of Khotän.

Pilgrims come annually to this three-day festival to celebrate and mourn the saint. Old men come to dance; young people come to the Ordam to meet each other; women come to pray to the saint for a child. The sick come to bury themselves in the sand around the site, which is thought to have healing powers. At this Islamic festival, music is everywhere: *dastanchi* singing tales of local heroes or famous lovers; *muqamchi* playing the *tämbur* five-stringed, long-necked lute and singing the *muqam*;[4] *mäddah* telling religious stories accompanying themselves on the *rawap* shorter plucked lute,[5] and many *ashiq*, religious mendicants, singing *hikmät*,[6] accompanying themselves on *sapaya* percussion sticks.

In the summer of 1995, researchers from the Xinjiang Arts Research Unit attended the Ordam Mazar and made video recordings of the musical activities which took place there. They estimated that some tens of thousands of people, the majority poor peasants, gathered at the shrine that year, arriving in this remote desert location, some from considerable distances, on trucks, donkey carts or on foot. This was the last time in recent years that the festival was held; the ban continues to the time of writing. The following descriptions are drawn from the video recordings they made.

---

[3]   See Feuchtwang (1991:21–3) for an exposition of the concept of sacred landscapes in China.

[4]   The Uyghur *muqam* (from the Arab *maqâm*) are large-scale suites consisting of sung poetry, stories, dance tunes and instrumental sections. Contemporary scholars refer to several distinct regional traditions maintained by the Uyghurs, but the most widespread and prestigious are the Twelve Muqam of the Kashgar-Yarkand region. See During and Trebinjac (1991) and Harris (2008) for a detailed study of formal aspects of the Uyghur Twelve Muqam.

[5]   At around 90cm long, the instrument has a small bowl-shaped body covered with skin, five or six metal strings which are plucked with a horn plectrum, and is decorated with ornamental horns (*möngüz*). There are several different types of Uyghur *rawap*, but they all belong to the *rubab* family of double-chambered lutes found in Iran, Central Asia and Northern India.

[6]   From the Arabic, lit. 'pieces of wisdom'.

Figure 6.1   Praying at a *mazar* in Qaraqash county near Khotän.

Scene One: Ashiq[7]

Late into the second night of the festival, in the courtyard of the mosque attached
to the tomb, a crowd of men have gathered to listen to a group of ashiq *musicians.*
Beginning the performance, an elderly Imam wearing a turban recites from the
Qur'an. The crowd makes the movement of ritual cleansing and gives the Islamic
*creed (*tawhīd*) in a drawn-out cry, 'La illahi ilallah'. A young* ashiq *wearing a flat*
cap plays the rawap. *He is accompanied by several men playing* sapaya *percussion*
sticks and one dap *frame drum. The musicians all seem slightly tranced. This piece*
is a version of Ushshaq Muqam, *one of the twelve great suites of Uyghur music.*
The ashiq *sings first the unmetered opening* muqäddimä *section of the* muqam
accompanying himself on the rawap. *He sings in a raw voice full of emotion. He is*
on the edge, but his playing is precise. The percussionists chime in with long cries
at end of his phrases. The all-male audience is quiet and calm, seated, smoking
cigarettes. A smoky fire lights the players. The percussionists are now deeply
tranced, the drummer makes his dap *leap in the air, one man twitches as he plays.*

---

[7]   The following descriptions are based on scenes videoed in 1995 by researchers
from the Xinjiang Arts Research Unit and viewed by the author at the Research Unit in
1996.

They move into the metered sections of the muqam, *singing together led by the* rawap *player, first the 7/8 rhythm of the first* mäshräp, *then the fast duple metre of the second* mäshräp. *The action and intensity of the musicians contrasts with the calm of the crowd. The rhythm of the drum changes, the percussionists give a rhythmic 'Woy! Woy! Woy!' They play with theatrical movements, up, left, right, rocking side to side. A long virtuoso section on the* rawap *follows, to an insistent drum beat. The piece comes to an end and the whole audience gives a long cry. Several men offer prayers blessing the festival.*

Amongst the Uyghurs the meaning of *ashiq* (lit. 'lover') differs somewhat from meanings in other parts of the Islamic world. Also known as *mäjnun* (one crazed by love), *diwanä*, dervishes or *qalandar* (mendicants), they are religious beggars and musicians who can still be found across the Xinjiang region, singing in town bazaars and especially congregating at the shrines where pilgrims are generous with their charity. Their signature instrument is the simple percussion stick *sapaya*, made from wood or ibex horn and hung with a pair of metal rings, but they may also play *tash*, a pair of flat stones struck together, and sometimes plucked lutes, usually the *rawap* or *tämbur*. The English missionaries Mildred Cable and Francesca French write colourfully of a group of *qalandar* encountered in the bazaar in the eastern town of Turpan in the 1930s:

> Above all the noise and shouting there can sometimes be heard a strange, weird, lilting chorus of men's voices. It comes from a band of *kalandars*, a group of strange, dishevelled men with long uncombed hair, dressed in fantastic costumes. One will have iron chains hanging to his arms which he shakes rhythmically as he moves, another will have a frame of hanging discs on which he plays a primitive accompaniment, another will knock pieces of bone together, marking time for the chant. They have sonorous voices, and though many are deformed and some blind in one or both eyes, they are strong creatures and greatly feared, no one daring to refuse their demand for money lest they call a curse down on him. These *kalandars* are a guild of professional beggars, and as they walk they sing old religious songs, always ending with the refrain, 'Allah, Allah-hu.' (Cable and French 1942:193)

The old religious songs to which Cable and French refer are the *hikmät* popularly sung by the *ashiq*, melodic vocal pieces which are also sung during the Sufi *sama* rituals over the rhythmic chants of the *zikr*.

Scene Two: Drums and Shawms

People are moving towards the tomb of Ali Arslan Khan, holding large coloured flags. This is a huge crowd, gathered for the culmination of the festival, the ritual of tugh körüshtürüsh *(meeting of the flags). The ritual is said to enact the bringing together of the head and body of Ali Arslan Khan after he was decapitated in battle. Several* naghra-sunay *(kettle drum and shawm) bands are playing. Many men in the crowd hold huge* dap *frame drums, over 50cm in diameter. The gathered crowds are climbing up the sand dunes towards the tomb in a long procession. There are five hills to cross. Women may climb the first two, then they roll down again, cleansing themselves of evil influence. The men continue towards the tomb, processing in village groups with their flags, led by* dap *constantly beating out rhythm. A man deep in trance runs before one group, half dancing, half urging them on, several others seem semi-ecstatic. A mountain of flags is being raised above the tomb, twenty metres high. The flags are pink, blue, red, white with black fringes, black tufts of fur on poles, reminiscent of Tibetan prayer flags.*

Sunay *and* dap *are being played and men are dancing. The drummers are competitive, displaying their skills, they hold the drums high above their heads and give theatrical flourishes. The tranced dancer twitches and moves his hands and legs in awkward shapes. He raises the cry 'Allah', and all join him. He weeps and shakes, kneels and speaks of his troubles, half frenzied. Others kneel and listen with respect, hands cupped. Some weep at his words and make the movement of ritual cleansing. One man sobs and breaks into song, a free recitative with long drawn-out notes in a high, hoarse voice; others make short speeches. In the crowd a young man plays a slow introductory section of a* sänäm *dance piece*[8] *on the* sunay. *Other* sunay *and* dap *join him for the dance section.*

The *naghra-sunay* kettle drum and double-reed shawm bands are probably the most widespread musical ensemble in the region, always playing outdoors to accompany many kinds of festive activities, usually with a solo *sunay* accompanied by two or more sets of *naghra* which beat out breathtakingly complex rhythmic variations.[9] These bands are thought to have accompanied the armies of the early Islamic Uyghur kings, and may have been introduced into Xinjiang from neighbouring Central Asia during the Qarakhan period alongside Islam. They are an important part of the Ordam festival, where three or more bands can be heard simultaneously playing in the central area of the festival, as if in competition, while men gather around them to dance the *sama* circling dance.[10] At the festival these bands play a variety of pieces from the popular repertoire including the piece

[8]   From the Arabic: 'carved image'. Suites of between six and thirteen folksongs played usually for dancing. Each oasis town has its own distinctive *sänäm* in the local singing style, but they are all related rhythmically, beginning with the same moderate four-beat dance rhythm and moving gradually into a faster metre. *Sänäm* are often played in a purely instrumental version by the *naghra-sunay* bands.

[9]   Uyghur *naghra-sunay* can be heard on *Music from the Oasis Towns of Central Asia. Uyghur Musicians of Xinjiang* (2000, track 8).

[10]   Samā (lit. 'audition') more commonly refers to the Sufi rituals involving *zikr*, but Uyghurs generally use this term to refer specifically to the dance. *Zikr* is described by Jean During as the practice of invocation through the repetition of a sacred word or formula. It may be silent or voiced, individual or collective. It is accompanied by rhythmic movements

Shadiyana ('rejoicing') which is specifically linked to Arslan Khan, thought to be the tune which played his armies into battle (Zhou 1999:71).[11]

Although the shawm has been singled out in orthodox interpretations of Islam as a particularly unclean (*harām*) musical instrument (Baily 1988:101–4), these drum-and-shawm bands play an indispensable role in religious festivals across Central Asia. Uzbek musicologist Alexander Djumaev reports that the Emir of Bukhara kept a band (*nakkarakhāna*) which played at dawn to mark the first day of Ramadan, and then each day at dusk to announce the breaking of the fast (2002:940). Until a few years ago, a similar band of *naghra-sunay* played annually at the festivals of Qurban and Rozi, from the roof of Kashgar's famous Idgah mosque, while huge crowds gathered in the square below to dance the *sama* circling dance. This large-scale public event is clearly related to the *sama* rituals performed by the Sufis in their *khaniqa* (lodges) and at the *mazar* festivals.

Another major shrine festival is held in southern Xinjiang in May during the mulberry season at the tomb of Imam Hasim, another eleventh-century martyr who died in battle against Khotan. Somewhat smaller than the Ordam festival, and lacking the *naghra-sunay* bands which so enliven that festival, this shrine is nonetheless the scene of much musical activity including *mäddah* telling tales from the Qur'an whilst accompanying themselves on *tämbur* lutes, *ashiq* singing to the accompaniment of *sapaya* percussion sticks, and Sufi *sama* rituals.

Scene Three: Circling and Speaking[12]

A large Sufi sama *ritual is being conducted in the middle of the day in the open air amongst the crowds at the festival. More than a hundred men are gathered in a tight circle, many wearing white loose gowns and turbans. At the centre of this group are mainly older men dancing the* sama, *moving in slow circles with their right arm raised, crooked at the elbow. The rest are gathered around in a circle, swaying to the beat, chanting the* zikr. *A small group of* hapiz *(reciters) are performing a series of long melodic chants (*hikmät *and* talqin*) over the rhythmic sound of the* zikr. *One of their melodies is familiar: the revolutionary folksong 'Yasha Gongchandang' ('Long Live the Communist Party'), originally a Sufi* hikmät *melody, borrowed and adapted to new revolutionary lyrics in the 1950s.*[13]

---

and special ways of breathing which are meant to circulate the body's energies (During 1989:136).

[11]   A version of Shadiyana for *dutar* can be heard on Abdulla Mäjnun (2003), *Mäjnun: Classical Traditions of the Uyghurs.*

[12]   These scenes were videoed at the Imam Hasim Mazar in 1997 by Rahilä Dawut, and viewed by the author in 2001.

[13]   Such appropriations were not uncommon in Xinjiang. See Harris (2001) for the history of a revolutionary shamanic ritual song in China. It seems that communist cultural workers of the 1950s were not troubled by the idea that old associations might cling to the melody when new lyrics have been affixed. The Sufi *hikmät*, with their typically rhythmic,

Across the way a smaller group of büwi *women ritualists, their shawls drawn over their heads, are conducting their own ritual, voices raised as if in competition with the men. They too accompany rhythmic* zikr *chants with their own melodic* hikmät.

As with *sama* rituals across the Islamic world, the Uyghur ritual is a powerful experience to undergo; participants emerge sweating from the vigorous movements of the dance, some fall into a trance-like state, and some give way to open expressions of grief. Uyghur Sufis sometimes refer to themselves as 'lovers of god' (*khodaning ashiqi*) in the classic Sufi sense, yet many Uyghurs who speak of the practice of *zikr* associate it less with religious zeal than with health, as in: 'the reason why my grandfather lived to be 120 years old is because he practised *zikr* every week and ate mutton every day.'[14] Sufi rituals are performed in contemporary Xinjiang not only at the shrine festivals, but also at regular weekly meetings in Sufi lodges (*khaniqa*), headed by hereditary *ishan* and situated in towns and villages around southern and eastern Xinjiang.[15] Uyghur Sufi lodges associate themselves with the Naqshbandiyya, Qaderiyya, and Chishtiyya orders which are found widespread around Central Asia, Pakistan and China. The centre of the large and influential Naqshbandiyya order is in Bukhara, where its members are drawn mainly from Tajik-speaking artisans. There they practise both silent and loud *zikr*, and the lyrics of their *hikmät* draw on mystical Persian poetry. The Qaderiyya order are strongest in the Ferghana-Tashkent region of Uzbekistan (Djumaev 2002:942), and they have put down strong roots in the neighbouring Kashgar-Yarkand region of Xinjiang.

From research on Sufi ritual in southern Xinjiang by the French scholar Thierry Zarcone (2002) and the Chinese musicologist Zhou Ji (1999) it is possible to build a picture of the complex relationship between Uyghur Sufi groups and political power in contemporary Xinjiang. Some of the major lodges of Xinjiang trace their individual genealogies back to the seventeenth century, when Sufi orders flourished under the patronage of the Khoja dynasty of Kashgar. Zarcone, however, suggests that the most influential Qaderiyya orders active in Xinjiang today were in fact founded by Uzbek Sufi sheikhs who fled from the Soviet Union in the first decades of the twentieth century to escape religious persecution in the aftermath of the Basmachi rebellion (2002:534).

Xinjiang's largest Sufi lodge, Teräkbagh Khaniqa, where 400 to 500 men meet regularly for Friday *sama*, is in the southern town of Yarkand. The lodge is situated on private land owned by Ishan Tukhsun Khoja, the sheikh of the lodge. Tukhsun Khoja traces his ancestry back to an associate of Afaq Khoja, one Khoja

---

stepwise melodies, well-suited to group singing, were eminently suitable material for reworking as a revolutionary song.

[14]   Rahilä Dawut, Interview, July 2000.

[15]   A Sufi *ishan* interviewed by Zhou Ji calculated that in 1995 over 20 Sufi lodges were active in the area surrounding the southern town of Qaghiliq alone (Zhou 1999:36).

Niyaz Sufi of the White Mountain (*aq sulugh*) Sufi order, whose tomb lies within the Teräkbagh compound. Tukhsun Khoja combines this illustrious ancestry with a considerable role in the contemporary political and religious bureaucracy of Xinjiang. His numerous political appointments (listed in full detail in Zhou Ji's account) include membership of the official Islam Committee (*yisilanjiao xiehui*) at national, regional and local level, as well as membership of the Yarkand Government Committee (*zhengxiehui*) (Zhou 1999:29). A second *ishan* leader of a major Sufi lodge in the neighbouring town of Qaghiliq (in Chinese: Yecheng) displays a similar, indeed related ancestry, and set of political titles. Their positions suggest that in recent decades the Xinjiang government has not sought to impose an outright ban on organised Sufi activities but rather to co-opt the leadership, who command considerable respect and influence in the community, into the system of government.[16]

At the Teräkbagh Khaniqa, Zhou Ji also interviewed the head *hapiz*[17] whose function in the *khaniqa* is to lead the melodic *hikmät* which accompany the *zikr* and whose position is hereditary. The lyrics of some of the *hikmät* are attributed to fifteenth- and sixteenth-century mystic poets such as Nawayi and Mäshräp, who wrote in Chagatay (the early Turkic literary language), as well as to the earlier writings of Ahmad Yassawi, founder of the Yassawiyya order whose tomb rests in the town of Turkestan in contemporary Kazakhstan. Many express mourning, often for the founder and former leaders of their Sufi lodge. Uyghurs call these Sufi *sama* rituals *hälqä-suhibät* (lit. 'circling and speaking'), while *zikr* refers specifically to the rhythmic chants given by the participants.[18] The form of the rituals as practised in Teräkbagh bears many similarities to descriptions of the rituals of the Yassawiyya order, centred in the town of Turkestan (Djumaev 2002:943). Further work remains to be done to trace the historical and contemporary links, and the musical continuities between Sufi orders in different parts of Central Asia, and as is clear from the distanced sources which I cite, such work is not easily accomplished in the present political climate on either side of the border.

Whilst the Uyghur Qaderiyya order draws on roots in the Ferghana Valley of contemporary Uzbekistan, the Chishtiyya order of Khotän in southern Xinjiang faces in another direction. This order has a large following in India, Pakistan and Afghanistan, whilst the tomb of its thirteenth-century founding saint, Hazrat Muinuddin Chishti, is found at Ajmer in Rajasthan. The order makes explicit use of music in its *sama* rituals, most famously amongst the *qawwali* of India and Pakistan (Qureshi 1986), as well as in Afghanistan (Baily 1988:154). The Chishtiyya order was brought to Khotän by merchants from India and Afghanistan

---

[16]   Zarcone's research suggests a similar situation, but he notes that Sufi orders are under constant surveillance, and that policy towards those with a history of opposition to Chinese rule has been harsher (2002:537).

[17]   Arabic: *ḥāfiz*, 'he who recites'.

[18]   The full cycle of *zikr* chants as performed in the *khaniqa* are transcribed by Zhou Ji (1999:31–4). The chants, frustratingly, are given only transliterated into Chinese characters.

in the nineteenth century, and its followers have maintained the practice of using musical instruments (including plucked lutes, wind and percussion) to accompany *sama* rituals (Zarcone 2002:537). Again, work remains to be done tracing musical links across borders, but some interesting work has been carried out tracing links between the *hikmät* of Chishtiyya *sama* rituals and the Twelve Muqam (Uyghur: *On Ikki Muqam*), the 'classical' musical suites which are generally regarded as national traditions of the Uyghurs. I will discuss these links further below.

Büwi

Büwi[19] are women ritualists found in almost every Uyghur village who conduct a range of minor home-based life-cycle and healing rituals. They also conduct *sama* rituals similar to the men's, where a single or small group of singers maintain the melodic *hikmät* while the gathered women dance *sama* and give the rhythmic *zikr* chants with a power and energy to match the men's gatherings. The Teräkbagh Khaniqa in Yarkand also contains a separate women's *khaniqa*, but more usually the women's rituals are conducted quite separate from the male world of Sufi lodges, often in private homes, and they do not possess an equivalent hereditary authority. Neither, apparently, have they been drafted into the government apparatus. However, the *büwi* are more numerous than the male Sufi groups, and are still found right across the Xinjiang region, including areas where the more formalised male traditions of Sufi ritual have died out. This may be partly due to the greater levels of secrecy imposed on these women even within Uyghur society. Trebinjac writes of the difficulties of gaining access to women's *zikr* rituals, and of the women begging her 'not to tell their husbands' of their activities (1995:67).

Exclusive to the women is the sung genre known as *monajat*,[20] widely considered by Uyghurs to be very beautiful and associated with grief and mourning. Groups of *büwi* can be found singing them at *mazar* festivals, accompanying themselves with *sapaya* percussion sticks, standing in a small circle, head scarves covering their faces, surrounded by crowds of women pilgrims who often weep as they listen and pile gifts of bread and cloth into the middle of the circle. The *büwi* are also frequently invited to conduct rituals in family homes. Such rituals include Qur'anic recitation (*qira'ät*) and *monajat* songs, and are requested by families who have had some small misfortune or illness, or who simply wish to affirm their religious faith. It is in this context that *büwi* have often fallen foul of local police enforcing the laws on 'illegal religious activities', and have been accused of conducting 'feudal superstition' and extorting money from gullible victims.[21]

---

[19] Literally a form of address to a respected older woman.

[20] 'Prayers of supplication' (During and Mirabdolbaghi 1991:22).

[21] Ildikó Bellér-Hann comments that Uyghur women's religious practices are commonly devalued and regarded as 'superstition' (2001a:15). See also Bellér-Hann's study of Uyghur female ritualists in Kazakhstan (2001b).

In contrast to the *hikmät* of the men's traditions and their relation to the prized *muqam* suites, Zhou Ji's analysis of several dozen recorded *monajat* suggests a diverse regionalised repertoire related to local folk song traditions (Zhou 1999:109). In terms of lyrics, equally, the use of language in the *monajat* draws less on the respected Chagatay literary tradition (*ghazal*) and more on idioms of folk poetry (*beyit*) or everyday speech. The following, composed by Büwi Muzäppärkhan, commemorates her mother:

Example 6.1   *Monajat*[22]

Özi huyluq	Good natured
Yuzi nurluq	Your face full of light
Közingiz cholpangha okhshash	Eyes like the morning star
Boyingizmu bäk pak idi	Your body very clean
Kättingiz uch bu jahandin	You have left this world
Sizge biz qandaq idi	How did we treat you?
Kättingiz kättär idi	You had to leave
Sa'adät khenim januz khenim	Sa'adät, dear lady
Bu makan ärdi khenim	This place is your husband, lady
Kätsing iding sän yighlitar sän	When you left you made us cry
Bäsh balang qandaq idi	How are your five children?
Mundaq turup sän oynisang	Left like this while you play

---

[22]   Sung by Büwi Muzäppärkhan; recorded (2001, Qaraqash) and transcribed by Rachel Harris.

I interviewed Büwi Muzäppärkhan in August 2001. A fine reciter of the Qur'an (learned from her father), and respected ritualist in the local community, she had been arrested several times on charges of feudal superstition, and released only after the intervention of her relatives and payment of fines/bribes. The large number of *büwi*, such as Büwi Muzäppärkhan, who practise across the region of Xinjiang indicates the continuing relevance of their rituals to the Uyghur villagers. Excluded from traditional male power structures such as the Sufi *khaniqa*, these women have simply continued to be marginalised and subject to harassment under the socialist state, in the pursuit of a calling which answers an ongoing need within rural communities.

Sacred and Secular

The majority of the musical styles, instruments and genres described above are not exclusive to the ritual context, and amongst the Uyghurs there is no sense musically in which one could delineate separate genres of 'ritual music'. The pieces played by the *naghra-sunay* bands at the Ordam Mazar are also played at the major Islamic festivals of Qurban and Rozi, in wedding processions where the bands play from the back of an open truck and even, in towns, to celebrate the opening of a new shop. Of course the notion of 'ritual music' in the Islamic context is fundamentally problematic.[23] Genres such as the Sufi *hikmät* and *büwi monajat* are certainly not conceptualised by their practitioners as *musiqa*, which would be most inappropriate to the ritual context, yet stylistically they are closely related to genres which definitely are *musiqa*, such as the *muqam* or local folksong.

The presence of such a wealth of musical activity at the Uyghur shrine festivals is particularly interesting because orthodox Islam forbids the performance of music at funerals or near big tombs, and forbids gatherings and entertainments at these places. As John Baily has pointed out, in Afghanistan one reason given by the Taliban for its ban on music was because the nation was deemed to be in mourning as it continued to suffer under civil war (2001:40; also this volume). In contrast, at the Uyghur shrine festivals many musical forms – not only the purely vocal, such as *hikmät* and *monajat*, which are less likely to be considered to be 'music', but also instrumental pieces (*näghmä*) – are specifically linked to mourning. Perhaps the most famous example is the piece 'Tashway', which is now part of the professional instrumental repertoire. The piece is attributed to a late nineteenth-century *ashiq* named Tashway, a religious mendicant and player of the *rawap* plucked lute, favourite instrument of the Uyghur narrative singers. Tashway is believed to have died in jail under the Qing imperial rule of Xinjiang. Tens of thousands of mourners are said to have attended his funeral, and processed after the body singing this piece. Zhou reports that prior to the 1950s, funeral

---

[23]   See Kristina Nelson's exposition of the '*samā* polemic' in historical and contemporary Arabic sources (2001, Chapter 3).

processions of Sufi adepts were commonly accompanied by groups of Sufi brothers chanting *zikr*, and suggests that the tale of Tashway may be related to this practice (1999:44).

Music and Spiritual Power in Central Asia

In the Central Asian context the ambivalent relationship between Islam and music has been discussed by several ethnomusicologists, in greatest detail in Afghanistan where the debate on the permissibility of music has historically been particularly sharp (Baily 1988, 2001 and this volume, Doubleday 1999, Sakata 1986). Amongst the Uyghurs the situation has historically been rather more relaxed, yet in reports from early twentieth-century Xinjiang one may find both sides of the debate represented in popular thought. One strand of the argument held that the hair of the ass of the Antichrist is made from the strings of musical instruments, which will entice people to follow him on the Day of Judgement; on the other hand, Uyghur musicians defended themselves with the belief that the prophet David was the inventor of music.[24] Contemporary attitudes to musicians are similarly mixed. Often regarded as disreputable and given to drink and drugs, women musicians in particular may be ostracised by the village community.[25] At the same time, prominent singers of the *muqam* have traditionally been treated with great respect. The emergence of a new class of high status, government-employed musicians in the song-and-dance troupes over the last 50 years has given a new gloss of respectability to musicianship, yet a huge gulf separates these people from the village *naghra-sunay* bands or the *ashiq* religious mendicants.

Sakata has argued that 'the notion of music in Afghanistan, like other cultural expression, is inextricably intertwined and based on religious meaning and interpretation' (1986:39). Ted Levin notes that amongst the Uzbeks (and this is also true of the Uyghur), musicians also commonly serve as poets, philosophers, comedians or mullahs. Thus, Levin suggests that for the Uzbeks music not only crosses the boundaries between but actively links the sacred and secular, and he illustrates this with the saying, '*Bir gāh xudāi rasuldan, bir gāh ghamzai usuldan* ["Once for Allah and the Prophet, once for merriment (lit. 'a seductive wink') and dance"]' (1996:63–4).

One of the very few historical sources on music in Xinjiang aside from Chinese imperial records makes clear the broad connection between music and spiritual power. The *History of Musicians* (*Tarikhi Musiqiyun*) was written by Mulla Mojizi

---

[24]   Jarring (1979, Prov.464.12R, Jarring Collection, Lund University Library), quoted in Bellér-Hann (2000:41). Compare such debates with Baily's study of popular attitudes to music in Afghanistan (1988:146–53).

[25]   See for example Sabine Trebinjac's account of the Khotän musician Mänglähkhan (2000:177–9).

in 1854–55 at the request of the Shah of Khotän, Ali Shir Hakim Beg.[26] Written in the style of histories of Sufi lineages (see Baldick 1993), the book contains a series of hagiographies of the famous musicians of Central Asia, going back to Kharz, descendant of Noah, who is regarded as another mythical creator of music, and up to the poet-musicians of the Chagatay era who are attributed as the creators of the *muqam*. The book records many miraculous tales, linking music making with the state of ecstatic union with God. For example, in the biography of Mawlana Sahib Bälikhi (d. 1440), musician at the court of Babur Shah in Kabul, Mojizi records that one day as Bälikhi played *Chol Iraq Muqam* for a *majlis* (festival) at Babur's court, a nightingale alighted on his *tämbur* plucked lute and began to sing, causing the audience to fall into trance and roll on the ground. The people became afraid and they stoned the nightingale to death: when the bird died, Bälikhi died. Mojizi also quotes from al-Farabi, the influential musical theorist: 'If you pray for a hundred years and do not receive abundance, take it from the strings of my *qanun* [zither].'[27] As Light points out, whilst al-Farabi is not well-known amongst scholars of Islamic music philosophy for discussion of music and spirituality, Mojizi's attribution places him firmly in the Central Asian Sufi tradition (1998:317).

The contemporary political ramifications of the impossibility of separating the sacred and the secular are illustrated by a current argument over the Twelve Muqam, the musical suites which are commonly held up as the jewel in the crown of Uyghur national culture. Zhou Ji argues that the *hikmät* sung in the *sama* rituals of the Chishtiyya Sufis in the Khotän region, and the songs of the *ashiq* religious mendicants are closely related musically to the free-metered opening *muqäddimä* section and final *mäshräp* metered dance sections of the Twelve Muqam. In his 1999 book on Uyghur ritual music, Zhou Ji has published transcriptions of part of a Sufi *sama* ritual conducted at the Imam Jafar al-Sadiq Mazar[28] in 1994 in which the *mäshräp* sections of *Rak Muqam* are sung to the accompaniment of *zikr* chants (Zhou 1999:248–66) (see Examples 6.2 and 6.3).

Both of the excerpts presented in Examples 6.2 and 6.3 employ the striking 7/8 rhythm characteristic of sections of the *muqam* and some Uyghur folk songs, and which uses hemiola over an asymmetric or *aqsaq* (limping) rhythm.[29] Although the melody is fitted slightly differently over the rhythm in the first sections of the two versions, they are clearly two renditions of the same piece.

---

[26]   A copy, made in 1919, was found in Khotän in 1950, and has since been translated into modern Uyghur and published in Xinjiang. Excerpts have been translated into English by Nathan Light (1998), and into French by Sabine Trebinjac (2000).

[27]   Translation by Nathan Light (1998:317).

[28]   This shrine, situated near Keriya in southern Xinjiang, is believed by the Uyghurs to be the tomb of the major Islamic saint Imam Jafar al-Sadiq, although he in fact died and was buried in Medina (Bellér-Hann 2000:33).

[29]   See During and Trebinjac's discussion of rhythm in the *muqam* (1991:17–18).

Example 6.2   *Sama* (adapted from the original cipher notation in Zhou 1999:255).

Example 6.3   *Rak Muqam*, first *mäshräp*, sung by Abdulla Mäjnun.[30]

From these examples it appears that the melodies used in Sufi *sama* rituals in the Khotän region, the songs of the *ashiq* mendicants, and the Twelve Muqam tradition are all drawing on the same stock of melody. Of course Zhou Ji's evidence might simply indicate that contemporary Sufi *hapiz* are incorporating the melodies of a well-known but separate *muqam* tradition into their rituals, but interviews with Uyghur musicians gathered by a number of researchers suggest a more complex

---

30   Transposed up a tone for ease of comparison.

historical relationship. Abdurishit, the son of a well-known *muqamchi* Qadirazi Muhämmät (1924–76) told me:

> My father, in order to learn *muqam*, *mäshräp* and many other things, wherever there were *ashiq*, wherever there were dervishes he would go to learn with them … and in that way he learned the full *muqam* – the *ashiq* know the *mäshräp* well.[31]

The Chinese musicologist Wan Tongshu, who made the first transcriptions of the seminal Turdi Akhun recordings of the *muqam* in the 1950s, has suggested that the *mäshräp* sections of the *muqam* originated with the songs of the *ashiq* (Xinjiang Weiwu'er Zizhiqu Wenhuating 1960:21, 54). Nathan Light quotes Qawul Akhun talking about how his father, Turdi Akhun, learnt the *mäshräp*:

> He would go to a *gulxan*, which is a house where they sold meat and tea and smoked *näšä* [hashish] … He went with the intention of learning Mäšräp songs, but they would not let him in if he did not smoke *näšä*. All of the performers were *ašiqs*. (1998:493)

Zhou Ji states that 'since the Middle Ages the development and transmission of the Uyghur Twelve Muqam has been closely related to the rituals of Sufi Islam' (1999:110).

The connection between the Twelve Muqam and the Sufi tradition is equally explicit in many of the lyrics of the Twelve Muqam which display the typical ambiguity of Sufi poetry, in which romantic love may serve as a metaphor for longing for the divine, and drunkenness represents intoxication with the divine. This is most clearly heard in the opening *muqäddimä* sections and the final *mäshräp* sections of the Twelve Muqam, the lyrics of which are mostly drawn from the Chagatay poets, as in the following, which are sung to the first *mäshräp* of *Charigah Muqam*:

> *Yarning köyida män diwanä boldum aqibät Alla*
> *Khälqi aläm aldida Alla biganä boldum aqibät Alla*
>
> *Bir zaman chäktim japa Alla qilargha säbrim qalmidi Alla*
> *Ay yuzning shävqigä Alla pärvanä boldum aqibät Alla*
>
> *Äy yaranlar yaru wäsli Alla meni äyläp dil khuma Alla*
> *Ishtiyaqing käypidä Alla mästanä boldum aqibät Alla*
>
> *Mustisil astanidä Alla mäykhanä boldum aqibät Alla*
> *Khälqi aläm aldida Alla wäyranä boldum aqibät Alla.*

---

[31] Abdurishit Qadirazi, Interview, Almaty, Kazakhstan, July 2003.

My love's flames, I have become a beggar, indeed Allah
Before the whole world I stand alone, indeed Allah

I have suffered for an age, Allah, my patience is ended, Allah
I have become a moth drawn to the beauty of your face, indeed Allah

Oh lovers, your desire, Allah, my heart is addicted, Allah
I revel in your pleasure, Allah, I have become a drunkard, Allah

In the city, Allah, I have become a wine shop boy, indeed Allah
Before the whole world, Allah, I have been ruined, indeed Allah.[32]

In other parts of Central Asia the musical and poetic links between Sufism and the 'classical' *maqam* traditions are well-documented. Writing on Uzbekistan, for example, Djumaev describes how from the sixteenth to the nineteenth centuries, there was a melding of musical genres such that Sufi *sama* rituals assumed new forms and came to incorporate parts of the *maqam* traditions (2002:937). During has also drawn attention to the Sufi roots of sections of the Bukharan *Shashmaqam*, notably the 'limping rhythm' *talqincha* which is based on the rhythms of *zikr* chants (1998a:125). In contemporary Xinjiang, however, the main thrust of political discourse works to obscure these links.

Rewriting the *Muqam*

Since the first recording sessions of the Twelve Muqam, undertaken by the Chinese musicologist Wan Tongshu with the *muqam* master musician Turdi Akhun of Yarkand, soon after the establishment of the People's Republic of China during the years 1951 to 1954, these musical suites have been canonised as the national 'folk classical' (*khaliq kilassik*) music of the Uyghurs. Wan's transcriptions, published in 1960, bore an introduction by Säypidin Azizi, Chairman of the Xinjiang Uyghur Autonomous Region until 1985:

> The 'Twelve Muqam' are a great treasure created through our ancestors – the Uyghur labouring masses – generations of hardship, struggle and experience …
> the reason why they are a treasure is that their content is deep and broad, they contain practically all the Uyghur national artistic forms, and they are a full set of twelve suites. (Xinjiang Weiwu'er Zizhiqu Wenhuating 1960:1–2)[33]

---

[32] Lyrics as sung by Abdulla Mäjnun (2003, track 7), translated by Aziz Isa and Rachel Harris.

[33] Translation from the original Uyghur by the author.

The Twelve Muqam project formed part of the wider Chinese Communist Party's policy of revising and promoting ethnic minority cultural forms according to new standards of 'national' culture. After the hiatus of the Cultural Revolution, the process of 'correctly carrying on' the Twelve Muqam, was resumed in 1978 with the establishment of the Twelve Muqam Research Committee (*On ikki muqam tätqiqat ilmiy jämiyiti*), and consolidated by the establishment in 1989 of the Xinjiang Muqam Ensemble, a troupe which now numbers some 120 musicians and dancers, dedicated to the revision and promotion of the Twelve Muqam. The drawn-out and hotly debated process of canonising the Twelve Muqam has given rise to a series of high profile conferences, publications (OIMTIJ 1992) and recordings (OIMTIJ 1994, 1997, Ministry of Culture 2002), and is still ongoing. It is not within the scope of this chapter to discuss the attempts to fix and order the repertoire, or the musical and stylistic changes wrought by the professional troupes. What is more relevant here are the revised versions of the lyrics performed by the troupes in order to minimise the religious content. A number of strategies were used, among them substituting texts from folk poetry or other historical texts.[34] In April 2003 a group of musicians from the Xinjiang Muqam Ensemble arrived in the UK to give a concert tour organised by Asian Music Circuit. The musicians told me that their programme had been vetted by the Xinjiang Cultural Bureau before they left and that all religious references had been (religiously) excised. It was notable, listening to their performances, how the traditional exclamations of '*Allah!*' had been substituted with '*dostlar!*' ('friends!').[35]

What is interesting in this process is the way in which Uyghur nationalist sentiment chimes with government preference for de-emphasising the religious aspects of traditional art forms in public performance. Zarcone has remarked on the confluence between Uyghur intellectuals and the government in anti-religious propaganda in Xinjiang, noting that whilst government attitudes are rooted in Marxist ideology and Uyghur intellectuals approach religion from a Muslim reformist point of view, these viewpoints converge in their representation of Sufism and Sufi-influenced popular religious practices as 'backward' or 'feudal superstition' (2002:537). The relationship between Sufi rituals, the *ashiq*, and the *muqam* causes considerable conceptual problems for many Uyghur nationalist intellectuals who raise up the *muqam* as the musical symbol of a long and civilised Uyghur culture but denounce the *ashiq* for their creed of *tark-i dunya* ('renouncing the world'), and their practice of performing ritual music and dances under the influence of hashish (ibid.:538).

---

[34]   Djumaev, writing on Soviet Uzbekistan, also notes the substitution of new texts in the *Shashmaqam* where the lyrics were considered too religious (1993:45).

[35]   These professional musicians are familiar with several sets of lyrics. At a private party in London, warmed by several bottles of brandy, the musicians launched into a superb rendition of the *Rak Muqam mäshräp*, interspersed with the traditional exclamations of '*Allah*' and '*Rassulillah*'.

In the field of history, Sufism also comes under attack, blamed by Uyghur nationalists for the downfall of the sixteenth-century Yarkand Khanate which they consider to be the last great Uyghur kingdom. This view of history has been strongly promoted through official culture, notably in the well-known film *Amannisa Khan*, based on a playscript by Chairman Säypidin Azizi. The film follows the life of the wife of Sultan Abdurashid Khan of the Yarkand Khanate, Amannisa Khan, who is attributed with playing a major role in the collection and ordering of the *muqam* in the sixteenth century. The sole historical source on Amannisa Khan is Mojizi's nineteenth-century text *History of Musicians*, yet the contemporary film neatly reverses the emphasis on Sufi mysticism in Mojizi's account and instead portrays Amannisa Khan as defender of the *muqam*, symbol of the Uyghurs' right to sing and dance,[36] against the attacks of the conservative Sufi elements in the Yarkand court who wished to place religious restrictions on music (Light 1998:338). A chance encounter in 2001 with a musician in the town of Yarkand, hometown of Amannisa Khan, is suggestive of the degree to which these views of Sufism and the revised versions of the Twelve Muqam have been internalised by sections of the Uyghur population. In conversation with Yusup Tokhti, an amateur *tämbur* player who had learned to play parts of the *muqam* through the cassette recordings released by the Xinjiang Muqam Ensemble (OIMTIJ 1994), a remark by my companion, the popular composer Yasin Muhpul, on the links between Sufi ritual and the *mäshräp* sections of the *muqam* provoked astonished disbelief and an outpouring of anger against the Sufis and their role in the Yarkand Khanate.

Controlling the Ritual Context

In the People's Republic of China the fate of popular religious activities has, to a certain extent, rested on definitions. The Chinese constitution enshrines the right to religious worship within the framework of the five acknowledged 'systematised religions' of Protestantism, Catholicism, Buddhism, Daoism and Islam. Hand-in-hand with this goes official intolerance of 'illegal religious activities' (*feifa zongjiao huodong*) and 'feudal superstition' (*fengjian mixin*), consistently linked in state propaganda to the 'backward' and 'uncivilised' and to social disorder. In practice, state intervention in ritual practices has ranged from the violent anti-superstition campaigns of the Cultural Revolution period, to more moderate strategies of propaganda and re-education (Anagnost 1994:227). Writing on Xinjiang, Béller-Hann has draw attention to the problematic nature of many popular Islamic ritual practices, such as the rituals of the *büwi*, which fall between classification as 'feudal superstition' and the politically neutral category of local 'folk customs' (*minsu*) (2001a:9).

---

[36]   Representations of singing and dancing ethnic minority peoples are ubiquitous in China's official media and popular culture. See Harris (2004:7–11).

In the case of the shrine festivals, the uneven situation across Xinjiang suggests that local decisions, rather than consistent state intervention, control these events. Zarcone has described attempts by the Xinjiang government to minimise the potential political threat of shrines and pilgrimage through limiting their influence and manipulating their symbolism (1999:234),[37] a strategy which parallels the revision and promotion of the *muqam*. Some of the major pilgrimage sites have been renovated and opened as tourist attractions, charging ticket prices which are too expensive for most locals to afford, and providing written introductions to the site in Uyghur, Chinese and English which offer officially-approved versions of the region's religion and history. This strategy enables the government to demonstrate publicly its support for Islam whilst limiting and controlling aspects of religious practice considered inimical to the state. Such development of tourist sites in Xinjiang may be read as a contesting of the symbolic landscape.[38] An article by Gardner Bovingdon recounts a poignant tale in which a group of young Uyghurs lose their way searching for a shrine and stumble upon a newly-built tourist site commemorating the exploits of the Chinese general Ban Chao (2001:95).

In parts of Xinjiang, local authorities have implemented policies of regulation and support over shrine festivals, ensuring a degree of government control over the activities. Since 1997, the Imam Hasim Mazar festival near Khotän has been regulated by the local government. A new road to the tomb has been built, pilgrims are sold tickets for entry to the festival, and local police oversee security. The festival is officially regarded as an opportunity to promote commerce and tourism, as well as to demonstrate official support for local 'folk customs'. However, in other parts of the region, policy has been more hard-line. As Xinjiang's political situation became increasingly tense during the 1990s, policy towards the shrine festivals became caught up in fears of the spread of Islamic fundamentalism (or Wahhabism)[39] and Uyghur separatism, which are regularly equated with violence and terrorism in government discourses. This issue was undoubtedly instrumental in a ban on the Ordam Mazar festival, imposed in 1997 and still in place at the time of writing. The large-scale *sama* dances performed at the festivals of Rozi and Qurban outside the main mosque in the town of Kashgar have also fallen foul of

---

[37]   Zarcone (1999) discusses the case of the Afaq Khoja Mazar in Kashgar, which Uyghurs venerate as the tomb of the kings of the Khoja dynasty, while Chinese sources refer to it as the tomb of the fragrant concubine (*xiangfei mu*), a princess of the Khoja dynasty who was married to the Chinese emperor, and hence a symbol of the 'unity of the nationalities'.

[38]   See Anagnost's discussion of ritual revival and government attempts to control popular ritual practices in southwest China in terms of a contesting of symbolic space (1994:222).

[39]   The extreme orthodox Wahhabi cult, which originates in Saudi Arabia, has become active in Central Asia in recent years, but the term is used loosely by the Central Asian authorities and media in a manner akin to the use of 'fundamentalist' in the Western media (Rashid 2002:45).

the local authorities' fear of large gatherings, and have not been permitted in recent years, replaced by carefully orchestrated events for middle-school children.[40]

The links made by the authorities between fundamentalism or Wahhabism and shrine pilgrimage are ironic given orthodox Islamic opposition to these popular traditions, and are indicative of the lack of knowledge of local religious customs amongst local officials. For example, the Hizb ut-Tahrir al-Islami (Party of Islamic Liberation), an underground Wahhabi organisation in Uzbekistan, is violently opposed to Sufi activities, especially the tradition of praying at shrines (Rashid 2002:122). In interview in 2001, Rahilä Dawut told me that local newspapers reported in 1999 that 'Wahhabis' had burnt down a shrine in Kashgar where women went to pray for children. In 2000, she encountered a woman at the Imam Hasim Mazar festival preaching to a crowd of curious but non-committal onlookers, telling them that worship of Sufi saints was the worship of human beings and against proper religious teaching.[41]

Elsewhere I have discussed the preoccupation of communist states, and more generally of modern nation states, with order (Harris and Norton 2002). The Xinjiang authorities, sensitive to national perceptions of the region as backward, chaotic and wild, have been particularly concerned with presenting a respectable face to the world at large. Arguably, official opposition to popular forms of religious expression lies as much in the sphere of aesthetics as politics. It is less any real political threat which the shrine festivals might pose, and more the 'disorderly' nature of their sights and sounds – the large crowds, the *naghra-sunay* and the ecstatic rituals of the Sufis – which prove so alarming to the authorities. These expressions – musical and ritual – of alternative forms of power are antithetical to the modernising, totalising mission of the nation state. Political developments in the region over the last decade, sharpened by global developments in recent years, have impelled stronger state efforts at controlling them. Yet revised and re-signified through the efforts of urban Uyghur politicians and musicians, distanced from popular expression, many of the musical forms at the heart of these ritual contexts are strongly promoted by the authorities as emblems of state support for Uyghur national culture. These forms do not supplant but exist side-by-side with the popular contexts and meanings which have persisted, despite varying degrees of political control and attempts at co-option, throughout the period of Chinese Communist Party rule.

---

[40] Dawut, Interview, Ürümchi, July 2001.
[41] Dawut, Interview, Ürümchi, July 2001.

Chapter 7

Jews, Women and the Power to be Heard: Charting the Early Tunisian *Ughniyya* to the Present Day

Ruth F. Davis

Hara Kebira, Djerba, 1978

The year is 1978. It is a midsummer afternoon and a little Jewish girl is celebrating her third birthday in the village of Hara Kebira (lit. 'little Jewish quarter') on the island of Djerba, just off the southeastern coast of Tunisia. Friends and relatives gather in the courtyard of the traditional Arab home; apart from a few infants, they are all women and young girls. The only male presence is the child's uncle, who lives and works in the house. Sweet foods and soft drinks are passed round, the children play with the birthday toys while the older guests, seated on a makeshift arrangement of plastic chairs, chat against the backdrop of Tunisian popular music blasting from a cassette recorder. Birthday candles are lit and blown out, the cake is cut and photos are snapped.[1]

By early evening, the cassette music has stopped and only a few close relatives remain; tentatively, I remind Mme X, reputedly the best singer amongst the Jewish women of Djerba, of her promise to sing.[2] The women draw together in an intimate gathering. The child's uncle emerges from the house with a *darbūka* (vase-shaped pottery drum) and holds it, skin-side down, over burning coals to improve the tone. He accompanies most of the songs while one of Mme X's daughters plays a *tār* (frame drum with jingles); both daughters join in the refrains. The atmosphere is animated and informal as the listeners encourage and prompt the singers.

---

[1]   This chapter is based on three periods of fieldwork: in Hara Kebira, Djerba in 1978, in Tunis in 1982–83, and in Hara Kebira and Tunis on several short visits between 1996 and 2001. My initial fieldwork in Djerba was carried out within the framework of a fieldwork training programme organised by the Free University of Amsterdam, and was funded by a grant from the University of Amsterdam. My fieldwork in Tunisia in 1982–83 was supported by a fellowship from the Social Science Research Council (US) and the American Council of Learned Societies. Subsequent field trips between 1996 and 2001 were supported by the University of Cambridge Travel Fund and research grants from Corpus Christi College Cambridge.

[2]   Mme X and her daughters asked me not to disclose their names.

Mme X assures me she is singing 'traditional Jewish' songs; the women call them '*chansons*' or, in Arabic, '*aghānī*' (sing. *ughniyya*; lit. 'song'[3]). All are in the Tunisian Arabic dialect; some are in *Franco-Arabe*, a mixture of Tunisian Arabic and French. One or two are by local Jewish personalities, including one by Mme X herself in which she laments the departure of her elder son who left Djerba to study medicine in Paris. Most, however, are associated with famous Jewish singers and composers who made their careers in Tunis during the first half of the twentieth century. One song, '*Ou Vous Étiez, Mademoiselle?*' has a special connection with Djerba: it was composed by Gaston Bsiri,[4] a relative of Mme X and uncle of Yaakov Bsiri, the island's chief Jewish musician, for a famous Jewish singer from Tunis called 'Dalel' or 'Dalila'.[5] As the evening draws in, Mme X sings:

> *Ou vous étiez, ou vous étiez, mademoiselle?*
> *Kull yawm asal 'alayki*
> *Oh ma belle, je vous aime*
> *Je deviens fou, ma bayn yiddiki*
> *Ma parole d'un homme, mademoiselle.*

> Where were you, where were you, mademoiselle?
> Every day I ask about you
> Oh my beauty, I love you
> I'm going crazy, in your arms
> My word as a gentleman, mademoiselle.[6]
> (Gaston Bsiri/Mme X, '*Ou Vous Étiez, Mademoiselle?*')

Typically, Mme X's songs are about the trials and tribulations of love and marriage, told from both male and female perspectives: they are based in real life situations and express real life emotions. In a song by Joseph Parientu, a rich Jew

---

[3]   The term *ughniyya* (pl. *aghānī*) is used in Tunisia to designate a type of song, usually in colloquial Arabic, with a strophic structure. The term applies equally to the songs sung on Djerba, those promoted by the Rashidiyya Institute both before and after Tunisian independence in 1956, and those constituting the staple repertory of the Tunisian state radio ensemble since independence (see below).

[4]   Tunisian names tend to be transliterated inconsistently in different sources. In the present article I use the forms used by the individuals concerned, if known. Otherwise I use forms commonly found in Tunisian published sources. When citing from a published source I use the form given.

[5]   '*Ou Vous Étiez Mademoiselle?*' is attributed to Mademoiselle Dalila on VSM, 1932: K 4680. References to VSM, Gramophone and Polyphon discs were provided by the Phonothèque Nationale, Centre des Musiques Arabes et Méditerranéennes, Sidi Bou Saïd, Tunisia.

[6]   I am grateful to Habib Gouja and Kathryn Stapley for their help in transcribing and translating the Tunisian song texts in this study.

from Houmt Souk, the main port and market town of Djerba,[7] the singer mourns the death of his beloved, a Djerban Muslim girl killed by her jealous cousin. In another, '*Ya Ghaliyya*' ('O My Precious One'), a young girl vows to remain faithful to her beloved, despite his many betrayals of her. This song was allegedly imported into Tunis by Jews from Tripolitania in the early years of the twentieth century;[8] it was subsequently recorded by the Tunisian Jewish singer Louisa Tounsia.[9] Other songs portray women who challenge or transgress conventional social roles. In '*Ma Nhabbshi N'aris*' ('I Don't Want to Get Married'), also sung by Louisa Tounsia, a young girl refuses to marry, insisting that she is better off remaining unattached and free in her father's home.[10] In '*Qalaqt w Mallit*' ('I'm Troubled and Fed Up'), by the Jewish singer-composer Cheikh El Afrit, a husband complains about his neglectful and indifferent wife, who has made his life a misery.[11]

Two weeks later, I attend the penultimate night of wedding celebrations in the groom's home. Yaakov Bsiri, Mme X's cousin, has been hired to sing Arabic songs accompanied by a band of Muslim and Jewish musicians.[12] The courtyard is filled with tables laden with steaming dishes, wine and *bucha* (fig spirits). The men and boys sit at the tables, while the women and girls are pressed against the walls on three sides. On a dais at the far end of the courtyard, the musicians sit in a semicircle around a table laden with *bucha* and beer. The band, which is amplified, comprises four men playing violin, accordion, *darbūka* and *tār*, with Bsiri accompanying himself on the *'ūd*. He begins each sequence of songs with an elaborate vocal improvisation in free rhythm, called *mawwal*, and the rest of the band join in the refrains. Amidst the stream of songs I recognise some that were sung by Mme X at her niece's birthday party, including Bsiri's version of '*Ou Vous Étiez, Mademoiselle?*'[13]

> *Ou étiez vous, ou étiez vous, ou étiez vous, mademoiselle?*
> *Kull yawm asal 'alayki*
> *Je vous aime, oh ma belle*
> *Je veux bientôt, ma bayn yiddiki*
> *Ma parole pour tu, mademoiselle.*

---

[7] Houmt Souk is about one and a half kilometres from Hara Kebira.

[8] This was confirmed by the Tunisian musicologist Salah el-Mahdi and various other Muslim musicians.

[9] Gramophone, 1945, catalogue number K4957.

[10] Gramophone, 1945, catalogue number K4921.

[11] Polyphon, 1935, catalogue number 45 885.

[12] Large-scale emigration of Tunisian Jews, which occurred in the aftermath of the creation of the state of Israel in 1948, Tunisian independence in 1956 and the Arab-Israeli war of 1967, had depleted the island of Jewish musicians. As a result, Djerban Muslims were normally invited to make up the band when Arabic songs were performed. In the present example, the accordion and violin were played by Muslims.

[13] Reproduced on Bchiri (2001:Track 18).

Where were you, where were you, mademoiselle?
Every day I ask about you
I love you, oh my beauty
I want soon [to be] in your arms
My word for you, mademoiselle.
(Gaston Bsiri/Yaakov Bsiri, '*Ou Vous Étiez, Mademoiselle?*')

I had first heard Bsiri sing at the celebrations for the Jewish festival of Lag b'Omar at the island's main synagogue known as the Ghriba (lit. 'stranger', 'lonely one') on the outskirts of Hara Sghira (lit. 'small Jewish quarter'), some seven kilometres inland from Hara Kebira. Each year, in late spring, pilgrims from mainland Tunisia and beyond gather at the miraculous synagogue, whose foundations are believed to contain relics from King Solomon's Temple, to celebrate the death of the second century Cabbalist Rabbi Shimon Bar Yochai. On this occasion, the Ghriba serves as a substitute for the actual tomb of Bar Yochai who was buried in Meron in Northern Israel.[14] The two-day celebrations provide a major commercial opportunity for the island's Muslims and Jews alike. The newly constructed hotels along Djerba's *zone touristique* are filled with Jews from Djerba and elsewhere in Tunisia who have emigrated to Israel and France, and the courtyard of the *fonduk* (caravanserai) adjacent to the synagogue, where the humbler pilgrims stay, is transformed into a holiday camp and bazaar. Streamers bearing Tunisian flags, huge portraits of President Bourguiba posted on the walls and a conspicuous array of policemen all serve to lend the occasion the character of a national holiday.

In the heat of the afternoon, a golden wagon bearing a five-tiered, hexagonal pyramid decorated with hundreds of candle holders is wheeled into the empty courtyard. As the crowd emerges from the midday siesta, two men playing *bendir* and *tār* mount the wagon while a small group of musicians playing *bendir*, *tār* and *darbūka*, led by Yaakov Bsiri on the *'ūd*, congregate below (see Figures 7.1 and 7.2). The crowd presses close. Someone tosses a coloured silk shawl to the *bendir* player on the wagon who makes as though to auction it. Cries of '*trois dinars*', '*cinq dinars*', and so on, rise above the crowd. At the highest bid, the musicians strike into tune, singing Hebrew songs, or *piyyutim*, the players on the wagon pivot around waving and beating their instruments, the *bendir* player flourishes the shawl and glasses of *bucha* are passed round. The shawl is draped over the wagon and a new one is offered for 'auction'.[15] By early evening, the wagon is completely covered with motley shawls. On the first day, it is wheeled into the Ghriba, the shawls are removed and the holders filled with burning candles. On the second day, the wagon, decked with shawls, is wheeled in a procession led by the

---

[14]   For detailed accounts of the Ghriba rituals and their significance see Udovitch and Valensi (1984:123–31) and, for their musical content, Davis (forthcoming).

[15]   The money thus raised is offered to the Ghriba and helps support the old men who spend their days studying and praying there.

Figure 7.1   Yaakov Bsiri singing *piyyutim* at the Ghriba celebrations, May 1978 (photograph by Ruth F. Davis).

Figure 7.2   Yaakov Bsiri addresses the crowd from the shawl-covered wagon at the Ghriba celebrations, May 1978 (photograph by Ruth F. Davis).

musicians, singing *piyyutim*, down the hill to Hara Sghira, where it comes to a rest in the courtyard of a synagogue. The musicians continue their singing until finally, the rabbi closes the proceedings with a speech in praise of President Bourguiba.

The following week, I record Yaakov singing his own selection of songs in the privacy of his home in Hara Kebira. He sings *piyyutim*, including some he sang at the Ghriba, accompanying himself on the *'ūd*. One such song, '*Shalom Nassim B'Eretz*' ('Let There be Peace in the Land'), adopts the tune of the popular Arabic song '*Andik Bahriyya, Ya Rais*' ('You Have Sailors, O Captain'). This song is generally associated with the well-known Lebanese singer Wadi el-Safi, whose version was frequently heard on Tunisian radio at the time.[16] According to Bsiri, however, '*Andik Bahriyya, Ya Rais*' was composed in Tunis in the 1920s by his uncle Gaston for the celebrated Tunisian Jewish singer Habiba Msika. Yaakov's story is endorsed by the Tunisian journalist and playwright Hamadi Abassi who describes Msika sitting cross-legged, dressed as a sailor, singing '*Andik Bahriyya, Ya Rais*' to rapturous audiences in the Municipal Theatre of Tunis (2000:11).[17] Another *piyyut*, '*Goeli Ya*' ('The Lord is my Redeemer'), is traditionally sung on the Sabbath and other religious holidays when the Torah is taken out of the ark and carried in a procession around the synagogue. This *piyyut* adopts the tune of Louisa Tounsia's song '*Ya Ghaliyya*' ('O Precious One'), sung by both Mme X at her niece's birthday party and Yaakov Bsiri and his band at the wedding celebrations.[18]

My visit to Djerba followed in the footsteps of the comparative musicologist from Berlin, Robert Lachmann, who made the first recordings on the island with an Edison phonograph in the spring of 1929. Lachmann focused his research on Hara Sghira, reputedly the older and holier of the two Jewish communities. Whereas Hara Kebira is associated with the Jewish migrations from Spain from the twelfth to the seventeenth centuries CE, the inhabitants of Hara Sghira trace their legendary origins to the exile of the Jews following the destruction of King Solomon's Temple in 586 BCE.[19] Hara Sghira's reputation for holiness is reflected in the extreme attitude of its rabbis towards musical instruments. While prohibitions on their use apply throughout Judaism, particularly on the Sabbath and religious holidays, in Hara Sghira, the mere presence of musical instruments is forbidden; thus Lachmann's 22 wax cylinder recordings are entirely vocal. In addition to examples of liturgical cantillation and *piyyutim*, sung exclusively by men, Lachmann's recordings include seven songs in the Judeo-Arabic dialect,

---

[16]   For music and text transcriptions comparing the Hebrew and Arabic versions, see Davis (1986:139–42).

[17]   I explore the complex performance history of '*Andik Bahriyya, Ya Rais*' in Davis 2009.

[18]   For music and text transcriptions comparing the Hebrew and Arabic versions, see Davis (1986:137–8, 2002:529–31).

[19]   A more modest version of the legend substitutes the exile following the destruction of the Second Jerusalem Temple by the Romans in 70 CE.

based on biblical and other themes relating to the lives of Jewish women; these songs were sung exclusively by women.[20]

Fifty years later, in Hara Kebira, men still sang *piyyutim*, both in and outside the synagogue, on religious holidays and other occasions considered holy such as the last night of wedding celebrations, after the ceremony. However, no-one could recall a distinctive repertory corresponding to Lachmann's Judeo-Arabic songs, sung exclusively by women. In the gatherings and celebrations that I attended, both men and women sang a similar repertory of secular songs in colloquial Tunisian Arabic called simply *chansons* or *aghānī*. Typically, these songs derived not from Djerba, but were associated rather with the popular, commercial repertory of well-known Jewish professional singers and composers active in Tunis during the latter decades of the French Protectorate. Their melodies sometimes reappeared in religious contexts set to Hebrew texts, as *piyyutim*.

In the following pages I chart my encounters with the early Tunisian *ughniyya* through two further periods of fieldwork: in Tunis, from 1982 to 1983, and on several brief visits to Tunis and Hara Kebira between 1996 and 2001. Born in the bars, cafés and music theatres of Tunis around the turn of the twentieth century, in a commercial musical environment dominated by Jews, the *ughniyya* was fostered by the early recording industry, eventually to become its favoured genre. In contrast to the traditional Tunisian art music repertory, called *ma'lūf*, whose public performance was confined to men, the principal exponents of the *ughniyya* included women who danced and sang, unveiled, to male audiences. In the 1930s, on the tide of the burgeoning nationalist movement, the Jewish-dominated culture of the *ughniyya* was subjected to hostile criticism by a predominantly Muslim, bourgeois musical public. The critics sought both to elevate the social and moral standing of public music making and, at the same time, to promote a more authentic 'Tunisian' musical culture, based on the *ma'lūf*. In November 1934, their goals were realised with the founding in Tunis of the Rashidiyya Institute, a non-commercial, government-funded music academy devoted to conserving and promoting the *ma'lūf* and encouraging high standards of new composition.[21]

After Tunisian independence in 1956, the Rashidiyya's project was taken up by the Ministry of Culture. As the contemporary mass media followed pan-Arab musical trends, the *ma'lūf* was officially designated the 'national' musical heritage and the early *ughniyya*, with its cosmopolitan associations, was denigrated by the entire musical establishment as decadent and corrupt;

---

[20] Lachmann's study based on his research on Djerba was first published posthumously in an incomplete English translation in 1940 (not all of the transcriptions were included). The complete work was subsequently published in the original German, edited by Edith Gerson-Kiwi (Lachmann 1978).

[21] The new institution was named after the eighteenth-century Ottoman patron and amateur of the *ma'lūf*, Muhammad al-Rashid Bey of Tunis. For a full account of the Rashidiyya's work and influence from its founding to the present day, see Davis 2004: 61–70, 71–4, 93–4, 96–102, 108–10.

in contrast, the *aghānī* promoted by the Rashidiyya before independence were hailed as popular classics. Meanwhile, mass emigration of Jews following the political upheavals of the mid-twentieth century and the ensuing Arab-Israeli wars, had depleted the country of its Jewish musicians.[22] By the late 1970s, when I first visited Djerba, the small Jewish community that remained were perpetuating a musical repertory elsewhere regarded as obsolete.

Following the *coup d'état* of 1987, known as *al-Taghrir* ('The Change'), the early *ughniyya* enjoyed a popular revival, prompting a reappraisal of previous attitudes. Marginalised by the musical establishment for over three decades, the artists and their songs became subjects of scholarly studies, popular biographies and CD compilations. Meanwhile, live performances of the subaltern repertory came to be associated with a radical group of all-female instrumentalists and singers called El 'Azifet (lit. 'the female instrumentalists'). In the light of these developments I argue that, far from constituting an aberration, as portrayed by the Rashidiyya and the post-Independence musical establishment, the early *ughniyya* is rooted linguistically, thematically and structurally in traditional Tunisian popular song; and that in their predilection for Egyptian modes and rhythms, the mixing of Western and Arab instrumental timbres and intonation, and the use of women's voices, the early Jewish pioneers of the *ughniyya* laid the musical foundations for subsequent developments in Tunisian popular song, through the twentieth century to the present day.

'*L'Âge de Décadence*': Perspectives from Tunis in the Early 1980s

In the early 1980s, I returned to Tunisia to research the Arab Andalusian tradition known as *ma'lūf*. When I played my Djerba recordings to musicians, journalists, cultural officials and other members of the musical establishment, in Tunis and elsewhere, they invariably spoke disparagingly of the secular Arabic songs. Many distanced themselves from the entire musical culture with which these songs were associated, referring to this as '*l'âge de décadence*'. Some expressed surprise that such songs were still current among the Jews of Djerba. Their attitude was underpinned by the official narrative outlined by Salah el-Mahdi in his book, co-authored with Muhammad Marzuqi (1981), on the Rashidiyya Institute, the first public, secular organisation devoted to Tunisian music. According to this narrative, Tunisian music during the 1920s and 1930s was in a state of decadence and decline. This had been caused in the first place by an unprecedented vogue for Egyptian and other Middle Eastern music,[23] imported to the capital by visiting celebrities since the early years of the twentieth century and promoted by the emerging record

---

[22] See footnote 12.

[23] Throughout this chapter, I use the term 'Middle Eastern' in the sense corresponding to the Tunisian *sharqiyya* and *orientale*, terms used to differentiate the music of Egypt and the surrounding Levant from that of Tunisia (*musiqa tunisiyya* or *musique tunisienne*).

market. Increasingly, Tunisian musicians were abandoning their own traditions and imitating the Egyptians, not only in their music but also in their dress and dialect (el-Mahdi and Marzuqi 1981:23–2, Farza n.d.:12, Shakli 1994:52–5, Moussali 1992:5–6). At the same time, the introduction of commercial recording in Tunis was encouraging the production of a new, inferior type of Tunisian song, characterised by trivial, vulgar and linguistically corrupt texts. Particularly deplorable, according to el-Mahdi, were those that degraded the Arabic language by mixing it with French (1981:25). Echoing el-Mahdi, Muhammad al-Saqanji criticises the songs of the time for their use of colloquial or 'relaxed' Arabic, their lightweight themes and their bacchic and erotic character (1986:16–24, cited in Moussali 1992:8–9). Similarly, Guettat describes how the corruptive influence of the record industry extended to the musicians themselves, 'a class of opportunists whose depraved behaviour and financial greed dragged the art of music and the status of the musician into a deplorable situation' (2000:238).

Professional musical activity in the early decades of the twentieth century was relegated primarily to Jews and to Muslims of low social status, typically barbers and other members of the lower artisan classes, who were generally considered to be of dubious moral standing. According to Sahli, 'the only people who got involved with music were those lacking all moral character and a few Jews, who monopolized the artistic milieu' (1975:25, quoted in Jones 1987:73). Typical public venues included music halls and theatres, traditional Arab cafés, bars and special *cafés chantants*, where audiences watching staged performances, seated in rows, were served drinks by waiters called *qahwaji* (lit. 'coffee server'; Shakli 1994:324–5). Muslims of higher social and moral repute generally confined their musical activities either to the *zwaya* (meeting places of Sufi brotherhoods), where the *ma'lūf* was cultivated alongside sacred musical repertories, or to the privacy of their homes.[24] Women were even more restricted than men. According to Jones,

> ... the only legitimate sphere of musical activity [for a woman] was within her husband's or father's guarded walls ... If a woman wanted to practise music professionally in public she would have to forfeit the comforts of family and respectability and accept the opprobrium dealt by orthodox and popular attitudes that failed to distinguish between singers and prostitutes. (1987:73)

Jewish women tended to be less confined socially than their Muslim counterparts, and whilst Muslim women did perform, it was Jewish women who, according to Shakli, provided the mainstay of professional female singers from the beginning of the twentieth century. Women were never engaged as instrumentalists and even for a Jewish woman, singing in public was considered undesirable: those who did so were for the most part driven by financial need (Shakli 1994:296). The legendary Jewish composer-singer Cheikh El Afrit reputedly forbade his sister to sing in the home for fear that she might eventually decide to pursue a career as a

---

[24]   See Davis (2004:6–7, 42–3) for descriptions of *ma'lūf* performances in the *zwaya*.

singer (Chaabouni 1991:26, cited in Shakli 1994:297). Female singers frequently doubled as dancers, a fact which doubtless contributed to their dubious reputation (Shakli 1994:297, Rizgui 1967:63). Rizgui describes certain bars in Tunis where prostitutes were hired to dance and sing, accompanied by bands of Jewish musicians, in order to encourage clients to drink (1967:96). The bars themselves were run by Jews who effectively monopolised the alcohol business at the time (Shakli 1994:307).

Continuing his narrative, el-Mahdi recounts how, in response to these conditions, Tunisian youth in particular reacted in defence of their traditional music, whose very identity appeared to be under threat, and how the great shaykhs of the *ma'lūf* rallied to the cause, turning their homes into private music clubs and schools. These grassroots efforts resonated with the activities of the patron and scholar of Arab music, Baron Rodolphe d'Erlanger, who turned his palace on the outskirts of Tunis into a centre of musical activity and research, and with the work of the International Congress of Arab Music held in Cairo in 1932, to which Tunisia sent a delegation.[25] They culminated, at the end of 1934, with the founding of the Rashidiyya Institute, aimed at both conserving and promoting traditional Tunisian music and encouraging high standards of Tunisian composition. Modelled on the idea of the Western conservatory (its immediate model was the French music conservatory founded in Tunis in 1896), the Rashidiyya set out not only to rescue Tunisian music but equally, to elevate the social status of musical activity. Presided over by the Mayor of Tunis and subsidised by the government of the Protectorate, the Rashidiyya provided for the first time in Tunisia a public secular environment where both amateur and professional musicians, regardless of gender, religion or social class, could participate without loss of dignity and respect.[26]

At the heart of the Rashidiyya's enterprise was its eponymous ensemble. Modelled in part on contemporary Egyptian ensembles, the Rashidiyya introduced a revolutionary new line-up for Tunisian music which essentially comprised an all-male instrumental section of several violins, one or two cellos, one or two double basses, various Arab melody instruments and percussion, and a separate chorus of male and female voices. Emulating the Western symphony orchestra, the instrumentalists played from notation and the ensemble was led by a conductor with a baton. With its regular rehearsal and concert schedule, including fortnightly public concerts on Saturday afternoons in the courtyard of the Institute, the Rashidiyya played a significant role in raising the social status of musical

---

[25]   The five members of d'Erlanger's *ma'lūf* ensemble, comprising *'ūd 'arbī*, *rabāb*, *naqqārāt*, *tār* and solo falsetto voice, were escorted to Cairo by the Syrian Shaykh 'Ali al-Darwish. For further details of the delegation and the effect of their participation on subsequent developments in Tunisian music, see Davis (1993:139–40, 2004:47–8).

[26]   The Rashidiyya included Jews and European Christians among its members. As discussed below, with rare exceptions, women were confined to singing roles, either as soloists or in the chorus.

performance. In the words of Muhammad Triki, the first leader of the ensemble, '*nous y allons ... comme à la mosquée*' (Guettat 2000:241–2).

The Rashidiyya focused its efforts on the *ma'lūf*. As Tunisia's most prestigious continuously surviving indigenous repertory, patronised by both the Ottoman aristocracy and Sufi brotherhoods, the *ma'lūf* was considered equivalent in social, historical, artistic and intellectual status to the Western classical tradition. It derived moral legitimacy, moreover, from being the only secular repertory admitted into the *zwaya*. In the heady nationalist climate of the time, the Rashidiyya promoted the *ma'lūf* both as an emblem of Tunisian musical identity and as the inspiration, if not the model, for the new Tunisian compositions performed by the ensemble. In contrast to the songs of the *ma'lūf*, which used literary Arabic interspersed with Tunisian dialect, the new songs – or *aghānī* – promoted by the Rashidiyya, generally adopted the various dialects of rural and urban Tunisia. And while the *ma'lūf* was sung by the chorus throughout, the new songs featured solo vocalists who were predominantly Muslim women. The first such soloist was the music theatrical star Chafia Rochdi, the only woman among the founding members of the ensemble. Rochdi was subsequently joined and eventually succeeded by some of the most popular media artists of the day including Fathiya Khayri, Oulaya, Na'ama and, most celebrated of all, the legendary Salayha, who replaced Rochdi as lead singer of the ensemble in 1941. Thereafter, Salayha sang exclusively for the Rashidiyya in return for a monthly retainer and free lodgings until her death in 1958.

For musicians, music journalists and the wider musical public of Tunis in the early 1980s, the artists associated with the Rashidiyya in the last two decades of the Protectorate represented the golden era of modern Tunisian song. Their names were recalled with nostalgia, their performances eulogised, and their songs received regular exposure on radio broadcasts and in live concerts given by the Rashidiyya and other major state ensembles. In contrast, for the Jews of Djerba it was the generation of Jewish singers and composers whose careers preceded, and in some cases ran parallel with, the Rashidiyya, which occupied a comparable status. From the perspective of the musical mainstream, the Jews of Djerba were caught in a time-warp. Uniquely, it seemed, this small island community was continuing to cultivate a repertory which elsewhere had been discredited and discarded as obsolete.

Perspectives Following 'The Change'

On 7 November 1987, 31 years after leading Tunisia to independence, President Habib Bourguiba was succeeded in a bloodless coup by Zine El Abidine Ben 'Ali. This landmark event, known as *al-Taghrir* ('The Change'), brought in its wake a gradual dissolution of the nationalist agendas of the previous regime, opening the way for more inclusive concepts of Tunisian cultural identity. A newfound nostalgia for the artistic and cultural expressions of the French Protectorate led, in the years immediately following 'The Change', to the revival and rehabilitation of musical repertories previously considered 'decadent'. This development was manifested in the reissuing of vintage recordings (both on locally produced cassettes and on internationally produced CDs, replete with liner notes), the emergence of a popular, journalistic and largely biographical literature, as well as various scholarly initiatives. Among the latter were Mourad Shakli's groundbreaking study of the Tunisian *ughniyya* (popular song) (1994), Bernard Moussali's research on the first decades of sound recording in Tunisia (1992), and other studies associated with the international inaugural conference of the Centre des Musiques Arabes et Méditerranéennes in Sidi Bou Saïd, near Tunis, in 1992.

At the forefront of the musical revival was the radical all-female ensemble El 'Azifet. Dubbed the first ensemble of its kind in Tunisia and the Arab world, El 'Azifet was founded in 1992 by the award-winning violinist Amina Srarfi, daughter of the eminent composer and former lead violinist of the Rashidiyya, Kaddur Srarfi (d.1977) and founder, in 1988, of the first officially recognised private music conservatory in Tunis. Srarfi acknowledges in our conversations that her projects are motivated by a mission to overturn entrenched gender roles; she describes El 'Azifet as her personal response to the fact that, despite enjoying equal educational opportunities in the state music conservatories, where their achievements equal and even exceed those of their male counterparts, female instrumentalists continue to be virtually excluded from participation in professional ensembles, including the major state-sponsored ensembles established since independence.

El 'Azifet is a showcase ensemble comprising some 12 to 15 conservatory-trained women, many of whom hold university degrees and pursue professions outside music. Dressed in regional costume, they play traditional Arab melody instruments and percussion, violins and bass, sometimes with piano; the instrumentalists double as chorus and, in keeping with El 'Azifet's primary focus on instrumental performance, there is no solo voice. Promoted by state institutions such as the Ministries of Culture and Tourism and the Municipality of Tunis, the ensemble performs in gala concerts and festivals throughout Tunisia and has made numerous trips abroad. Paradoxically, in view of the ensemble's radical agenda, to the mainstream political establishment El 'Azifet represents not so much a challenge to conventional social norms as a tribute to Tunisia's enlightened, progressive stance towards women. In 1993, in recognition of her various musical initiatives, culminating in El 'Azifet, Amina Srarfi was awarded the title Officier du Mérite Culturel by President Zine El Abidine Ben 'Ali.

Srarfi specialises in the various repertories with which her father, Kaddur Srarfi, was associated throughout his professional life. In addition to the *ma'lūf* and the new songs promoted by the Rashidiyya under the Protectorate, these include the songs Srarfi performed in his formative years in the 1920s and 1930s (the so-called '*âge de décadence*') when he was apprenticed to ensembles of Jewish musicians. Thus, El 'Azifet's programmes draw from the same pool of 'traditional Jewish' songs as were sung by Yaakov Bsiri and Mme X on Djerba. Among Amina's favourites are songs of the Jewish singer-composer Cheikh El

Afrit, those of the tragic Jewish diva Habiba Msika,[27] and those she describes as '*chansons franco-tunisiennes*'. Associated primarily with Jewish musicians, the latter mirror the practice common among Arabic-speaking urban populations during the Protectorate of colouring their speech with French. When applied to song lyrics, as in Gaston Bsiri's '*Ou Vous Étiez, Mademoiselle?*', this Franco-Arabic dialect was considered by doyens of the Rashidiyya as the ultimate linguistic corruption. Yet *chansons franco-tunisiennes* were also composed by Muslims, including some who, like Kaddur Srarfi, were later to become leading lights of the Rashidiyya. '*Vous Dansez Madame*' by Muhammad Triki, the original leader of the Rashidiyya and one of its most distinguished composers, is a staple of El 'Azifet's programmes:

> *Vous dansez madame*
> *Vous dansez monsieur*
> *Ana nghanni bi chant*
> *Je suis amoreux.*
>
> *Anoreux f'ir raqs*
> *Ma'a madame gentille*
> *Son mari thibb tqullu non cheri*
> *Nurqus 'al-angham*
> *Permettez monsier.*
>
> *Vous dansez madame ...*

You dance, madame
You dance, monsieur
I am singing a song
I am in love.

Dancing amorously
With a nice lady

She wants to call her husband 'my darling'
We dance to the melodies.

You dance, madame ...
(Srarfi/Triki, '*Vous Dansez Madame*')[28]

---

27 Habiba Msika died in 1939, burned alive whilst asleep in her house, which was set alight by a jealous lover.

28 El 'Azifet (n.d. [1998]:Track 3).

In recent years, Amina Srarfi has extended the ensemble's repertoire to include songs from the *turāth al-sha'biyya* (lit. 'popular heritage'), traditional anonymous songs in colloquial Tunisian Arabic, passed down within families from one generation to the next. The linguist Kathryn Stapley suggests that, in their use of colloquial Arabic, their thematic content reflecting real-life emotions and experiences, and their strophic/refrain structure, the *turāth al-sha'biyya* songs may be considered forerunners of the commercial popular songs of the early twentieth century such as were sung by Yaakov Bsiri and Mme X on Djerba.[29]

In a recent article on Tunisian women musicians, Laurel Lengel focuses on a category of *turāth al-sha'biyya* which she describes as 'resistance songs' (2004:225). Traditionally sung at all-female gatherings celebrating the various wedding rituals for the bride, such songs present the downside of conventional marital life and its relationships (for example, the jealous husband, the vicious mother-in-law) from the woman's point of view. As Lengel observes, these songs provide a safe medium though which women have traditionally expressed resistance, or *nushuz* (lit. 'rebellion') to their subservient position in marriage and society at large (2004:214ff.). In '*Amati*' ('Slave Woman'), introduced by Lengel in the context of the *lutiyya* (henna ceremony), where it is sung by the bride's female relatives as they apply henna to her hands and feet, a young girl refuses the hand of her jealous suitor. Transferred to the concert stage by El 'Azifet, '*Amati*' is clearly related thematically to Gaston Bsiri's '*Ma Nhabbhsi N'aris*' ('I Don't Want to Get Married'), recorded by Louisa Tounsia[30] and sung by both Yaakov Bsiri and Mme X on Djerba.

> Why do you have to feel jealous?
> Do you think I am your slave?
> Don't follow me around
> I don't want to be connected to you
> I don't want to be related to you
> And so go away, leave me alone.
>
> I don't want you, you're a jealous man
> I don't want to marry a jealous man
> You always accuse me
> I'm not promiscuous.
> (Srarfi, '*Amati*' [extracts]; cited in Lengel 2004:213).[31]
>
> *Ma nhabbshi n'aris ma nhabbsh nitjawwiz*
> *Ma nhabbshi rajul yahkum fiyya ...*

---

[29] Personal communication, July 2005. See also Stapley 2002.
[30] Gramophone, 1945: K4921.
[31] Lengel does not provide the Arabic text.

Fayn nimshi y'amil assas
Bi-rigadi was sarabu l-'aysuyya
La la ma nhabbshi rajul yahkum fiyya ...

I don't want to get married. I don't want to get married
I don't want a man telling me what to do ...

Wherever I go he'll have people watching me
Ten policemen and the commander
No, no, I don't want a man telling me what to do ...
(Gaston Bsiri/Yaakov Bsiri, '*Ma Nhabbhsi N'aris*' [extract])[32]

Musical Genesis of the *Ughniyya al-Tunisiyya*

Dismissed by the Rashidiyya and the post-independence musical establishment as an era of decadence and decline, the early decades of the twentieth century emerge, in the light of their repertory's renewed popularity, as the formative period of the *ughniyya al-tunisiyya* (*chanson tunisienne* or Tunisian popular song). It was during these decades, when professional musical activity was dominated by Jews, that the female solo vocalist acquired a status in performance equivalent to that of her male counterpart, while the use of Middle Eastern modes and rhythms, and the practice (so deplored by purists of the Rashidiyya) of combining Western instruments of fixed pitch with traditional Arab ones, were established as standard features of the genre that was to dominate Tunisian professional musical activity until the present day.[33]

In his pioneering study of the *ughniyya al-tunisiyya*, Shakli describes it as 'a short strophic song with lines of regular metre and a refrain' (1994:17). It is the refrain, recurring each time to the same melody, that, he contends, is the defining feature of the genre, distinguishing it from the *muwashshah*, the principal poetic genre of the *ma'lūf*.[34] Like the *ma'lūf*, the Tunisian *ughniyya* is based on a system of melodic modes called *maqāmāt* (sing. *maqām*) and rhythmic-metric cycles with

---

[32] Reproduced on Bchiri (2001:Track 16).

[33] Shakli observes that 'in Tunisia, the *ughniyya* is apparently if not the sole, then at least the most important area of musical production and consumption of the twentieth century' (1994:17).

[34] See Davis (2004:6) for a description of the musical structure of the *muwashshah*. Tunisian scholars generally describe the Tunisian *ughniyya* as derived from the *fūndū* (pl. *funduwwāt*; lit. 'joyous'), a type of 'semi-classical' song associated with the *ma'lūf*. Originating in the late nineteenth century, *funduwwāt* are also characterised by a couplet/refrain structure. Unlike the *ughniyya*, however, the *fūndū* is typically based on the *maqāmāt* of the *ma'lūf*; the individual couplets are generally in different *maqāmāt*, and they are separated by elaborate vocal improvisations called *'arūbī* (Shakli 1994:180–81).

distinctive patterns of accentuation called *iqā'āt* (sing. *iqā'*). In contrast to the major and minor scales of Western music, based on tones and semitones, the *maqāmāt* include, in addition to these, intervals of approximately three quarters of a tone falling at variable degrees between the two. The traditional Tunisian *maqāmāt* and *iqā'āt* are those of the 13 *nūbāt* (large-scale vocal suites) that constitute the core repertory of the *ma'lūf*; also included are four additional *maqāmāt*, believed to represent 'incomplete' *nūbāt*.[35] From the eighteenth century onwards, however, *muwashshaḥat* representing Turkish and other Middle Eastern *maqāmāt* and *iqā'āt* were absorbed anonymously into the *ma'lūf* under Ottoman influence. The new songs were generally performed independently of the *nūbāt* in smaller song cycles called *waslāt* (sing. *wasla*, lit. 'chain'). Thus, the emulation of Middle Eastern music by Tunisian composers in the early twentieth century was no new phenomenon, but rather an expansion and continuation of a pre-existing trend. It was rather the unprecedented intensity, scope and degree of that emulation, its association with a new commercial musical culture centred on the emerging genre of *ughniyya* and, to top it all, the concurrent neglect of the traditional repertory, that together the traditionalists found so unacceptable.

By the mid-1930s, when the Rashidiyya embarked on its mission to re-establish the *ma'lūf* as the foundation for new Tunisian composition, the use of Egyptian *maqāmāt* and *iqā'āt* had become entrenched amongst Tunisian composers. The predominantly long, slow *iqā'āt* of the *nūbāt* made scant inroads into the *ughniyya*, essentially conceived for dancing.[36] And while the Rashidiyya's efforts to promote the traditional Tunisian *maqāmāt* met with more success, their revival by no means displaced the use of Middle Eastern *maqāmāt* among even the most dedicated of the Rashidiyya's composers. Both the ensemble's original chorus master and most distinguished composer, Shaykh Khemais Tarnane (d.1966), and its original leader, Muhammad Triki, composed in Egyptian *maqāmāt* for the ensemble, as did subsequent leaders such as Salah el-Mahdi, Abdelhamid Belalgia and Muhammad Sa'ada.

Middle Eastern *maqāmāt* and *iqā'āt* have continued to dominate the Tunisian *ughniyya* to the present day. According to Shakli, they constitute 'the natural medium of expression for Tunisian composers, and the melodic universe in which singers feel most at ease' (1994:139–40). Apparently, 90 per cent of the songs recorded by the radio ensemble[37] since the early 1970s are based on Egyptian

---

[35]   See Davis (1996:426, 428–9 and 2004:5, 13–15) for discussion and illustration of the *iqā'āt* and *māqāmat* of the *ma'lūf*.

[36]   Exceptions are the relatively fast duple *barwal* and *dkhul barwal* (Shakli 1994:90). Tunisian folk rhythms, traditionally associated with dancing, were also used in the early *ughniyya* and remain popular today (ibid.:87). Shakli notes that only five or six Middle Eastern rhythms are used regularly in the Tunisian *ughniyya*, the most popular being *malfuf*, *wihda*, *dwik* and *masmudi* (ibid.:93–6).

[37]   The in-house ensemble of the ERTT (Établissement de la Radio et Télévision Tunisienne) is generally referred to as the 'radio ensemble'.

maqāmāt, while contemporary stars of the *ughniyya* such as Amina Fakhet and Dhikra Mohamed sing only in these *maqāmāt* (ibid.). Critics lamenting the loss of identity in Tunisian song have long observed that the only element that defines the genre as Tunisian is its use of the Tunisian Arabic dialect.

European instruments of fixed pitch were introduced into Tunisian music in the late nineteenth century, when *ma'lūf* ensembles typically comprised a *rabab*, *'ūd 'arbī*, *naqqārāt* and *tār*. The instrumentalists doubled as singers, sometimes joined by one or two vocal soloists. Gradually, the violin began to replace the *rabab*, and more radically, despite their inability to produce the variable pitches of the *maqāmāt*, instruments of fixed pitch such as the harmonium and piano were added. Musicians and audiences evidently found no contradiction in the fact that, whilst the voice, *'ūd* and violin articulated the intervals of the *maqāmāt*, the keyboard instruments played the same melody in equal temperament. In the first commercial recordings of Tunisian *aghānī*, made in 1908 by Zonophone (the French subsidiary of Gramophone), the accompanying ensemble typically comprised an *'ūd 'arbī*, violin, harmonium or piano, *naqqārāt* and *tār*. This heterogeneous combination of traditional Arab and European instruments, particularly those of fixed pitch, was a speciality of Jewish musicians 'eager to free themselves from the constraints of the traditional modes and scales, and equally attentive to the acoustical quality of the Western instruments and the extent of their ambitus' (Moussali 1992:4). Gradually, this line-up became standard among ensembles of the period. Meanwhile, other Arab instruments such as the *'ūd sharqī* (lit. 'eastern lute'),[38] *qānūn* (from the 1920s) and *nāy* (from the 1930s) were added under the influence of Egyptian ensembles, as were the Tunisian percussion instruments *darbūka* and *bendir*.

The use of Western instruments in Arab music was particularly controversial among European reformers at the time. From his palace in Sidi Bou Saïd on the outskirts of Tunis, the European patron and scholar Baron Rodolphe d'Erlanger countered the 'corruptive' effects of this trend, both in his writings and in his own *ma'lūf* ensemble, which excluded European instruments altogether.[39] At the 1932 Cairo Congress, the European-dominated Committee of Musical Instruments recommended that the equal-tempered piano and the cello, both widely used in Egyptian music, be outlawed from Arab music ensembles.[40] When it was founded in the mid-1930s, the Rashidiyya ensemble was revolutionary in Tunisian music for its expanded size, its instrumental doublings, its introduction of cellos and double basses and its separate mixed chorus. Despite the obvious influence of the European orchestra, however, the Rashidiyya – exceptionally among Tunisian ensembles of the time – followed the line of the European purists by excluding instruments of fixed pitch.

---

[38]   The standard five- or six-stringed *'ūd* used throughout the Arab world today.

[39]   D'Erlanger targets in particular the piano, harmonium and fretted mandolin (1949:341). See footnote 25 above for details of his *ma'lūf* ensemble.

[40]   See Racy (1991:76–9) for a detailed account of the discussions and disagreements among the Congress participants relating to the use of these instruments.

After Tunisian independence in 1956, the Rashidiyya provided the model for new state-sponsored amateur ensembles, whose activities centred on the *ma'lūf*.[41] The trend for accompanying *aghānī*, however, was set by the radio ensemble which, taking the Rashidiyya as its basic model, added to this line-up an eclectic mix of percussion such as drum kit and bongo drums, as well as fixed pitch instruments such as accordion, guitar and piano. Later, electronic instruments such as the electric guitar, keyboard and synthesiser were also introduced.[42] Until the advent of private studios in the 1980s, virtually all recordings of *aghānī* were made by the radio ensemble in the studios of the ERTT.

The extent to which European instruments of fixed pitch have become identified with Tunisian music, both practically and conceptually, is reflected in the account by Mourad Shakli, Tunisia's leading authority on the *ughniyya*, of the introduction of the piano and harmonium into Tunisian ensembles in the late nineteenth century. Acknowledging this development as an event of 'revolutionary' significance, Shakli describes it as an example, not of Westernisation, but rather of 'Tunisification' of the European instruments (1994:201–2). Similarly, the use of the synthesiser in Tunisian ensembles since the 1960s may be seen not so much as a local manifestation of a pan-Arab musical trend as, rather, a modern-day extension of a traditional instrumental practice rooted in Tunisia's colonial past.

Conclusion

It was precisely their marginalised social status that empowered the predominantly Jewish professional musicians and singers of Tunis in the early twentieth century to exploit the commercial opportunities offered by the emerging record industry and the public entertainment venues of the Protectorate, for their artistic ends. By selectively engaging with the new musical influences from the Eastern and European Mediterranean, and adapting these to the textual conventions of traditional urban popular song, these musical pioneers established the essential characteristics of the *ughniyya*, the genre that was to dominate Tunisian musical activity to the present day.

For Tunisians steeped in the traditional musical culture of the *ma'lūf*, no less than for the Baron Rodolphe d'Erlanger in his self-styled Moorish palace, the new commercial musical developments threatened the very identity of Tunisian music. By the 1930s, in the light of the prevailing nationalist ideology, the defence of that identity began to be perceived not so much as an artistic preference as a moral imperative. Modelled on the European music conservatory, the Rashidiyya achieved a new social legitimacy for music making, empowering Muslims and

---

[41]   I discuss these ensembles and their activities in Davis (1997:6–11, 2004:71–6).

[42]   Technological advances have since enabled the synthesiser to emulate the microtonal intervals of the *maqāmāt*, thus transforming the keyboard into an instrument of variable pitch. See Rasmussen (1996:352–7).

non-Muslims alike to engage publicly in performances of the *ma'lūf* and to participate in the creation and performance of new Tunisian songs. Despite their use of predominantly Egyptian modes and rhythms, and their performance by an ensemble featuring European bowed strings and other instruments typically played in Egyptian ensembles, the new songs of the Rashidiyya were regarded as Tunisian and they were included in concerts devoted to the *ma'lūf*. In contrast, the songs of their Jewish predecessors were discredited by the Rashidiyya as 'foreign' and corrupt.

After independence in 1956, the new state radio ensemble set the standard for the Tunisian *ughniyya*; modelled on Egyptian film orchestras, the ensemble openly embraced Egyptian styles. With the mass emigration of Tunisian Jews in the 1950s, the songs with which they were associated dropped out of mainstream Tunisian musical life. However, among the remaining Jews on the island of Djerba, they acquired the status of 'traditional Jewish songs' serving as nostalgic reminders of a bygone era.

The relaxation of nationalist agendas following the *coup d'état* of 1987 was accompanied by a reawakening of cultural and artistic values associated with the Protectorate. Thus the early *ughniyya* enjoyed a nostalgic revival in mainstream society: its songs and personalities received renewed exposure through the reissuing of vintage recordings, as well as in popular and scholarly writings. In the early 1990s, empowered by her prestigious musical lineage and establishment credentials, Amina Srarfi challenged the continuing taboo surrounding public performances by female instrumentalists with the founding of El 'Azifet, whose founding members are typically conservatory-trained university graduates who 'follow their careers as doctors, dentists, university teachers, chemists, etc.'.[43] Like the founding fathers of the Rashidiyya, they dissociate themselves from the professional musical world by presenting themselves as amateurs; and like the Rashidiyya, El 'Azifet performs under the auspices of Tunisian governmental organisations on official occasions, rather than for private or commercial functions.

For Amina Srarfi, the songs of the early Jewish pioneers hold a privileged place in her father's legacy: they were the songs of his formative years. Thus in performances by El 'Azifet, the songs of the Jewish diva Habiba Msika and the Jewish singer/composer Cheikh El Afrit essentially belong to the same urban musical heritage as those by artists of the Rashidiyya, including Kaddur Srarfi himself, and they have equal status in the ensemble's programmes, which also include items of the *ma'lūf*. Formerly despised by the mainstream musical establishment, the early *aghānī* are associated today, through El 'Azifet, with a radical, progressive tendency within that establishment. In the musical culture of contemporary Tunis they represent a distinctive aspect of the Tunisian musical heritage, and a unique phase in Tunisia's urban musical past.

---

[43] CD liner notes, El 'Azifet (n.d. [1998]).

Chapter 8
Music and Politics in North Africa

Tony Langlois

Introduction

The three Maghreb states to be discussed in this chapter each have unique cultural and political histories. At the same time, they have important characteristics in common which justify considering them as a single region. Morocco, Algeria and Tunisia are all predominantly Muslim Mediterranean states which have achieved full political independence in the last 50 years. Their post-colonial experiences have been different, but all three have had to manage issues such as migration, politicised religion, economic change and other problems facing states in the process of establishing a sense of national identity. As both a medium and barometer of cultural change, music has been involved in the outworkings of these issues, and here I intend to outline this relationship using examples from the wide range of musical traditions that co-exist in the region.

Throughout the Maghreb, it is interesting to note that whilst musical meanings are framed by political discourses, these issues are rarely confronted explicitly through the music itself. However, the mere broadcast of songs in 'Berber' languages might be considered an assertion of non-Arab political identity even though the lyrics themselves are quite innocuous, or even meaningless, to Arab speakers.[1] Although ethnic 'Arab' and 'Berber' listeners may well apprehend the music quite differently, both would be aware that the very fact of its broadcast was significant in political terms. So politics permeates North African music in complex, diffuse ways, power being most frequently manifested through the (generally unspoken) rules which regulate when music can or cannot be performed, who is permitted to perform, and where and when it is appropriate to listen to it.

In this chapter I will investigate the relationship between music and power by pursuing three main strands. Firstly, I will identify some of the key social discourses in the region that relate most to music, focusing primarily on concepts of nationhood, religion and language. Secondly, I will consider three very different musical genres, examining their relationships to these discourses and thus their

---

[1] As Goodman demonstrates in her analysis of the song '*A Vava Inouva*' ('My Little Father'; 1976) by Algerian singer Idir (2005). The song text is in Tamazight, the Berber language of Idir's home district of Kabyle.

significance as genres in relation to one another.[2] Finally, I will consider the global – or at least 'transcultural' – factors which have influenced these musics to varying degrees, as well as the socio-political context in which they exist.

Following Bourdieu (1984) and Hall (1997a), amongst others, it is my view that cultural, and therefore political, meanings are sustained by the experience of difference. Thus musical genres and practices, in distinguishing tastes, define their consumers as communities of shared knowledge and interest. Often, though imprecisely, these overlap with social categories such as class, 'race' and gender. This is particularly apposite in the context of North Africa, where social boundaries relating to class and gender tend to be fairly rigid. For each of the genres discussed below I will show how they map, in both sound and practice, onto specific social groups, which themselves may represent political positions. The first musical genre to be considered will be the *andalus* art music tradition, variations of which can be found in urban centres throughout North Africa. *Andalus* has an esteemed position in each state, partly because it is considered a link to a golden age in 'Andalousiya' (medieval Islamic Spain). The genre bears similar connotations of sophistication and heritage to those attached to Western classical music and is taught to middle-class children in much the same way. I will describe its sometimes ambivalent relations with class, state and Islam. Equally ambivalent is the magico-musical role of the *g'nâwa*, the focus of my second case study. The *g'nâwa* are a black ethnic minority whose musical performances involve 'folk' interpretations of Islam and include psychotherapeutic practices. Through musical ritual, the *g'nâwa* facilitate emotional catharsis amongst poorer women and the most excluded men in Moroccan society. In doing so, I will argue that they effectively bind themselves and their audiences into these marginal social positions. Lastly, I will consider the political implications of *raï*, a music of the urban poor that has (somewhat problematically) become a fêted 'world music'. *Raï*'s syncretic nature raises issues of cultural hybridity and local identity which, during Algeria's recent decade of political trauma, have proved particularly difficult to resolve. Before discussing these three examples further – and in order to contextualise them – I will first describe the broader cultural and political characteristics of the region.

Historical Background

Despite a number of commonalities, the political and economic histories of Algeria, Morocco and Tunisia differ in important respects. For example, Morocco is governed by a constitutional monarchy with a very high rural population (with around 40 per

---

[2]   It would have been possible to choose between dozens of distinct musical traditions from the region to make much the same points. The decision to focus on *andalus*, the music of the *g'nâwa* and *raï* was based on my familiarity with these traditions, which have featured in my own research since the early 1990s.

cent involved in agricultural production).[3] Algeria, by contrast, was introduced to industrialisation by French colonists, adopted centralist socialism on independence in 1962, has an overwhelmingly urban population and is largely dependent economically upon petrochemical exports. Tunisia, a much smaller country with fewer natural resources, has attempted, both diplomatically and economically, to serve as a bridge between the West and the Arab world. Over the last 20 years, international tourism has been a major contributor to the Tunisian economy.

At the same time, these adjacent Arab states have shared significant formative experiences that continue to influence current political and cultural discourses. These include colonisation by European nations on the other side of the Mediterranean,[4] large-scale economic migration (often to these same countries), technological development, revolution and independence. In spite of recent constitutional reforms throughout the region, none of these countries have seen a significant change of political regime since the 1960s. At the time of writing (2007), the Algerian government is still effectively run by its military and the FLN (National Liberation Front), the party that led the revolution against the French. Tunisia, also dominated by the party that brought it independence (the Constitutional Democratic Rally), has had only two Presidents in this period. The present Moroccan A'alawi dynasty has held power since the 1790s, despite the French/Spanish Protectorate of the twentieth century. Although Morocco has a longer history of independence than its neighbours, all three countries are relatively young as nation states, the region having been previously dominated by successive empires including the Romans and Ottomans.[5] During the most recent European colonisation, religion and language became key areas of distinction between indigenous North Africans and settlers. Consequently both Islam and the Arabic language have become central features of national identity in the independent Maghrebian states.

---

[3]   CIA World Factbook, <www.cia.gov/library/publications/the-world-factbook/geos/mo.html#People> (accessed 13/08/08).

[4]   French Protectorates governed Tunisia between 1883 and 1956 and Morocco between 1912 and 1956. Spain also controlled large parts of northern and southern Morocco and continues to hold two peninsular enclaves on the Mediterranean coast. Algeria was more comprehensively colonised than its neighbours, being politically linked to the French mainland. Although French culture was introduced in each case, the settlers themselves were ethnically diverse: many were Spanish and came seeking refuge from Franco's regime.

[5]   Historically, political power was centred in rich cities and the powerful elites that controlled their hinterland. Various local dynasties exercised control over key trade routes by patronising tribal groups living in the hills and plains between the cities. Inevitably such alliances fluctuated regularly. Modern national borders were largely established and maintained by colonial powers and some of these remain of doubtful legality. The most divisive boundary dispute between countries of the Maghreb concerns the Western Sahara, once a Spanish Protectorate, which is claimed by both Morocco and the indigenous Saharawi people. A mass occupation of the territory by Moroccan citizens took place in 1975, an event celebrated as the 'Green March'. Algeria continues to support pro-independence Polisario guerrillas, whilst the United Nations is charged with resolving the dispute. See Stora (2002).

Religion and Political Culture

As discussed by many previous writers, Islam as an ideology proposes moral and legal codes which do not always sit comfortably alongside civil legislation in contemporary North African states.[6] Though various schools of religious jurisprudence interpret *Shari'a* law in different ways, their moral right to criticise or even oppose secular government is widely accepted in the Maghreb. Indeed, this role is considered a healthy balance to secular authority and its potential excesses. However, the full integration of religion and nation into an Islamic state tends to appeal mostly to those with the smallest stake in the political *status quo*.[7] Each state has attempted to manage religious activities, typically by suppressing its most radical manifestations whilst placating more moderate voices. Nevertheless, Islam has been used many times throughout the region as the banner for either political reform or resistance.[8] For example, Algerian rebels who adopted a radical interpretation of Islam, were almost certainly influenced by individuals who had been involved in the actions of the Mujahedin against the Soviet occupation of Afghanistan in the 1980s. The recent war of mutual attrition between armed rebels and the Algerian government has come close to outright civil war on many occasions over the last ten years.[9] In Morocco, the figure of King has long combined both secular and religious authority in one person. As a *sharif*, the royal line claims descent from the Prophet Mohamed so exploiting the political capital afforded to elite and religious lineages of many kinds in the region. Nominally a constitutional head of state, in fact the King has considerable personal authority and is extremely vigilant regarding potential threats to his regime.[10] The Tunisian government

---

[6]   See, for example, Vatim (1987), Hourani (1991) and Munson (1993).

[7]   Some political parties in Morocco favour the integration of religion and state but they are not politically strong and most are obliged to work alongside the government. Nevertheless, it has been suggested to me that these movements are partly financed by interests outside the country and some are very active in building up support in the poorer urban neighbourhoods.

[8]   See Gellner (1981).

[9]   Amongst other economic problems, increasing unemployment and fewer opportunities for emigration led to widespread civil unrest in the late 1980s. General elections scheduled for 1992 were cancelled when it became clear that parties campaigning for Islamic political reform were likely to win a majority. A decade of extreme violence, allegedly carried out by both government forces and rebel factions such as the GIA (Armed Islamic Group) and FIS (Islamic Salvation Front), had left over 80,000 dead by 1997 (Amnesty International Report MDE 28/023/1998, <http://web.amnesty.org/library/eng-dza/index>, accessed 05/12/04). This has since risen to 150,000 according to BBC reports (<http://news.bbc.co.uk/2/hi/middle_east/country_profiles/790556.stm>, accessed 12/01/05). Most of these casualties have been civilians.

[10] During the early decades of independence, several assassination attempts and plots against the King were ruthlessly crushed (See Waterbury 1970). These attacks were mostly from left-wing factions who at the time considered the monarchy anachronistic. Perhaps

also keeps a tight rein on potential dissent although under Bourguiba's 30-year presidency the country developed increasingly secular policies in keeping with aspirations to play a key diplomatic role in the region. More recently, religious opposition groups have been invited to play a role in government, a policy which has served both to placate critics and to compromise their potential to challenge the current balance of power.

It is important to note that religious practices are much more diverse than those presented in orthodox discourses. Alongside the 'Islam of the mosque' (itself far from monolithic) many popular forms exist, particularly – but by no means exclusively – in rural areas. Many of these practices and beliefs, which syncretise with more orthodox viewpoints, are generally deemed 'ignorant' by religious and state authorities. 'Maraboutic Islam' (cults following practices established by charismatic individuals) tends to appeal to the most powerless in society, and Sufism (esoteric spiritualism) to a well educated but small minority. And since governments do not seem to consider these practices to be as threatening as blatantly politicised movements, only extreme forms, bordering on 'sorcery', are considered illegal under civil law.

The relationship between religious discourse and political authority has considerable impact upon the values associated with musical practices in these countries. As Nasr (1997) and al-Faruqi (1985) explain, each musical style can be placed conceptually on a moral scale, ranging from acceptable (*halāl*) to unacceptable (*harām*). Consequently, all acts of musical production or consumption, whether by individual *or* state, can be interpreted as adopting a position on such a continuum. Where it is possible neither to condone nor to suppress *harām* musical practices, North African regimes tend to turn a blind eye to their existence, whilst nevertheless monitoring their activities.

Language and Identity

The political significance of language, with its key role in identity construction, inevitably impacts upon any music involving song. Reflecting its indigenous ethnic mix and historical influences, local dialects of Arabic contain many

---

ironically, it is now 'socialist' Algeria that is under assault from radical Islamic groups. Traditionally, the Sultan (later 'King') of Morocco maintained his authority in a politically and ethnically diverse country by continually undermining potential allegiances against him and defeating opposition militarily. History has shown that complacent regimes were soon replaced by tribal alliances, frequently coalesced around charismatic religious leadership. Waterbury (1970) and Gilsenan (1990) investigate the significance of charisma and descent in Maghrebi politics. The persistence of the current dynasty is in many ways a testimony to its powers of surveillance and its ability to play the 'religious card' effectively. See also Vatim (1987) and Munson (1993) for discussions of political and religious discourse in Morocco.

influences, primarily from French, Spanish and Berber languages. Several Berber languages are spoken in the Maghreb, including Tamazight, Amazigh and Tifinagh, each associated with specific regions. In Morocco, where the promotion of cultural diversity might strategically prevent alliances which threaten the regime, minority languages and musics are tolerated and to some extent supported by the state. By contrast, in Algeria, which since independence has tended more towards institutional centralisation, Berber languages and identities have not been officially acknowledged until very recently, and only after considerable civil strife.[11] Colloquial Arabic (or *derija*), with its rich vernacular, exists in localised forms throughout the Maghreb and is the generally preferred medium for everyday communication. However, *derija* is rarely written or broadcast on state networks, where standard (international) Arabic dominates. In addition, French is still regularly used in many areas of business and education and North Africans have long been avid consumers of Francophone television broadcasts on satellite stations. Consequently, policies to promote and 'improve' the standard of Arabic used in Maghreb states have been largely ineffective.[12] The use of standard Arabic is probably weakest in Algeria, where French colonisation was most intense and educational developments inclined towards a 'modernity' framed essentially in terms of Western capitalism (Bourdieu 1977, Ottaway and Ottaway 1970). This is important in political and musical terms because movements seeking Islamic reform have portrayed linguistic pluralism as evidence of cultural and moral degeneracy. In the recent period of political unrest, editors of French language newspapers in Algeria have been attacked, as have teachers using French in technical education.[13] Just as Islamic essentialism promotes orthodoxy in dress and behaviour, so purity of language has been engaged as a moral and political cause.

This cursory exploration of the North African cultural and political context is intended to provide a backdrop to the following discussion of musical practices. Since it is my contention that the political significance of these musics is both contextual and relational, the influences of such powerful cultural discourses as religion, nationhood and language will affect each genre differently, as they do the social groups with which they are associated.

---

[11]   The Berber enclave of the Kabyle Mountains has been the main focus of protests against Arabisation in Algeria. This struggle for a distinct cultural identity inevitably goes against the pressure for increased linguistic homogeneity that has come from political Islamists. See, for example, Goodman (1996).

[12]   See Maghraoui (1995).

[13]   See Maghraoui (1995).

Andalus: **Art Music and Social Class**

Tlemçen, an ancient hill-town overlooking the border between Algeria and Morocco, is considered the traditional home of *gharnâti*, a form of *andalus* art music that had its origins in the courts of the Umayyad Caliphate of Granada in Muslim Spain (Andalousiya). Like other closely-related schools of *andalus* music that are found across North Africa from Morocco to Libya, *gharnâti* is believed to have been brought to North Africa by migrants fleeing the Christian *reconquista* of Spain in the fourteenth and fifteenth centuries.[14] The repertoire is comprised of suites (*nûbât*) of songs and instrumental interludes named after the mode (*tab'*) in which they are played and the music is performed in ensembles which typically include the *oud* (lute), *kamenja* (bowed fiddle held upright on the player's knee), *rebab* (a low-pitched bowed lute), *târ* (frame drum) and *derbûka* (goblet drum). Though specialist singers may perform virtuoso parts, instrumentalists also serve as a chorus.

Whilst detailed discussion of *andalus'* long history lies beyond the scope of this chapter, even a brief outline of the last century will show how the role of the music has changed. It is quite likely that in both Andalusian and Maghrebian courts, professional Jewish musicians played a key role in maintaining the musical tradition. The *reconquista* being as prejudicial against Jews as 'Moors', many migrated with their masters to the powerful cities of the Maghreb. *Andalus* remains a quintessentially urban music. As the elite classes who patronised the *andalus* tradition lost political influence during the colonial period, so their music also suffered in terms of status and support. By the 1930s, the Algerian *mâlûf* from the eastern district of Constantine had become associated with low-status drinking clubs and hostels (*f'ndouk*). During the 1950s, however, pro-independence movements through cultural associations gradually rehabilitated the genre, presenting it anew as a distinctly indigenous art form with historical links to a pre-colonial era when Moorish civilisation flourished.

Since Maghrebi independence in the late 1950s and early 1960s, *andalus* has enjoyed a privileged status. Since most of the Jewish population left the Maghreb during this period (especially following the Six Day War in 1967), their role in preserving the tradition has tended to be overlooked. In their absence, the music became emblematic of a new national identity, providing a model of 'high culture'

---

[14] The entire *andalus* repertoire is often ascribed to a single originator, the legendary composer Zyriab, who travelled from Baghdad to the western caliphate in the ninth century. The original collection is said to have comprised 24 suites of songs and extended instrumental passages, each with a specific modal structure and associations with a particular time of day, colour, cardinal humour and so on. Current repertoires are theoretically derived from the remnants and regional variations of this corpus. Contemporary schools of *andalus* include the *al-âla* tradition in Algiers, the *mâlûf* in Constantine, *çana fassiya* in Fez, *gharnâti* in Tlemçen, *fann* in Libya and the *nûbat* of Tunis. For details of the historical and stylistic distinctions between these schools, the reader is referred to Guettat (1980) and Poché (1995).

to rival (or perhaps supplant) that of Europeans, authenticated by an unbroken historical tradition.[15] In each of these countries, *andalus* has been promoted through state conservatories and is recorded and broadcast by national networks. Music festivals and competitions at both local and pan-Maghrebian levels maintain fidelity to these traditions. Modern manifestations of regional 'schools' differ not only in repertoire but also stylistically as a result both of national policies towards music and the nature of local patronage. Possibly under the influence of Ottoman and other Arab art musics, Tunisian and Libyan schools of *andalus* have tended towards large ensembles, often with specialised choirs whose aesthetic includes a preference for precise musical unison. This may be related in part to the early transcription of the repertoire and the centralisation of music education.[16] By contrast, since the complete Moroccan repertoire has only recently been transcribed, it is generally taught orally and there is a distinct tendency towards heterophony, performers being relatively free to ornament the melody according to their abilities. To suggest that the normative relationship between individual and community in each country is replicated in these musical aesthetics would be rather conjectural without further research. Nevertheless, it is interesting to note that the comparatively 'free market' economy of music in Morocco appears to encourage competition, both between ensembles and the musicians within them. In more centralised political regimes such as Algeria, where *andalus* ensembles are largely state-supported, this element of competition, and degree of musical heterophony, is noticeably less apparent.

My own involvement with *andalus* musicians has been in the cities of Tlemçen and Oran in western Algeria and Oujda in eastern Morocco, both places where the *gharnâti* school is well established. Interestingly, most of the non-musicians that I talked to in these cities were at the very least ambivalent towards *andalus* music or disliked it, despite (or perhaps because of) its privileged status. Whilst many acknowledged *andalus* to be a 'national treasure', very few chose to listen to it, saying that they found the language of the songs antiquated and dull compared with more contemporary genres. The music had no associations with the 'modernity' that young people in particular aspired to: it was rarely heard in cafés or cassette shops and, above all, was rarely danced to. I also found that on both sides of the Algerian-Moroccan border, the music retained strong associations with the town of Tlemçen and its social elite. In contrast, by far the most popular musical style

---

[15]   The fixed nature of the basic repertoire has not prevented considerable creativity within it. Each *nûba*, played in its entirety, would require hours to perform. Instead, contemporary ensembles tend to perform excerpts from different *nûbât*, and sometimes from different traditions, in order to make concerts more interesting to listeners. Also, within the *gharnâti* school there has developed an extensive repertoire of '*hawzi*' pieces, which apply the general style of the *andalus* tradition to more popular songs and contemporary language. See Schuyler (1978) for a description of the *andalus* performed in other Moroccan regions and Davis (1996) for a discussion of Tunisian cultural policy regarding *andalus*.

[16]   See Davis (1996).

in the region was *raï*, a self-consciously eclectic and colloquial genre that will be described later in this chapter. I found such strong class associations striking and when I attended performances of *andalus* discovered that these preconceptions were often borne out by both performers and audiences.[17] These associations are perhaps not so surprising in Morocco where class hierarchies are marked. Nevertheless, the association with Tlemçen, a city in an inaccessible neighbouring nation state, suggested that cultural and economic links with traditional political centres were more resilient than one might have expected.

As traditional patrons of the arts, the Moroccan upper classes have strongly influenced the status of particular musical genres, have financially supported the ensembles of favoured musicians and more recently, influenced government policies on music performance and education. In Algeria, where traditional power relations were deliberately and deeply undermined by the colonial regime (which was itself replaced in the 1960s by socialist-style collectivist programmes), it was remarkable to find that the old elite classes of Tlemçen still retained esteem in the present era. I was also intrigued by the persistent associations made between *andalus* and this social group.[18] On a number of occasions, I accompanied the director of the Oran Cultural Centre to visit his counterpart at the Tlemçen Maison de la Culture in order to secure the loan of ancient instruments for display in an exhibition. In the course of these negotiations, it became clear that although Oran is now a much larger and more important city in the region, the visitor showed considerable deference, both to the Tlemçen Maison de la Culture and its director, who responded rather coolly towards his guests. After several visits, and in order to finally clinch the deal, the Orani director finally felt it necessary to stress his own familial links with Tlemçen and his personal commitment to the *gharnâti* tradition. What emerged through these and similar observations was that this form of *andalus* was strongly associated on both sides of the border with a social group which retained the cultural capital of a political structure that had not officially existed for generations.

In Algeria, *andalus* has occupied an ambivalent position since the recent political crisis. In a context in which rebel groups challenge the government's political and moral legitimacy, any music promoted by the state as a national treasure was unlikely to thrive. In the 1990 local elections, the Islamic Salvation Front (FIS) won control over many local authorities, including Tlemçen. In addition to promoting the ideal of an Islamic state, the policies of the FIS included improving

---

[17] After attending rehearsals of Oran's *Association Andalousiya* ensemble on a few occasions, it became clear that most of the young people who made up the group were well educated and drawn from the city's middle class. It also emerged that many of their families were indeed originally from Tlemçen. Learning to play *andalus* music is considered an important accomplishment for young boys and girls of this class, and most had studied for several years before joining adult ensembles in Oran or Oujda.

[18] See Ottaway and Ottaway (1970) for a detailed description of Algeria's post-colonial socialist reforms.

local services, challenging corruption and training the unemployed. When starved of financial resources by central government, they drew upon networks of local volunteers and independent funds from abroad.[19] FIS-controlled municipalities redirected resources from the arts to local services, leaving established conservatories, and therefore art musics, with little financial support. After the second round of the general elections was cancelled in 1992, the military-backed government banned the FIS and widespread violence ensued. This period of crisis itself made arts funding difficult to justify and with the imposition of a night-time curfew in many Algerian cities, the market for most 'officially sanctioned' music rapidly dried up. Although musicians continued to learn, rehearse and play *andalus* on a voluntary basis, the drastic reduction of state funding and possibilities for performance undermined the genre's privileged status. Reliance upon central funding is a common feature of the Algerian economy and although the black market positively thrived on the country's difficulties, *andalus* does not have the popularity necessary to fall back on alternative commercial sources. Conservative religious factions did not single out *andalus* for attack, but rather it has been left to wither without the state support it once enjoyed, and this has effectively weakened its symbolic value as a vehicle of Algerian national heritage.

Elsewhere in the Maghreb, where opposition groups have not resorted to force to the same extent as in Algeria, *andalus* retains a position of cultural prestige, although it does not enjoy much more popularity with the general public. The Moroccan ensembles with which I was involved were most active during Ramadan, rehearsing nightly in the weeks leading up to the holy month.[20] Regular public performances took place throughout Ramadan and many of these were financially supported by local government. Considerable competition existed between the various ensembles in Oujda for the best virtuoso performers. As free-market professionals, sought-after musicians rehearsed with several ensembles in the lead up to Ramadan, finally opting for the group most likely to pay the highest fee or with the most prestigious and numerous performances. As well as *andalus*, many musicians also performed other styles (including, when required, Western pop music). The busiest period in a professional musician's calendar, apart from Ramadan (which can fall at any time of the year), was the late summer wedding season. What is evidently different between the situation in Algeria and that of Morocco, is the extent to which the cultural economy is centralised: whereas Algeria has fostered excellence through state sponsored conservatories, the Moroccan government effectively supports the best musicians that arise through competition. In both cases, however, *andalus* is a genre which requires patronage,

---

19   See Davis (1992).

20   It should be noted that these musicians were all men. Although young women do learn to play and sing *andalus* in conservatories, I never saw adult women perform in Morocco and only once in Algeria. This is partly because of the moral stigma attached to being a paid musician, as well as the fact that public exposure is considered undignified for a woman. In addition, women are traditionally discouraged from playing wind instruments.

either from elites or from governmental structures. Unlike the case of more popular genres, the sale of recordings is inadequate to sustain a large industry, and although there is growing international interest in *andalus* (particularly in Spain) this is insufficient to give the genre commercial independence. Inevitably then, the music is implicated with regimes of power, and in Algeria *andalus* has suffered as a consequence of this association.

Gender, 'Race' and the *G'nâwa*

In music, as in many other fields of social activity, gender segregation is common in North Africa, a dynamic that creates strong social bonds within single-sex sets and palpable discursive opposition between them. Independent Algeria's early enthusiasm for socialist-style 'progress' extended beyond the economy and education and attempted, with moderate success, to encourage gender equality amongst its citizens.[21] Observers might consider that Algerian women enjoy a more 'modern' lifestyle than their 'traditional' counterparts in Morocco: they are more likely to drive cars, have greater access to education and in the cities tend to wear clothes that, though a little more modest, would not seem out of place in western Europe. Modernist aspirations encouraged though education and government rhetoric persuaded many Algerians to consider neighbouring countries as less 'developed' than themselves, though changed circumstances on both sides of the border in recent years have called this view into question.[22] As increasing numbers of Moroccan women are entering higher education and becoming active in government, so the cultural polarisation arising from the Algerian conflict has led to increasing conservatism. In the 1990's, Algerian women had become the target of verbal and even physical intimidation for engaging in such activities as hairdressing, wearing Western dress and working outside the home. Much of this aggression came at the time from supporters of the FIS, though legislation such

---

[21]   Gender relations in Algeria and Morocco are partly fixed in statutes called the 'Family Code' which include such areas as inheritance, divorce and child custody legislation. Reforms of the Algerian code in the 1980s was widely criticised by local women's organisations for being discriminatory and too influenced by Islamist lobbies (Lyes Si Zoubir, 'Twenty Years of the Family Code', in *Le Monde Diplomatique*, on-line journal, March 2004, <http://mondediplo.com/2004/03/07familycode?var_recherche=zoubir>, accessed 31/08/09).

[22]   'Development' here tends to be gauged in terms of literacy, health, industrialisation and the privileging of an urban, rather than rural, lifestyle. Whilst these were seen as positive characteristics, many Algerians that I spoke to acknowledged that this modernist sensibility is to some extent a legacy of colonisation. In fact, many idealised the 'simple', 'pious' life of the tribespeople of the deep south, who lived 'like real Arabs'. Such dilemmas were characteristic of conflicting discourses in Algeria between a romantic traditionalism and a glamorous modernism.

as the Family Code (1984) indicated the government's own retreat from its liberal 1960's policies.

The strong tendency towards gender segregation in North Africa has ensured that many kinds of music exist which are primarily associated with women, typically in the context of quasi-religious events and social gatherings where women are involved as both performers and audiences.[23] For example, the *medahat* are professional female musicians from the Algerian-Moroccan border region who play, sing and dance at single-sex pre-nuptial parties. Their performances reputedly convey marital advice to the young bride-to-be, and the wider female community share the *baraka* (blessing) generated by her change of social status.[24] Another important area of women's music making relates to 'folk' religious practices. Although not officially prescribed, it is more common for men to attend mosques than women in North Africa; instead, women tend to observe religious practices at home, in keeping with customary modesty in the public arena. Among the poorer classes in both Algeria and Morocco, groups of women often visit the shrines of local saintly figures, or *marabout*. Through such 'pilgrimages in miniature' women seek the intercession of saints in their practical problems or perhaps obtain the advice of the shrine's guardian (who often belongs to the lineage of the *marabout*). Visits also provide a legitimate opportunity to socialise with the women of their quarter.[25]

For several months during the mid 1990s, I was often the only man in an audience of nearly one hundred who attended Thursday afternoon performances by a *g'nâwa* troupe in Oujda, Morocco. These took place in a small walled enclosure, where women and their children sat bunched together on floor rugs. The *g'nâwa* ethnic group are a small black community who live in certain districts of Moroccan towns. Only men performed at these events, although *g'nâwa* women collected donations and helped members of the audience who through the ritual process became distressed. The *g'nâwa* are thought to be descended from slaves or mercenaries brought from sub-Sahara centuries ago.[26] The name *g'nâwa* suggests 'Guinean' or other West African origins and this connection is supported by similarities in religious practices, instruments and musical structure. It is also possible that a proportion simply migrated north from the Sahel during the colonial period and have since occupied the cultural niche of *g'nâwa* for economic

---

[23]   In order to illustrate a form of gender discourse which is broadly common throughout North Africa, I have chosen a socio-musical example where this discourse is most clearly illustrated. Inevitably, gender relations are manifested differently in rural and urban settings, and in different nation states, ethnic groups and social classes. Nevertheless, at the risk of over-essentialising these relations, I would contend that the presence and influence of such a discourse is identifiable throughout the Maghreb.

[24]   See Naceri and Mebarki (1983).

[25]   See Schaeffer-Davis (1983) and Langlois (1998).

[26]   See Schuyler (1981) and Baldassarre (1995).

reasons.[27] The popular discourse supporting this specialist role associates black people in general with dangerous supernatural powers, a double-edged stereotype which defines a racial group by ascribing unusual qualities to it.[28] *G'nâwa* troupes have exploited this reputation, and in so doing position themselves as intermediaries between the physical world and supernatural domains. Reflecting this dynamic between the *g'nâwa* and mainstream society, their music and even their instruments remain distinct from those used in other North African genres. For example, where pentatonic tunings or the *genbri* (also known as a *hajhouj*, a box-shaped lute which sounds in the bass register) are used in non-*g'nâwa* musical styles, they often represent explicit references either to the *g'nâwa* themselves or to the social and spiritual context with which they are associated.

G'nâwa performances in Oujda had a simple structure, the aesthetic and psychological efficacy of which depended on a web of complimentary beliefs and practices. Each musical piece would begin with an introduction to the melodic theme played on the *genbri*. The sound of the lute was augmented by several pairs of large metal castanets known as *qaqarbat*. After some minutes, a few women stumbled forward from the crowd to a small space in front of the musicians where they danced in a rigid, flailing manner, uttering occasional cries and loosening their clothes. For perhaps ten minutes, the tempo gradually increased to the point where the nucleus of the original melody was reduced to a bass ostinato over the roar of *qaqarbat*. Finally, as dancers swooned one at a time into the arms of audience members, the music came to an abrupt end, followed by a brief recitation of the names of local maraboutic saints, the prophet Mohamed and Allah.[29] The afternoon would be taken up with maybe a dozen repetitions of this pattern, though the melodies varied and different dancers came forward each time. The melodies themselves are derived from traditional *g'nâwa* suites, each associated with a specific symbolic colour, a maraboutic shrine and a type of affliction.[30] As women heard the melody and chanted the name of the saint linked to their own problems,

---

[27] The *g'nâwa* themselves maintain that they are descended from Bilal, the Prophet Mohamed's first *muezzin*, who was a black Nubian. Some even claim hereditary maraboutic powers, although since these are generally transferred deliberately (for example, by anointing a chosen individual successor with spittle), this is clearly not an automatic function of lineage alone. Both of these assertions seek to invert the low status ascribed to black people in North Africa, and allow *g'nâwa* performers to claim legitimacy in precisely the same way as other religious and political leaders, through association with an esteemed spiritual lineage.

[28] This accords with Stuart Hall's (1997a:223–79) views on essentialising racial difference.

[29] See Schuyler (1981) and Langlois (1998) for further descriptions of *g'nâwa* ceremonies.

[30] In the comprehensive liner notes accompanying Antonio Baldassarre's (1995) excellent recordings of *g'nâwa* musicians in Casablanca and Marrakech, he explains the complex relationship between the music, *djinn* and other spiritual entities.

they become entranced, dancing until the spirit (*djinn* or *m'louk*) causing these problems left them or were propitiated.

In my view, such events essentialise both physical and emotional difference, marginalising both poorer women and the *g'nâwa* themselves from orthodox (masculine) religious discourses. Just as the *g'nâwa* are excluded on the basis of their association with profane supernatural domains, this context enables women to exhibit precisely the emotionalism which is commonly believed to distinguish them from male 'rationality' and self-control.[31] Participation in such cathartic rituals reinforces an essentialised gender distinction, by which women are to some extent represented as less 'civilised' than men. Women who actively observe Islamic practices tend to do so in their own homes or otherwise take part in 'folk religious' practices such as those provided by the *g'nâwa*. The fact that Moroccan *g'nâwa* performers are licensed by local authorities and carry cards identifying their profession as 'traditional musicians' suggests tacit state approval of these clearly heterodox religious practices, such regulation also affording some degree of surveillance and control. Maraboutism (and religious movements generally) have so frequently become politicised that it would be reckless to leave them entirely to their own devices.[32] On quite a different level, such practices (and including several non-*g'nâwa* institutions which perform similar functions) enable a collective act of solidarity by some of the most disempowered in North African society. Since most of the women present would have known which melodies were associated with particular afflictions, they could tell which of the dancers had been abandoned or were childless, ill or depressed, and so on. The support offered to each fainting dancer amounted to a gesture of solidarity within the community. Moreover, because these events take place out of doors, the sound of (what is effectively) collective grievance could be heard throughout the quarter by men and women alike. As a *political* gesture this is admittedly oblique, but given the circumstances of these women, is perhaps as vocal a 'protest' as is possible.[33]

In Algeria, as in Morocco, musicians from black ethnic minorities often function as mediators between the spirit world and women. Amongst those involved in such activities, performing troupes such as Les Frères Kakabou in Oran play a key role in summer wedding celebrations. The musicians involved here are more likely to be first or second generation migrants from the deep south of Algeria, and these origins are marked through both instrumentation (ensembles usually comprise several different sized clay goblet drums) and dress. Conceptually, *kakabou* music lacks the *g'nâwa*'s complex metaphysical

---

[31]   See also Deborah Kapchan's (2003) discussion of women's emotional response to music in Morocco.

[32]   See Waterbury (1970), Gellner (1981) and Gilsenan (1990) for detailed discussion of this phenomenon.

[33]   Lewis (1986) presents an invaluable comparative study of the politics of female possession cults in Africa. See, in particular, Chapter 7.

associations with colours, suites and *m'louk*, but otherwise these troupes play a comparable role to black musicians across the border. Performance during pre-wedding female gatherings brings about an entranced state amongst listeners, who dance to the point of collapse. In Oran, demand for *kakabou* performances at weddings regularly exceeds the pool of musicians from this community. Consequently, young, unemployed Arab men (who visibly do not belong to this ethnic minority) often form their own '*kakabou*' groups, dress like authentic 'southerners' and perform in pre-wedding events. Each summer Thursday evening (being the start of the Algerian weekend, the favoured night for wedding celebrations), these groups can be seen playing from the back of pick-up trucks leading wedding motorcades winding noisily across the city. These bands provide seasonal income for (typically underemployed) young men, although I was told that they are not paid as well as genuine 'southerners', most of whom reside in the *Medina j'dida* quarter of Oran. Clearly, one doesn't have to be black to play *kakabou* music, but the ethnic exoticism carries a kudos that makes their performances more sought after.

Just as *andalus* orchestras have acquired the connotations of elite social classes and their political interests, so other, very different styles of music are associated with lower classes. In the case of the *g'nâwa*, the niche of musician/ritual specialist provides a living, which until relatively recently has been mostly at the very margins of society. The ritual interaction of poor women and black men during *g'nâwa* events binds gender, class and racial stereotypes in a choreographed performance of ecstatic abandon. That this physical response is almost the complete opposite of that expected at an *andalus* event can hardly be coincidental, manifesting as it does the *actual* lack of control which poorer Moroccan women have over their own lives. Likewise, the use of language and understandings of religion are as distinct as the musics themselves. In political terms, these musical activities are not merely markers of differing taste but performances of almost entirely separate world views.

The one field of North African culture in which these otherwise distinct physical responses to religious music may be said to overlap is amongst the Sufi *zawia* (brotherhoods), where men perform long *dhikhr* rites leading to ecstatic trance states. These numerous organisations have a long and complex relationship to power in North Africa (see Gellner 1969, Gilsenan 1990) and vary in important regards from one another. Moreover, each North African state has its own approach to Sufism. Given its recent history, Algeria remains understandably wary of popular Islamic movements, whereas in the last decade the Moroccan government has actively supported certain 'approved' forms of Sufism as a preferred alternative to religious-political fundamentalism.

Raï, Technology and Modernity

So far I have described musical genres and practices which tend to correspond more or less with specific social groups. In principle, there are few reasons why middle-class men shouldn't attend *g'nâwa* ceremonies but on the whole they don't, just as poorer women tend not to listen to *andalus*. Such are the distinctions between class, 'race' and particularly gender in North Africa that the cultural domains outlined above remain fairly discrete and therefore relatively easy for governments to monitor. Since the third genre to be discussed knows few such bounds, it has raised a number of problematic issues relating to morality, language and identity. *Raï* is a form of popular music most associated with the cities of western Algeria and eastern Morocco, but which is now also consumed internationally as part of the 'world music' phenomenon. On a superficial level *raï* is influenced by many global styles, from Egyptian art music to reggae, but at its structural and original core the music combines elements from local wedding musics and Western pop.

In the late 1940s and 1950s, *raï* (lit. 'my opinion') referred to a traditional style featuring women singers accompanied by flute (*gaspah*) and drum (*guellal*).[34] These *cheikha*'s were most likely *medahat* performers who had moved from the 'female only' market to entertaining men in the clubs of colonial Oran. In this morally-dubious cabaret environment – one of the few places where men and women, Arabs and Europeans, mixed – many stylistic fusions took place involving elements of jazz and Latin American musics, French *chanson*, Bedouin rhythms and even *andalus*.[35] After independence, urban musical tastes shifted towards emulating American guitar groups, but in the early 1980s disco electronics were also drawn into the mix and a new 'pop-*raï*' emerged, spurred by the growth of cheap cassette recording technology and a European *émigré* market hungry for Algerian recordings. The *raï* of this period posed significant dilemmas for the Algerian government. The authorities were prepared to tolerate the existence of a nocturnal *demi-monde* of cabarets and brothels, so long as it remained invisible. Although technologically dislocated from this scene, the *raï* music which emerged from it was considered lewd and tasteless. The songs often referred to frustrated passion, illicit sex and drunkenness, either explicitly or by innuendo, and the fact that they were sung by both men and women was even more shocking.[36] As if the themes of these songs weren't contentious enough, *raï*'s use of the vernacular language contributed to its notoriety. If the classical Arabic of the Qur'an is considered to be the purest form of the language, and for many the literal word of God, then the *derija* dialect with its loan words, 'corrupted' grammar and street

---

[34]   The reader is referred to Virolle (1995), Daoudi and Miliani (1996) and Tenaille (2002) for good descriptions of early *raï*.

[35]   The pianist Maurice el Medioni became locally famous for syncopating melodies from *andalus* suites with popular Afro-Cuban rhythms.

[36]   Virolle (1995) and Tenaille (2002) both provide a useful analysis of *raï* lyrics during this period.

slang, occupied the opposite end of this moral scale. At the same time, *derija* is also the language of domestic spaces and the neighbourhood (*houma*). Unlike *andalus*, where passionate sentiments might be expressed in a literary form, *raï* tended to be prosaic and coarse. During the early 1990s, knowledge that women played *raï* cassettes inside the home could scandalise male heads of families, whose duty it was to maintain honour by ensuring the separation of domestic and public domains (Langlois 2005).

As *raï* moved from the private to public sphere, the Algerian government responded by banning its broadcast. However, it encountered numerous obstacles to effective censorship. Recordings were produced outside state control (in the back rooms of shops, for example) and distributed on street corners. *Raï*'s popularity, both at home and abroad, also proved problematic for the government. With less explicit lyrics, *raï* quickly became the preferred music for weddings, initially in the border region and very soon wherever North Africans had settled in Europe. Whilst the Algerian government could ban *raï* from its own national radio and television stations, it could not prevent it being broadcast on stations like Medi 1, based in Nador in neighbouring Morocco.[37] As complete censorship proved impossible, a compromise was eventually reached whereby broadcast was permitted on condition that cassette sales were taxed and lyrics toned down.[38] The government's approach may partly have been a matter of accepting the inevitable, but at this time of economic crisis they may also have sought favour with the urban youth who were the largest consumers of *raï*, had the smallest stake in society and were most attracted to political alternatives.[39] If this was the case, then it was a risky strategy, since appearing to condone such an obviously disreputable form of music played into the hands of the regime's many critics. This may well have been the outcome, since even though the songs themselves became 'cleaner', more sentimental and less sexually-explicit, *raï* never shook off its 'immoral' associations. In his study of masculinity in Oran, Schade-Poulson describes how young men intending to 'mend their ways' by a return to praying at the mosque had first to forego the temptations of alcohol, women and listening to *raï* (1999:149).

---

[37]   *Raï* is also produced in studios on the Moroccan side of the border, although this is not perceived as problematic within Morocco, where *raï* is less popular than *cha'abi* and other genres, and is generally considered an 'Algerian' music. The towns of eastern Morocco are so distant from its other major cities that there are strong economic, familial and cultural links across the border, despite the border's official closure since 1995.

[38]   See Schade-Poulson (1999) and Tenaille (2002).

[39]   During the 1990s, over 60 per cent of the Algerian population was under 20 years of age. This age group suffered the highest level of unemployment and young people were most attracted to alternative political movements. Because of the economic crisis, young women were more likely than ever to marry overseas, into Maghrebi families resident in Europe. The same option was not open to young men who, underemployed, often remained in prolonged dependency in the family home.

Early *raï* singers doubtless benefited from the publicity that the genre's notoriety brought them and yet it was inevitable that they would become unwitting participants in the political turmoil that engulfed Algeria from the late 1980s. Even the most outspoken songs, though critical of social restrictions in a general sense, avoided overt political statements. Nevertheless, as political and cultural views became increasingly polarised, *raï* became associated with notions of cultural hybridity and modernity that in themselves had become problematic for many Algerians. Supporters of political Islam certainly considered *raï* a debased form of entertainment which exhibited both local immorality *and* 'Western values'. Whilst many people in Oran told me that they were rather ashamed that such a 'low' form of music had achieved international success, it nevertheless seemed clear that *raï*'s social role in weddings and even its very syncretic nature were distinctly local characteristics. Just as *derija* is a patois derived from many sources and Oranaise culture more generally draws upon both local and global features, so *raï* also reflects this complex and uncertain post-colonial mix of influences. As I have argued elsewhere (Langlois 1996), those elements of *raï* that suggest 'modernity' to listeners (for example, the use of synthesised, rather than native flute sounds) are often used rather cosmetically in local music production.[40] Despite a veneer of electronic instrumentation, Algerian *raï* generally adhered to traditional sonorities, and melodic and rhythmic structures. This allowed musicians to seamlessly adapt well-known popular and even religious songs into their repertoire. Such indigenous characteristics of the music would not protect it from a political critique which disapproved of music *per se*. Moreover, *raï*'s (global) syncretism and (local) immoral associations made it a highly visible target for insurgents. Many singers received death threats and several concert halls used for *raï* performances outside Oran were burned down in the early 1990s. Star performers such as Khaled and Mami, who had already become famous outside the country, left Algeria. Due to reduced opportunities for performance or intimidation, others retired or turned to other musical genres and some have even been killed. In September 1994 Cheb Hasni, certainly the most famous star of the *sentimentale* style of *raï*, was shot dead outside his home in Oran for (according to his detractors) 'spreading evil across the earth'. Two years later, Ahmed Baba, the genre's most celebrated record producer, was also assassinated in Tlemçen (Tenaille 2002).

Raï's political significance, by which I mean its widely perceived relations to political discourses, does not stem from its associations with specific social groups so much as its contradiction of such compartmentalisation. Had *raï* remained in those liminal spaces ascribed to it (weddings and nightclubs), had its vulgarity remained hidden and parochial, then its political significance may well have been quite different. Such controversy as *raï* has generated stems from its problematic visibility at least as much as from its content *per se*. *Raï* presents Algeria (and to

---

[40]   Since most recording studios operate on a small scale for quick turnover, they are reluctant to take bold creative risks. Consequently, the greatest source of innovation in contemporary *raï* arguably comes from music produced outside North Africa.

some extent, North Africa generally) as a vibrant but contradictory cultural space. At once highly local in language, theme and structure (songs from Oran regularly mention specific streets and quarters of the city) but with the 'exotic' trappings of Western pop, *raï* is a trans-Mediterranean phenomenon in ways that other Maghrebi genres are not. *Raï* produced in France now addresses frustrations experienced in the housing estates of Lyons more than the Vieux Port quarter of Oran, its themes of loss, psychological conflict and disenfranchisement as applicable to diasporic North African culture as they are to indigenous youth. In a political environment where 'modernities' are not only perceived to have failed, but are under assault by proponents of hyper-traditionalism, *raï* demonstrates in many, doubtless unintended ways, the *bricolage* that most Algerians actually inhabit.

The Politics of Music Production and Consumption

As elsewhere in the world, new media technologies have had a considerable impact on the ways in which music is produced and consumed in North Africa. Pop *raï* owes its very existence to developments in recording and broadcasting technology, and in particular the fact that these have proved difficult for the authorities to control.[41] On the production side, cassette (and now digitally-based) recording systems have enabled multi-tracking, sampling and – with stereo sound – spatial experimentation, all techniques which are more apparent in *raï* than in other genres. In contrast to recordings of *andalus*, which aim to reproduce 'ideal performances' of relatively large ensembles with little apparent editing, the *raï* aesthetic typically involves a solo singer accompanied by synthesised instruments, prominent electronic drums and a non-naturalistic spatial orientation of sound. In short, the object of the recording here is not to emulate a live performance but to employ novel, even disorienting techniques. In the case of *g'nâwa*, since the ritual event itself is so central to its meaning, this music is broadcast infrequently, although there are commercial recordings which attempt to reproduce 'live' performances in a studio.[42] Not only do such different uses of technology appeal to varying audiences, but to some extent they also reflect differing notions of authenticity. For example, whilst *andalus* recordings demonstrate respect for artistic heritage – even

---

[41] For comparative material and discussion on this theme the reader is referred to Manuel (1993) and Keil (1994).

[42] Cheap recording technology has made it economically viable to produce small numbers of cassettes for local audiences. Consequently, music produced in regional languages or local styles do exist and are popular with urban migrants from these communities as well as with the home market. Although unmediated *g'nâwa* music does not have mass appeal, some characteristic features of the genre can be heard in other contexts, often signifying a degree of 'otherness'. For example, the popular Moroccan *cha'abi* group, Nass El Ghiwane (members of which have even been imprisoned in the past for political views expressed in their songs), use a *genbri* alongside a banjo and percussion instruments.

if neither the tradition nor the recording process are as straightforward as they are made to appear – *raï*'s 'authenticity' is based rather upon a local interpretation of modernity. More in tune with global styles, production techniques are influenced by 'foreign' *raï*, MTV and Levantine Arab pop, though musical structures and themes maintain continuity with familiar local sounds and consumption contexts.

The global impact of modern communication technologies upon local discourses and practices is by now well documented and it goes without saying that this window on the world has changed the ways in which North Africans see themselves and others. However, one general aspect of this phenomenon, which relates to the effect of media in the domestic environment, is worth highlighting here. In the Maghreb the home is broadly considered a feminine, family-oriented environment, whilst men tend to occupy public spaces from an early age. Satellite television and music broadcasting technologies in the home have effectively undermined the ability of men to protect the moral sanctity of domestic space through 'mutual surveillance'.[43] Although the sexes remain physically apart, it is no longer possible for this conceptual barrier to be convincingly maintained. The implications of such changes for gender politics have yet to be seen.

Conclusions

The most potent political discourses in contemporary North Africa relate to concepts of the nation state (often conflated with 'nationalised institutions' such as the presidency or official religion), to radical Islam, 'global modernity' and, to a less universal extent, to class, gender and 'race'. Each of the musics described in this chapter bear particular relations to these discourses, and consequently to one another. Whilst the Moroccan and Tunisian regimes have managed to either appropriate, placate or stifle potential threats to the current political *status quo*, this has proved much more difficult in Algeria. Because of its specific socio-cultural connotations, music itself becomes politically discursive, and this is particularly evident in cases where music engenders patterns of social activity or fosters ways of thinking and feeling about such core tropes as gender.[44] It is because music and musical practices are able to reinforce or challenge attitudes and behaviour that they have agency in identity formation. This process, however, is unpredictable and not easy for governments (let alone musicians) to control. As I have argued above, *andalus* is presented in each of the Maghreb countries as an inclusive symbol of national identity, and yet it nevertheless continues to be associated with urban elites. Though officially disapproved of, the activities of the *g'nâwa*

---

[43]   See Langlois (2005) and Hadj Moussa (2003).

[44]   Both Abu-Lughod (2002) and Armbrust (1996) discuss the role of the mass media in defining 'modern sensibilities' in an Egyptian context. This approach is particularly useful to music research, where political impact is most observable in the expression of emotions and behavioural practices.

are tolerated, partly because they are hard to regulate but also, I have suggested, because they serve a useful cathartic purpose and reinforce the boundaries between marginal and mainstream (that is, Arab, male) society. *Raï*, rendered problematically ubiquitous through new recording and broadcasting technologies, posits an ambiguous identity which in its crudest form is unacceptable to those responsible for national culture.

Interestingly, a correlation might be drawn between such musical discourses and the physical responses they engender, supporting Foucault's (1977) view that through culture the body becomes the ultimate site of political control. To take an example, both musicians and audiences at *andalus* performances typically respond with restraint, manifesting a respectful, static state of audition.[45] In contrast, the appropriate response to the music of the *g'nâwa* is emotional abandon. Once again, this is formalised: dancers do not suffer *uncontrolled* fits, but instead move rhythmically in a way that *suggests* trauma. It is hardly coincidental that audiences for *andalus* concerts tend to be predominantly male and that the concerts take place in public spaces, whilst mostly women attend *g'nâwa* events which are kept out of public sight, if not hearing. Equally characteristically, *raï* dancing is eminently social, usually involving small, single-sex groups rather than couples. Like the music itself, dance here combines traditional elements associated with wedding celebrations with the 'glamour' of the Western nightclub. The movements made in dancing to *raï* may be mildly sexually suggestive, but actual contact between dancers of different sexes rarely takes place.[46] As physical responses are not 'fixed' to these musics in all contexts (or for all time), it is reasonable to suggest that their current associations are, in part, a product of the social and political environment in which they exist. I suggest that this correlation between musical genre, social position and expressive behaviour may be a common principle in North African countries, though the musical styles themselves may be quite different. Musical genres have come to be strongly associated both with the groups that participate in them and with the behaviour they elicit, and consequently have connotative political meaning in relation to one another.

---

[45] This controlled response to music is reminiscent of the ideal emotional state of audition (*samā'*) as described by Rouget (1985:264–70) and Racy (2003:56).

[46] At Algerian weddings which I have attended, male and female dancers do mix, although most guests are from the families of the bride or groom and they are closely observed by family elders. Where supervision is light it is not uncommon for fights to break out between jealous young men. Such fights tend mostly to be over issues of pride and I have not seen them result in physical injury.

Chapter 9

Singing against Silence: Celebrating Women and Music at the Fourth Jasmine Festival

Wendy S. DeBano

Introduction

The Jasmine Festival (Jashnvāreh-ye Gol-e Yās) is a weeklong festival of women's music that began in 1999, one of the first national festivals of women's music in Iran. The festival, which features art and folk musics, is held annually at one of Tehran's most prestigious concert halls, the Tālār-e Vahdat, and is timed to coincide with the birthday of Fatemeh, the daughter of the Prophet Mohammad and wife of the first *Shi'eh* Imam, Ali. Open only to female performers and audiences, this event is a unique occasion on which women, performing for and with other women, work to negotiate complex government policies and changing social views regarding women, music and performance. This chapter, which focuses on the social and performance dynamics of the Fourth Jasmine Festival in 2002, examines the ways in which participants view and represent themselves, and provides a microcosmic example of how social hierarchy, music practice and 'doing gender'[1] are mutually constitutive in Iran. The festival's empowering potential and emergent pluralism[2] can only be fully understood by acknowledging the somewhat limiting and potentially divisive parameters of the festival and by investigating the ways in which individual agents and social institutions conflict or cooperate in this context. Based on my interviews with festival organisers for 2002 and previous years, participants, staff and audiences, as well as attending privately-held meetings of music advocates, other music events during the same period, and observations at every concert in the 2002 festival series,[3] a number of points become clear. First, a great deal of ambivalence still exists towards the musical activities of women in Iran; second, state agencies and policies directly and profoundly affect women's musical lives; third, there is a disjunction between official mandates and actual practice; fourth, despite

---

[1]   An expression which emphasises the performative aspects of gender and the fact that gender is 'an activity accomplished through routine social interaction' (Andersen 2003:409).

[2]   Nooshin (2005b) has discussed this phenomenon with regard to rock music, and there are some parallels in the Jasmine Festival.

[3]   The author is grateful to the American Institute of Iranian Studies for their fellowship support during this period.

the inherent challenges, women are increasingly active and vocal as performers and aficionados; and finally, notwithstanding externally imposed limits, the Jasmine Festival is nonetheless empowering for many of its participants.

The degree to which the Jasmine Festival and similar events are regarded as empowering or otherwise depends largely on the cultural and historical perspective of the viewer, as well as their general positioning in relation to Iranian social hierarchies. Moreover, it is important to note that attitudes towards women and music are far from monolithic, nor do they emerge from an historical vacuum, as will be discussed below. In some cases, rifts over questions concerning the fundamental form that Iranian culture and society should take have been so pronounced that Iranians have found themselves oceans apart, both figuratively and literally.[4] Such differences explain conflicting views about the 'women-only' nature of the Jasmine Festival, criticised by some as an imposed form of gender segregation but viewed by others as an important tool for women's empowerment. Likewise, diverse perspectives on the role of music in society and competing notions of musical aesthetics account for simultaneous claims that events such as the Jasmine Festival are one of the most effective ways to foster Iranian music or, alternatively, have the effect of stunting artistic freedom. In this discussion, I will focus on both the state's expedient use of the festival for distinct national and religious agendas, as well as the ways in which advocates embrace the festival as a means of promoting women's greater participation in musical spheres.

Women and Music in Iran: Attitudes and Debates

While a detailed discussion of concepts such as Islamic feminism and feminism in Iran lies well beyond the scope of this chapter, the following analysis of the Fourth Jasmine Festival is strongly informed by such paradigms. Musical traditions and institutions on the one hand, and gender constructs on the other, were both dramatically affected by the sweeping changes that followed the 1979 Revolution, and later, by the gradual reforms and liberalisation associated with the election of President Khatami in 1997.[5] In particular, state-dictated changes after 1979 dramatically altered many aspects of daily life for certain groups including 'ethnic' minorities, women and musicians. Even before the revolution, these groups were located on the periphery of powerful social institutions and their full participation in society was often limited by the state's intertwined social and political agendas. However, post-1979 changes worked to place many already-marginalised groups

---

    [4]   I refer here to the large Iranian diaspora population. Views on such issues are often very diverse, whether between Iranians in Iran and in diaspora or even amongst those living in the same place.

    [5]   Changes in the post-1979 period are only touched on briefly here. Youssefzadeh (2000) provides an in-depth discussion of the role of official music organisations with regard to the transmission of music.

in an even more tenuous position. The specific implications for women and musicians will be discussed below.

Because gender constructs always operate in relation to other social hierarchies, women's experiences during and after the revolution depended greatly on factors such as ethnic background, religion, class, age, education and so on. For example, for women from relatively conservative religious backgrounds, state-mandated rules concerning gender segregation, dress and other aspects of social conduct worked to open up educational and employment opportunities that had not existed before 1979.[6] By enforcing 'propriety' (according to post-revolutionary social mores) in public venues such as schools and offices, women from relatively conservative families were able to participate in the public arena with greater ease than before, and were thus more likely to encounter a more diverse range of people and ideas than had previously been the case.[7] Post-revolutionary reconfigurations of gender norms and ideals also had a significant impact on musical practice.

In the rapidly changing socio-cultural atmosphere of the early 1980s, gender norms and ideals were not the only contested social issues: the appropriate role of music and the status of musicians were the subject of much debate and resulted in new laws circumscribing musical practice and transmission. For instance, there was a prolonged ban on all popular music, public solo female singing in front of mixed gender audiences was forbidden and the material culture associated with music – particularly instruments and sound recordings – was carefully monitored.[8] Explicit government permission was (and still is) required for all public concerts, sound recordings and publications on music. Many musicians, especially those with strong connections with the pre-revolutionary regime, left Iran and some of those who remained discontinued their performances altogether.[9]

---

[6] It is important to note that conservative *Shi'eh* families represent a gamut of class associations. Thus, it would be incorrect to conflate the religiously conservative lower-class families (unlikely to attend the Jasmine Festival partly because of cost, but also because of negative attitudes towards music) with the elite families of leading clerics and government officials (who may also generally frown on music, but many of whom are more open to, and able to afford to attend, cultural events sponsored by the state).

[7] While such women were unlikely to become professional musicians, some took music lessons from teachers approved by the Ministry of Culture and Islamic Guidance. Also, women from this background would be more likely to accept employment at public cultural venues, working as entrance guards, ushers, stage hands and so on. For example, one usher with whom I spoke, and who lives in a poor area of south Tehran, told me that she was grateful for her job, not only because she enjoyed the work, meeting people, and seeing the concerts, but also because it was 'honest pay'.

[8] Women sing in groups (sometimes as small as duets or trios) in front of mixed gender audiences, but solo singing in front of men is officially prohibited. Of course, actual musical practice, especially as it occurs in the privacy of a home or studio, does not always adhere to official mandates.

[9] The superstar pop singer Googoosh is a prime example of this. Although very active as a performer since childhood, Googoosh ceased singing publicly after the revolution.

Just as the Iranian Revolution was not an isolated or simple historical event, so Iranian society has not remained static in the intervening period. The situation of music has changed dramatically since the early 1980s and by the summer of 2002, when the Fourth Jasmine Festival took place, government restrictions on music had eased considerably.[10] Indeed, even before the election of President Khatami in 1997, some musicians, especially those representing art music (*musiqi-e sonnati*) and folk (*mahalli*) traditions, were supported and promoted by the government as part of what some have hailed as a post-1979 renaissance of indigenous music. After 1997, significant policy changes occurred. For instance, certain kinds of Iranian pop music were legalised and, within specific parameters of style, performance and lyrics, a number of local pop musicians (mainly men) have emerged.[11] Indications of the greater acceptance and promotion of women musicians include the emergence of festivals such as the Jasmine Festival,[12] the rising prominence of female performers, the increasing role of women in official cultural institutions and as music educators, and the growing number of female music students. However, much of this is less the result of advocacy on the part of the government but rather speaks to the hard work and diligence of particular artists, teachers and promoters. Most of the musicians that I spoke to, both male and female, argued that while the relative liberalisation since 1997 has led to some improvements, musicians still face many financial and institutional barriers: state policies and bureaucracy work to reinforce social biases against both music and female performers, and the process of establishing oneself as a musician remains overly dependent on personal contacts. Among government-sanctioned musicians, there is a clear hierarchy based on an individual's musical pedigree, talent, popularity and willingness to navigate state institutions. Those who wish to continue their careers are obliged to work within state parameters. At the same time, better-known artists are often allowed greater leeway – in terms of performance liberties, venue access, repertoire and so on – than their less prestigious counterparts.

Since leaving Iran in 2000 (and settling in Toronto, Canada), Googoosh has undertaken a number of concert tours in North America and Europe.

[10]   The fact that Iranians nowadays carry musical instruments quite openly in public is one indicator of shifts, both in government policy and also in terms of general social attitudes towards music.

[11]   As discussed by Nooshin elsewhere in this volume.

[12]   As well as devoting segments of national mixed gender festivals such as the Fajr Festival (which started in 1989) to women, there have since 1997 been a handful of national women's festivals including the 2003 Festival of Women's Regional Music and the 2005 Lady of Paradise Festival (Jashnvāreh-ye Bānu-ye Behesht) which had the stated goal of featuring music from various tribes. It is important to note that in addition to these state festivals, women perform regularly at many concerts for both mixed gender and women-only audiences. However, *any* public concert, even if it doesn't have the visibility of a national festival concert series, requires state permission and review.

The Dynamics of Participation and Representation at the Jasmine Festival

Officially sponsored by the Ministry of Culture and Islamic Guidance (Vezārat-e Farhang va Ershād-e Eslāmi),[13] in conjunction with the ministry's Music Center (Markaz-e Musiqi) and the Society for Iranian Music (Anjoman-e Musiqi-e Iran), the Fourth Jasmine Festival for Women (Chahāromin Jashnvāreh-ye Gol-e Yās Vizheh-ye Banuvān) was organised by Fariba Davudi (herself a musician) and included 12 all-female groups.[14] The festival was held at Tehran's Tālār-e Vahdat (Unity Hall), one of the most prestigious concert halls in the capital and the daily performances, which featured two concerts every evening, ran between 31 August and 6 September 2002.[15] Aurally, the festival's diversity followed that of other state-sponsored festivals, with the difference that it was women's voices that resonated in the hall.[16] Conceptually and visually, the festival was framed and promoted as a woman's space within a broad national and religious context.

---

[13]   Known as Vezārat-e Ershād for short. All public concerts need official permission (*mojavvez*) from this ministry. Those in charge of venues where live music is performed, even if this is only a restaurant, can be fined for allowing unauthorised performances. This point was explained to me after witnessing an incident between a restaurant owner and two Afghani musicians in Neyshapour, a city in northeastern Iran, in 2002. After noticing that two unauthorised performers were busking on his property, the restaurant owner chased the pair off the premises, repeatedly beating them with kitchen implements and the *daff* (frame drum) that he had grabbed from one of the players. I was told that neither the restaurant owner nor those of us at the table who had encouraged and enjoyed the musical performance were 'responsible' for this altercation. Rather, it was the fault of the musicians (who were obviously destitute refugees) who had not obtained official permission.

[14]   The festival organiser varies from year to year (Pari Maleki was the organiser for the first festival in 1999). Whilst Davudi was in charge of organising the 2002 festival, she worked closely with other musicians and concert hall staff in putting the programme together.

[15]   According to the solar *khorshidi* calendar (used predominantly in Iran and Afghanistan), these concert dates ran between the 9th and 15th of the month of *Shahrivar* in the year 1381 (31 August – 6 September 2002). According to the Arabic lunar calendar (referred to locally as *tārikh-e hejri-e qamari*), the festival occurred between the 22nd and 28th of the month of *Jamādi* in the year 1423.

[16]   The ensembles which performed at the festival were as follows (listed in order of performance): Tanburnavāzān-e Zakhmeh, led by Shirin Mohammadi; Naghmeh, led by Azar Hashemi and featuring Naghmeh Gholami as vocalist; Sahar, featuring the singer Shakeh Aghamal and Niloofar Badrikuhi on piano; Pari Rokh, featuring the singer Pari Zanganeh with Fariba Javaheri and Azadeh Gorgani on piano; Chehel Daff, led by Fariba Rostamzadeh (Gharibnejad) and featuring Sudabeh Amani as vocalist; Golbāng, led by Behnaz Zakeri and featuring Parvin Sabet (Keshavarz) as vocalist; Viyan Sanandaj, led by Shohleh Kordnejad and featuring Neshat Mojtahedi as vocalist; Neyriz, led by Maliheh Sa'idi and featuring Hurvash Khalili as vocalist; Shāteriān-e Tabriz, featuring Shayesteh Ahmadi as vocalist; Zhivār, featuring the ensemble leader and vocalist Kalaleh Shaykh al-Eslami (Zhivar); Tazro, with orchestral leader Sorur Zarigar and featuring the singers Qodsi

The Fourth Jasmine Festival was enveloped by notions of the 'ideal' *Shi'eh* woman and of the nation according to post-revolutionary social mores and gender ideologies. As Kandiyoti has observed, nationalism often brings mixed blessings for women:

> Women's stake in nationalism has been both complex and contradictory. On the one hand, nationalist movements invite women to participate more fully in collective life by interpolating them as 'national' actors: mothers, educators, workers, and even fighters. On the other hand, they reaffirm the boundaries of culturally acceptable feminine conduct and exert pressure on women to articulate their gender interests within the terms set by nationalist discourse. (1996:9)

Only women are allowed to attend the festival, which is always timed to coincide with the birthday of Fatemeh, the daughter of the Prophet Mohammad and wife of the first *Shi'eh* Imam, Ali.[17] Fatemeh's significance as a female role model is unparalleled elsewhere in *Shi'eh* Islam, and in post-revolutionary Iran she has become a gendered symbol of nation.[18] And since Fatemeh's birthday is an important holiday for *Shi'eh* Muslims, schools, government offices and businesses are closed and there are commemorative celebrations and events throughout the country.[19] Given the strong association between Fatemeh's birthday and the Jasmine Festival, it is interesting that some of the ensembles which participated in the festival, including the predominantly Armenian group Sahar, represented non-Muslim religious groups who would not otherwise celebrate this *Shi'eh* holiday.

Graphic and symbolic representations of Iran's religious and cultural diversity were absent from the promotional materials for the festival, as were any images of musical instruments or female performers. On posters, billboards and ticket jackets, the only symbol evoking music was the image of a treble clef. For those unfamiliar with music notation, the significance of this central image was obfuscated by its

Moshiri and Mahin Afjam; and Orkestr-e Majlesi-e Fārsi, led by Purandokht Khalaj Tehrani and featuring the singer Sedigheh Emadi.

[17]   In 2002, Fatemeh's birthday celebration (observed according to the *hejri* calendar) fell on Thursday 29 August (20 *Jamādi* 1423). By coincidence, that of Ayatollah Khomeini (celebrated according to the *khorshidi* calendar) also happened to fall on the same day (29 August 2002/7 *Shahrivar* 1381).

[18]   Fatemeh was also the mother of the second and third *Shi'eh* Imams, Hassan and Hossein. Being the only one of Mohammad's offspring to have children, Fatemeh is the sole point of origin for all who currently claim to be descendants of the Prophet. Fatemeh's birth date is also currently used to mark Mother's Day in Iran, ritually recollecting, emphasising and reinscribing her role as a loyal mother, wife and daughter. Prior to the revolution, Mother's Day was used to promote the gender ideologies of the Pahlavi regime.

[19]   Banners with proclamations such as '*Yā Fatemeh*!' ('O Fatemeh!') are not only displayed on government buildings and mosques, but also adorn private buildings, public streets and even car windows. Because of the celebratory nature of this holiday, many consider music to be not only permissible, but very appropriate.

likeness to the jasmine flower (see Figure 9.1). In festival materials, the image of the jasmine – rife with feminine associations – was embedded in the colours and a graphic design similar to that of the Iranian flag, thus serving to articulate the nationalism surrounding the festival.[20]

Figure 9.1   Billboard in front of Tālār-e Vahdat (Tehran) publicising the Fourth Jasmine Festival (photograph by the author, summer 2002).

Although a few of the pieces performed at the festival specifically addressed Islamic or nationalistic themes, the musical content was not exclusively focused on *Shi'eh* sound art,[21] nor on women's musical traditions. With the exception of two concerts devoted to European classical music, the repertoire of the remaining ten scheduled concerts was directly tied to state-sponsored forms of Iranian art and folk musics. Moreover, even though some of the ensembles had been founded with the specific purpose of promoting women's access to musical training and performance, many of those who performed at the festival were simply the female contingent of

---

[20]   The Iranian flag features a tulip-shaped rendition of *Allah* ('God') in the centre of bold green, white and red stripes. Since the revolution and the ensuing Iran–Iraq war (1980–88), tulips have come to symbolise (predominantly male) martyrs.

[21]   I use the term 'sound art' here to avoid the potential conundrum that the term 'religious music' evokes in an Islamic context (for further discussion of this, see Sakata 1983, al-Faruqi 1985 and Nelson 1985). In front of an all-female audience, women's solo recitation of the Qur'an, prayers or other religious texts is perfectly acceptable and takes place both in private and in public, for example in the women's section of mosques.

otherwise mixed ensembles.[22] Festival repertoire was neither exclusively associated with women's musical traditions nor composed by women.

Even after being formally invited to perform at the festival, ensembles still had to tailor their image, repertoire and modes of representation in order to obtain official permission from Vezārat-e Ershād (see Figure 9.2). For example, prior to the festival, musicians had to provide officials at the ministry with their biographies, group photographs, a detailed concert programme, sample recordings, a transcription of all Persian lyrics and transcriptions and translations of non-Persian lyrics. Although many of the folk musicians had experience performing Iranian art music, the groups performing Kurdish, Azeri and Armenian musics made a point of choosing repertoire unique to their respective traditions, further emphasising their regional identities by using distinctive performance styles, modes of introduction, staging and dress.

Figure 9.2   Tanburnavāzān-e Zakhmeh, photograph submitted to Vezārat-e Ershād for review prior to the Fourth Jasmine Festival (photograph reproduced by kind permission of Shirin Mohammadi).

---

[22]   For example, five days prior to their performance at the Fourth Jasmine Festival (on 11 *Shahrivar* 1382), the group Chehel Daff ('Forty Daffs') performed in its entirety with both male and female members at a mixed gender celebration on the eve of Fatemeh's birthday (6 *Shahrivar* 1382) held at a large tennis stadium in the Enqelāb Sports Complex (Majmueh-ye Varzeshi-ye Enqelāb) in northern Tehran. This celebration was attended by thousands of people, mostly government employees, and featured speeches by government officials, including President Khatami, as well as the performances by Chehel Daff and other folk and pop music groups.

If there was one unifying factor among the groups present at the festival, it was not their repertoire or stage presentation, but the fact that they all shared a high level of education and training, had developed strong ties to government-sponsored cultural organisations and they performed to an elite audience. Given the relative diversity of groups and repertoire represented, the performers' biographies were strikingly similar in a number of ways: firstly, the fact that many had achieved post-secondary degrees in music, generally from state-funded universities; second, the extent to which performers had cultivated ties to official organisations, especially national radio, cultural centres and music schools; and, third, the number of musicians who had appeared at national and international venues, including some who had performed at the United Nations' Fourth World Conference on Women, held in Beijing in 1995. In a country where only a small percentage of the population is able to secure entrance to university, the educational achievements of the performers immediately indicates a high level of knowledge and competency, as well as skill and experience in negotiating various types of governmental bureaucracy. The prestige of the festival was marked not only by the privileged status of the performers, but the audience as well. Ticket prices (30,000 *rial*s, equivalent to about $3.78 [US] in 2002) effectively worked to exclude many from the lower classes. For a country where the average annual income in 2002 was $2,000, where 21 per cent of the population lived in poverty[23] and where there was an unemployment rate of 12.2 per cent,[24] the cost of attending one evening, much less the entire concert series, was prohibitive.

Interestingly, while festival performers and audiences shared similar class backgrounds, there were clear differences in attitudes concerning acceptable audience behaviour and the type of conduct considered befitting to the musical venue. This resulted in tension between some members of the audience who were unwilling to relinquish sonic control of the event, and the festival organiser, performers and other audience members who felt they had a right to quash what they regarded as boorish behaviour. Festival audiences were repeatedly admonished for rustling chip bags, bringing noisy children and clapping along to the music. In fact, the audience was specifically asked several times by the festival organiser to extend respect to the performers by being absolutely silent during performances. These requests were framed within the parameters of teaching appropriate listening etiquette to the audience. After one impassioned plea, some members of the audience responded by simply clapping along more loudly, an action which resulted in glares and derogatory remarks from others in the audience. Although this disruptive behaviour was regarded by many as being disrespectful towards the performers, it is important to contextualise the response of noisy audience

---

[23] World Bank (2004), 'Iran Data at a Glance', <www.worldbank.org/data/countrydata/aag/irn_aag.pdf> (accessed 15/04/05).

[24] International Monetary Fund (2004), *Islamic Republic of Iran: Statistical Appendix*, prepared by Abdlelali Jbili, Vitiali Kramarenko, Lynge Nielsen, José Bailén and Mitra Farahbaksh, <www.imf.org/external/pubs/ft/scr/2004/cr04307.pdf> (accessed 18/04/05), p. 3.

members. Given the relatively prohibitive entrance fees, it can be assumed that most of the audience were committed listeners. Thus, in this specific instance, boisterous clapping was not necessarily indicative of disrespect for the music and musicians, but rather was perhaps a sign that some audience members were determined to express themselves in and on their own terms.

Of all the factors shaping the Fourth Jasmine Festival, the gendered prohibitions surrounding dress and musical performance – factors which are very important considerations in public mixed gender settings – had little or no bearing on the festival. For instance, due in part to the pervasive heterosexism of Iranian society, the perceived sensuality and sexual implications of women's singing and uncovered bodies which are of such central importance at mixed gender gatherings are simply not an issue at women-only events. Men are physically excluded from all-female venues and their potential for future 'voyeurism' is kept in check by banning all recording equipment. Before audiences were admitted to the venue, concert hall staff ensured that no men – regardless of whether they were a performer's spouse, son or brother, or an unrelated member of the stage crew – remained on the premises. Like other public facilities, Tālār-e Vahdat has separate entrances for men and women and security checks are conducted by same-sex guards. Bag checks and pat-downs ensure that cameras and other recording devices such as mobile phones are not taken into the performance space. Even though audience members complained about this invasive practice, certainly the recording and public dissemination of events would be detrimental not only for the festival organiser and staff, but quite possibly for the performers and audiences as well. For instance, upon entering the auditorium, many audience members cast off their 'proper' Islamic attire such as jackets and scarves; some even donned 'Tehran chic' for the occasion.[25] While the women-only nature of the festival made some participants feel more comfortable, the absence of (male) sound engineers meant that numerous technical problems during performances remained unresolved, the lack of female engineers in itself being one consequence of the gendered division of labour. In fact, the only man in the vicinity of Tālār-e Vahdat during performances was the guard stationed at the iron gates in front of the hall, whose role was to prevent unauthorised members of the public from entering, thus making the Fourth Jasmine Festival inaudible and invisible to all but its female participants.

---

[25]   This term, taken from an online review of the Jasmine Festival, aptly encapsulates the clothing styles many Iranian women wear at social events. 'Tehran chic' is evocative of the most glamorous contemporary fashion magazines across the globe. See Shadi Vatanparast (1381[2002]), 'Behind the Curtains: A Look at Women, Music and the Fourth Annual Women's Yaas Music Festival', *Bad Jens: Iranian Feminist Newsletter*, December 2002, <www.badjens.com/newissue/a4.htm> (accessed 15/04/05).

Ambivalence about Women and Music: Historical Context and Recent Changes

Attitudes towards women and music in Iran are very complex, and have changed greatly in recent decades and continue to do so. To some extent, women engaged in state-approved musical pursuits today are far less stigmatised than those who performed during the preceding Pahlavi period (1925–79).[26] Despite positive changes, however, ambivalent attitudes towards music and female musicians are still prevalent and were often articulated in the planning stages and actual presentation of the Jasmine Festival.[27] Such attitudes have clear historical precedents and help to explain why music has so often been overlooked in accounts of women's lives in pre-revolutionary Iran. To understand performative aspects of gender in Iran, and music's potential role as a tool in women's empowerment, it is important to situate post-revolutionary attitudes about women and music with an eye both to the historical context and to recent changes.

Ambivalence towards both music and female musicians continues to have a direct impact on women's participation in musical spheres, access to training and performance venues, choices about repertoire and representation and women's ability to control some of the most basic aspects of their musical lives. Notwithstanding some important exceptions,[28] very few publications focus exclusively on women musicians and music scholarship has lagged well behind the emergent documentation on women's involvement in other spheres, most notably Iranian literature.[29] This lack of documentation promotes a type of silence

---

[26]   When I presented my findings about the Jasmine Festival at the 2004 conference of the International Society for Iranian Studies in Bethesda, Maryland (United States), audience members, many of whom were highly educated women who had grown up in pre-revolutionary Iran, commented that they were surprised at how radically attitudes to women and music had changed during their own lifetime. That music might provide a potential forum for women's empowerment had been unthinkable just decades ago.

[27]   For instance, there were many delays in receiving official permission to hold and publicise the 2002 festival. As a result, some ensembles received final confirmation of the programme only a few weeks before the festival itself and had little time to finalise their performances or prepare supplementary written materials for the programme. While festival organisers and participants (both from 2002 and previous years) have noted that delayed permissions are not uncommon in Iran regardless of the venue or the musicians involved, in this case, the repeated stalling carried a clear message that the whole concert series might be cancelled and the likelihood of its continuation was dependent upon the caprices of the state. Limits on promotional materials – in content, scope and prominence of advertising – are also indicative of such ambivalence.

[28]   See, for example, Zohreh Khaleqi's monograph on Qamar ol-Molouk Vaziri (1994) and Tuka Maleki's chronology of women in Iranian music (2001).

[29]   See Najmabadi (1990), Milani (1992) and Talattof (2000). As Talattof has noted with regard to post-revolutionary Iranian literature, 'Since the late 1980s literature has become a particularly important medium for women's self-expression because public space

about women's musical lives and experiences, a silence that is symbiotically tied to the state parameters and ideologies that permeate music festivals.[30]

Since musical training is a clear prerequisite for involvement in festivals such as that discussed here, the extent to which women have access to training is an important issue. The serious pursuit of a musical education, even if it does not lead to a professional career, has long been somewhat suspect regardless of the musician's sex, but particularly for women.[31] In fact, it wasn't until 1925 that a select group of Iranian women were first allowed to study music in a school setting, after Ali Naqi Vaziri secured special permission from the government to open a private school of arts for women.[32] Vaziri's early classes were comprised solely of extended family and friends, and it was only very gradually that women began to participate in public musical life, an arena that was considered to be male. Even now, the majority of performers, lyricists and composers are male and, indeed, concerns about transgressing the boundaries of respectable behaviour continue to reflect gender norms and expectations. The following anecdote illustrates the fact that even a figure such as Mehrangiz Manouchehrian, Iran's first female senator, a lawyer and one of the most highly celebrated feminists of the Pahlavi era, ceded her musical pursuits because of the stigma attached to female performers: 'As she got older, she studied music, learning several instruments. But she realized she could never be a performer – the only female musicians playing in public were regarded as loose women' (Howard 2002:57). Such derogatory attitudes prevailed right up until the eve of the revolution, despite the ever increasing public prominence of female performers on government-controlled media.

Due in part to the chaos that permeated all social and educational institutions at the time and due in part to the contested role and status of music and musicians, music education was, at least initially, impacted in a negative way by the revolution and the ensuing Iran–Iraq war. However, by the 1990s, select musics (especially Iranian art music and to a lesser degree, Western art music) were being actively taught both at university level, and also at cultural centres (*farhangsarā*). At the present time, many opportunities exist for male and female musicians. There are numerous privately owned music schools in Tehran and the provinces, such as that run by the Kamkar family, and as long as musicians are both licensed by and pay fees to the government, they are allowed to conduct lessons in their home.

---

for discussion and debate has been extremely limited' (2000:140). I would argue that the same is true for music.

[30]   Related issues of omission are discussed by DeBano (2003, 2004) and Youssefzadeh (2004).

[31]   By discussing the following attitudes towards music and professional musicians, I do not mean to imply that such attitudes are confined to Iran or the Middle East.

[32]   The information about Vaziri and his music school are taken from Khoshzamir (1979:113–14) who cites a June 1977 interview with Mrs Badri Vaziri (Vaziri's daughter) as his source. This same information (without the specific citation of 1925) is found in Khaleqi (1956:234–8) and reiterated by Maleki (2001:180).

Musical training is not only important in terms of increasing the presence of women in musical life, but can in fact be a significant tool for women's empowerment. Teachers that I've talked with who have participated in the Jasmine Festival proudly describe how their students' outlook on life, their degree of assertiveness, and even their posture, have changed noticeably in the course of their lessons. Likewise, I have seen many cases where students embrace music as a sole refuge from social and familial pressures, and their teachers – male and female – are important role models.[33] As the enthusiastic audiences at the Jasmine Festival demonstrated, even women who choose not to pursue formal musical training can be very vocal fans.

Assessing the Potential for Empowerment at the Jasmine Festival

To understand fully the implications of women's continued participation as teachers and performers, and how this affects the Jasmine Festival, it is important to examine the internally and externally imposed silences of female musicians. These selective silences are spawned both by the fact that the Jasmine Festival is sponsored by the state and that it is a women-only event. On the one hand, some female musicians refuse to participate in state-run festivals on the basis that they are unable to control many parameters of the performance. Other musicians do not participate in festivals that segregate women, which are often considered to be inferior to and less profitable than men's performances,[34] and thus potentially unrewarding artistically and economically.

Given current government restrictions, some artists are concerned that their participation may signal complicity with state-imposed gendering of musical spheres and thereby compromise their artistic or professional standing. By limiting the performance venues available to female musicians, women often lack access to what are construed as being more 'serious' venues;[35] likewise, when men

---

[33] These students, many of whom have no intention of becoming professional musicians, include not only younger students (in their teens and twenties) but also middle-aged women. Such students are enthusiastic, demonstrate a strong personal connection to their instructor and are avid concert-goers whose support often extends to their teachers' wider circle of colleagues and mentors.

[34] Although I was unable to ascertain exact figures for this festival, I frequently heard complaints that female groups earned less than comparable all-male or mixed gender ensembles would have. Furthermore, I was told that participation fees were exorbitant compared with groups' incomes from their percentage of ticket sales, thus making each group's total income from performances only nominal.

[35] As noted earlier, the Jasmine Festival features some of the most highly trained and talented female musicians in Iran and is held at Tālār-e Vahdat, one of the most exclusive venues in the country. Generally speaking, however, women-only groups are not usually awarded this level of prestige.

are excluded from women's music venues, potential collaboration and exchange among musicians can be stifled.[36] As Pari Maleki, one of the first female vocalists to receive an official permit to perform in post-revolutionary Iran, and a strong supporter of the Jasmine Festival in the past, explains:

> I used to give concerts for women. But I've come to believe that joint concerts with men co-singers (and mixed audience) are better because the manoeuvrability in women's music has been narrowed. I mean the level of performance in exclusively-women programs cannot be as high as it is otherwise.[37]

Other active performers and teachers, such as the singer Afsaneh Rasayi, often perform abroad rather than be limited to women-only contexts in Iran.[38] Those who choose to participate in women-only contexts often do so in the hope that their involvement will pave the way for greater freedoms in the future, and also out of a sense of obligation to their female audiences.

Some studies of women-only festivals outside Iran suggest that these types of festivals can be extremely important sites where women can develop and celebrate their musical and technical skills and repertoires by and for women, as well as fostering women-oriented audiences.[39] Similarly, Veronica Doubleday, who has discussed the negative impact of gender segregation on music in Afghanistan, has also pointed to the potential benefits of all-female gatherings: 'Middle Eastern women often enjoy the privilege of all-woman space, a setting which facilitates the power of female solidarity and provides the principal context for music-making' (1999:102–3).

Although the music at the 2002 Jasmine Festival did not represent a women-created or 'women-centred' repertoire, it is true that the women-only space of the festival, while externally imposed, was used by the organiser, performers,

---

[36]   It should be noted, however, that such collaboration regularly takes place outside the context of women-only groups and festivals.

[37]   Quotation from 'Close-up with First Post-revolution Woman Vocalist: Traditional Music Enjoys Relatively High Standard', *Iran Daily*, 14 September 2003, cited on <www. khonya.com/htmls/engpage/interv_irandaily.htm> (accessed 14/04/05) (original in English). Both Maleki and Afsaneh Rasayi (another prominent vocalist) have expressed these sentiments, not only in published interviews but also in person when I visited their teaching studios in August 2002.

[38]   It should be noted that Rasayi has performed and recorded in Iran with the ensemble Hamāvāyān which comprises vocalists Mohsen Keramati, Afsaneh Rasayi and Homa Niknam in addition to Ali Samadpour (supporting vocal and *dammām*), Daryush Zargari (*tombak*) and Hossein Alizadeh (*tār* and *tanbur*). Given the prohibitions on the solo female voice, it is interesting that on the album *Rāz-e No* ('New Secret'), whilst the two female vocalists, Rasayi and Niknam, don't technically sing 'solo' for more than a few seconds (since one of the other two vocalists are often singing as well or echoing a previous phrase), nevertheless, the voices of all three performers can be clearly distinguished (Alizadeh 1998).

[39]   *Radical Harmonies*, 2004, dir. Dee Mosbacher, San Jose, CA: Wolfe Video.

concert hall staff and audiences not only to bond, but to reinterpret and challenge gender norms and hierarchies. The events surrounding and defining the festival demonstrated that the 'feminine' ideals promoted and reinforced by the state are certainly more prescriptive than descriptive. When women participate in musical activities, whether as performers, as students or as music aficionados, they are clearly acting as vocal agents on their own behalf. Whether at events such as state-run festivals, or in the privacy of music lessons and rehearsals, silence is simply not part of the musical equation.

Ultimately, differing attitudes towards female musicians, their training and their performances not only impact on the content and presentation of the Jasmine Festival, but continue to reflect and inform debates about the future role of women and music in Iran. The very same behavioural codes that shape attitudes towards music in Iran are closely tied to those involved in the social construction of gender. In this regard, those who participated in the Jasmine Festival were not simply passive victims of the state or of patriarchal society, but rather active social agents who, despite many obstacles, make choices about their lives, their representation and the terms in which they will collaborate with or challenge existing norms. Given the parameters within which they must navigate their careers and daily interactions, their accomplishments are truly extraordinary. For these reasons, the dynamics of women's music making in Iran merit further examination since they offer potentially useful paradigms for social theory and action.

Conclusion

This chapter has sought to highlight the gendered construction of musical experience in Iran as encapsulated in the Fourth Jasmine Festival. In this context, simply belonging to a particular musical tradition and actively claiming one's identity as a female performer, or even as a music aficionado, involves an often precarious balancing act in which performers must negotiate shifting governmental policies and complex notions of music and self. Despite the fact that women's participation in music has been clearly circumscribed, I would argue that the various issues of representation and identity that surround and internally structure the Jasmine Festival work to heighten its transformative social potential, which is profound, both for members of the musical community and beyond. Through music and its performance, female musicians and their audiences grapple with the realities of state and social marginalisation while at the same time actively asserting their individual and collective notions of self and society. For many, the Jasmine Festival is a 'safe place' to share not only their music, but also their experiences, their struggles and their creative vision, both with other musicians and with their audiences. Less experienced musicians use the festival to network professionally with veteran performers and to develop and reaffirm deeply personal and symbolic ties to their mentors. For more veteran performers, participation in the festival underscores their central role in respective musical communities as artists and leaders, thereby validating their personal and professional struggles as well as their lifelong contributions.

The broader social implications of the Jasmine Festival are inherent in its historical and cultural significance. Even the idea of a nationally endorsed 'respectable' forum for female musicians would have been unimaginable in prior decades, and certainly in prior generations. As such, the successes and challenges associated with the Jasmine Festival provide a model for previously marginalised individuals and social groups seeking to express their emerging roles and realise their own visions of the future.

Chapter 10
'Tomorrow is Ours':
Re-imagining Nation, Performing Youth in the New Iranian Pop Music

Laudan Nooshin

Prelude: 'How Precious Can a Concert Be?'

In her November 2002 review of a pop concert in Tehran which appeared in the on-line arts magazine tehranavenue.com, Naghmeh Taqizadeh reports on the ticket-buying frenzy which preceded a series of concerts by the up-and-coming Arian Band. Arian presented a total of 14 concerts over seven nights in Tehran's Milad Hall. According to official sources, an unprecedented 28,000 tickets were sold in the first six hours and tickets were subsequently available on the black market at ten times the box office price.[1] Describing the extremes to which some went to obtain tickets, a rather bemused Taqizadeh asks, 'How precious can a concert be?'[2] In this chapter, I attempt to answer this question by examining various aspects of Arian's music, including some of the reasons for the band's popularity and the ways in which the band uses the performative – and transformative – power of music to explore a range of contemporary issues. Drawing on analysis of lyrics, music and live performance, as well as personal interviews with musicians, audiences and band members, Arian's music will be considered in the context of the post-1997 reform movement, an emergent youth culture and ongoing debates within Iran about the role of civil society and changing notions of national identity.[3]

---

[1]   Interview with Mr Taqavi, Director of the company Tiraj-e Film, on *Arian Band Live in Concert* (Arian Band, DVD, Tarane Sharghee Cultural & Artistic Company, 2003).

[2]   Naghmeh Taqizadeh (2002), 'How Precious Can a Concert Be?' <www.tehranavenue.com/at_city_queue.htm> (accessed 21/11/04).

[3]   The material presented in this chapter is based on several periods of fieldwork in Iran between 1999 and 2008.

Introduction: 1997 and its Aftermath

Arian Band was born out of the specific socio-cultural environment which followed the May 1997 landslide presidential election victory of Mohammad Khatami. After almost 20 years of austerity, Khatami's presidency ushered in a period of liberalism which included profound changes in cultural policy, with far-reaching implications for music in particular. As I have discussed elsewhere, one of the most remarkable changes was the legalisation of pop music – which had been banned in public since the 1979 Revolution – and the subsequent development of a local pop music industry.[4] Not only did this legalisation allow the government to take control of the pop music market, but many Iranians welcomed what came to be known as '*pop-e jadid*' ('the new pop') as an alternative to imported diaspora pop which had dominated the black market since the early 1980s and was increasingly regarded as disconnected from life in Iran.[5] Legalisation was followed by decentralisation, and decentralisation led to something unforeseen by the government: alongside the newly legalised 'mainstream' pop, there emerged a new grassroots 'alternative' music movement, strongly rock-oriented and predominantly urban, cosmopolitan and middle-class.[6] Several bands which began in this way became assimilated into the musical mainstream as a result of commercial success; others, either unable to gain government authorisation or who remained outside the mainstream by choice,

---

[4]   It should be noted that some forms of popular music – diaspora and pre-1979 Iranian pop, as well as Western commercial popular music broadly defined – remained, and remain, prohibited (see Nooshin 2005a). In this chapter, I use the term 'pop' as it is used in Iran, that is to refer to mainstream, mediated, commercial pop music. The broader category of 'popular music' as I use it here also encompasses a range of other styles such as rock, metal and hip-hop which are largely unauthorised by the government and therefore mainly circulate 'underground'; discussion of the latter lies outside the scope of this chapter.

[5]   There are interesting parallels elsewhere in the Middle East with the post-1997 legalisation of pop music in Iran. In 1985, for example, the Algerian government unexpectedly relaxed its opposition to *rai*. As Gross, McMurray and Swedenburg note, '… at the same time that officialdom brought *rai* in from the periphery and claimed it as part of the national patrimony, it attempted to tame, contain and mainstream the music' (1996:124). Unlike Iran, however, this required a cleaning up of what were widely regarded as risqué lyrics. Similarly, Stokes discusses the use of a previously marginalised musical style – *arabesk* – by the Özal government in Turkey for specific political objectives (1994c:26). Returning to Iran, there are also parallels with the government appropriation, and subsequent development, of the local film industry in the early 1980s, see Nooshin (2005a:252–3, 265, 2008:70).

[6]   Some indication of the astounding growth in the local market is given by Youssefzadeh (2003), according to whom half of all music permit applications submitted to the Ministry of Culture and Islamic Guidance (Vezārat-e Farhang va Ershād-e Eslāmi) in 2002 were for recordings of pop music. Since 1986, all commercial recordings and public performances of music have required such government authorisation.

have found other ways of reaching audiences through 'underground' networks and particularly through the Internet.[7]

Khatami represented the so-called 'reformist' section of a government which had been (and continues to be) marked by deep fissures and internal power struggles since the creation of the Islamic Republic in 1979; and internal divisions have been particularly acute in relation to matters of cultural policy which have formed the focus of contestation between reformist factions on the one hand and 'conservative' factions on the other.[8] Two imperatives were central to the agenda of the post-1997 reform movement: the development of a civil society infrastructure in Iran, and the normalising of Iran's international relations. Both are relevant to the discussion of this chapter. With regard to civil society, many writers have noted the growing importance of pluralist thinking in Iranian social and political life in recent years and the increasing number of non-state organisations. Some have even suggested that an increasingly decentralised social space and more empowered civil institutions are crucial to Iran's future stability, as a counterbalance to the central power of the state.[9] During his eight-year presidency (1997 to 2005), Khatami invested a great deal in promoting the civil society agenda and even published on the subject of Islam and civil society.[10] In this way, the civil society 'discourse' became inextricably associated with Khatami and his followers. The growth of civil society in Iran has important implications for music, as will be discussed below. In particular, as a symbol of the new civil voice, the grassroots music movement can be understood as both emanating from, and contributing to, the new mood of pluralism and diversity.

Another important aspect of the post-1997 period has been the growth of a distinct and visible youth culture,[11] manifested in various ways, including media and other commercial products aimed at young people: magazines (for example, *Iran Javān* ['Young Iran']) and television and radio programmes, including a dedicated radio channel (Radio Javān); a growing number of social venues and events where young people can meet (cafés, parks, concerts, chic shopping malls and so on); as well as the ubiquitous jeans, mobile phones and other indicators of a modern-cosmopolitan lifestyle. Alongside this, increased access to satellite technology (from the early 1990s) and the Internet (from the late 1990s) enabled many young people to re-connect with the outside world after two decades of

---

[7]   See Nooshin (2005b).

[8]   See Dorraj (2001), Alinejad (2002), Moslem (2002) and Tarrock (2002).

[9]   See Amirahmadi (1996:90) and Banuazizi (1995:576).

[10]   See, for example, Khatami (2000). Khatami's inaugural speech is published in *Civil Society* V1(69):7–9 (1997). There is an extensive literature on the development of civil society, both in Iran and the Middle East in general and the reader is referred to Banuazizi (1995), Norton (1995), Amirahmadi (1996), Kamali (1998), Bashiriyeh (2001), Gheytanchi (2001), Kamrava (2001), Sajoo (2002) and Chaichian (2003).

[11]   Continuing a fledgling youth culture which began in the 1960s but which went through a period of hiatus (at least in the public domain) during the 1980s and much of the '90s.

relative isolation.[12] Notwithstanding the still strong social divisions, both in terms of class[13] and the urban/rural divide, there is an increasing self-awareness among young people, what might be termed a youth consciousness. One of the propelling forces behind this is demography: the birth rate rose sharply in the early 1980s and an estimated 70 per cent of the population is currently under the age of 30.[14] Moreover, whilst a sizeable section of the population has no memory of life before 1979, the cosmopolitan outlook inherited from this period has remained and become more widespread.[15] Unsympathetic to the predominantly authoritarian and confrontational style of governance, many young people have become disillusioned both with the government's failure to address issues such as unemployment and social alienation and the inability of the reform movement to effect genuine economic and social change, particularly after so much hope was invested in it after 1997. At the same time, one of the most interesting social phenomena in Iran today is that young people and women, previously the two most disenfranchised sections of society, are increasingly making their presence felt in the public domain.[16]

After many years of largely ignoring the needs of young people, the government has, somewhat late in the day, started to acknowledge the significance of this so-called 'third generation' (Alinejad 2002:35). The easing of restrictions on pop music was a clear indication of this; but the legalisation could only work (for the government) if the music could be centrally controlled. One way of doing this was to insert pop music into an official framework, as seen for example in the inclusion of a pop music section, *musiqi-e 'elmi-e rooz*,[17] in the government-sponsored

---

[12]   Since 2001, blogging has become immensely popular in Iran. Indeed, according to Khiabany and Sreberny, 'Persian bloggers number in the hundreds of thousands, making Persian amongst the top five most popular languages of the global blogosphere' (2007:563).

[13]   And which points to the emergence of distinct youth cultures (in the plural), a topic which, however, lies beyond the scope of this chapter.

[14]   At the time of the 1996 Iranian census, 60.04 per cent of the population was under the age of 25 (Statistical Centre of Iran, <www.sci.org.ir/portal/faces/public/sci_en/sci_en.Glance/sci_en.pop>, accessed 17/09/06). Recently published statistics from the 2006 census show a sharp drop to 50.24 per cent under the age of 25 (<www.sci.org.ir:80/portal/faces/public/sci_en/sci_en.Glance/sci_en.pop>, accessed 03/09/08). United Nations statistics (most recently available for 2002) give a figure of 32 per cent of the population under the age of 15 (<http://cyberschoolbus.un.org/infonation3/menu/advanced.asp>, accessed 08/01/07). Young adults and city dwellers represent two of the largest sections of Iran's population (Naficy 2002:55).

[15]   For further discussion of Iran's emerging youth culture see Mousavi Shafaee (2003:191–3), Basmenji (2005), Varzi (2006) and Khosravi (2007).

[16]   See Alinejad (2002:26) and Dabashi (2001:269). These are the very sections of society from which Khatami gained much of his support (Naficy 2002:55, Dabashi 2001:269).

[17]   Literally 'scientific music of the day'. The use of the term *'elmi* ('scientific') in this context is very interesting. Elsewhere, I have discussed the ways in which the term

Fifth Festival of Youth Music, held in December 2003. Announcing the festival, the monthly music magazine *Honar-e Musiqi* reported that the pop music section would include 'musical styles such as *mardomi* [lit. 'of the people'], jazz, blues, rock, etc.'.[18] Noting the increasing involvement of young people in grassroots bands, Dr Mohammad Sarir, one of the festival organisers, defended the inclusion of pop music in the festival and suggested that misunderstanding about pop music in the past had obscured the fact that works of good quality can emanate from any musical style; interestingly, the pop music section only included invited groups (presumably to avoid music of inferior quality).[19] Not surprisingly, young musicians that I spoke to were wary of centrally-organised events, both because of uncertainty about government motivations and concerns over loss of control, as well as a general reluctance to be associated with officialdom.

Arian Band: '*Ye bahooneh barāye khoondan*' ('An excuse to sing')[20]

And so to Arian. Formed in 1999, Arian is a prime example of a grassroots band which is very much a product of the reform period. Indeed, the band's creative output to date has been both framed and shaped by the reform period: its first album was published in 2000, the first official concert was held in April 2000 at the Talār-e Harekat Hall in Tehran, and its third album was published less than a year before Khatami's term as president ended.[21] But Arian is not just any pop band. From its humble grassroots beginnings, Arian has become a phenomenon and through its artistic success and promotion by the company Tarane Sharghee

---

has been used to validate music in a traditionally hostile religious environment (Nooshin 1996:80,121), but this is the first time that I have encountered this adjective as a descriptor for pop music. More often, the term has been used to designate Iranian music as the unscientific 'Other' of Western classical music (see Nooshin 2005a:263).

[18]   'The Fifth Festival of Youth Music', *Honar-e Musiqi* 48:55 (November 2003). Translation by the current author.

[19]   The results of the (competitive) festival are announced in a later issue of *Honar-e Musiqi* (volume 50:51, January/February 2004).

[20]   From the lyrics to '*Bahooneh*' ('Excuse'), *Arian II*, track 6; lyrics by Sharareh Farnejad, Ali Pahlavan and Ninef Amirkhas; music by Payam Salehi. Some of Arian's songs can be heard on www.arianmusic.com (accessed 03/01/08).

[21]   At the time of writing, Arian's line-up was as follows: Ali Pahlavan (voice and acoustic guitar) and Payam Salehi (voice and acoustic guitar), the two founders of the band, Siamak Khahani (violin), Ninef Amirkhas (keyboards), Sharareh Farnejad (acoustic guitar and backing vocals), Alireza Tabatabaee (drum kit), Borzou Badihi (percussion), Sanaz Kashmari (backing vocals) and Sahar Kashmari (backing vocals). For further information on the history of the band, see www.arianmusic.com. The four albums to date are: *Gol-e Aftābgardoon* (*The Sunflower*, 2000), *Arian II – Va Ammā Eshgh …* (*Arian II – And Now Love …*, 2001), *Tā Binahāyat* (*Till Eternity*, 2004) and *Bi To Bā To* (*Without You, With You*, 2008). All four albums are published by Tarane Sharghee Cultural & Artistic Company.

has been projected to national significance. As well as its four albums, Arian has toured extensively in Iran and abroad – the first post-revolutionary pop band to do so – and has attracted a large fan-base, both at home and among diaspora Iranians. No Iranian pop band to date has generated such a level of 'hype'.

Whilst there is no direct connection between Arian and the reform movement, I'm interested in the ways in which Arian's musical discourses were very much 'of the moment' in the early 2000s and were concerned with many of the same imperatives: building a diverse civil space, responding to a growing youth culture and rethinking notions of national belonging in an increasingly global environment. Arian was not the only band to emerge in the post-1997 period, but it became the most popular, and indeed has been imitated by a number of 'clone' boy-girl bands, none of which have quite managed to capture the spirit of the nation in the way that Arian has.[22] For this reason, I focus exclusively on Arian in the second half of this chapter, and primarily on songs selected from the first two albums (published 2000 and 2001). As Lipsitz observes,

> Culture enables people to rehearse identities, stances, and social relations not yet permissible in politics. But it also serves as a concrete social site, a place where social relations are constructed and enacted as well as envisioned. Popular culture does not just reflect reality, it helps constitute it. (1994:137)

In the same way, far from simply reflecting the reality of contemporary Iran, I would suggest that the music of Arian has played an important role in imagining and ultimately creating new realities.

So, how does Arian do this? What makes Arian's music so interesting is that it draws on some of the distinctive aesthetic paradigms developed through the grassroots movement, and largely associated with alternative 'underground' bands, but presented here in a mainstream 'overground' context. In particular, this involves challenging some of the long-accepted and unquestioned norms of Iranian pop music, including: a new group ethos with named bands whose collective identity transcends individual members and which contrasts strongly with the solo singer cult which has tended to dominate Iranian pop; a move towards greater stylistic eclecticism in contrast with the rather formulaic sounds of mainstream pop; and the growing presence of women, mainly as backing singers but also increasingly as instrumentalists and composers, something which can also be seen to some extent in mainstream pop.[23] All of these changes resonate with the idea of a more diverse and inclusive social domain and I'd like to consider each in turn before

---

[22]   Such groups include Gap Band, Rama, Part Music Group and Tika Band (see discography).

[23]   Indeed, there are some all-female pop bands. In August 2004, I attended a concert by one such band, Mashyana (led by Ghazal Kianinejad), performing to an all-female audience at the Talār-e Vahdat, one of Tehran's most prestigious concert venues.

discussing the lyrical content of Arian's songs which, like much post-1997 pop, is central to the band's appeal.[24]

Arian has a strong group ethos. In interview, band members regularly emphasise the collaborative nature of their work. Payam Salehi, for example, explains that the band wanted to show that it is possible to carry out group work in Iranian pop music, 'If there is compromise and a love of one's work, it is definitely possible to do this', and he assents to the interviewer's suggestion, 'So, it seems that group work is the basis and the main meaning of your coming together'.[25] Notwithstanding a number of pop/rock bands before 1979, the group format (as opposed to solo singer and anonymous backing group) is relatively new to Iran and many bands have found it hard to sustain long-term relationships. As such, the public discourses through which Arian members convey an awareness of the need for co-operation and compromise in order to make the group work is interesting. As Ali Pahlavan explains, 'If we have any problem in the group, we sit together around a table and discuss it. We may even shout at each other, but we resolve the problem there are then and when we come out we are friends as before.' This, he suggests is the '*ramz-e māndegār-e Arian*' ('the key to Arian's longevity'). An important theme which emerges from these interviews is the bond of friendship between band members, which is presented as central to the cohesion of the group. The interviews also reveal the extent to which music, lyrics and arrangements, whilst they may originate with one or more members of the group, are always open to whole group discussion and negotiation, 'nothing in the group is the work of one person' (Ninef Amirkhas, keyboard player and arranger). In the context of contemporary Iran, this image of a democratic group putting into practice ideas of collaborative decision-making, co-operation and equality, is highly significant.

One of the most striking emblems of this 'performance of unity/democracy' is that the two lead singers, Ali Pahlavan and Payam Salehi, regularly divide the sung text between them, alternating in a symbolic musical sharing. This provides a refreshing contrast with the usual dominance of the solo singer in Iranian music generally, and is both central to the visual narrative of the band on stage and unique to Arian (see Figure 10.1).[26] Moreover, 'discourses of co-operation' can be found within the repertoire itself, as for example in the lyrics to the exquisite and highly poetic '*Ageh Dasthām-o Begiri*' ('If You Take My Hands'),[27] which can be interpreted both literally as a straightforward love song and as a figurative 'taking of hands' and a symbol of co-operation. Such layering of multiple meanings in Arian's lyrics will be discussed below.

---

[24]   For further discussion of these aesthetic paradigms in the context of 'underground' grassroots bands, see Nooshin (2005b:485–9).

[25]   All quotations in this section are from interviews on *Arian Band Live in Concert*, a commercial DVD recording of one of the autumn 2002 concerts (Tarane Sharghee, 2003), and are translated from Persian by the author.

[26]   Although at least one 'clone' band, Tika Band, has adopted this technique in some songs.

[27]   *Gol-e-Aftābgardoon*, track 3; music and lyrics by Ali Pahlavan.

Figure 10.1   Photograph of Arian in concert in Vancouver, January 2005 (by kind
                permission of Tarane Sharghee).

In terms of style, Arian's music is grounded in a clearly recognisable Iranian
pop idiom but, like many other contemporary – particularly grassroots – bands, also
draws on a range of other (predominantly Western popular) styles, including jazz
(for example, in '*Hamrāz*', *Arian II*, track 11), techno ('*Royā-ye Sepid*', *Arian II*,
track 10), latin/flamenco ('*Gharibe*', *Gol-e Aftābgardoon*, track 4 and '*Bahooneh*',
Arian II, track 6), and rock ('*Iran*', *Arian II*, track 7). In particular, and again like
many grassroots bands, Arian avoids the heavy nostalgia which permeates much
mainstream pop. As well as having access to a wider range of music than ever
before, particularly through the Internet, the more liberal atmosphere since 1997
has led many musicians to experiment stylistically. At the same time, this new
eclecticism has revived the long-standing debate on Iranian commercial popular
music as a form of cultural dependency and an imitation of the West, particularly
since most musicians do tend to look westwards in their search for new sounds.
Such views have been widely expressed in recent years, both by the religious
lobby and by some classical musicians who regard the post-1997 legalisation
of pop music as a 'dumbing down' of the culture and a weakening of national
identity.[28] In contrast, for many listeners and for pop musicians themselves, this

---

[28]   For example, the *Honar-e Musiqi* article referred to above is followed directly by an
item expressing anxieties over the 'dangers' (*khatar*) of 'decadent'/'degenerate' (*mobtazal*)
music, which is contrasted with 'healthy' (*sālem*) music ('The Leader of Tabriz's Youth
Majlesi Orchestra: "The Danger of Music's Diversion Towards Decadence is Increasing"',

music has become indigenised, acquiring local meanings and regarded as firmly rooted at 'home'.

Regarding the involvement of women musicians, Arian was the first post-1997 band to include a woman – Sharareh Farnejad[29] – as instrumentalist and composer/ lyricist (in addition to the more usual female backing vocalists, of which there are two). Whilst the presence of women, particularly Sharareh, is significant, their role is somewhat ambiguous, especially since two of the three are largely in the background. The only song in Arian's repertoire to deal specifically with gender issues, 'Mādar' ('Mother'),[30] links notions of motherhood and nation – and thus might be regarded as empowering – but also serves to re-inscribe existing gender roles. Any discussion of gender in post-1997 pop music should be understood in the context of the remarkable increase in the number of women musicians in Iranian classical music (musiqi-e assil) since 1979, and the growing social presence of women more generally. Certainly, Sharareh serves as a prominent role model and, as already noted, a number of mixed gender bands have followed in Arian's footsteps.

Lyrics: '*Yek ālam harf-hāye tāzeh*' ('Lots of new things to say')[31]

One of the most appealing aspects of Arian's music is the lyrics, through which the band explores a range of issues, sometimes including subtle social comment of the kind which for centuries has allowed Iranian artists, particularly poets, to challenge the establishment without contesting it directly.[32] Arian thus follows a well-trodden path: on the one hand, listeners are given the interpretive space to project their own meanings onto the music; on the other, many of the implied meanings are well understood by audiences accustomed to reading a great deal into very little.

Honar-e Musiqi 48:55, November 2003). See Nooshin (2005a) for further examples of published critiques of this kind.

[29] The wife of co-founder and lead singer, Ali Pahlavan.

[30] *Gol-e Aftābgardoon*, track 5; music and lyrics by Payam Salehi.

[31] From '*Bahooneh*', see footnote 20. All translations of song texts in this chapter are by the current author.

[32] Classical singers have often drawn on the double meanings of Persian poetry, something which was particularly evident in the early 1980s. Within commercial popular music there is little tradition of direct social or political comment with the exception of a few singers in the late 1970s, most notably Farhad and Dariush (see Shay 2000:85). According to Shay, before 1979 Iranian pop was a music whose 'sanitized lyrics … form a relatively "safe" or "innocuous" body of music' (ibid.:68). In contrast to this, he discusses the use of political satire and critique in traditional forms of popular music, often in improvised comic music-theatre such as *siyāh-bāzi* (ibid.:62); such songs were rarely broadcast on radio and after 1979 were banned alongside Westernised popular music, but continued to be performed in private (ibid.:66). Mention should also be made of earlier forms of popular music which provided political commentary, specifically the revolutionary anthems composed at the time of the 1906 Constitutional Revolution (see Chehabi 1999).

In this context, lyrics such as 'open the window', 'tomorrow is ours' and 'an excuse to sing' become laden with meaning. Arian's songs are not overtly challenging but their subtle messages speak volumes to those attuned to contemporary Iran. Indeed, Arian derives much of its credibility through being seen to work within the system rather than against it in the manner of 'underground' bands. Many of my interviewees suggested that such an approach, which privileges gradual erosion over direct confrontation, is more artistically satisfying and more effective in the long term.[33] Moreover, in addressing issues such as nation, family and religion, Arian has shown itself to be in touch with the everyday concerns of Iranians; and since its repertoire also includes many ostensibly straightforward love songs, it has avoided being labelled as a band which deals only with social issues.

Arian explores a range of issues in its songs, from commemorating the martyrs of the Iran–Iraq war in the opening track – 'Setāreh' ('Star') – of its debut album, to subtly commenting on the traditional antipathy of the religious establishment towards music, which since 1979 has had significant implications for Iranian musicians. For example, the song 'Bahooneh' ('Excuse') is a song about singing, the 'excuse to sing' being 'to plant happiness in hearts/to reach the whole world, all that the heart wants to say, in a single song'.[34] In the guise of a love song, 'Bahooneh' is a self-reflective commentary in which the band gives itself permission to sing. Another example of typically ambiguous lyrics can be found in 'Panjereh' ('Window'),[35] which begins in a down-beat mood – 'You say our world is full of sorrow ... Our words have become full of sadness, our hearts break easily' – and presents images of dark nights and black clouds. Half way through the verse, however, the mood changes: 'But in the dark, cold and silent night, look – the sky is full of stars ... When love and hope enter hearts/They fill with happiness and all talk becomes sweet'. This is followed by the chorus and the main hook-line, 'Open the window, sing of love and hope'. Like so many of Arian's songs, 'Panjereh' can be read simultaneously on different levels: as a straightforward love song ('If you say your heart is lonely, if you say you're cold every night/If your pain and sadness are overflowing ... Call out to love'); as an appeal to recognise good in everything: stars in the apparently dark night, dancing leaves in the autumn wind, a happy song in the falling rain; or perhaps as a call to 'open the window' of social freedom or even engagement with the outside world. Arian's third album (*Tā Binahāyat*, 2004) includes a song appealing for world peace sung in three languages, English, Arabic and Persian (see Nooshin 2008).

---

[33] As Brian Ward observes in the context of protest music in the United States, '... crude agit-prop sloganeering quickly became wearing for an audience and creatively unrewarding for the artists. It was far more effective to describe a situation which illustrated an injustice ... or simply tell a tale of beauty, love and decency achieved against the odds of poverty and oppression' (1998:415).

[34] The original Persian is: '*shādi-o too del-hā neshoondan/Harf-e del ro bā yek tarāneh, beh hameh donyā resoondan*'.

[35] *Arian II*, track 2; music and lyrics by Ali Pahlavan. See p. 267 for the lyrics.

Elsewhere there are moments of self-reflexive irony, with song texts commenting on poetic double meanings: '*Telesm*' ('The Spell'), to all intents and purposes a love song, is full of textual references to Arian's earlier songs and includes the following line, 'But for how much longer will we have to talk of flowers/hiding in stories what our hearts want to say?'[36]

Arian's success lies, to some extent, in the variety of its song texts, from love songs to those dealing with topical issues, through to songs which validate the band as upholders of national and family 'values' and lend it a 'healthy' and 'wholesome' image. This can be seen in songs such as '*Mādar*' ('Mother') and '*Mowlā Ali Jān*'[37] (the former presenting an iconic figure of the self-sacrificing mother and the latter dedicated to the highly revered and cherished Shi'eh Imam Ali), as well as in the regular references to religion and religious symbolism, both in their music and lyrics, in performance and in interview. Other Iranian pop musicians have in recent years turned to religious symbols and texts, the best known being Ali Reza Assar. Indeed, some of my interviewees suggested that this religious 'turn' is partly motivated by the likelihood of the Ministry of Culture and Islamic Guidance being more sympathetic to religiously-oriented pop music. Whether for the benefit of officialdom, in order to appeal to audiences or from personal conviction, Arian's shrewd choice of themes have enabled it to negotiate tricky ground: to gain official approval whilst also maintaining public credibility. For obvious reasons, band members are generally unforthcoming on such questions. Payam Salehi perhaps came closest to this in interview, 'If we have new things to say, maybe we can make some hearts happy and say something new in the music of our country.'[38] Above all, Arian is regarded as a band whose lyrics are both thoughtful and thought-provoking; the logo on its website describes the band as providing 'Entertainment for Mind and Soul'.

A Precious Music …

There would seem to be a number of reasons, therefore, for Arian's popularity, including a winning combination of meaningful lyrics, up-beat and memorable tunes, imaginative arrangements, talented musicians and professional presentation. In addition, and despite its commercial success, the band has managed (until very recently, at least) to preserve a grassroots 'feel' and a sense of being in touch with ordinary people, partly through a carefully crafted image and partly through the song lyrics, as already discussed. The band's juxtaposition of highly poetic texts with often quite colloquial language reinforces this 'down to earth' image.

---

[36]   *Ta Binahāyat*, track 5; music and lyrics by Ali Pahlavan. The original Persian is: '*Vali cheghad ākheh bāz, bāyad az gol-hā goft/Harf-hāye del-o penhooni too ghese-hā gotf*'.

[37]   *Gol-e-Aftābgardoon*, track 6; music by Ali Pahlavan and Payam Salehi; lyrics by Darab Pahlavan.

[38]   *Arian Band Live in Concert* (DVD, Tarane Sharghee, 2003).

Asked why they liked Arian's music, audience members interviewed during one of the autumn 2002 concerts responded by focusing on the 'happy' (*shād*) qualities of the music, the fact that the band members are young and have good voices, as well as the variety of songs, which were regularly described as *ghashang* ('beautiful') and *sālem* ('healthy'),[39] clearly reflecting the wholesome image which Arian has cultivated, and mentioned above.[40] In describing the music as *mardomi* ('of the people'), another interviewee highlighted an important factor in Arian's success: the perception of the band as autonomous and in control of its music.[41] The fact that the music and lyrics are (with a few exceptions) composed by band members, often collaboratively, also contributes to this perception.

At the same time, and notwithstanding its undisputed success – indeed largely because of it – Arian has recently come under criticism. As part of an emerging entrepreneurship in Iran, Arian was one of the first bands to be 'signed' to a commercial company and sponsored by a multinational corporation, the electronics company LG. The display of promotional banners at the autumn 2002 concerts was quite novel to Iranian audiences,[42] as seen in interviews with audience members who were asked for their views on this kind of sponsorship. Some suggested that commercial success has started to distance the band from its grassroots origins, a view shared by many individuals that I spoke to. Certainly, Arian has a much more 'corporate' image now in comparison with the early years, something which can be seen on its website, which at the time of writing included product advertising, including an advertisement for the 'Arian Fast Food and Coffee Shop' (located in Rud-e Hen, to the East of Tehran), managed by the band's percussionist Borzou Badihi.

An interesting aspect of Arian's broad appeal is that its music reaches across social boundaries, particularly those of class and religion; such divisions are still strong in Iran, particularly between the relatively affluent, cosmopolitan and often secular middle classes, and the more traditional, religious sectors of society.[43]

---

[39]   Particularly in comparison with imported diaspora pop, often known as '*los angelesi*' music, which for many has somewhat vulgar and 'cheap' overtones. Unlike a number of local pop bands which are increasingly producing *los angelesi* style dance music, Arian has avoided dance rhythms with potentially vulgar associations.

[40]   All quotations from audience members are taken from *Arian Band Live in Concert* (DVD, Tarane Sharghee, 2003).

[41]   People that I spoke to often used the term '*mardomi*' to describe Arian's music and lyrics; see also the interview with Mr Taqavi referred to above.

[42]   And presented an interesting juxtaposition alongside the ever-present pictures of Ayatollahs Khomeini and Khamenei which are displayed above the stage in all public performance venues. Whilst commercial sponsorship is fairly well established in areas such as film and sport, this is the first time that a commercial company has become an ongoing sponsor of a music group.

[43]   Questions of class are extremely complex and it isn't always possible to map divisions of social background onto monetary wealth, particularly with changes following

Whilst little ethnographic work has been carried out in this area, it is clear that the post-1997 legalisation and the emergence of a local industry has lent pop music a social acceptance, and started to attract an audience, among sectors of Iranian society which would previously have been unlikely to listen to it – with its associations of secularity, affluence, decadence and Westernisation – let alone attend a concert.[44] In particular, as mentioned above, the recent changes have served to reframe pop music within discourses which locate it 'at home'. Class and other social divisions in Iran are visibly marked through dress codes (particularly for women), and it is interesting that whilst the 2002 concert DVD shows a primarily middle-class audience, there are also audience members from ostensibly more traditional, religious backgrounds, with women wearing the enveloping *chador* veil and without make-up.[45] Given the difficulties in securing concert tickets and the fact that these can be prohibitively expensive for certain sections of the population, the concert audience is not necessarily representative of the wider market for Arian's music. At the same time, the presence of individuals who, not so long ago would have been entirely absent from such settings is significant. It is also interesting to note that whilst Arian's music is aimed primarily at young people, the lyrics in particular have attracted a broad audience in terms of age as well, something which can again be seen on the concert DVD; rather touchingly, several older women interviewed said that '*Mādar*' ('Mother') was their favourite Arian song.

The final section of this chapter will focus on two specific songs in order to explore the ways in which Arian addresses contemporary, and sometimes contentious, issues through its musical and textual discourses.

Performing Nationhood: '*Iran*'[46]

The song '*Iran*' begins with the sound of a radio dial being turned: someone is searching for something. As the invisible dial turns, the listener is offered

---

the 1979 Revolution and the emergence of a new social layer of traditional, religious '*nouveau riche*'.

[44] A number of writers have pointed to this trend, going back as far as the late 1980s. Chehabi, for example, suggests that pop music's popularity 'is not confined to westernized citizens' (2000:166), and he cites Ian Brown's work with Iranian child prisoners of war (in Iraq, 1987), largely from poor, religious backgrounds, amongst whom Iranian pop music was very popular.

[45] Something which would be very unusual among the relatively affluent, secular and cosmopolitan 'North Tehrani' women.

[46] *Arian II* (2001), track 7; lyrics by Farimeh Radmand; music by Payam Salehi, Ali Pahlavan and Ninef Amirkhas; see p. 265 for the lyrics (translations by the current author); the music can be heard on www.arianmusic.com. This is the only song on the album *Arian II* not set to lyrics by a member of the band. The discussion which follows is based primarily on the versions of songs as recorded on Arian's albums. With the exception of a medley at the end of the concert, the DVD comprises songs already released on CD (and therefore

scattered fragments, including part of the title track of Arian's first album (*Gol-e Aftābgardoon*), a voice announcing (in English) 'Arian Band's second album', and finally a few seconds from the introduction to the popular anthem '*Ay Iran*' which has the status of an unofficial national anthem and is immediately recognisable by Iranians.[47] This fades out to make way for the song proper: high electric guitar (Hendrix-style) over a low pulsating bass riff setting the mood for the entry of a heavy rock drum beat which dominates for much of the piece. When the voices enter, they present an anthem-like unison – male and female voices symbolically united – on the word 'Iran', which is stressed and repeated. This unison chorus continues throughout, alternating with solo lines shared by Ali Pahlavan and Payam Salehi. Only in the third verse does the mood become more reflective, but at the end of the verse the rock beat returns with a vengeance. The instrumental sections between verses feature solo violin in jazz-rock style, with solo electric guitar at the end of the song.[48] The final few bars effect a sudden change of mood and a return to the opening of '*Ay Iran*' played softly on solo electric guitar. Together, the fast tempo, the strong bass riff and the rock drum beat make this Arian's most strongly rock-influenced song to date.

Effectively, '*Iran*' is a patriotic rock anthem-cum-love song which draws heavily on a romanticised vision of Iran's ancient heritage and the country's geographical beauty. A number of thematic strands run through the lyrics, including references to Iran's historic literature, notably the national epic, the *Shahnameh*,[49] in the form of the heroic characters Siavash, Rostam, Kaveh and Arash,[50] and the fabled lovers Farhad and Shireen. The historical narrative also includes the palaces

---

familiar to the audience), but incorporating some minor musical and textual changes, some of which are referred to here. The increased speed of some songs is particularly noticeable.

[47]   Composed in 1944, music by Ruhollah Khaleqi, lyrics by Hossein Gol-e Golab. According to a number of informants, this song has in recent years been used in a variety of fora to voice patriotic sentiments. Prohibited during the 1980s and early '90s, '*Ay Iran*' has been officially tolerated by the government since the late 1990s and is now broadcast on radio and often performed in ceremonial gatherings or at the end of concerts. One informant told me that it has even become popular for '*Ay Iran*' to be sung at birthday parties. Certainly, many Iranians feel a close affinity with this song and consider that it should be Iran's official national anthem. When it was played over loudspeakers at the end of an evening display at the ancient site of *Takht-e Jamshid* (Persepolis, near Shiraz) which I attended in the summer of 2000, the audience spontaneously joined in with enthusiastic singing and clapping.

[48]   The DVD concert performance includes an extended *ad lib* solo section (which is not on the CD recording) performed by guest electric guitarist Saman Emami.

[49]   By the poet Ferdowsi (*c*.940–1021 CE).

[50]   The reference to Arash the archer, who sacrificed his life in drawing the boundaries between ancient Iran and neighbouring Turan, is particularly significant in relation to this discussion of new configurations of nationhood. The original story of Arash is told in the *Avesta*, the ancient sacred writings of Zoroastrianism.

of *Chehel Sotoun* (in Esfahan) and *Takht-e Jamshid* (Persepolis), both symbolic of Iran's former power and in the case of the latter the pre-Islamic heritage.[51] Another theme is the country's diverse geography (forests, mountains, sea coasts) and beauty ('land of light and the sea'; 'you are the *koh-i nor*[52] in the treasure chest of the world'; 'the glowing redness of the sunset'). The pervading romantic narrative is particularly evident in lines such as 'you are my only homeland' and 'my love for you is the blood in my veins', as is the theme of separation ('I don't want to be separated from you'),[53] which reveals a diasporic consciousness unusual in the new pop. The subject position continually shifts from Iran to a diasporic viewpoint, for example 'wherever I am in the world' and 'When I am far from here, I weep the sorrow of separation/I keep all your beauties in my mind'. This interweaving of home and diaspora serves both to insert the latter into a broader concept of nationhood, and to reach out to the large audience of Iranians abroad.[54]

In order to understand the significance of '*Iran*', one needs to consider it both in relation to the earlier discussion of stylistic diversity and in the context of the long-standing contestation over questions of nationhood in Iran. Of particular significance is what I have elsewhere called 'the play of identities' (Nooshin 2005a:235), the ways in which those in power have emphasised, or conversely downplayed, different aspects of Iranian identity in pursuit of particular political agendas. For example, the Pahlavi monarchs (r. 1925–79) emphasised Iran's pre-Islamic heritage, partly in order to validate their own claim to power, and also, significantly, in an attempt to disempower the clergy, at the same time seeking to forge a national identity which was largely secular, cosmopolitan and modernist. The reaction against this after 1979 was seen in official discourses which, in contrast, emphasised an all-encompassing Islamic identity and (at least in rhetoric) a rejection of modernity and cosmopolitanism. After 1997, such discourses became strongly contested as Iran re-established its international relations and opened up

---

[51] This referencing the pre-Islamic heritage is similar to that found in the *sorud*s ('anthems') of the 1930s as described by Chehabi (1999:148).

[52] Literally 'mountain of light' in Persian, once the largest known diamond in the world and now part of the British Crown Jewels.

[53] There are interesting parallels here with Chehabi's discussion of nationalistic poetry at the time of the 1906 Constitutional Revolution. The poet 'Aref, for example, 'substituted the homeland for the beloved or the panegyrised king, and the people for the lovers' (1999:145).

[54] Communication with Iranian music outlets in London have indicated a high level of demand for post-1997 local pop, with Arian's music being the most sought after. In interview, Arian's manager (and director of Tarane Sharghee), Mohsen Rajabpoor, indicated the band's desire to reach an international audience, both Iranians and others. Asked whether Arian would be able to compete abroad with well-established diaspora musicians, he responded, 'We bring the scent of Iran. Wherever members of Arian give concerts, for those Iranians who live in that country they bring an offering of Iran' (*Arian Band Live in Concert*, DVD, Tarane Sharghee, 2003). It will be interesting to see how this popularity impacts on the already complex issues of identity, cultural ownership and belonging.

to the outside world, prompting heated debate on what it means to be Iranian in the twenty-first century and on Iran's place in the global arena.

Whilst a full discussion of nationalist discourses lies outside the scope of this chapter,[55] its relevance here lies in the ways in which Arian, through its music, continues the debate on nationhood. What makes '*Iran*' so interesting is that it is the only song in the band's repertoire to refer directly to questions of nationhood, and is also their most conspicuously rock-based song. If, as Taylor suggests, 'texts of whatever variety aren't merely texts, but statements that need to be understood, both as texts and as culturally and historically specific utterances' (2001:9), then we need to ask why Arian should have chosen a musical idiom so closely associated with modernity – and since 1979 represented in official discourses as the very antithesis of national identity – to set this particular song. What does the choice of musical style mean? Following Taylor's argument that such choices are not arbitrary, and acknowledging that my reading is one of several possible interpretations of the 'text', I would suggest that the particular significance of '*Iran*' is that for the first time since the post-1979 government set about de-coupling modernity from nationhood through official discourses, these concepts have been symbolically reunited in a locally-produced pop/rock song.[56] The decision to set a fusion of rock and Iranian pop in the specific context of a patriotic song tells us a great deal about Arian's desire to weave modernity and nationhood into a single narrative, effectively projecting an alternative vision of nationhood in which modernity, youth, popular culture and cosmopolitanism are brought in from the 'margins', and presenting a subtle challenge to dominant discourses of nationhood which have tended to exclude them.[57] This is perhaps less obvious in the lyrics, which depend on a number of stock signifiers of nationhood, but becomes clear in the up-front choice of musical style. Just as Lipsitz discusses the 'complex connections linking the nation with the imagi-nation' (1994:137), so this song serves as a 'register for the changing dimensions and boundaries' (ibid.:126) of national identity, and in so doing continues a long tradition of music as central to

---

[55]   But see Kashani-Sabet (1999), Ansari (2003), Keddie (2003) and Ahmadi (2004, 2005), among others. Holliday (2007) discusses the contestation of national identity during the reform period.

[56]   To my knowledge, '*Iran*' was the first post-1997 local pop song to directly address issues of nationhood. However, there is a strong tradition of pop music used as a vehicle for expressions of national belonging, in both pre-1979 and diaspora pop (see <www.iranian.com/Music/Patriotic/index.html> for a listing; accessed 08/01/07). In diaspora, such expressions usually focus on ex-patriate nostalgia for a lost homeland, sentiments which are often regarded with antipathy in Iran itself. Arian was also one of a number of bands which wrote songs for the Iranian national team ahead of the 2006 football World Cup: '*Ey Jāvidān Iran*' ('Eternal Iran') was originally available through the band's website and has recently been included in the 2008 album *Bi To Bā To*.

[57]   For a consideration of similar issues, see Ramnarine's discussion of the new centrality of previously marginalised 'Others' to concepts of 'Britishness' (2004).

the mediation of Iranian identity. In providing a public platform on which a 'new set of national symbols' (Marashi 2002:102) can be played out, and in engaging with the ongoing debates over nationhood which marked the reform period, '*Iran*' is very much of its time and because of this takes on heightened meanings.[58]

It is clear from the ecstatic reception to the song (on the concert DVD) that such meanings are not lost on audiences. Moreover, framed between references to '*Ay Iran*' (at the beginning and end), the song seems to offer itself up as an alternative national anthem. After the song, Payam Salehi addresses the audience: 'Friends, this love of Iran, our love of this holy land runs in all of our veins' (to the strains of '*Ay Iran*' in the background), thus reinforcing the link between the band and nationhood. Indeed, the very name Arian symbolises this; as Salehi explains in interview, 'We wanted to choose a name which would show our love of Iran. First, we chose 'Arya', and then because we are a group we decided on 'Aryaian' [plural], which became shortened to Arian'.[59] It is significant that Arian is the first Iranian pop band to embed such a signifier of nationhood in its name and thus its very identity. In placing itself and its music at the heart of a national narrative, the band simultaneously draws on signifiers of nation and 'rootedness' on the one hand (Persian lyrics and poeticism, Iranian rhythms and melodies) and indices of modernity on the other (stylistic eclecticism, 'Western' instruments and sound technology, highly choreographed concert staging, commercial sponsorship). In part, the former serves to validate the music and to set it up in contrast to diaspora pop, often described as less 'rooted' than post-1997 local pop.

There are two further points to note here. First, at the same time that Arian challenges dominant configurations of national identity, it continues to seek authentication through 'traditional' symbols of nation in a way which would be hard to find parallels with in British pop music, for example. That the band should have chosen to set a text such as '*Iran*' in the first place is indicative of the fact that nationhood remains a contested space. Second, there are some telling silences in the text of '*Iran*'. In emphasising a shared (pre-Islamic) history over both regional cultural differences and other dimensions of Iranian identity (in particular, religion), the song privileges a primarily secular and Persian-centric view of that identity. In part, the absence of religious signifiers reflects a growing secularism among young people, but also serves to emphasise a shared nationhood over regional, ethnic and religious differences. Further, whilst the song references Iran's

---

[58] For discussion of a much earlier linking of modernity and nation-building by musical modernisers of the early Pahlavi period, see Chehabi (1999). There is a considerable literature on modernisation and concepts of modernity in Iran during the Pahlavi period, and in particular the autocratic policies adopted by Reza Shah during the 1930s, for example see Cronin (2002) and Atabaki and Zürcher (2003). For further discussion of modernity in Iran, the reader is referred to Martin (1989), Boroujerdi (1996), Shayegan (1997), Mirsepassi (2000), Tapper (2000), Alinejad (2002) and Vahdat (2002).

[59] *Arian Band Live in Concert* (DVD, Tarane Sharghee, 2003). The word 'Iran' derives from the same root as Aryan.

geographical diversity, this is a geography devoid of people. Again, this might be understood as a reaction to official policies which, since 1979, have promoted a romanticised view of rural areas and of Iran's ethnic diversity in the national imagination, evidenced for example in the large number of recordings of regional music published in recent years and in the predominant choice of rural settings for Iranian films.[60] In making no reference to the nation's cultural diversity, '*Iran*' harks back to an earlier form of nationalism in which such diversity is subsumed within the dominant Persian culture.[61]

Performing Youth: '*Fardā*'[62]

As discussed above, the development of a youth culture in Iran has been an important factor in the emergence of groups such as Arian. Notwithstanding its broad appeal, Arian's music is aimed primarily at young people and speaks to their aspirations. Not only does Arian place youth at the centre of its lyrical narrative but a number of its songs specifically address issues of concern to young people. One of the most interesting examples of this is '*Fardā*' ('Tomorrow'), the final track on Arian's first album. The first verse presents images of animals and plants (fish, dove, flower bud) in various states of discomfort (alone, sitting in the rain), which in the chorus and later verses are contrasted with more positive phrases such as 'Let the tired bud escape from the corner of the flowerpot', 'Let your warm hands be protection for the dove', 'blue sky', 'until tonight the sky becomes filled with the moon and stars', 'with you, this autumn is spring again' and 'It's time for the flowers to smile'. Drawing on the well-established symbolic association of flowers with youth in Iran, the final line alludes to the many years of austerity, particularly during the 1980s and the war with Iraq when public displays of joy were frowned upon, effectively declaring, 'now it's time for young people to be happy again'. The chorus itself comprises a rising melodic sequence which builds up to a climax on the words '*fardā māl-e māst*' ('tomorrow is ours'). With its message of hope for the future, this song presents an unambiguous statement of youth presence, the meaning of which is quite clear to listeners, and a fitting culmination to Arian's debut album: the last word, so to speak. As with '*Iran*', the audience reception (on the concert DVD) is rapturous, especially when the band unexpectedly change the last line of the chorus to '*emshab shab-e māst*' ('tonight is our night'), heightening the level of excitement and further intensifying the special ambience created by

---

[60]   Although it could be argued that this has not been translated into the enfranchisement of Iran's many regional ethno-linguistic and minority religious populations. At the same time, Banuazizi suggests that rural areas have benefited greatly in recent years from government projects aimed at improving living standards (1995:571–2).

[61]   See Chehabi (1999:148).

[62]   *Gol-e Aftābgardoon* (2000), track 10; music and lyrics by Ali Pahlavan; see p. 266 for the lyrics; the music can be heard on www.arianmusic.com.

the shared concert experience with the inclusiveness of the word 'our'. Whilst 'Fardā' is not stylistically challenging in the way that 'Iran' is, the up-beat mood reinforces the optimistic message of the lyrics, and the line 'Come and open the windows facing towards tomorrow' places the agency firmly on young people themselves.

As mentioned earlier, in moving from amateur grassroots to professional status, Arian has largely preserved its down-to-earth feel which, at least in the early years, presented what might be described as a 'boy/girl next door' image, a previously unimaginable role model for others. One might even suggest that Arian's significance for young people is not unlike that of the Beatles and other Euro-American pop/rock bands of the 1950s and 1960s. This is youth speaking to youth, rather than being addressed from above. All of the band members are in their twenties and early thirties and therefore belong to the generation which grew up under the Islamic Republic and which experienced the rupture of revolution and war. As such, there is a shared experiential bond between musicians and audience which is largely missing in the consumption of diaspora pop in Iran.

The message of 'Fardā' should thus be understood in the context of a largely disillusioned youth, for whom this music perhaps represents a way of reclaiming a sense of self. As discussed in the context of 'Iran', the shifting of new pop from periphery to centre serves as an important symbol of youth enfranchisement; and at the same time reflects the government's intense awareness of the need for young people to feel included within the national vision. 'Fardā' both reflects and serves to foster a growing confidence and positive self-image in the face of dominant discourses which for many years denied youth culture any value.

Concluding Comments: Opening the Windows?

President Khatami's term of office ended in the summer of 2005 when he was succeeded by conservative President Ahmadinejad. The preceding eight years of reform had had long-term implications for music in Iran and the election was followed by a period of uncertainty among musicians. However, whilst Ahmadinejad and his followers had threatened to clamp down on manifestations of Western culture, and many have reported continuing difficulties, particularly for those applying for performance or recording permits, there have been few dramatic changes since 2005. The demographic pressure of a sizeable youth population which has lived through the reform period and includes a significant cosmopolitan element, is simply too strong to allow a return to the austerity of the 1980s. Still, the battle for the soul of Iran goes on between reformist and conservative factions, not least on questions of cultural policy and national identity. And Arian continues its work; the band released its fourth album, *Bi To Bā To* (*Without You, With You*) in the summer of 2008, which includes a track recorded in collaboration with British singer Chris de Burgh, as well as the song

'*Ey Jāvidān Iran*' ('Eternal Iran'), written in support of the Iranian national football team for the 2006 World Cup.

In conclusion, post-1997 liberalism played a crucial role in creating the conditions under which pop music could be transformed from peripheral 'Other' to a music occupying the centre space of Iranian cultural life and from a symbol of cultural imperialism (before 1997) to an icon of nationhood. Nowhere can this be seen more clearly than in the music of Arian, which has been shaped by and has in turn helped to shape public discourses associated with the reform movement, including an increasingly diverse civil domain and the promotion of open debate, tolerance and plurality. Blending a cosmopolitan consciousness with a strong sense of the local, Arian has come to symbolise a newly emerging civil order by literally reclaiming public space in the name of civil society, a space in which to debate and contest dominant discourses so deeply implicated in the exercise of power. As well as offering young people a music to call their own and giving a voice to those who have long been excluded by the 'dominant mythologies' (Stokes 1994c:21), Arian's music serves as a 'repository of alternative visions of reality' (Stokes 2003a). Just as McClary writes about the ways in which music allows for 'new ways of articulating possible worlds through sound ... demonstrating the crucial role music plays in the transformation of societies' (1985:158), so through their music – whether singing about nationhood, youth or democracy – new visions of the future are being imagined, explored and performed: an inclusive vision which simultaneously embraces local and global, tradition and modernity, religious and secular. Whilst much of this is still at the symbolic level, I would argue that the very act of imagining is prophetic of the genuine enfranchisement to come. In exploring the link between the production of meaning and the dynamics of power in contemporary Iran, Arian's music raises important questions about the relationship between sound structure and social structure, and how music becomes a site for the public expression of ideas which can't be expressed elsewhere. This is music's power and its prerogative. From this perspective, there can only be one answer to Taqizadeh's question, 'How precious can a concert be?' Very.

Lyrics to '*Iran*' [63]

Chorus   *Iran, Iran, Iran. Iran, Iran, Iran.*

Verse 1   *Iran-e hamisheh jāvid, sarzamin-e noor o daryā*
               To khodet ye kooh-e noor-i, tooyeh ganjineh-ye donyā
               Parchamet ye eftekhāhreh, oon bālā too owj-e abrā
               Hamisheh bā man mimooneh, oon seh rang-e nāb-e zibāt.

Verse 2   *Iran*
               Vatanam faghat toi to, har jāy-e donyā keh bāsham
               Eshgh-e to khoon-e too rag-hām, nemikhām az to jodāsham
               Vakhti keh az eenjā dooram, boghze ghorbat-o mibāram
               Hame-ye ghashangiāt-o, too-ye zehnam misepāram.

Chorus   *Iran, Iran, Iran. Iran, Iran, Iran.*

Verse 3   *Ghese-ye Farhad o Shireen, ghese-ye eshgh-e Siavash*
               Oon abar mardhā-ye āshegh, Rostam o Kaveh o Arash
               Yād-e jangal, yād-e koohā, Chehel Sotoun o Takht-e Jamshid
               Sāhel-e daryā kenār o, sorkhi-e ghoroob-e khorshid.

Chorus   *Iran, Iran, Iran, Iran. Iran, Iran, Iran.*

Chorus   Iran, Iran, Iran, Iran. Iran, Iran, Iran.

Verse 1   Iran, the everlasting land of light and the sea
               You are the *koh-i nor* in the treasure chest of the world
               Your flag is a pride, up there above the clouds
               Your three beautiful colours will always remain with me.

Verse 2   Iran
               You are my only homeland, wherever I am in the world
               My love for you is the blood in my veins, I don't want to be separated from you
               When I am far from here, I weep the sorrow of separation
               I keep all your beauties in my mind.

Chorus   Iran, Iran, Iran. Iran, Iran, Iran.

Verse 3   The story of Farhad and Shireen, the story of Siavash's love
               Those great men of love, Rostam, Kaveh and Arash
               Remembering the forests, remembering the mountains, Chehel Sotoun and Persepolis
               The beaches of the sea coast and the glowing redness of the sunset.

Chorus   Iran, Iran, Iran, Iran. Iran, Iran, Iran.

---

[63] By kind permission of Tarane Sharghee. Translations by the current author (note that the lyrics often use colloquial Persian, therefore the transliterations given do not always accord with 'standard' written Persian).

Lyrics to '*Fardā*' ('*Tomorrow*')[64]

Verse 1   *Sedā kon māhi-e tanhā-ye too-ye tong-e boloor o*
Sedā kon shabnam-e gol barg-e sepid-e ārezoo
Sedā kon kabootari rā keh neshasteh zir-e bāroon
Yā keh oon ghonche-ye tanhā keh neshasteh too-ye goldoon.

Chorus   *Begoo ay gol keh dobāreh, een khazoon bā to bahāreh*
Vakht-e labkhand-e golās, begoo fardā māl-e māst.

Verse 2   *Bezār tā māhi-e tanhā keh too tong-e gham asir-e*
Too-ye daryā-ye voojoode, tā dobāreh joon begireh
Bezār az gooshe-ye goldoon, ghoncheh-ye khasteh rahāsheh
Sar panāh-e oon kabootar, dasthā-ye garm-e to bāsheh.

Chorus   (as above)

Verse 3   (as Verse 1)

Chorus   (as above)

Verse 4   *Biyā vo panjere-hāye roo be fardā-hā ro vā kon*
Too-ye āsemoon-e ābi ghāsedak-hā rā sedā kon
Begoo ay gol keh dobāreh, een khazoon bā to bahāreh
Begoo tā āsemoon emshab, por sheh az māh o setāreh.

Chorus   *Vakht-e labkhand-e golās, begoo fardā māl-e māst*
Māl-e māst, māl-e māst.

Verse 1   Call the lonely fish in the crystal bowl
Call the dew on the white petal of hope
Call the dove sitting in the rain
Or the lonely flower bud in the vase.

Chorus   Oh, flower, say that with you, this autumn is spring again
It's time for the flowers to smile, say that tomorrow is ours.

Verse 2   Let the lonely fish, who is captive in the bowl of sadness
Find strength again in the sea of existence
Let the tired bud escape from the corner of the flowerpot
Let your warm hands be protection for the dove.

Chorus   as above

Verse 3   as Verse 1

Chorus   as above

---

[64]   By kind permission of Tarane Sharghee.

Verse 4   Come and open the windows facing towards tomorrow
Call to the dandelion seeds[65] in the blue sky.
Oh, flower, say that with you, this autumn is spring again
Say it, until tonight the sky becomes filled with the moon and stars.

Chorus   It's time for the flowers to smile, say that tomorrow is ours
It's ours, it's ours.

Lyrics to '*Panjereh*' ('*Window*')[66]

Migi donyā-ye mā, por az ranj o ghameh, tamām-e zendegi, ghoseh va mātameh
Delam gerefteh bāz, az een shab-hāye tār, az abr-hāye siyāh, zemestoon o bahār
Che ghamgineh ghooroob, che delgireh khazoon
Az gham por shodeh harf-hāmoon, āsoon mishkaneh del-hāmoon
Amā too shab-e tār, keh sard o bi sedāst, bebin keh āsemoon, por az setāre-hāst
Bā āhang-e khazoon, mirakhsand barg-hā bād, bāroon mibāreh bāz, bā naghmeh-hāye shād
Vakhti eshgh o omid, mishinan too del-hā
Shādi por misheh too ghalb-hā, shireen misheh hameh harf-hā.

Chorus   *Panjereh ro vā kon, bekhoon az eshgh o az omid*
Az gol-e sorkh o, atr-e yās, az niloofar-hāye sepid
Panjereh ro vā kon, bekhoon az payiz o bahār
Az shab o rooz o, az ghooroob, az shoor o shogh-e entezār
Ageh migi tangeh del-e tanhāt, ageh migi sardam hameh shab-hāt
Ageh shodeh labriz gham o dard-hāt, gham o rahā kon.

Vakhti keh shab-e to shab-e tār-e, nadāri too shab-hāt ye setāreh
Vakhti del too sinat bigharār-e, eshgh o sedā kon. Eshgh ...
Eshgh o sedā kon, gham o rahā kon.

Chorus   *Panjereh ro vā kon, bekhoon az eshgh o az omid*
Az gol-e sorkh o, atr-e yās, az niloofar-hāye sepid
Panjereh ro vā kon, bekhoon az payiz o bahār
Az shab o rooz o, az ghooroob, az shoor o shogh-e entezār
Panjereh ra vā kon, eshgh o sedā kon, gham o rahā kon
Panjereh ro vā kon, gham o rahā kon ...
Panjereh ro vā kon, eshgh o sedā kon ...
Panjereh ro vā kon ... panjereh ro vā kon, eshgh o sedā kon ...

You say our world is full of sorrow and sadness, all of life is worry and regret
Once again my heart is heavy at these dark nights, these black clouds, winter
    and spring

---

[65]   *Ghāsedak* literally means 'little messenger' and refers to the fluffy seed heads of the dandelion plant.

[66]   By kind permission of Tarane Sharghee.

How sad is the dusk, how disheartening autumn
Our words have become full of sadness, our hearts break easily
But in the dark, cold and silent night, look – the sky is full of stars
With the song of autumn, the wind dances the leaves, it's raining again with a
    happy song
When love and hope enter hearts
They fill with happiness and all talk becomes sweet.

Chorus   Open the window, sing of love and hope
Of red flowers, of the perfume of jasmine, of the white lilies
Open the window, sing of autumn and spring
Of night and day, of dusk, of the excitement and thrill of waiting
If you say your heart is lonely, if you say you're cold every night
If your pain and sadness are overflowing, let go of sadness.

When your night is dark, without even a single star
When your heart is restless, call out to love. Love …
Call out to love, let go of sadness.

Chorus   Open the window, sing of love and hope
Of red flowers, of the perfume of jasmine, of the white lilies
Open the window, sing of autumn and spring
Of night and day, of dusk, of the excitement and thrill of waiting
Open the window, call out to love, let go of sadness.

Chapter 11

The Power of Silent Voices:
Women in the Syrian Jewish Musical Tradition

Kay Kaufman Shelemay

Introduction

In much of the Jewish and Islamic Middle East, women have been constrained by religious precept from participating publicly in musical performance. This chapter explores one such case study in detail – the Syrian Jewish paraliturgical hymn tradition known as the *pizmonim* (sing. *pizmon*) – and seeks to amplify women's otherwise 'silent voices' in order to achieve a fuller understanding of power relations within that tradition.[1] While the *pizmonim*, and the broader world of Syrian Jewish musical and ritual life which these songs anchor, are generally perceived as exclusively male domains, I will argue that women occupy roles vital to the processes of transmission and maintenance of tradition. My approach will draw in part on a theoretical framework for evaluating power relations proposed by James P. Scott, who uses the term 'public transcript' as 'a shorthand way of describing the open interaction between subordinates and those who dominate' (Scott 1990:2). Alongside a public transcript, Scott suggests that there exists

---

This chapter is dedicated to the memory of Adrienne Fried Block, pioneer in the study of women and music, and of Johanna Spector, pioneer of Jewish musical studies.

[1]   The research process for this project began as a collaborative one with my then graduate students at New York University in the mid-1980s. We worked closely in a team effort with musicians of the Syrian community, almost all amateur aficionados of the *pizmon* tradition (See Shelemay 1988). After the conclusion of the team project, I continued research on my own with members of the community in Brooklyn, Mexico City and Jerusalem. While we had interviewed only one woman during the collaborative stage of the project, during the late 1980s and the early '90s I purposefully interviewed a number of women in the United States and elsewhere. I also attended many domestic rituals and family occasions, which provided an experience of life inside the Syrian Jewish family and ritual cycle absent from the team project. It was only while writing a book about music and memory in the Syrian tradition (Shelemay 1998) that I began to appreciate the importance of the silent voices of women within that tradition. I thank Ellen T. Harris, Judith Tick, Sylvia Barack Fishman, Maureen McLane, Sarah Weiss and Steven Kaplan for their useful comments and suggestions on drafts of this paper. I thank also those who gave stimulating feedback following colloquia at Wesleyan University, University of North Carolina, Chapel Hill, Harvard University, the Peabody Institute and The University of Florida.

a 'hidden transcript', a 'discourse that takes place "offstage", beyond direct observation by powerholders' (1990:4). Gender relations in the Syrian Jewish *pizmon* tradition can be usefully analysed in these terms, encouraging us to explore the 'hidden transcripts' that women perpetuate alongside and in dialogue with the more public world of music making perpetuated by men. At the same time, however, we need to move beyond Scott's emphasis on structural aspects of dominance and resistance to unravel the relationship of public and hidden notions of power within an explicitly performative domain of musical culture.

Following an introduction to the musical tradition at the core of this discussion, the second section of this chapter will follow established patterns for the historiography of women in interrogating religious ideology, social process and repertory (Tick 2001:520). The third section will explore selected *pizmon* texts for insights into how women are represented within the songs, while the fourth will present ethnographic data providing new insights into female roles which may escape notice if inquiry is restricted only to music making in public domains or within performance events. The conclusion will propose that in situations where women are excluded from composing and performing music, particularly in sacred styles with sex segregation, repertory analysis and ethnographic interviews can provide surprising revelations, exposing the intimate knowledge that women acquire of musical traditions in which they do not obviously participate.[2] The chapter suggests that women's silence does much more than simply mask a 'hidden transcript', and may in fact provide insights into how women exercise power within the tradition.

Shadowing this discussion of the Syrian Jewish *pizmon* tradition is its transmission in diasporic settings. From its inception in medieval Aleppo, the *pizmon* was a cultural and musical hybrid that wed Jewish linguistic and religious content to Arab musical and expressive domains; its use of popular Arab melodies within a Jewish religious context also united seemingly incompatible streams of secular and sacred within *pizmon* composition and performance. By the early twentieth century, *pizmonim* began to travel as Syrian Jews migrated worldwide. Today, the *pizmonim* are no longer extant in Syria due to the departure of the entire Jewish community from their historical homeland, but the songs continue to be actively sustained by Syrian Jews living in North and South America, Israel and other locales.[3] A search for Syrian women's voices at the turn of the twenty-first century must therefore be dually situated: within a dynamic, transnational setting and within the realm of memory that retains a strong and deep connection to its Middle Eastern roots.

---

2   A pioneering effort to interview women about Syrian Jewish social history is found in Zerubavel and Esses (1987), where the authors discuss the frequency with which women describe themselves as silent, 'as not being able to speak' (533).

3   From its inception in the late nineteenth century, recording technology played an important role in musical transmission among Syrian Jews worldwide. This subject is too complex to address here, but is explored in detail in Shelemay (1998).

Introducing the *Pizmonim*

The *pizmon* repertory incorporates well over five hundred songs, some dating from the sixteenth century but many composed in the nineteenth and twentieth centuries. The *pizmonim* are *contrafacta*, their melodies borrowed primarily from Arab secular songs, their texts newly composed in Hebrew. Today the *pizmonim* constitute the primary surviving traces of a Judeo-Arab identity dating back more than a thousand years. That this hybrid identity is still nurtured by many Syrian Jews in diaspora and regularly celebrated in song speaks to the persistence of an expressive culture rendered marginal by nearly a century of intense conflict in the Middle East. *Pizmon* texts praise God, quoting and paraphrasing Jewish literature and liturgy as well as referencing Jewish folklore and custom. The texts further contain names of individuals within the Syrian community, including family genealogies, and provide allusions to the occasions for which they were commissioned and on which they were first performed. *Pizmonim* have been composed exclusively by men and most were commissioned to celebrate life-cycle occasions as experienced by their male honourees, including circumcisions, *bar mitzvah*s, weddings, holidays and miscellaneous other special communal events.

Performing *pizmonim* brings Syrian Jews together as a community and many of the song texts explicitly prescribe aspects of a traditional male life-cycle, as can be seen, for example, in the text of *pizmon* '*Yehi Shalom*' ('*May There Be Peace*'). Composed in the nineteenth century and performed regularly since that time at the beginning of circumcision ceremonies for male infants, the song is dedicated 'To the father of the son':

> May there be peace within our walls, tranquility in Israel.
> In a favorable sign did a son come to us, in his days shall the redeemer arrive:
>
> May the boy be refreshed, in the shadow of Shaddai [Almighty God] will he lodge.
> And the Torah [Five Books of Moses] he then will examine, he will teach the religion to all that ask.
>
> May his fountain be blessed, his life span shall be lengthy.
> May his table be ordered, and his offering shall not be defiled.
>
> His name will go out in all directions, when he grows he will be a strong man.
> And let him be a member of those that fear God, let him be in his generation like Shmuel.
>
> Until old age and hoariness, he shall be plump with all manner of goodness.
> And peace to him and much love, 'Amen,' so will say the Lord.

The circumcised in his nation will live for his father and mother.
And may his God be with him and with the whole House of Israel.[4]

The text of '*Yehi Shalom*' contains obvious references to the circumcision ceremony as well as substantial intertextuality.[5] The first line is based on Psalm 122:7, 'May there be peace within your walls, tranquillity in your palace'. The expression 'May his table be ordered' is a pun on the name of the authoritative sixteenth-century Jewish legal code, the *Shulchan Aruch* (lit. 'set table'), written by Rabbi Josef Karo. The reference to the 'generation like Shmuel' alludes to a rabbinic saying that the greatness of each prophet is relative to his own generation. Thus the text both celebrates the circumcision ritual and prescribes the future for the newborn baby boy, whose observance and transmission of religious law, the text affirms, ensure that he will prosper.

This song is located within, and seeks to perpetuate, a patriarchal system, invoking the infant to grow into a strong man, in the mould of the biblical forefathers. It sets forth a public transcript based on Jewish religious ideology, which is reaffirmed through male observance of religious law and practice. Many of the double meanings that pervade the text move beyond simple intertextuality to constitute what Scott has termed a 'third realm' of group politics located strategically between the open and hidden transcripts (1990:18–19). While Scott connects this 'third realm' to subordinate or resistant aspects of the hidden transcript, in the Syrian *pizmon* one finds the public transcript reinforced by a further layer of meanings. The close textual relationship of *pizmon* '*Yehi Shalom*' to the rite of circumcision and male power is further underscored by its melodic setting, an Arab melody in *maqām Sabā*, the melodic category traditionally used by Syrian Jews at the circumcision ceremony.[6] The distinctive melodic contour of *Sabā*, incorporating two neutral intervals at the second and sixth scale degrees, provides an audible musical marker reinforcing the strong textual associations within the song text and its ceremonial settings.

With the exception of the final *pizmon* stanza, which enjoins the infant to live for 'his father and mother', there appear to be no references to women either within the text or its layers of double meanings. Yet there is a hidden allusion to women's subordinate roles. This is found in the third English verse, alongside the most overt reference to male physiology, 'May his fountain be blessed', drawn from Proverbs 5:18. Although not quoted in the *pizmon*, the proverb reads: 'Let your fountain be blessed; Find joy in the wife of your youth – A loving doe, a graceful mountain goat. Let her breasts satisfy you at all times; Be infatuated with love of her always'

4   Shelemay (1998:260); translated by Joshua Levisohn.

5   I thank Joshua Levisohn for explicating these references and preparing the translation of '*Yehi Shalom*'.

6   The association of *maqām Sabā* with the circumcision ceremony derives from the liturgical use of this mode when the biblical reading for the day mentions circumcision. See Shelemay (1998:155–6).

(JPS 1999:1607). This *pizmon* text closes the circle of male power on multiple levels. Only men sing the *pizmonim* in public, whether during the synagogue service, at domestic rituals or at celebrations. All the historical evidence, initial ethnographic observation and preliminary textual analysis, then, suggest that this is a tradition composed by males, for males, about males. The *pizmon* can be said to openly reflect and sustain the dominant role of men in Syrian Jewish life, where males hold positions of both prestige and power (Ortner 1996b:146), legitimised by Jewish legal and ritual precepts. Certainly the *pizmon* also provides a signal challenge for ethnographic research that privileges musical performance as the central unit of analysis.[7]

Understanding Women's Silence: The Impact of Ideology on Musical Practice

What recourse do scholars have when there is apparently no musical performance by women, public or private? Several paths are open, requiring first and foremost an exploration of why women are silent. Here one encounters the manner in which religious ideology informs – and transforms – both musical and social practices.

Women do not usually sing publicly within Orthodox Jewish communities due to a dictum termed *kol isha*, which states '*kol b'isha ervah*', literally 'the voice of a woman is a sexual incitement' (Koskoff 2001:126).[8] While the genesis of *kol isha* is generally attributed to a sixth-century Babylonian Talmudic scholar's response to a passage from the Song of Songs (2:14) that reads, 'Let me see thy countenance, let me hear thy voice, for sweet is thy voice and thy countenance is comely', a series of controversies about the dictum, its legal sources and issues relating to its meaning have left it open to debate and reinterpretation throughout history. Attitudes towards and applications of *kol isha* vary between and even within different Orthodox communities, but in general the dictum prohibits public musical performance by women. The social and musical outcomes often attributed

---

[7]   In their introduction to the first section of *Music and Gender* (Moisala and Diamond 2000), entitled 'Music Performance and Performativity', the editors stress the centrality of performance to the study of music and gender as well as to ethnomusicology in general (21). While women's absence from performance prodded me to write this chapter, my approach here has more in common with the second section of the same volume which focuses on narratives and 'telling lives' (97). A recent collection of essays on women and music in Mediterranean cultures (Magrini 2003) similarly seeks to move away from long-time representations of Mediterranean women in the anthropological literature as 'silent, passive, and marginal figures' (13).

[8]   See Koskoff (2001:126–34) for a more extended and nuanced discussion of *kol isha* as understood and practised in an Orthodox Hassidic community in New York City. The ban in current Orthodox Hassidic practice, as studied by Koskoff, extends primarily to men hearing the singing (not speaking) voices of all women past puberty outside of their families. See also Berman (1980).

to *kol isha* by members of the community include the separate seating of women in the synagogue, often behind a screen or other barrier, and the banning of female performers at gatherings of men. *Kol isha* is maintained to differing extents in Syrian Jewish communities, depending on individual and familial patterns. However, segregated seating is universally observed in Syrian synagogues and women generally do not sing in the same room with the men, even at the festive Sabbath afternoon songfests (termed *Sebet*) held in private homes. Many Syrian Jewish men, especially those of an older generation, are not accustomed to hearing women sing in public.[9] For instance, one elderly Syrian man, who wished to remain anonymous, described for me his reaction to encountering a female singer while visiting an Arab nightclub in Los Angeles: 'She got up to perform. And it was the first time in my life I ever, ever heard a female or soprano singer. Never did …'.

The position of women in Syrian Jewish musical life thus reflects clearly marked gender roles, deriving primarily from *kol isha* and other ritual injunctions regarding female purity. Moreover, it seems likely that Jewish dicta against public performance by Syrian Jewish women were reinforced historically by similar prohibitions in Islamic societies within which this Jewish community long resided.[10] Constraints on women in public performance continue to be a subject of debate.[11] While many women within the Syrian Jewish community perceive roles dramatically differentiated by sex as complementary, others within the community perceive the status of Syrian women to be an example of marked power asymmetry. Both perspectives will be discussed below.

The many issues surrounding the ideology of gender and its implications for musical behaviour and social interaction also render more complex the role of the fieldworker. As a woman and ethnographer, I experienced substantial discomfort over these gender constraints. Similar tensions have been noted by other female fieldworkers as they moved between insider and outsider perceptions of gender asymmetries and inequities. Ethnomusicologist Ellen Koskoff has explicitly addressed the challenge of representing Hassidic women in contexts within which

---

[9]   Stricter observance of *kol isha* has been reported recently in certain segments of the Orthodox world in the United States, where it has given rise to controversy and opposition. See Fishman (2000:50–53).

[10]   Doubleday (1988) and van Nieuwkerk (2003) have published relevant case studies of female performers in Afghanistan and Egypt respectively. The similarities likely derive from long-time proximity which led to exchange in many domains of Jewish and Islamic musical thought and practice. The connections between Islamic and Jewish theoretical and philosophical writings about music are summarised in Shiloah (1992:53–9).

[11]   Sylvia Barack Fishman has carried out research regarding attitudes toward *kol isha* in Orthodox communities, observing: 'As it is colloquially understood within the Orthodox community today, prohibitions clustered around the concept of *kol isha* laws prohibit observant men from hearing women's voices in songs that have erotic valence. The fact that Orthodox environments must acknowledge such concerns and deal with them is one important boundary between Orthodox and non-Orthodox Jewish feminists' (2000:48).

the fieldworker herself is uncomfortable.[12] Similarly, anthropologist Faye Ginsburg commented on her personal ambivalence during a study of Syrian women's rituals, which were problematic to her as a Jew and as a feminist. Both Koskoff and Ginsburg include interpretations of these gender asymmetries in a manner congruent with the values of the Orthodox Jewish communities they studied, particularly as they were explained and mediated by (female) insiders. Koskoff explicates Hassidic women's understanding and support of *kol isha* as part of a larger balance of power (1993:155–6), while Ginsburg draws on the frequently articulated Jewish concept of *tsniut*, which is translated from the Hebrew as 'modesty', to reconcile the gender asymmetry from an insider's perspective. Through the Syrian women with whom she worked, Ginsburg came to understand that there are 'realms of general and ritual activity that are to be shielded from the eye of the outsider, and that are characterized by an internalized devotional attitude that transcends individual volition or desire for recognition' (1987:542). Moreover, according to Ginsburg, members of the Syrian community consider there to be a type of 'equity' between public male ritual performance (such as singing *pizmonim*) and more private female practices, such as dressing modestly or maintaining Jewish laws in the home. I will return to the concept of *tsniut* below, but would simply observe here that the enforced boundaries of Syrian women's musical, social and ritual activities are effectively 'naturalised'[13] by concepts such as *kol isha* and *tsniut* for insiders to the tradition, despite their clear vulnerability to external critique as frameworks oppressive to women. Like Ginsburg, I also gathered ethnographic data concerning dichotomous male and female roles in Syrian Jewish life and the ways in which this division of responsibility is perceived by many Syrian Jews to 'carry equal and complementary weight in the ongoing life of the community' (Ginsburg 1987:543).

Despite the fact that the relationship between Syrian men and women in the musical domain appears to mirror that encountered in other aspects of Jewish ritual practices – men predominate in the public domain, while women are involved either in hidden or in separate spheres altogether – I would like to avoid theorising this relationship only in terms of the more obvious binaries. Ethnographic observation and interviews construct a picture that includes moments in which male prestige and power are affirmed, but also of much more subtle interactions. The data also provide ample evidence that Syrian women are implicated much more directly than it might initially appear, for example, in *pizmon* transmission.

Here, it is instructive to consider the writings of anthropologist Sherry Ortner, who has criticised the limitations of evaluating women either in relation to a

---

[12]   Koskoff suggests integrating differing perspectives of ethnographer and insiders in order 'to call attention to the many intentional or unintentional biases through which all so-called raw data are filtered' (1993:163).

[13]   This expression is borrowed from Yanagisako and Delaney's exploration of 'naturalising power', defined as the ways in which differentials of power can appear to be 'natural, inevitable, even god-given' (1995:1). See Scott (1990:75–6) for an enumeration of other discussions of the naturalisation of patterns of domination.

male dominant social order or, alternately, as a resistant (usually morally better) agenda (1996a:16). In the Syrian instance, as in the case studies discussed by Ortner (1996b), one finds movement between these poles as well as a great deal of activity in an ambiguous middle zone. Ortner's discussion, coupled with Scott's notion of a 'third realm' cited above, are extremely helpful in moving discussion away from binary models of either male or female hegemony to acknowledge what Ortner describes as the making and remaking of gender relations over the course of time through interactions characterised by shifting power relations and moments of solidarity (1996a:19).

Just as there are expectations for the Syrian Jewish male life-cycle, there are equally strong prescriptions for a woman: that she will marry (usually at a very tender age), raise a good number of children and oversee a traditional Jewish household (see Ginsburg 1987:542, Zenner 1983:177–8). On occasion, these expectations are echoed in song.

Songs that Speak: Perspectives of Women from Three *Pizmonim*

The following section presents specific examples of the ways in which women are invoked and represented in *pizmon* texts. The first example is a famous wedding *pizmon* from turn of the twentieth century Aleppo; the second and the third examples, less well-known *pizmonim* composed in twentieth-century Brooklyn for *bar mitzvah*s. Printed collections of *pizmon* texts have circulated among Syrian communities worldwide since the second quarter of the twentieth century. In 1964, a new edition titled *Sheer Ushbahah Hallel Ve-Zimrah* ('*Song and Praise, Praise and Song*', hereafter abbreviated *SUHV*), based on previous written collections plus additions from the oral tradition, was prepared and published in New York under the guidance of a Brooklyn cantor named Gabriel Shrem. A sixth edition of *SUHV* was issued in 1993.[14]

Pizmon 'Melekh Raḥaman'

It is noteworthy that the first personal dedication in *SUHV*, that which introduces *pizmon* '*Melekh Raḥaman*', mentions a woman (Shrem 1988:168). '*Melekh Raḥaman*' was composed around the turn of the twentieth century in Aleppo by Rabbi Raphael Taboush in honour of his student, Moses Ashear, for whom he was also a personal mentor and close friend. The Hebrew text of '*Melekh Raḥaman*' conveys familiar religious imagery, seeking God's protection for the people of Israel and portraying the Sabbath as Israel's bride, a common image in Jewish literature. The English translation is as follows:[15]

---

[14]   The references here are to the fifth edition, 1988.

[15]   Unless otherwise indicated, the information about '*Melekh Raḥaman*' discussed here was provided by Albert Ashear on 19 July 1989. The complete Hebrew text can be

Merciful King, protect, pray thee, and redeem a people that awaits You.
Oh Rock, rebuild forever the pleasant city; through it He will gain honor.

Pray accept, a song out of love, when I sing,
before the bridegroom, with beautiful bride,
a helpmate has [surely] come for him.
May he rejoice with her always,
the bride of Moses, the daughter of Jacob, an upright man.

Give thanks, faithful people, with the voice of rejoicing,
to God, He is great yet hidden.
He is, forever, my shepherd and deliverer, in every epoch and age.
From his mercies, I shall behold a beauty.
May the blessing of Abraham be granted me, Oh Lord, forever.
Constant Father. I shall surely ask of the Faithful One.
Let my glory shine, speedily, as in the days of Solomon.[16]

The song is dedicated to 'the pleasant groom, Rabbi Moshe Ashear, on the day of his marriage to Ṣalaḥah, daughter of Yaʻakov Shamaʻa'. An acrostic spells the name 'Moshe', honouring the bridegroom. Within the *pizmon*, however, Ṣalaḥah is mentioned only indirectly as a (beautiful) bride and a daughter: she is at once defined by the family she leaves and the one that she will join. Other women important in Ashear's life are also named in the song, including his mother, Samḥan, said to be represented by the Hebrew word '*yismaḥ*' (lit. 'may he rejoice'), and his sister Rinah ('[the voice of] rejoicing').[17] Abraham is both the biblical patriarch and the bride's brother. Interestingly, Ashear's father (Joseph), who died at an early age, is not mentioned; however, the names of the groom's brothers, Shaul (lit. 'I shall surely ask') and Shlomo (Solomon), are included.

The reference to the bride by name in the dedication is unusual. In 1912, Moses Ashear immigrated to New York City, where he served as cantor until his death in 1940. Several months after her husband's departure, pregnant and with several young children in tow, Ṣalaḥah travelled from Aleppo to New York. Shortly after her arrival, she gave birth to a son, Albert, whom she nicknamed 'Amerik'. 'You are the seed of Aleppo and the fruit of America', she later told him. If her husband Moses linked the *pizmon* tradition of Raphael Taboush in Aleppo with that of the New World, Ṣalaḥah Ashear also connected their families and associated rituals over time and space. In ethnographic interviews, several Syrian women credited Moses Ashear with initiating the Saturday afternoon

---

found in Shelemay (1998:211).

[16] Shelemay (1998:211); translated by Geoffrey Goldberg and James Robinson.

[17] Note that some names clearly evident in the original Hebrew text are much more difficult to recognise in translation. However, names can be disguised in Hebrew as well, as is the case here with Samḥan, represented by '*yismaḥ*'.

Sebet celebration in New York City.[18] While it cannot be confirmed, Ṣalaḥah Ashear seems likely to have been the first to actually mount a *Sebet* in New York City at her home.

Pizmon 'Yeḥidah Hitna'ari'

Moses Ashear composed numerous *pizmonim*. One of the most interesting, if not the most widely performed, *pizmon 'Yeḥidah Hitna'ari'*, was prepared for the *bar mitzvah* of Joseph Saff in 1933.[19] Cantor Ashear led a rendition of the song as young Joseph was called forward during the *bar mitzvah* ceremony. During an interview (23 October 1984), Joseph Saff explained that there were many names of family and friends within the song.[20] A partial translation of the song is as follows:

> *You, the one and only, stir yourself,*
> *An end to your trouble, enough, enough.*
> *Put on your strength and awake,*
> *And come to me, to me.*
> *Eat my honey with my honeycomb,*
> *In the garden of my fields, my fields.*
> *Pasture my kids.*

> The God of my father, my help
> Who rides the heavens, the heavens,
> Let Him adorn me with my crown,
> And [make like] suckling babes my enemies, my enemies.
> He will continue to gather my scattered ones,
> For they have lasted long, my days, my days,
> And I await my salvation.

---

[18] Sheila Schweky disagreed, claiming that the *Sebet* was also celebrated in Aleppo before Syrian Jews left the country (Interview, 27 January 1988). For an interesting discussion of 'variants' in life experience narratives, see Bowers (2000:149).

[19] The song is today forgotten by all but its elderly honouree, its lack of popularity attributed by most to shortcomings in its melody, which is considered both difficult and lacking in appeal. Even Joseph Saff, when performing the song during an interview, remarked: 'After you sing the first stanza, the music is repetitious down the line and you'll get bored with it. Honestly, I'm bored with it. I never sing the whole song. I usually sing the first, second, third, fifth and last [verses]' (Interview, 4 December 1984).

[20] See Shelemay (1998:174–7), where the Hebrew text printed by Ashear for the *bar mitzvah* is annotated with superscript numbers that correspond to Saff's detailed comments about the song's contents and meaning. The complete English translation of the text is also presented in Shelemay (1998:172–4).

You, the one and only ...

Rejoice with me, my mother,
My brothers and my sisters.
For on this day today I enter,
On the [first] day of the fourteenth of my years,
To serve him with my prayer,
In my heart and on my lips,
With the community of my congregation.

You, the one and only ...[21]

While there is no direct reference to a woman in the song's dedication (as there is in '*Melekh Raḥaman*'),[22] the opening words of the song provide a clear reference to its female subject. The first two lines translate as 'You, the one and only, stir yourself/An end to your trouble, enough, enough'. This is an admonition to Joseph Saff's mother, who headed a family in crisis and to whom the song is actually addressed. Joseph's father died in 1927 when Joseph was seven, leaving a young widow barely in her thirties with six young children. It was customary for a Syrian Jewish woman in mourning to wear black for a period of six to nine months and to remain in the house for perhaps the first two or three months after bereavement. When '*Yeḥidah Hitna'ari*' was composed in 1933, Mrs Saff had not left her home for six years. Her friends and sisters evidently took her children shopping for clothes and Joseph remembers that he did much of the family grocery shopping. '*Yeḥidah Hitna'ari*' seeks to restore a woman to her traditional role, the care and nurturing of her children. Mrs Saff is referred to indirectly in the song; her maiden name, Shalom, is incorporated only within the last two lines.

If the *pizmonim* generally celebrate and commemorate life-cycle events, this song promotes a return to everyday life for the mother. Mother, brothers and sisters are enjoined to rejoice, despite a reference to their being 'left alone' in a later verse of the song. The song also paraphrases in a later verse the traditional view that a woman's 'performance of commanded things' is of the greatest importance and the mother is called on to return to these responsibilities while taking comfort in her children.

---

[21] Shelemay (1998:172–3); translated by Geoffrey Goldberg and James Robinson.

[22] The dedication and the song text contain an unusually large number of names, all men from Saff's family and social circle. The printed version of the song distributed by Ashear at the *bar mitzvah* highlighted these names in upper case Hebrew letters to ensure that they were recognised (see Shelemay 1998:174–7).

Pizmon 'Mizzivakh Tanhir'

Lest we construct too valedictory a picture of a song tradition in which women, while only indirectly acknowledged, are valorised, let us return to a more complex example of gender asymmetry and male domination. Like '*Yeḥidah Hitna'ari*', many *pizmonim* have names in them, but they are usually more difficult to decipher. Names are often disguised, transformed or even divided between lines of the sung text.

A woman's name, hidden in another *pizmon* by Moses Ashear, '*Mizzivakh Tanhir*' (Example 11.1), has given rise to an anecdote circulated in several versions:

> So now … you're going to laugh when I tell you … You see … this [*pizmon*] is for a *bar mitzvah*. The *talmid* [student], his name was Ṣion, and the father was Shemuel, and the family's name is Nasar … Now look at the second verse where it says '*shem el nora yinṣereni*', you see it? '*Shem el*' is Shemuel, that's the father. '*Yinṣereni*' is Nasar, the family name. '*Ṣion*' [same line] is the boy that's getting *bar mitzvahed*. Now he mentioned all the family. Abraham [two lines down] is probably his other son. Now he [Shemuel Nasar] goes over to the guy [composer Moses Ashear], and he says: 'Where did you put my wife's name?' His wife's name was Sanyar, a Syrian name. He's looking all over the book, he doesn't see it. So [Ashear] says, 'Over here, now … I'm going to sing the song, just that part, where your wife's name is'. So he goes like this: '*Beḥodesh nisan yar'eni*' [in the month Nisan]: He says, 'I cut her off in the middle!' (Meyer Kairey, 12 December 1984)

Example 11.1   Transcription of an extract from *Pizmon 'Mizzivakh Tanhir'*.

be - ho - desh ni -   san   yar - 'e - ni

In one of the other versions of this tale that circulates in the community, the story ends with a more graphic and sexist line. After showing the father the way in which the wife's name is split between two words, the composer's comment is reputed to have been, 'I even spread her legs for you'.

'*Mizzivakh Tanhir*' provides an example that is doubly provocative. Names are of paramount importance in the Syrian tradition, with children named after paternal and maternal grandparents, living and deceased. Both women and men are enormously proud of this tradition and every Syrian woman I interviewed made it a point to mention that granddaughters had been named after her. The inclusion of her name provides evidence of a deep-seated respect for Sanyar. That the wife's name can be heard when sung, yet seen only with difficulty within the written text is further testimony of a respectful gesture. Until the late twentieth century, most Syrian Jewish women did not study or read Hebrew. Most spoke a language that the community colloquially terms 'Syrian', a Judeo-Arabic vernacular. Sanyar would certainly have heard her name in this song when it was performed and noted it with pride. That the song today is discussed in the context of a sexist tale may provide evidence of changes over time in the *pizmon* tradition, or expose a moment in which the respectful public transcript gives way to disrespectful elements otherwise masked.

An exploration of selected *pizmon* texts reveals that women are occasionally a muted presence within some songs, a presence which is circumscribed by tradition and posited within their traditional roles in Syrian society as daughters, sisters, wives and mothers. Song texts written by men thus provide only a limited, and quite conventional, window on the power of women in Syrian Jewish life; indeed, their representations in these contexts are consistent with the public transcript. It is to the testimony of the women themselves that one must turn in search of a hidden transcript and for more substantive insights.

The *Pizmonim* in Women's Lives

Beyond their primary responsibility for running the household and caring for children, women plan and mount the various life-cycle celebrations, such as the *Sebet*, that are an integral part of Syrian ritual and domestic life. Women further maintain Syrian culinary traditions that are at the centre of these observances. These responsibilities were undertaken universally by Syrian Jewish females of past generations and are still rigorously maintained by most today in a community that continues to privilege ceremonial observances, both to conserve strong family ties and to maintain marked social boundaries with outsiders. However, this traditional perspective on Syrian Jewish women's roles appears to understate their impact beyond the confines of their own family units, the activities they undertake to nurture their broader communities and their work alongside their husbands as dictated by economic necessity. Oral histories carried out with Syrian women, particularly those of the generation which emigrated from Syria, document that many worked alongside their spouses, shared business decisions and often instigated moves to other diaspora communities (Sutton 1988:240–48).

Musical involvement by Syrian women derives almost exclusively from their traditional roles in planning and participating in domestic ceremonies and family occasions; they have no formal role in synagogue governance or its rituals. However, many young girls acquire knowledge of *pizmonim* by attending synagogue services with their fathers before they reach puberty, and within their homes many actively participate in music making. Adult women also maintain close contact with the male musical world through the activities of their children, especially through their sons.

The hidden, but active role of women within the *pizmon* tradition can best be reconstructed through a close look at *pizmon*-related domains in which Syrian women are active.[23] Domains that emerge as important to the transmission of *pizmonim* include the following: (1) ensuring the physical continuity of the community; (2) controlling life-cycle ceremonies; (3) maintaining culinary production; (4) sustaining knowledge of *pizmon* source melodies; (5) conserving oral histories; and (6) experiencing moments of public prestige.

Many women joined in singing *pizmonim* and other Hebrew song repertories with their families.[24] The late Sophie Cohen recalled:

> My father would go to the synagogue; he'd come back, make *kiddush* [blessing over wine] and pray on the bread, and we'd have a nice feast. And then we'd sing all these songs after we'd finished our dinners, the Saturday *pizmonim* … Every Saturday we used to sing the same songs, but on holidays they had extra songs. At *Shabbat* [Sabbath], at holidays, of course they always sang in my family. And I'd join in sometimes. I used to join in when they used to sing. (Sophie Cohen, 28 February 1985)[25]

Syrian women conserve tradition through mounting domestic ceremonies, displaying their array of special foods as a framework for the musical content. That women prepare and serve food at rituals such as the *Sebet*, while men sing at these same events, is of signal importance.[26] Indeed, in Sophie Cohen's memory, food and song converge as complementary domains of experience.[27] Music and food share a semantic field relating to aesthetics: both the *pizmonim* and Syrian food should be 'sweet' not sour. *SUHV* is dedicated to the memory of the 'sweet singer of Israel' (Cantor Moses Ashear) and to the holy songs 'which are sweeter even than honey and the honeycomb' (Shelemay 1998:39). Songs sung in the various

---

[23] See Diamond (2000) for discussion of the ways in which feminist scholarship has used oral histories for exploring the 'performance of gender and the gendering of performance' (99). I concur with Diamond's two assertions: first, that oral narratives must be heard or read in terms of what is desired, not just in terms of what has been done; and second, that music and gender are sites for negotiating a place within communities that tend to reinforce certain values and behaviours as normative (100).

[24] Interview, Isaac Cabasso, 13 November 1984.

[25] Sophie's two brothers, the late Hyman Kaire (14 March 1985) and Meyer Kairey (6 November 1984), offered similar testimony. Sophie also remembered that when she would overhear her father teaching her brothers to sing *pizmonim*, she would sing along by ear.

[26] In a study of Syrian Jewish women in Mexico City, Paulette Kershenovich writes that 'From the perspective of the women of this study, the fact that they cook and prepare for holidays and special occasions means that it is they who are the ritual experts and the guardians of traditions' (2002:119).

[27] See Shelemay (1998) for further discussion of the role of memory in the *pizmon* tradition as well as the complex relationship of memory to historical reconstruction.

Arab *maqāmāt* are said to be 'sweetened' by improvisation, just as food can be sweetened with sugar. The experience and memory of song are reinforced and strengthened through food, with which it shares a network of associations. In this way, too, the male world of musical performance and female world of ritualised cuisine merge and become wholly interdependent.[28]

Like many young girls, Sophie Cohen also went to the synagogue with her father, where she loved to listen to the liturgy. When she was a child, she would sit with her father among the men, but was relegated to the ladies' section before adolescence. Around this time, her attendance at the synagogue fell off and, without knowledge of Hebrew, Sophie's musical interests shifted from the *pizmonim* to the Arab songs that were the source for *pizmon* melodies. She remembers listening to Arab music on the radio while working at her sewing machine in the New York City garment industry, and later to Arab music on cassette tapes at home 'all night long'.

The interest and knowledge of Syrian Jewish women concerning Arab music has been one of the most active ways in which they participate in the *pizmon* tradition, and which has tied them to what is considered to be the authentic 'source' (*makor*) of the *pizmonim*.[29] Women are at once the physical source of the community through procreation, they produce the community's food and nourishment, and their relationship with Arab music is one with the source of the songs. Here we might pause to consider that women's power in relation to the broader religious tradition, as well as its music, can be termed 'generative'. On the other hand, men's power derives from more 'performative' domains.

One Syrian woman deeply knowledgeable about Arab music was Gracia Haber, a great niece of Aleppo *pizmon* composer Raphael Taboush. Haber, who was 80 years of age and blind in 1989 when she sat for an interview at her home in Brooklyn, New York, spent her days listening to the soundtracks of Arabic language musical films on videotape. In the course of the interview, she insisted on showing me one of these videos, during which she alternately sang along with and narrated the action, translating from Arabic to English. Gracia Haber said: 'It's very important … You will enjoy the music, I'm telling you. The wording, it's worth listening to them, the stories. I have tapes, stories and singing.'[30] Like other

---

[28]   Recipes are also transmitted in a manner similar to the *pizmonim*. The *pizmon* book contains blank pages at the back to accommodate the texts of newly composed *pizmonim*; similarly, the women of the Syrian community in New York collectively publish a cookbook, entitled *Festival of Holidays: Recipe Book* (1987), with blank pages at the end of each section so that 'everyone can add her own recipes' (Sheila Schweky, 27 January 1988).

[29]   According to Moses Tawil, one of the most accomplished singers in the Syrian community, 'I sing them [the *pizmonim*] in Arabic, which is the authentic song. Which gives it the authentic flavour, because invariably, it could change in the translation. I'm not talking about the translation of the words, and passing the melody, but the authentic *makor*, the base [lit. 'the source'] is the Arabic and that's that' (Moses Tawil, 6 November 1984).

[30]   Gracia Haber, 31 January 1989.

women interviewed, Gracia Haber provided a wealth of oral knowledge about the *pizmon* tradition. She told stories she had learned from women in her family, especially from her grandmother, sharing important details concerning *pizmon* history completely absent from the testimony of Syrian men. The historical knowledge of Haber and other women suggests that women's oral/historical narratives are a corollary of and complement to the male narratives embedded within the *pizmon* texts.[31] For example, Haber volunteered detailed information concerning the life and musical practices of her great uncle, Raphael Taboush. Her narrative began with an account of her grandfather, Abraham, and his siblings in Aleppo and sketches the genesis of Taboush's involvement with the *pizmonim*:

> And the third one was my grandfather Abraham ... And then the young, the fourth one was Rabbi Raphael Taboush. And the fifth one was Joseph Taboush. So those three older ones were very successful in their business. And the two younger ones, they were spoiled. They used to run around, they don't want to do anything. And the older one, Hakham Raphael [Learned Raphael], used to go to places where there were Syrian songs, Arabic songs that he loved tunes. And he wanted to get the tunes in his head. Always. So every time they hear there's a wedding or a party by the Arab, they, he used to go there. He has some friends that goes with him. And he already finished his Hebrew school, but not the higher [school] to be a Rabbi. When he ran, one day, they were gonna be, they caught them, why they're Jewish and they came to the Arab village? So they send the police after them. And he got so scared he ran, breathing very fast, he washed his face with cold water, he was very hot, and he became blind.
>
> I don't know [why he became blind], that's what they, my grandmother told me. That's Abraham's wife. So, and he became blind, and then he used to go with his friend also to listen to the music. One day then his friend didn't show up. So it was a Saturday, so one of them was going to *shul* [synagogue], another friend was going to *shul*, he told him, 'Raphael, you want to go with me to *shul*, because your friend didn't show up?' He says, 'Yes, I'll go with you to *shul*.' Since that day, he never left the *shul*. He loves it. He had tunes in his head, and every time there was a wedding, or there was a *bar mitzvah*, or a *bris* [circumcision], he used to, in Hebrew, translate the words. The music is in Arabic, but the wording was Hebrew. And that's how we start the *pizmonim*. And for every occasion, there is another *pizmon* that he used to make.

So, from the oral testimonies of Gracia Haber and Sophie Cohen, we hear the voices of Syrian women who learned *pizmonim* as children, became aficionados

---

31   This is not to imply that women did not participate in other ways to recording narratives. Edwin Seroussi documents the activity of Sephardic Jewish women who collected folksong texts, describing in detail the manuscript notebooks of Emily Sene, who 'became an archivist perhaps in part to compensate for her own inability to sing' (Seroussi 2003:202).

of the Arab tunes that were their sources and who remain unique repositories of oral histories about the past.

In terms of public music performance by women, the picture is much less clear. Stories circulate about only one woman in the Brooklyn Syrian community who sang in public, and who belonged to one of the premier families of amateur musicians: Sarah Tawil. Blind since childhood, Sarah initially spoke of her love of singing Arab songs, not the *pizmonim*:

> I used to sing the very high Syrian singing because my Dad, he used to buy me the better records so I should learn it. He used to love to hear me singing. You know, every Saturday, they used to come by us, my uncles, all our friends. We used to sit down from twelve o'clock until sunset ... To tell you the truth *pizmonim* I don't know ... Most of my singing was Syrian Arabic and Hebrew, my songs ... (Sarah Tawil, 30 March 1989)

However, other aspects of Sarah's testimony suggest that she did in fact know *pizmonim* and related repertoires, and that indeed, she may also have once publicly challenged the observance of *kol isha*. Sarah Tawil described a Sabbath evening *Havdalah* ritual around 1945 at a Jewish resort hotel in the Catskill Mountains of New York, as follows:[32]

> Then, the Rabbi Kassin tell me, he says, 'Sarah, would you like to, uh, to say [=sing] *Havdalah*, please, you know the *pizmonim* they say in *Havdalah*?'
>
> And they have the *hazzan* [cantor], can I tell you, you know, and he was screaming his head off. And as a *hazzan*, really, really who is not a great voice, no. But his voice, it doesn't make you happy, that's it, I don't know. I heard *hazzanim* [cantors], you know. Yiddish *hazzanim*, I hear it, and I know them. I know who had the great voice.
>
> Anyway, the Rabbi went so tired of this, listening to him, so he turned to me, please Sarah, say some *Havdalah*. So this *hazzan*, he put his hands like that in his ear, and he said 'Oh, no, a woman singing! Oh, I don't like a woman singing!'
>
> So OK, and you know what I do, I said, heh, and I opened my mouth and I start the '*B'motzaei Yom Menucha*'. The guy, and you know what, he closed his ear, and he was going. Listen to that! So when he heard, he came back and he sat in the room. He said ...
>
> So we have a friend here who is very upset at him. He said, 'Why did you do that in the first place?' He says, 'I didn't know you had such a great voice.'

---

32 I note that this may in fact be considered a subversive move, or at least that it has been constructed as such in Sarah Tawil's testimony. That she reports that the Rabbi encouraged her to sing is also surprising, although it is useful to consider one scholar's comment that despite religious precepts in Jewish communities, people don't necessarily observe them in practice (Loeb 1996:64). That this event took place outside a formal synagogue context may be another relevant factor in the departure from tradition.

He says, 'You know or you don't know, or you won't do that to your kind of people. Why should you do that?'

There was gonna have a big fight in that place and I said this *Havdalah*. (Sarah Tawil, 30 March 1989)

Through these accounts, one can began to understand some of the ways in which women participated actively in Syrian Jewish musical life, providing their own counterpoint to the male transcript of a woman doing only 'commanded things'. Women of younger generations have continued these patterns, reporting that 'I'm no different than all those women. I've learned by just being there, enjoying the music, and yeh, humming along and singing' (Interview, Joyce Kassin, 30 March 1989). Some women have contributed new songs within the home. For instance, Sheila Schweky recalls that her father would ask her to teach Israeli songs she had learned in school to the family after dinner (Interview, 27 January 1988).[33] Moreover, the increasing involvement of women in learning Hebrew and *pizmonim* in the late twentieth century has led a few to think about *pizmon* composition. Joyce Kassin noted:

> Every once in a while I'll hear a song and I'll say, oh gosh, that would be great for a *pizmon* ... One day I'm going to take a little book along with me and every time I hear those songs I'm going to jot them down so that when the time comes that I really would love to get a *pizmon* written for some occasion or another ... I'm gonna pick the proper song. (30 March 1989)

Women therefore stand in a complex relationship to the *pizmonim*. Constrained on most occasions from participating publicly in musical life, they acquire musical repertories in the home and synagogue and perpetuate them indirectly by sustaining domestic rituals and by listening to Arab music. This picture is consistent with a framework of gender relations shaped by *tsniut* (modesty). There is also evidence that power and prestige are not derived solely from musical activity in the public realm (Ginsburg 1987:542). In some *public* contexts, the *absence* of musical activity appears to mark a woman's special power. For instance, at the end of the Syrian Jewish funeral (during which there is no singing), a ram's horn (*shofar*) is blown for the deceased man to 'keep the *mazikim* [evil spirits] away' (Interview, Gabriel Shrem, 9 January 1986). In contrast, no ram's horn is blown for a deceased woman because, in the words of community member and singer of *pizmonim*, Gabriel Shrem, 'the women, they go straight to heaven – they don't need no nothing'.

---

[33]   It may be of more than passing interest that Seroussi notes that Emily Sene's folksong collection, cited above, reflects 'new Sephardi song' (2003:206). It seems possible that while women conserve memories of the past, they may also under certain circumstances act as agents for change. An appreciation of the role of women in transmitting tradition does not necessitate stereotyping their contribution in conservation as conservative in content.

Conclusions

In the case of the Syrian Jewish community, gender differences established and explained through religious edict are reaffirmed and performed through song. When women appear in song texts, they exist as defined through their relationships to men, as mothers, wives, sisters, daughters and aunts. At the same time, they are also celebrated in ways which are shaped by the same tradition, within a framework that commemorates and values procreation and biological continuity. Women are celebrated for their achievements, whether as a bride or as mother of the *bar mitzvah* boy. They are also enjoined to reclaim their traditional duties in situations, such as the Saff family tragedy, when they have been unable to fulfil these responsibilities.

How should asymmetrical gender relations be interpreted by a scholar, and how can one reconcile the conflicting positions of different Syrian women? Few have rebelled against the silencing of their voices in ritual contexts or confronted the power asymmetry that this situation perpetuates. Even those who have resisted these gender constraints appreciate a women's power within Syrian tradition. For instance, one young woman who left the Syrian Jewish community to become a Rabbi has begun to reconsider her relationship with her community and 'to slowly reenvision the community from one that I saw as only patriarchal and oppressive, to one of complexity in its weave of Middle Eastern tradition and "America", of a patriarchal facade and hidden, yet tangible female power' (Esses 1992:13).

It is also clear that through mounting rituals, explicating history and transmitting the Arab tunes on which *pizmonim* are based, many Syrian women achieve deeply meaningful participation in Syrian religious life. Music is evidently a crucial source of emotional and spiritual affirmation, at once embedding and sustaining their involvement, as one comment from a Syrian Jewish woman living in Mexico City indicates:

> They're [the *pizmonim*] so pretty, and when you hear them all together … it makes me closer to where we came from, to my roots. I feel it, even though I was born in the United States, and my parents came [from Aleppo] at a very young age … I always feel it every time I'm sitting in the *shul* [synagogue] and listening to the prayers. Maybe because I heard them ever since I can remember, since I was a young child. And the way everyone is together, and understands, and sings with one voice, that means a lot to me. It makes me feel part of a tradition that was before, is now, and probably will continue for many, many years. That won't be lost. As long as they keep it up each year, year after year after year. That's going to keep up forever, as long as there is a Hebrew nation or our people exist. I think so, from father, to son, to grandchild. This is nothing I've thought about a lot. Just a feeling you have when you're there. (Ruth Cain, 7 September 1992)

This quotation suggests that some Syrian Jewish women may enjoy their deepest moments of connection with the *pizmonim* when they themselves are silent, when they sit and listen to the songs within the traditional boundaries of *kol isha*. From the perspective of a scholar, one could further suggest that the notion of *tsniut* (modesty) is a deep-seated Syrian Jewish value, manifested in multiple domains of Syrian Jewish culture through the masking of meanings. This is certainly the case when Syrian Jews surreptitiously borrow Arab melodies and domesticate them with new Hebrew texts, when they quietly display their Arab identity through quoting beloved Arabic proverbs and eating Middle Eastern cuisine, and when they sing Jewish prayers improvised in Arab *maqāmāt*. In many ways, one might argue, the most meaningful aspects of the Syrian Jewish identity are those which are not on open display, but are intensely private, including the role of women in musical life. As Ginsburg has noted, '... a community in which religious behavior that an outsider might see as polarized into public and private spheres is experienced by insiders as continuous, through the concept of *tsniut*, which links visible religious performance with the less visible practices in the home ...' (1987:546). She continues, 'Syrian Jewish women are not passively accepting a sexist status quo. Rather, they are actively meeting new circumstances by constructing an order in which their biological and social experiences of being female are integrated gracefully and powerfully into communal life' (ibid.).

While Syrian women are formally subordinate within a religious and ritual framework, they are not powerless. Rather, they perceive themselves to be privy to knowledge and bearing responsibility for practices that cannot survive without them. Although their roles may have emerged in the interstices of dominant practice, Syrian women have fashioned a powerful role for themselves, within a space that is ideologically sanctioned and consistent with community notions of modesty.

The *pizmonim* have, throughout Syrian Jewish history, been sites of mediation and reconciliation; they have generated and sustained both public and hidden transcripts and have at the same time provided the most enduring symbol of this ongoing dialectic. For centuries, these songs have united the separate worlds of Jewish and Arab experience in historical Syria. For the last one hundred years in diaspora, *pizmonim* have perpetuated memories of the Syrian Jewish past within new homelands and through new technologies. As they have done since their inception, the *pizmonim* have moved constantly across boundaries of secular and sacred expression within Syrian Jewish tradition itself, eliciting reverence during sacred moments in the synagogue and engendering rejoicing at festive parties. That the *pizmonim* and their transmission have provided a locus in which male and female power joined forces to sustain a community is perhaps, in the end, not so surprising.

Bibliography

Abassi, Hamadi (2000), *Tunis Chant et Danse 1900–1950*, Tunis: Alif – Les Éditions de la Méditerranée et les Éditions du Layeur.

'Abd al-Fattah, Abu Idris Muhammad bin (2001), *'Ilm al-Tilawa (The Science of Reciting the Qur'an)*, Cairo: Dar al-'Aqida.

Abdo, Geneive (2000), *No God But God: Egypt and the Triumph of Islam*, New York: Oxford University Press.

Abed-Kotob, Sana (1995), 'The Accommodationists Speak: Goals and Strategies of the Muslim Brotherhood in Egypt', *International Journal of Middle East Studies*, 27(3), 321–39.

Abu-Lughod, Lila (1983), 'Finding a Place for Islam: Egyptian Television Serials and the National Interest', *Public Culture*, 5, 493–513.

—— (1989), 'Bedouins, Cassettes and Technologies of Public Culture', *Middle East Report*, 159(4), 7–11, 47.

—— (2002), 'Egyptian Melodrama-Technology of the Modern Subject?', in Faye Ginsburg, Leila Abu-Lughod and Brian Larkin (eds), *Media Worlds*, Berkeley, CA: University of California Press, pp. 115–33.

—— (2004), *Dramas of Nationhood: The Politics of Television in Egypt*, Chicago, IL: University of Chicago Press.

Agawu, Kofi (1992), 'Representing African Music', *Critical Enquiry*, 18, 245–66.

—— (2003), *Representing African Music: Postcolonial Notes, Queries, Positions*, New York: Routledge.

Ahmadi, Hamid (1383[2004]), 'Din va Melliyat dar Iran: Hamyari ya Keshmankesh?' ('Religion and National Identity in Iran: Fellowship or Discord?'), in Hamid Ahmadi (ed.), *Iran: Hoveiat, Melliyat, Qumiat (Iran: Identity, Nationality, Ethnicity)*, Tehran: Institute for the Research and Development of Social Sciences, pp. 53–114.

—— (2005), 'Unity and Diversity: Foundations and Dynamics of National Identity in Iran', *Critique*, 14(1), 127–47.

Aini, Sadriddin (1926), *Namunai Adabiyoti Tojik (A Sample of Tajik Literature)*, Moscow: Chopkhona-i Nashriyot-i Markaz-i Itihod-i Jumohir-i Shurawi-i Sosyolisti.

Alinejad, Mahmoud (2002), 'Coming to Terms with Modernity: Iranian Intellectuals and the Emerging Public Sphere', *Islam and Christian-Muslim Relations*, 13(1), 25–47.

Allison, Lincoln (1996), 'Power', in Iain McLean (ed.), *The Concise Oxford Dictionary of Politics*, Oxford: Oxford University Press, pp. 396–9.

Amirahmadi, Hooshang (1996), 'Emerging Civil Society in Iran', *SAIS Review*, 16(2), 87–107.

Anagnost, Ann (1994), 'The Politics of Ritual Displacement', in Charles Keyes, Laurel Kendall and Helen Hardacre (eds), *Asian Visions of Authority: Religion and the Modern States of East and Southeast Asia*, Honolulu, HI: University of Hawaii Press, pp. 221–56.

Andersen, Margaret L. (2003), *Thinking About Women: Sociological Perspectives on Sex and Gender* (6th edition), New York: Pearson Education.

Ansari, Ali (2003), *Modern Iran Since 1921: The Pahlavis and After*, Edinburgh: Pearson Education.

Anwar, Raja (1989), *The Tragedy of Afghanistan: A First-hand Account*, London: Verso.

Apperley, Alan (1996), 'Foucault, Michel', in Iain McLean (ed.), *The Concise Oxford Dictionary of Politics*, Oxford: Oxford University Press, p. 187.

Ardener, Edwin (1975), 'Belief and the Problem of Women', in Shirley Ardener (ed.), *Perceiving Women*, London: Malaby Press, pp. 1–27.

Armbrust, Walter (1996), *Mass Culture and Modernism in Egypt*, Cambridge: Cambridge University Press.

—— (2000), 'Introduction: Anxieties of Scale', in Walter Armbrust (ed.), *Mass Mediations: New Approaches to Popular Culture in the Middle East and Beyond*, Berkeley, CA: University of California Press, pp. 1–31.

Atabaki, Touraj and Eric Jan Zürcher (2003), *Men of Order: Authoritarian Modernization Under Atatürk and Reza Shah*, London: I.B. Tauris.

Attali, Jacques (1985), *Noise: The Political Economy of Music* (translated by Brian Massumi), Minneapolis, MN, University of Minnesota Press. Originally published 1977.

Aulas, Marie-Christine (1982), 'Sadat's Egypt: A Balance Sheet', *MERIP Reports*, *no. 107: Egypt in the New Middle East*, 6–18, 30–31.

Austern, Linda Phyllis and Inna Naroditskaya (eds) (2006), *Music of the Sirens*, Bloomington, IN: Indiana University Press.

Author unknown (1996), 'Kabul Cinemas Closed', *The Muslim*, 15 July 1996.

Averill, Gage (1989), 'Haitian Dance Bands, 1915–1970: Class, Race, and Authenticity', *Latin American Music Review*, 10(2), 203–35.

—— (1997), *A Day for the Hunter, A Day for the Prey: Popular Music and Power in Haiti*, Chicago, IL: Chicago University Press.

'Awaḍ, Maḥmuud (1969), *Umm Kulthūm Allatī Lā YaʿRifuhā Aḥad* (*The Umm Kulthūm that Nobody Knows*) (1st edition), Cairo: Akhbār al-Yawm.

Ayubi, Nazih (1980), 'The Political Revival of Islam: The Case of Egypt', *International Journal of Middle East Studies*, 12, 481–99.

—— (1983), 'The Egyptian "Brain Drain": A Multidimensional Problem', *International Journal of Middle East Studies*, 15(4), 431–50.

Ayubi, Safarmuhammad (1989), 'Falaki Dashtu Daman' ('Falak of the Plains and of the Mountains'), *Adabiyot va San'at*, 49(626), 10.

Baily, John (1981), *The Annual Cycle of Music in Herat*, London: Royal Anthropological Institute.

—— (1988), *Music of Afghanistan: Professional Musicians in the City of Herat*, Cambridge: Cambridge University Press.

—— (1996), 'Using Tests of Sound Perception in Fieldwork', *Yearbook for Traditional Music*, 28, 147–73.

—— (2001), *Can You Stop the Birds Singing? The Censorship of Music in Afghanistan*, Copenhagen: Freemuse.

—— (2003), 'Ethnomusicological Fieldwork in Kabul to Assess the Situation of Music in the Post-Taliban Era', unpublished report to the British Academy's Committee for Central and Inner Asia.

Baldassarre, Antonio (1995), Liner notes to CD *Les Maîtres du Guembri-Gnawa Lila, Volume V*, Nanterre: Al Sur.

Baldick, Julian (1993), *Imaginary Muslims: The Uwaysi Sufis of Central Asia*, London and New York: I.B. Tauris.

Balzer, Marjorie M. (1994), 'From Ethnicity to Nationalism: Turmoil in the Russian Mini-Empire', in James R. Millar and Sharon L. Wolchik (eds), *The Social Legacy of Communism*, Washington, DC: Woodrow Wilson Center Press and Cambridge University Press, pp. 56–88.

Banuazizi, Ali (1995), 'Faltering Legitimacy: The Ruling Clerics and Civil Society in Contemporary Iran', *International Journal of Politics, Culture and Society*, 8(4), 563–78.

Barat, Qurban (ed.) (1986), *12 Muqam Tekistliri* (*Texts of the Twelve Muqam*), Ürümchi: Shinjang Yashlar-Ösmürlär Näshriyati.

Barthes, Roland (1972), *Mythologies*, London, Cape.

Bashiriyeh, Hossein (2001), 'Civil Society and Democratisation during Khatami's First Term', *Global Dialogue*, 3(2/3), 19–26.

Basmenji, Kaveh (2005), *Tehran Blues: Youth Culture in Iran*, London: Saqi Books.

Bečka, Jiri (1980), *Sadriddin Ayni: Father of Modern Tajik Culture*, Napoli: Istituto Universitario Orientale, Seminario di Studi Asiatici Series Minor 5.

Becquelin, Nicolas (2004), 'Criminalizing Ethnicity: Political Repression in Xinjiang', *China Rights Forum*, 39–46.

Bellér-Hann, Ildikó (2000), *The Written and the Spoken: Literacy and Oral Transmission among the Uyghur*, Berlin: Anor.

—— (2001a), 'Making the Oil Fragrant: Dealings with the Supernatural among the Uyghurs in Xinjiang', *Asian Ethnicity*, 2(1), 9–23.

—— (2001b), 'Rivalry and Solidarity among Uyghur Healers in Kazakhstan', *Inner Asia*, 3(1), 73–98.

Bennett, Tony, Simon Frith, Lawrence Grossberg, John Shepherd and Graeme Turner (eds) (1993), *Rock and Popular Music: Politics, Policies, Institutions*, London: Routledge.

Bennigsen, Alexandre and S. Enders Wimbush (1985), *Mystics and Commissars: Sufism in the Soviet Union*, Berkeley and Los Angeles, CA: University of California Press.

Berliner, Paul (1977), 'Political Sentiment in Shona Song and Oral Literature', *Essays in Arts and Sciences*, 6, 1–29.

Berman, Saul J. (1980), 'Kol Isha', in Leo Handman (ed.), *Rabbi Joseph H. Lookstein Memorial Volume*, New York: Ktav Publishing, pp. 45–66.

Bernstein, Jane A. (ed.) (2003), *Women's Voices Across Musical Worlds*, Boston, MA: Northeastern University Press.

Blacking, John (1965), 'The Role of Music in the Culture of the Venda of the Northern Transvaal', in M. Kolinski (ed.), *Studies in Ethnomusicology, Volume 2*, New York: Oak Publications, pp. 20–52.

Blum, Stephen (1975), 'Towards a Social History of Musicological Technique', *Ethnomusicology*, 19, 207–31.

Bohlman, Philip (1993), 'Musicology as a Political Act', *The Journal of Musicology*, 4, 411–36.

—— (2002), *World Music: A Very Short Introduction*, Oxford, Oxford University Press.

—— (2007), *The Silence of Music*, British Library/Royal Holloway Lectures in Musicology 2006/7, February/March 2007.

Born, Georgina and David Hesmondhalgh (2000), 'Introduction: On Difference, Representation, and Appropriation in Music', in Georgina Born and David Hesmondhalgh (eds), *Western Music and Its Others: Difference, Representation, and Appropriation in Music*, Berkeley, CA: University of California Press, pp. 1–58.

Boroujerdi, Mehrzad (1996), *Iranian Intellectuals and the West: The Tormented Triumph of Nativism*, Syracuse, NY: Syracuse University Press.

Bosworth, Clifford Edmund (1995), 'Samanids: History, Literary Life and Economic Activity', in C.E. Bosworth, E. van Donzel, W.P. Heinrichs and G. Lecomte (eds), *The Encyclopaedia of Islam, New Edition, Volume 8*, Leiden: E.J. Brill, pp. 1025–9.

Bourdieu, Pierre (1977), *Algeria 1960*, Cambridge: Cambridge University Press.

—— (1984), *Distinction: A Social Critique of the Judgement of Taste*, London: Routledge.

Bovingdon, Gardner (2001), 'The History of the History of Xinjiang', *Twentieth Century China*, 26(2), 95–139.

Bowers, Jane (2000), 'Writing the Biography of a Black Woman Blues Singer', in Pirkko Moisala and Beverley Diamond (eds), *Music and Gender*, Urbana, IL: University of Illinois Press, pp. 140–65.

Brenninkmeijer, Olivier A.J. (1998), 'International Concern for Tajikistan: UN and OSCE Efforts to Promote Peace-Building and Democratisation', in Mohammad-Reza Djalili, Frédéric Grare and Shirin Akiner (eds), *Tajikistan: The Trials of Independence*, Richmond, Surrey: Curzon Press, pp. 180–215.

Buchanan, Donna (1995), 'Metaphors of Power, Metaphors of Truth: The Politics of Music Professionalism in Bulgarian Folk Orchestras', *Ethnomusicology*, 39(3), 381–416.

Bukhari, al- (2000), 'Sahih al-Bukhari', in *Hadith Encyclopedia* (CD-ROM), Cairo: Harf.

Bulk, Ahmad al- (1992?), *Ashhar Man Qara'a al-Qur'an fi al-'Asr al-Hadith* (*The Most Famous Qur'an Reciters in the Modern Era*), Cairo: Dar al-Ma'arif.

Bussman, Hadumod (1996), *Routledge Dictionary of Language and Linguistics* (translated by Gregory and Kerstin Kazzai Trauth), London: Routledge.

Cable, Mildred, with Francesca French (1942), *The Gobi Desert*, London: Hodder and Stoughton.

Castelo-Branco, Salwa el-Shawan (1980), 'The Socio-Political Context of al-Mūsīka al-'Arabiyyah in Cairo, Egypt: Policies, Patronage, Institutions, and Musical Change (1927–77)', *Asian Music*, 12(1), 86–129.

—— (1984), 'Traditional Arab Music Ensembles in Egypt Since 1967: "The Continuity of Tradition Within a Contemporary Framework"?', *Ethnomusicology*, 28(2), 271–88.

—— (1987), 'Some Aspects of the Cassette Industry in Egypt', *World of Music*, 29(2), 32–45.

—— (2001), 'Performance of Arab Music in Twentieth Century Egypt', in Virginia Danielson, Scott Marcus and Dwight Reynolds (eds), *Garland Encyclopedia of World Music, Volume 6, The Middle East*, New York: Garland Publishing, pp. 557–62.

Ceribasic, Naila (2000), 'Defining Women and Men in the Context of War: Images in Croatian Popular Music in the 1990s', in Pirkko Moisala and Beverley Diamond (eds), *Music and Gender*, Urbana, IL: University of Illinois Press, pp. 219–38.

Chaichian, M.A. (2003), 'Structural Impediments of the Civil Society Project in Iran: National and Global Dimensions', *International Journal of Comparative Sociology*, 44(1), 19–50.

Chehabi, Houshang (1999), 'From Revolutionary *Tasnif* to Patriotic *Sorūd*: Music and Nation-Building in Pre-World War II Iran', *Iran*, 37, 143–54.

—— (2000), 'Voices Unveiled: Women Singers in Iran', in Rudi Matthee and Beth Baron (eds), *Iran and Beyond: Essays in Middle Eastern History in Honor of Nikki R. Keddie*, Costa Mesa, CA: Mazda, pp. 151–66.

Chvyr, Ludmila (1993), 'Central Asia's Tajiks: Self-identification and Ethnic Identity', in Vitaly Naumkin (ed.), *State, Religion and Society in Central Asia: A Post-Soviet Critique*, Reading: Ithaca Press, pp. 245–61.

Clayton, Martin (2001), 'Introduction: Towards a Theory of Musical Meaning (in India and Elsewhere), *British Journal of Ethnomusicology* (special issue on Music and Meaning), 10(1), 1–17.

Cobban, Helena (1984), *The Palestinian Liberation Organization*, Cambridge: Cambridge University Press.

Coplan, David (1985), *In Township Tonight! South Africa's Black City Music and Theatre*, London, New York, Johannesburg: Longman, Ravan Press.

Cowan, Jane (1990), *Dance and the Body Politic in Northern Greece*, Princeton, NJ: Princeton University Press.

Creswell, K.A.C. (1969), *Early Muslim Architecture*, Oxford: Clarendon Press.

Cronin, Stephanie (ed.) (2002), *The Making of Modern Iran: State and Society Under Riza Shah, 1921–1941*, London: RoutledgeCurzon.

Currid, Brian (2000), '"A Song Goes Round the World": The German *Schlager* as an Organ of Experience', *Popular Music*, 19, 147–80.

Dabashi, Hamid (2001), *Close Up: Iranian Cinema, Past, Present and Future*, London: Verso Press.

Danielson, Virginia (1990), 'Min al-Mashayikh: A View of Egyptian Musical Tradition', *Asian Music*, 22(1), 113–28.

—— (1997), *The Voice of Egypt: Umm Kulthum, Arabic song, and Egyptian Society in the Twentieth Century*, Chicago, IL: University of Chicago Press.

Daoud, Ibrahim (ed.) (1997a), *Al-Qur'an fi Misr* (*The Qur'an in Egypt*), Cairo: Toot.

—— (1997b), 'Shaykh Mustafa Isma'il', in Ibrahim Daoud (ed.), *Al-Qur'an fi Misr*, Cairo: Toot, pp. 27–34.

Daoudi, Bouziane and Hadj Miliani (1996), *L'Aventure du Raï: Musique et Société*, Paris: Inédit.

Darimi (2000), 'Sahih Darimi', in *Hadith Encyclopedia*, Cairo: Harf.

Davis, Hannah (1992), 'Taking Up Space in Tlemçen: The Islamist Occupation of Urban Algeria – Interview with Rabia Bekkar', *Middle East Report*, December, 11–15.

Davis, Ruth F. (1986), 'Some Relations Between Three *Piyyutim* from Djerba and Three Arab Songs', *The Maghreb Review*, 11(2), 134–44.

—— (1993), 'Tunisia and the Cairo Congress of Arab Music, 1932', *The Maghreb Review*, 18(1–2), 135–44.

—— (1996), 'The Arab-Andalusian Music of Tunisia', *Early Music*, 24(2), 423–37.

—— (1997), 'Cultural Policy and the Tunisian *Ma'lūf*: Redefining a Tradition', *Ethnomusicology*, 41(1), 1–21.

—— (2002), 'Music of the Jews of Jerba, Tunisia', in Virginian Danielson, Scott Marcus and Dwight Reynolds (eds), *The Garland Encyclopedia of World Music, Volume 6, The Middle East*, New York: Garland Publishing, pp. 523–31.

—— (2004), *Ma'lūf: Reflections on the Arab Andalusian Music of Tunisia*, Lanham MD: Scarecrow Press.

—— (2009), 'Time, Place, and Jewish music: Mapping the Multiple Journeys of "*Andik Bahriyya, Ya Rais*"' , in Philip V. Bohlman and Marcello Sorce Keller (eds), *The Musical Anthropology of the Mediterranean. In Memory of Tullia Magrini*, Bologna: CLUEB, 47–58.

—— (in press), 'Time, Place and Memory: Music for a North African Jewish Pilgrimage', in Eric Levi and Florian Scheding (eds), *Music and (Dis)placement*, Lanham MD: Scarecrow Press.

Dawuti, Reyila [Dawut, Rahilä] (2001), *Weiwuerzu Mazha Wenhua Yanjiu* (*Research on Uyghur Shrine Culture*), Ürümchi: Xinjiang Daxue Chubanshe.

DeBano, Wendy S. (2003), 'Singing against Silence: Celebrating Women and Music in Iran', Paper Presented at the 48th Annual Meeting of the Society for Ethnomusicology, Miami, Florida, 5 October 2003.

—— (2004), 'Hearing the Voices of the Present and Performing Collective Futures: Women, Music and Empowerment in Iran', Paper Presented at the International Society for Iranian Studies Biennial Conference, Bethesda, Maryland, 29 May 2004.

—— (2005), 'Enveloping Music in Gender, Nation, and Islam: Women's Music Festivals in Post-Revolutionary Iran', *Iranian Studies*, 38(3), 441–62.

de Jong, Frederick (1978), *Turuq and Turuq-Linked Institutions in Nineteenth-Century Egypt: A Historical Study in Organizational Dimensions of Islamic Mysticism*, Leiden: E.J. Brill.

D'Erlanger, Rodolphe (1930, 1935, 1938, 1939, 1949, 1959), *La Musique Arabe* (6 volumes), Paris: Librarie Orientaliste Paul Geuthner.

DeWeese, Devin (1993), *An Uvaysi Sufi in Timurid Mawarannahr: Notes on Hagiography and the Taxonomy of Sanctity in the Religious History of Central Asia*, Bloomington, IN: Indiana University Press.

Diamond, Beverley (2000), 'The Interpretation of Gender Issues in Musical Life Stories of Prince Edward Islanders', in Pirkko Moisala and Beverley Diamond (eds), *Music and Gender*, Urbana, IL: University of Illinois Press, pp. 99–139.

Djumaev, Alexander (1993), 'Power Structures, Culture Policy, and Traditional Music in Soviet Central Asia', *Yearbook for Traditional Music*, 25, 43–66.

—— (2002), 'Sacred Music and Chant in Islamic Central Asia', in Virginia Danielson, Scott Marcus and Dwight Reynolds (eds), *The Garland Encyclopedia of World Music, Volume 6, The Middle East*, New York: Garland Publishing, pp. 935–47.

Dorraj, Manochehr (2001), 'Iran's Democratic Impasse', *Peace Review*, 13(1), 103–7.

Doubleday, Veronica (1988), *Three Women of Herat*, London: Jonathan Cape.

—— (1999), 'The Frame Drum in the Middle East: Women, Musical Instruments and Power', *Ethnomusicology*, 43(1), 101–34.

—— (ed.) (2008), *'Sounds of Power': Musical Instruments and Gender*, Special Issue of *Ethnomusicology Forum*, 17(1).

Dresden, Mark (1983), 'Sogdian Language and Literature', in Ehsan Yarshater (ed.), *The Cambridge History of Iran, Volume 3/2: The Seleucid, Parthian and Sasanian Periods*, Cambridge: Cambridge University Press, pp. 1216–29.

Dudoignon, Stéphane A. (1998), 'Political Parties and Forces in Tajikistan, 1989–1993', in Mohammad-Reza Djalili, Frédéric Grare and Shirin Akiner (eds),

Tajikistan: The Trials of Independence, Richmond, Surrey: Curzon Press, pp. 52–85.

Dunya, Ibn Abi al- (1938), 'Dhamm al-Malahi' ('The Condemnation of Entertainments'), in *Tracts on Listening to Music* (translated by James Robson), London: Royal Asiatic Society.

During, Jean (1989), *Musique et Mystique dans les Traditions de L'Iran*, Paris and Tehran: Institut Français de Recherche en Iran.

—— (1993a), 'Musique, Nation et Territoire en Asie Interieure', *Yearbook for Traditional Music*, 25, 29–42.

—— (1993b), Liner notes to CD *Tajik Music of Badakhshan/Musique Tadjike du Badakhshan*, Musiques et Musiciens du Monde. Auvidis/UNESCO, CD 8212.

—— (1998a), *Musiques d'Asie Centrale. L'Esprit d'une Tradition*, Arles: Cité de la Musique/Actes Sud.

—— (1998b), Liner notes to CD *Tadjikistan: Chants des Bardes/Songs of the Bards*, Archives Internationales de Musique Populaire, 51, Musée d'Ethnographie, Genève. Lausanne: VDE-Gallo, CD 973.

—— and Sabine Trebinjac (1991), *Introduction au Muqam Ouigour*, Bloomington, IN: Indiana University Research Institute for Inner Asian Studies.

—— and Zia Mirabdolbaghi (1991), *The Art of Persian Music*, Washington, DC: Mage Publishers.

Egyptian Ministry of Information (1999), 'SonoCairo', in *al-I'lam al-Misri wa al-Alfiyya al-Thalitha* (*Egyptian Media and the Third Millennium*), Cairo: Egyptian Ministry of Information, pp. 170–87.

Erlmann, Veit (1985), 'Black Political Song in South Africa: Some Research Perspectives', *Popular Music Perspectives*, 2, 187–209.

—— (1991), *African Stars: Studies in Black South African Performance*, Chicago, IL: University of Chicago Press.

—— (1996), *Nightsong: Performance, Power and Practice in South Africa*, Chicago, IL: Chicago University Press.

—— (1999), *Music, Modernity, and the Global Imagination: South Africa and the West*, New York: Oxford University Press.

ERTU (2004), *al-Kitab al-Sanawi 2004* (*2004 Yearbook*), Cairo: Egyptian Radio and Television Union.

Esses, Dianne O. (1992), 'A Hunger for Syrian "Exotica"', *The Melton Journal*, 25 (autumn), New York: Jewish Theological Seminary, pp. 12–13.

Fadl, Bilal (1997), 'Ahzan Surat Yusuf … wa (Mandabat) Shuyukh al-Naft' ('The Sorrows of the Qur'anic Chapter "Yusuf" and the Wailing of the Petroleum Shaykhs'), in Ibrahim Daoud (ed.), *Al-Qur'an fi Misr*, Cairo: Toot, pp. 105–10.

Fakhouri, Jozef (n.d), *Abd al-Halim Hafiz: I'dad wa Tadwin*, Beirut: Dar al-Sharq al- Arabi.

Farid, Majid (1994), *Nasser, The Final Years*, Reading: Ithaca Press.

Farmer, Henry George (1929), *A History of Arabian Music*, London: Luzac & Co. (reprinted 1973).

—— (1957), 'The Music of Islam', in Egon Wellesz (ed.), *New Oxford History of Music, Volume 1, Ancient and Oriental Music*, London and New York: Oxford University Press, pp. 421–77.

al-Faruqi, Ibsen Lois (1985), 'Music, Musicians and Muslim Law', *Asian Music*, 17(1), 3–36.

—— (1987a), 'The Cantillation of the Quran', *Asian Music*, 19(1), 2–25.

—— (1987b), 'Quran Reciters in Competition in Kuala-Lumpur: Islamic Chant', *Ethnomusicology*, 31(2), 221–8.

Farza, Belhassan (n.d.), 'Al-Mūsīqā al-Tūnisiya fi'l Qarān al-'Ashrīn' ('Tunisian Music of the Twentieth Century'), in *Al-Turāth al-Mūsīqī al-Tūnisī* 6, Tunis: Wizārat al- Shu'ūn al Taqāfiyya/Ministère des Affaires Culturelles, 3–12.

Fathulloev, S. (1991), 'Asrori "Falak"-ro Na Tu Donivu Na Man …' ('You Do Not Know the Secrets of "Falak" and Neither Do I …'), *Adabiyot va San'at*, 22(703), 11.

Feld, Stephen (1994a), 'From Schizophonia to Schismogenesis: On the Discourses and Commodification Practices of "World Music" and "World Beat"', in Charles Keil and Steven Feld (eds), *Music Grooves: Essays and Dialogues*, Chicago, IL: University of Chicago Press, pp. 257–89.

—— (1994b), 'Notes on "World Beat"', in Charles Keil and Steven Feld (eds), *Music Grooves: Essays and Dialogues*, Chicago, IL: University of Chicago Press, pp. 238–46.

Feldman, Walter (1992), 'Central Asia: Music', in Ehsan Yarshater (ed.), *Encyclopaedia Iranica*, 5, Costa Mesa, CA: Mazda, pp. 240–42.

Fernandes, Leonor (1988), *The Evolution of a Sufi Institution in Mamluk Egypt: The Khanqah*, Berlin: Klaus Schwarz Verlag.

Festival of Holidays: Recipe Book (1987), Brooklyn, NY: Sephardic Community Center.

Feuchtwang, Stephan (1991), *The Imperial Metaphor: Popular Religion in China*, London: Routledge.

Fishman, Sylvia Barack (2000), *Changing Minds: Feminism in Contemporary Orthodox Jewish Life*, New York: American Jewish Committee.

Foucault, Michel (1977), *Discipline and Punish: The Birth of the Prison*, Harmondsworth: Penguin.

—— (1980), *Power/Knowledge: Selected Interviews and Other Writings 1972–1977*, ed. Colin Gordon, Brighton: Harvester Press.

Fragner, Bert G. (1994), 'The Nationalization of the Uzbeks and Tajiks', in Edward Allworth (ed.), *Muslim Communities Reemerge: Historical Perspectives on Nationality, Politics, and Opposition in the Former Soviet Union and Yugoslavia*, Durham, NC: Duke University Press, pp. 13–32.

—— (2001), 'Soviet Nationalism: An Ideological Legacy to the Independent Republics of Central Asia', in Willem van Schendel and Erik J. Zürcher (ed.),

Identity Politics in Central Asia and the Muslim World, London and New York: I.B. Tauris, pp. 13–33.

Frishkopf, Michael (2002), 'Islamic Hymnody in Egypt: *Al-Inshād al-Dīnī*', in Virginia Danielson, Scott Marcus and Dwight Reynolds (eds), *The Garland Encyclopedia of World Music*, *Volume 6*, *The Middle East*, New York: Garland Publishing, pp. 165–75.

—— (n.d.), *The Development of Egypt's Phonogram Manufacturing Industry: Muhammad Fawzy, Misrphon, and Sawt al-Qahira (SonoCairo)* (manuscript in preparation).

Frith, Simon (1978), *The Sociology of Popular Music*, London: Constable.

—— (1983), *Sound Effects: Youth, Leisure and the Politics of Rock*, London: Constable.

—— (1988), *Music for Pleasure: Essays in the Sociology of Pop*, Cambridge: Polity Press.

—— (ed.) (1989), *World Music, Politics and Social Change*, Manchester: Manchester University Press.

—— (1996), 'Music and Identity', in Stuart Hall and Paul du Gay (eds), *Questions of Cultural Identity*, London: Sage, pp. 108–27.

Frye, Richard Nelson (1975), 'The Sāmānids', in R.N. Frye (ed.), *The Cambridge History of Iran*, *Volume 4: From the Arab Invasion to the Saljuqs*, Cambridge: Cambridge University Press, pp. 136–61.

Gaffney, Patrick D. (1994), *The Prophet's Pulpit: Islamic Preaching in Contemporary Egypt*, Comparative Studies on Muslim Societies, 20, Berkeley, CA: University of California Press.

Garofalo, Reebee (ed.) (1992), *Rockin' the Boat: Mass Music and Mass Movements*, Boston, MA: South End Press.

Geertz, Clifford (1973a), 'Ethos, World View, and the Analysis of Sacred Symbols', in *The Interpretation of Cultures*, New York: Basic Books, pp. 126–41.

—— (1973b), 'Ideology as a Cultural System', in *The Interpretation of Cultures*, New York, Basic Books, pp. 193–233.

Gellner, Ernest (1969), *Saints of the Atlas*, Chicago, IL: University of Chicago Press.

—— (1981), *Muslim Society*, Cambridge: Cambridge University Press.

Ghafurov, Bobojon (1983/1985), *Tojikon, Volumes 1–2*, Dushanbe: Nashriyoti Irfon. Originally published 1972.

Gharib, Gharib Ali (2001), *Mu'assasat al-Risala – 2001 Catalog*, Cairo: Mu'assasat al-Risala li al-Intaj wa al-Tawzi' al-Islami.

Ghazali, Abu Hamid Muhammad b. Muhammad al- (1901), 'Emotional Religion in Islam as Affected by Music and Singing' (translated by Duncan B. Macdonald), *Journal of the Royal Asiatic Society*, 22, 195–252, 705–48; 23, 1–28.

Gheytanchi, Elham (2001), 'Civil Society in Iran: Politics of Motherhood and the Public Sphere', *International Sociology*, 16(4), 557–76.

Ghoib, Muhammad (1989), 'Mushkiloti Ansambli "Falak"' ('The Problems of the "Falak" Ensemble), *Adabiyot va San'at*, 36(615), 10.

—— (1990), 'Kushoishi "Savti Falak"' ('The Debut of "Savti Falak"'), *Adabiyot va San'at*, 18(647), 10.

Gilroy, Paul (1987), *There Ain't no Black in the Union Jack: The Cultural Politics of Race and Nation*, London: Routledge.

—— (1993), *The Black Atlantic: Modernity and Double Consciousness*, London: Verso.

Gilsenan, Michael (1990), *Recognizing Islam*, London: I.B. Tauris.

Ginsburg, Faye (1987), 'When the Subject is Women: Encounters with Syrian Jewish Women', *Journal of American Folklore*, 100, 540–47.

Gladney, Dru (2004), 'Responses to Chinese Rule: Patterns of Co-operation and Opposition', in Frederick Starr (ed.), *Xinjiang: China's Muslim Borderland*, New York and London: M.E. Sharpe, pp. 375–96.

Glick-Schiller, Nina and Georges Fouron (1990), 'Everywhere we go we are in Danger: Ti Manno and the Emergence of a Haitian Transnational identity', *American Ethnologist*, 17(2), 329–47.

Goodman, Jane (1996), 'Dancing towards "La Mixite": Berber Associations and Cultural Change in Algeria', *Middle East Report*, July, 16–19.

—— (2005), *Berber Culture on the World Stage: From Village to Video*, Bloomington, IN: Indiana University Press.

Gordon, Joel (2000), 'Nasser 56/Cairo 96: Reimagining Cairo's Lost Community', in Walter Armbrust (ed.), *Mass Mediations: New Approaches to Popular Culture in the Middle East and Beyond*, Berkeley, CA: University of California Press, pp. 161–81.

—— (2002), *Revolutionary Melodrama: Popular Film and Civic Identity in Nasser's Egypt*, Chicago, IL: Center for Middle East Studies.

Gourlay, Kenneth (1978), 'Towards a Reassessment of the Ethnomusicologist's Role in Research', *Ethnomusicology*, 22, 1–35.

Graham, Stephen (2004), 'Conservative Backlash as Afghan TV Airs First Female Singer in 10 Years', *The Independent*, 14 July 2004, 34.

Gramsci, Antonio (2001), *Quaderni del Carcere (Prison Notebooks)*, *Volumes 1–4*, ed. Valentino Gerratana, Torino: Giulio Einaudi Editore. Originally written 1929–35; first published 1975.

Gross, Joan, David McMurray and Ted Swedenburg (1996), 'Arab Noise and Ramadan Nights: *Rai*, Rap and Franco-Maghrebi Identities', in Smadar Lavie and Ted Swedenburg (eds), *Displacement, Diaspora and Geographies of Identity*, Durham, NC: Duke University Press, pp. 119–55.

Grossberg, Lawrence (1991), 'Rock, Territorialization and Power', *Cultural Studies* (special issue on The Music Industry in a Changing World), 5(3), 358–67.

Grout, Donald J. and Claude V. Palisca (2001), *A History of Western Music* (6th edition), New York, Norton.

Guettat, Mahmoud (1980), *La Musique Classique du Maghreb*, Paris: Sindbad.

—— (2000), *La Musique Arabo-Andalouse. L'Empreinte du Maghreb*, Paris: Éditions El-Ouns.

Gulrukhsor (Safieva) (1971), 'Vatan', *Sado-i Sharq*, 3, Dushanbe: Union of Writers of Tajikistan, p. 38.

Häbibulla, Abdurähim (1993), *Uygur Etnografiyisi* (*Uyghur Ethnography*), Ürümchi: Shinjang Khälq Näshriyati.

Hadj Moussa, Ratiba (2003), 'New Media and Politics in Algeria', *Media, Culture and Society*, 25, 451–68.

Hall, Stuart (1996), 'Introduction: Who Needs "Identity"?', in Stuart Hall and Paul du Gay (eds), *Questions of Cultural Identity*, London: Sage, pp. 1–17.

—— (1997a), 'The Spectacle of the "Other"', in Stuart Hall (ed.), *Representation: Cultural Representations and Signifying Practices*, London: Sage/Open University, pp. 223–79.

—— (1997b), 'The Work of Representation', in Stuart Hall (ed.), *Representation: Cultural Representations and Signifying Practices*, London: Sage/Open University.

Hamam, Ahmad (1996), *Rihlati ma'a al-Qur'an: al-Shaykh Muhammad Gabril* (*My Journey with the Qur'an: Shaykh Muhammad Gabril*), Cairo: Dar al-Madina al-Munawwara.

—— (2000), *Sufara' al-Qur'an* (*The Qur'an's Ambassadors*), Volume 1, Cairo: Markaz al-Raya.

Hamm, Charles (1989), 'Afterword', in Simon Frith (ed.), *World Music, Politics and Social Change*, Manchester: Manchester University Press, pp. 211–16.

Hansen, Miriam (1991), *Babel and Babylon: Spectatorship in American Silent Film*, Cambridge MA: Harvard University Press.

Harris, Rachel (2001), 'From Shamanic Ritual to Karaoke: The (Trans)migrations of a Chinese folksong', *CHIME*, 14, 48–60.

—— (2004), *Singing the Village: Memories, Music and Ritual amongst the Sibe of Xinjiang*, Oxford and New York: Oxford University Press.

—— and Rahilä Dawut (2002), 'Mazar Festivals of the Uyghurs: Music, Islam and the Chinese State', *British Journal of Ethnomusicology*, 11(1), 101–18.

—— and Barley Norton (2002), 'Red Ritual: Ritual Music and Communism. Introduction', *British Journal of Ethnomusicology*, 11(1), 1–8.

—— (2008), *The Making of a Musical Canon in Chinese Central Asia: The Uyghur Twelve Muqam*, Aldershot: Ashgate.

Hassan, Dawoud (1999), 'The Voice that Draws Thousands: Lawyer-turned-Imam Mohammad Gibril Attracts Unprecedented Crowds to the Continent's Oldest Mosque', *Cairo Times*, 23, 3.

Hassaneyn, Adil (1995), *Abd al-Halim Hafiz: Ayamna al-Hilwa*, Cairo: Amadu.

—— (n.d.), *Wataniyat: Aghani wa Ash'ar*, Cairo: Amadu.

Hawkins, Joyce M. and Robert Allen (eds) (1991), 'Power', in *The Oxford Encyclopedic English Dictionary*, Oxford: Clarendon Press, pp. 1135–6.

Hebdige, Dick (1979), *Subculture: The Meaning of Style*, London: Methuen, Routledge.

Heneghan, Tom (1986), 'Afghan Nightlife: Swinging Till 10', *International Herald Tribune*, 6 June 1986, 2.

Herzfeld, Michael (1991), 'Silence, Submission, and Subversion: Towards a Poetics of Womanhood', in Peter Loizos and Evthymios Papataxiarchis (eds), *Contested Identities: Gender and Kinship in Modern Greece*, Princeton, NJ: Princeton University Press, pp. 79–97.

Heyworth-Dunne, J. (1939), *An Introduction to the History of Education in Modern Egypt*, London: Luzac & Co.

Hilawi, Muhammad 'Abd al-'Aziz al- (1984?), *Kayfa Tujawwidu al-Qur'an wa Turattiluh Tartilan* (*How to Recite the Qur'an*), Cairo: Maktabat al-Qur'an.

Hirschkind, Charles (2004), 'Hearing Modernity: Egypt, Islam, and the Pious Ear', in Veit Erlmann (ed.), *Hearing Cultures: Essays on Sound, Listening and Modernity*, Oxford: Berg, pp. 131–51.

—— (2006), *The Ethical Soundscape: Cassette Sermons and Islamic Counterpublics*, New York: Columbia University Press.

Hogwood, Christopher (1977), *Music at Court*, London: The Folio Society.

Holliday, Shabnam (2007), 'The Politicisation of Culture and the Contestation of Iranian National Identity in Khatami's Iran', *Studies in Ethnicity and Nationalism*, 8(3), 27–44.

Homer (1996), *The Odyssey* (translated by Robert Fagles, Introduction and Notes by Bernard Knox), London: Penguin Classics.

Hourani, Albert (1991), *History of the Arab Peoples*, London: Faber & Faber.

Howard, Jane (2002), *Inside Iran: Women's Lives*, Washington DC: Mage Publishers.

Human Rights Watch (2003), *'Killing You is a Very Easy Thing for Us'*, Human Rights Abuses in Southeast Afghanistan, Washington, DC, London and Brussels: Human Rights Watch.

Husari, Mahmud Khalil al- (196x), *Ahkam Qira'at al-Qur'an al-Karim*, Cairo: Maktabat al-Turath al-Islami.

Hussein, Mahmoud (1977), *Class Conflict in Egypt 1945–1970* (translated by Michel Chirman, Susanne Chirman, Alfred Ehrenfeld and Kathy Brown), New York: Monthly Review Press.

Hyman, Anthony (1984), *Afghanistan Under Soviet Domination, 1964–83* (2nd edition), London: Macmillan.

Ibn Hanbal, Ahmad (2000), 'Sahih ibn Hanbal', in *Hadith Encyclopedia* (CD-ROM), Cairo: Harf.

Ibn Majah (2000), 'Sahih ibn Majah', in *Hadith Encyclopedia* (CD-ROM), Cairo: Harf.

Ibrahim, Saad Eddin (1996), *Egypt, Islam and Democracy: Twelve Critical Essays*, Cairo: American University in Cairo Press.

al-Imrussi, Magdi (1994), *A'iz al-Nass*, Cairo: al-Tab'a al-Rab'ia.

Infitah (1986), 'Egypt's Infitah Bourgeoisie', *MERIP Reports, no. 142: Wealth and Power in the Middle East*, 39–40.

Jahangiri, Guissou (1998), 'The Premises for the Construction of a Tajik National Identity, 1920–1930', in Mohammad-Reza Djalili, Frédéric Grare and Shirin

Akiner (eds), *Tajikistan: The Trials of Independence*, Richmond, Surrey: Curzon Press, pp. 14–41.

Jalilzoda, Ibrohim (1985), *Odina Hoshim*, Dushanbe: Nashriyoti Irfon.

Jaris, Muhammad Makki al- (199x), *Nihayat al-Qawl al-Mufid fi 'Ilm al-Tajwid*, Cairo: Maktabat Tawfiqiyya.

Jawad, Nassim and Tadjbakhsh, Shahrbanou (1995), *Tajikistan: A Forgotten Civil War*, London: Minority Rights Group International Report.

Johansen, Julian (1996), *Sufism and Islamic Reform in Egypt: The Battle for Islamic Tradition*, Oxford Oriental Monographs, Oxford: Clarendon Press.

Jones, Charles (1996), 'Ideology', in Iain McLean (ed.), *The Concise Oxford Dictionary of Politics*, Oxford: Oxford University Press, pp. 233–4.

Jones, L. Jafran (1987), 'A Sociohistorical Perspective on Tunisian Women as Professional Musicians', in Ellen Koskoff (ed.), *Women and Music in Cross-Cultural Perspective*, Urbana, IL: University of Illinois Press, pp. 69–83.

JPS (Jewish Publication Society) Hebrew–English Tenakh (1999), Philadelphia, PA: Jewish Publication Society.

Kaemmer, John A. (1989), 'Social Power and Musical Change among the Shona', *Ethnomusicology*, 33(1), 31–45.

Kamali, Masoud (1998), *Revolutionary Iran: Civil Society and State in the Modernisation Process*, Aldershot: Ashgate.

Kamrava, Mehran (2001), 'The Civil Society Discourse in Iran', *British Journal of Middle Eastern Studies*, 28(2), 165–85.

Kandil, Magda (1999), 'Towards a Theory of International Labor Migration: Evidence from Egypt', in Mark Tessler (ed.), *Area Studies and Social Science: Strategies for Understanding Middle East Politics*, Bloomington, IN: Indiana University Press, pp. 81–101.

—— and M. Metwally (1990), 'The Impact of Migrants' Remittances on the Egyptian Economy', *International Migration*, 26(2), 159–81.

Kandiyoti, Deniz (1996), 'Contemporary Feminist Scholarship and Middle East Studies', in Deniz Kandiyoti (ed.), *Gendering the Middle East*, New York: Syracuse University Press, pp. 1–27.

Kapchan, Deborah (2003), 'Nashat: The Gender of Musical Celebration in Morocco', in Tulia Magrini (ed.), *Music and Gender: Perspectives from the Mediterranean*, Chicago, IL: University of Chicago Press, pp. 251–66.

Karomatov, Faizulla and Nizom Nurdzhanov (1978–86), *Muzïkal'noe Iskusstvo Pamira* (*Musical Art of the Pamir*), Moscow: Izdatel'stvo 'Sovetskiy Kompozitor'.

Kashani-Sabet, Firouzeh (1999), *Frontier Fictions: Shaping the Iranian Nation, 1804–1946*, Princeton, NJ: Princeton University Press.

Keddie, Nikki R. (2003), *Modern Iran: Roots and Results of Revolution*, New Haven, CT: Yale University Press.

Keil, Charles (1994), 'People's Music Comparatively: Style and Stereotype, Class and Hegemony', in Charles Keil and Steven Feld (eds), *Music Grooves*, Chicago, IL: Chicago University Press, pp. 197–217.

Kelly, Michael (1994), 'Introduction', in Michael Kelly (ed.), *Critique and Power: Recasting the Foucault/Habermas Debate*, Cambridge, MA: MIT Press, pp. 1–16.

Kepel, Gilles (1993), *Muslim Extremism in Egypt: The Prophet and Pharaoh*, Berkeley, CA: University of California Press.

Kerman, Joseph (1985), *Musicology*, London: Fontana.

Kershenovich, Paulette (2002), 'Evoking the Essence of the Divine: The Construction of Identity Through Food in the Syrian Jewish Community in Mexico', *Nashim*, no. 5, *Gender, Food, and Survival*, 105–28.

Khalafallah, H. (1982), 'Unofficial Cassette Culture in the Middle-East', *Index on Censorship*, 11(5), 10–12.

Khaleqi, Ruhollah (1335[1956]), *Sargozasht-e Musiqi-ye Iran* (*The History of Iranian Music*), Tehran: Ebn Sina.

Khaleqi, Zohreh (1373[1994]), *Ava-ye Mehrabani: Yadavari-e Qamar ol-Moluk Vaziri* (*Voice of Kindness: In Memory of Qamar ol-Moluk Vaziri*), Tehran: Donya-ye Madar.

Khalil, Atiya Abd al-Khaliq and Nahid Ahmad Hafiz (1984), *Fann Tarbiyat al-Sawt wa 'Ilm al-Tajwid* (*The Art of Training the Voice and Science of Tajwid*), Cairo: Maktabat al-Anglu al-Misriyya.

Khatami, Mohammad (2000), *Islam, Dialogue and Civil Society*, Canberra: Centre for Arabic and Islamic Studies (The Middle East & Central Asia), Australian National University.

Khiabany, Gholam and Annabelle Sreberny (2007), 'The Politics of/in Blogging in Iran', *Comparative Studies of South Asia, Africa and the Middle East*, 27(3), 563–79.

Khoshzamir, Mojtaba (1979), 'Ali Naqi Vaziri and His Influence on Music and Music Education in Iran', unpublished PhD thesis, University of Illinois at Urbana-Champaign.

Khosravi, Shahram (2007), *Young and Defiant in Tehran*, Philadelphia, PA: University of Pennsylvania Press.

Koen, Benjamin D. (2003a), 'Devotional Music and Healing in Badakhshan, Tajikistan: Preventive and Curative Practices', PhD thesis, Ohio State University.

—— (2003b), 'The Spiritual Aesthetic in Badakhshani Devotional Music', *The World of Music*, 45(3), 77–90.

—— (2005). 'Medical Ethnomusicology in the Pamir Mountains: Music and Prayer in Healing', *Ethnomusicology*, 49(2), 287–311.

Koepke, Bruce (2000), 'Covert Dance in Afghanistan: A Metaphor for Crisis', in Mohd Anis Md Nor (ed.), *Asian Dance: Voice of the Millennium*, Kuala Lumpa: University of Malaya, pp. 92–107.

Kosacheva, Rimma (1990), 'Traditional Music in the Context of the Socio-Political Development in the USSR', *Yearbook for Traditional Music*, 22, 17–19.

Koskoff, Ellen (1987), 'An Introduction to Women, Music and Culture', in Ellen Koskoff (ed.), *Women and Music in Cross-Cultural Perspective*, Urbana, IL: University of Illinois Press, pp. 1–23.

—— (1993), 'Miriam Sings Her Song: The Self and the Other in Anthropological Discourse', in Ruth A. Solie (ed.), *Musicology and Difference: Gender and Sexuality in Musical Scholarship*, Berkeley and Los Angeles, CA: University of California Press, pp. 149–63.

—— (2001), *Music in Lubavitcher Life*, Urbana and Chicago, IL: University of Illinois Press.

Lachmann, Robert (1940), *Jewish Cantillation and Song in the Isle of Djerba*, Jerusalem: Azriel Press, Archives of Oriental Music, Hebrew University.

—— (1978), *Gesange der Juden auf der Insel Djerba*, ed. Edith Gerson-Kiwi, Yuval Monograph Series no. 7, Jerusalem: Magnes Press.

Lane, Edward W. (1973), *An Account of the Manners and Customs of the Modern Egyptians* (5th edition), ed. Edward Stanley Poole, New York: Dover Publications.

Langer, Susanne K. (1957), *Philosophy in a New Key* (3rd edition), Cambridge, MA: Harvard University Press.

Langlois, Tony (1996), 'The Local and Global in North African Popular Music', *Popular Music*, 15(3), 259–73.

—— (1998), 'The Gnawa of Oujda: Music at the Margins in Morocco', *The World of Music*, 40(1), 135–56.

—— (2005), 'Outside-In: Music, New Media and Tradition in North Africa', in Kevin Dawe and David Cooper (eds), *The Mediterranean in Music: Critical Perspectives, Common Concerns, Cultural Differences*, Lanham, MD: Scarecrow Press, pp. 97–114.

LaTowsky, Robert J. (1984), 'Egyptian Labor Abroad: Mass Participation and Modest Returns', in *MERIP Reports, no. 123: Migrant Workers in the Middle East*, 11–18.

Lazarus-Yafeh, Hava (1983), 'Muhammad Mutawalli al-Sha'rawi – A Portrait of a Contemporary 'Alim in Egypt', in Gabriel Warburg and Uri M. Kupferschmidt (eds), *Islam, Nationalism, and Radicalism in Egypt and the Sudan*, New York: Praeger, pp. 281–97.

Lengel, Laura (2004), 'Performing In/Outside Islam: Music and Gendered Cultural Politics in the Middle East and North Africa', *Text and Performance Quarterly*, 24(3–4), 212–32.

Leppert, Richard and Susan McClary (eds) (1987), *Music and Society: The Politics of Composition, Performance and Reception*, Cambridge: Cambridge University Press.

Levin, Theodore (1979), 'Music in Modern Uzbekistan: The Convergence of Marxist Aesthetics and Central Asian Tradition', *Asian Music*, 12(1), 149–58.

—— (1984), 'The Music and Tradition of the Bukharan Shashmaqam in Soviet Uzbekistan', unpublished PhD thesis, Princeton University.

—— (1993), 'The Reterritorialization of Culture in the New Central Asian States: A Report from Uzbekistan', *Yearbook for Traditional Music*, 25, 51–9.

—— (1996), *The Hundred Thousand Fools of God: Musical Travels in Central Asia (and Queens, New York)*, Bloomington, IN: Indiana University Press.

Lewis, I.M. (1986), *Religion in Context*, Cambridge: Cambridge University Press.

Lewisohn, Leonard (1997), 'The Sacred Music of Islam: *Samā'* in the Persian Sufi Tradition', *British Journal of Ethnomusicology*, 6, 1–33.

Light, Nathan (1998), 'Slippery Paths: The Performance and Canonization of Turkic Literature and Uyghur Muqam Song in Islam and Modernity', unpublished PhD thesis, Indiana University.

Lings, Martin (1983), *Muhammad: His Life Based on the Earliest Sources*, London: Allen & Unwin.

Lipsitz, George (1994), *Dangerous Crossroads: Popular Music, Postmodernism and the Poetics of Place*, London: Verso.

Loeb, Lawrence D. (1996), 'Gender, Marriage, and Social Conflict in Habban', in Harvey Goldberg (ed.), *Sephardic and Middle Eastern Jewries*, Bloomington, IN: Indiana University Press, pp. 56–76.

Ma Binyan (1983), 'Nanjiang Mazha he Mazha Chaobai' ('Shrines and Shrine Worship in Southern Xinjiang'), *Xinjiang Kexue Yanjiu*, 1.

Maghraoui, Absalem (1995), 'Algeria's Battle of Two Languages,' *Middle East Report*, January, 23–6.

Magrini, Tullia (ed.) (2003), *Music and Gender: Perspectives from the Mediterranean*, Chicago, IL: University of Chicago Press.

el-Mahdi, Salah and Muhammad Marzuqi (1981), *Al-Ma'had al-Rashīdī Li-l-Mūsīqā al-Tūnisiyya*, Tunis: Wizārat al-Shu'ūn al-Taqāfiya/Ministère des Affaires Culturelles.

Mahfuz, Talib and Abd al-Wahhab al-Zahrani (2002), 'al-'Ajmi: Imam al-tarawih bi Jami' Khadim al-Haramayn al-Sharifayn bi Jadda' ('al-'Ajmi: The Leader of Tarawih at the Khadim al-Haramayn al-Sharifayn Mosque in Jedda'), '*Ukaaz*, 8 November 2002, 30.

Maleki, Tuka (1380[2001]), *Zanan-e Musiqi-e Iran az Astureh ta Emruz* (*Women of Iranian Music from the Legendary Time up to Now*), Tehran: Ketab-e Khorshid.

Manuel, Peter (1993), *Cassette Culture, Popular Music, and Technology in North India*, Chicago, IL: University of Chicago Press.

Marashi, Afshin (2002), 'Performing the Nation: The Shah's Official State Visit to Kemalist Turkey, June to July 1934', in Stephanie Cronin (ed.), *The Making of Modern Iran: State and Society Under Riza Shah, 1921–1941*, London: RoutledgeCurzon, pp. 99–119.

al-Marīnī, Abū Bakr (ed.) (1975), *Umm Kulthūm: Mu'jizat al-Qarn al-'Ishrīn fī 'āla al-Nagham wa-al-Talḥīn*, Casablanca: Dār al-Sulm ī Aḥmad.

Marshak, Boris Ilich and Numan Negmatovich Negmatov (1996), 'Sogdiana', in Boris Anatolevich Litvisky (ed.), *History of Civilizations of Central Asia*,

Volume 3: The Crossroads of Civilizations: A.D. 250 to 750, Paris: UNESCO Publishing, pp. 233–82.

Martin, Vanessa (1989), *Islam and Modernism: The Iranian Revolution of 1906*, London: I.B. Tauris.

McClary, Susan (1985), 'Afterword: The Politics of Silence and Sound', in Jacques Attali, *Noise: The Political Economy of Music* (translated by Brian Massumi), Minneapolis, MN: University of Minnesota Press, pp. 149–58.

—— (1991), *Feminine Endings: Music, Gender and Sexuality*, Minneapolis, MN: University of Minnesota Press.

McCracken, Allison (2001), 'Real Men Don't Sing Ballads: The Radio Crooner in Hollywood, 1929–1933', in Pamela Wojcik and Arthur Knight (eds), *Soundtrack Available: Essays on Film and Popular Music*, Durham, NC: Duke University Press, pp. 105–33.

Merrell, Floyd (2001), 'Charles Sanders Peirce's Concept of the Sign', in Paul Cobley (ed.), *The Routledge Companion to Semiotics and Linguistics*, London: Routledge.

Merriam, Alan (1964), *The Anthropology of Music*, Evanston, IL: Northwestern University Press.

Meyer, Leonard B. (1967), *Music, the Arts, and Ideas: Patterns and Predictions in Twentieth-Century Culture*, Chicago, IL: University of Chicago Press.

—— (1989), *Style and Music: Theory, History, and Ideology*, Philadelphia, PA: University of Pennsylvania Press.

Middleton, Richard (1990), *Studying Popular Music*, Open University Press.

Milani, Farzaneh (1992), *Veils and Words: The Emerging Voices of Iranian Women Writers*, New York: Syracuse University Press.

Millward, James (2004), 'Violent Separatism in Xinjiang: A Critical Assessment', *Policy Studies*, no. 6, Washington, DC: East-West Center.

Mirsepassi, Ali (2000), *Intellectual Discourse and the Politics of Modernization: Negotiating Modernity in Iran*, Cambridge: Cambridge University Press.

Mitchell, Richard (1969), *The Society of the Muslim Brothers*, Oxford: Oxford University Press.

Mitchell, Timothy (1988), *Colonising Egypt*, Cambridge: Cambridge University Press.

—— (2002), *Rule of Experts: Egypt, Techno-Politics, Modernity*, Berkeley, CA: University of California Press.

Moisala, Pirkko and Beverley Diamond (eds) (2000), *Music and Gender*, Urbana, IL: University of Illinois Press.

Morsy, Soheir A. (1988), 'Islamic Clinics in Egypt: The Cultural Elaboration of Biomedical Hegemony', *Medical Anthropology Quarterly*, 2, 355–69.

Moslem, Mehdi (2002), *Factional Politics in Post-Khomeini Iran*, Syracuse, NY: Syracuse University Press.

Mousavi Shafaee, Seyed Masoud (2003), 'Globalization and Contradiction Between the Nation and the State in Iran: The Internet Case', *Critique: Critical Middle Eastern Studies*, 12(2), 189–95.

Moussali, Bernard (1992), 'Les Premiers Enregistrements de Musique Tunisienne par les Compagnies Discographiques', unpublished paper read at the colloquium *Liens et Interactions entre les Musiques Arabes et Méditerranéennes*, Programme d'Inauguration du Centre des Musiques Arabes et Méditerranéennes, Hotel Abou Nawas, Gamarth, Tunisia, 9–12 November 1992.

Muhammadi, Musohib Muzaffar (1991), 'Surude, Ki Sūz Nadorad, Surud Nest!' ('A Song That Has No Grief, Is Not a Song!'), *Adabiyot va San'at*, 17(698), 5.

Munson, Henry (1993), 'The Political Role of Islam in Morocco (1970–1990)', in George Joffe (ed.), *North Africa: Nation, State and Region*, London: Routledge, pp. 87–102.

Murad, Mustafa (199x), *Ta'lim al-Qur'an al-Karim* (*Teaching the Glorious Qur'an*), Cairo: Dar al-Rawda.

Muslim (2000), 'Sahih Muslim', in *Hadith Encyclopedia* (CD ROM), Cairo: Harf.

Naby, Eden (1973), 'Tajik and Uzbek Nationality Identity: The Non-literary Arts', in Edward Allworth (ed.), *The Nationality Question in Soviet Central Asia*, New York, Washington, DC and London: Praeger Publishers, pp. 110–20.

Naceri, K. and Y. Mebarki (1983), *Introduction à l'Étude du 'Madhar' La Chanson 'Raï' dans le Festivities de Marriage á l'Oran*, unpublished Masters thesis, Department of Sociology, University of Oran.

Nada, Atef Hanna (1991), 'Impact of Temporary International Migration on Rural Egypt', *Cairo Papers in Social Science*, volume 3, 14, Cairo: AUC Press.

Naficy, Hamid (2002), 'Islamizing Film Culture in Iran: A Post-Khatami Update', in Richard Tapper (ed.), *The New Iranian Cinema: Politics, Representation and Identity*, London: I.B. Tauris, pp. 26–65.

Najmabadi, Afsaneh (ed.) (1990), *Women's Autobiographies in Contemporary Iran*, Cambridge, MA: Harvard University Press.

Nasr, Seyyed Hossein (1995) 'Oral Transmission and the Book in Islamic Education: The Spoken and the Written Word', in George N. Atiyeh (ed.), *The Book in the Islamic World: The Written Word and Communication in the Middle East*, Albany, NY: State University of New York Press, pp. 57–70.

—— (1997), 'Islam and Music: The Legal and the Spiritual Dimensions', in Lawrence E. Sullivan (ed.), *Enchanting Powers: Music in the World's Religions*, Cambridge, MA: Harvard University Press, pp. 219–35.

Nelson, Kristina (1985), *The Art of Reciting the Qur'an*, Austin, TX: University of Texas Press.

—— (2001), *The Art of Reciting the Qur'an* (2nd edition), Cairo: American University in Cairo Press.

Nettl, Bruno (2005), *The Study of Ethnomusicology: Thirty-one Issues and Concepts* (2nd edition), Urbana, IL: University of Illinois Press.

Niyazi, Aziz (1993), 'The Year of Tumult: Tajikistan after February 1990', in Vitaly Naumkin (ed.), *State, Religion and Society in Central Asia: A Post-Soviet Critique*, Reading: Ithaca Press, pp. 263–89.

Nooshin, Laudan (1996), 'The Processes of Creation and Re-Creation in Persian Classical Music', unpublished PhD thesis, Goldsmiths' College, University of London.

—— (2005a), 'Subversion and Countersubversion: Power, Control and Meaning in the New Iranian Pop Music', in Annie Randall (ed.), *Music, Power, and Politics*, New York: Routledge, pp. 231–72.

—— (2005b), 'Underground, Overground: Rock Music and Youth Discourses in Iran', *Iranian Studies*, 38(3), 463–94.

—— (2008), 'The Language of Rock: Iranian Youth, Popular Music, and National Identity', in Mehdi Semati (ed.), *Media, Culture and Society in Iran*, New York: Routledge, pp. 69–93.

Norton, Augustus Richard (ed.) (1995), *Civil Society in the Middle East*, Leiden: E.J. Brill.

Nourzhanov, Kirill (2000), 'Politics of National Reconciliation in Tajikistan: From Peace Talks to (Partial) Political Settlement', in David Christian and Craig Benjamin (eds), *Silk Road Studies IV. Realms of the Silk Roads: Ancient and Modern*. Proceedings from the Third Conference of the Australasian Society for Inner Asian Studies (A.S.I.A.S), Macquarie University, September 18–20 1998, Turnhout, Belgium: Brepols, pp. 161–79.

O'Connell, John M. (2004), 'Sustaining Difference: Theorizing Minority Music in Badakhshan', in Ursula Hemetek, Gerda Lechleitner, Inna Naroditskaya and Anna Czekanowska (eds), *Manifold Identities: Studies on Music and Minorities*, London: Cambridge Scholars Press, pp. 1–19.

On Ikki Muqam Tätqiqat Ilmiy Jämiyiti [OIMTIJ] (1992), *Uyghur On Ikki Muqam Häqqidä* (*About the Uyghur Twelve Muqam*), Ürümchi: Shinjang Khälq Näshriyati.

Oren, Michael B. (2002), *Six Days of War: June 1967 and the Making of the Modern Middle East*, Oxford: Oxford University Press.

Ortner, Sherry B. (1996a), 'Making Gender', in Sherry B. Ortner (ed.), *Making Gender: The Politics and Erotics of Culture*, Boston, MA: Beacon Press, pp. 1–20.

—— (1996b), 'Gender Hegemonies', in Sherry B. Ortner (ed.), *Making Gender: The Politics and Erotics of Culture*, Boston, MA: Beacon Press, pp. 139–72.

Ottaway, David and Marina Ottaway (1970), *Algeria: The Politics of a Socialist Revolution*, Berkeley, CA: University of California Press.

Pacholczyk, Jozef M. (1970), 'Regulative Principles in the Koran Chant of Shaikh 'Abdu'l-Basit 'Abdu's-Samad', unpublished PhD thesis, University of California, Los Angeles.

Peña, Manuel (1985), *The Texas-Mexican Conjunto: History of a Working-Class Music*, Austin, TX: University of Texas Press.

Petkov, Steven (1995), 'Ol' Blue Eyes and the Golden Age of the American Song', in Steven Petkov and Leonard Mustazza (eds), *The Sinatra Reader*, Oxford: Oxford University Press, pp. 74–84.

Pickthall, Mohammed Marmaduke (1953), *The Meaning of the Glorious Koran: An Explanatory Translation*, New York: New American Library.

Poché, Christian (1995), *La Musique Arabo-Andalouse*, Paris: Cité de la Musique/ Actes Sud.

Poliakov, Sergei (1992), *Everyday Islam: Religion and Tradition in Rural Central Asia* (translated by Anthony Olcott), New York and London: M.E. Sharpe.

Potter, Pamela (1998), *Most German of the Arts: Musicology and Society from the Weimar Republic to the End of Hitler's Reich*, New Haven, CT: Yale University Press.

Powers, Harold (1979), 'Classical Music, Classical Roots, and Colonial Rule: An Indic Musicologist Looks at the Muslim World', *Asian Music*, 12(1), 5–39.

Qadi, Shukri al- (1999), *'Abaqirat al-Tilawa fi al-Qarn al-'Ashrin* (*The Greats of Qur'anic Recitation in the Twentieth Century*), Cairo: Matabi' Dar al-Tahrir li al-Tab' wa al-Nashr.

Qalamuni, Abu Dharr al- (ed.) (2000), *Fa Firru ila Allah: La Malja' min Allah Illa Ilayhi* (*Hasten to God: There is No Refuge from God Except with Him*), Cairo: Dar al-Fajr lil-Turath.

Qureshi, Regula B. (1986), *Sufi Music of India and Pakistan*, Cambridge: Cambridge University Press.

—— (2002), *Music and Marx: Ideas, Practice, Politics*, New York: Routledge.

Rabinow, Paul (1975), *Symbolic Domination: Cultural Form and Historical Change in Morocco*, Chicago, IL: Chicago University Press.

Racy, Ali Jihad (1976), 'Record Industry and Egyptian Traditional Music: 1904– 1932', *Ethnomusicology*, 20(1), 23–48.

—— (1977), 'Musical Change and Commercial Recording in Egypt, 1904–1932', unpublished PhD thesis, University of Illinois.

—— (1991), 'Historical Worldviews of Early Ethnomusicologists: An East-West Encounter in Cairo, 1932', in Stephen Blum, Philip V. Bohlman and Daniel M. Neuman (eds), *Ethnomusicology and Modern Music History*, Urbana and Chicago, IL: University of Illinois Press, pp. 68–91.

—— (2003), *Making Music in the Arab World: The Culture and Artistry of Tarab*, Cambridge: Cambridge University Press.

Rahimov, Ismatullo (1986), 'Maqomi Jovidonī' ('Eternal *Maqom*'), *Adabiyot va San'at*, 51(271), 15.

—— (1987), 'Ansamble, Ki Der Boz Intizorash Budem' ('An Ensemble We Were Long Waiting For'), *Adabiyot va San'at*, 12(284), 13.

Rahman, Fazlur (1979), *Islam* (2nd edition), Chicago, IL: University of Chicago Press.

Rajab, Subhon (1990), 'Guli Dar Sang Rusta' ('The Flower that Grew Amid the Rocks'), *Adabiyot va San'at*, 33(662), 13.

Rajabi, D. (1986), 'Az Har Boghe Yak Shingil' ('A Bit from Every Garden'), *Adabiyot va San'at*, 26(246), 14.

Rajabov, Askarali (1989), *Az Ta'rikhi Afkori Musiqii Tojik (Asrhoi xii–xv)* (*On the History of Tajik Music Theory (12th–15th Centuries)*), Dushanbe: Nashriyoti 'Donish'.

Ralls-MacLeod, Karen and Graham Harvey (eds) (2000), *Indigenous Religious Musics*, Aldershot: Ashgate.

Ramnarine, Tina (2004), 'Imperial Legacies and the Politics of Musical Creativity', *The World of Music*, 46(1), 91–108.

Randall, Annie J. (2005), (ed.) *Music, Power, and Politics*, New York: Routledge.

Rashid, Ahmad (2000), *Taliban: Islam, Oil and the New Great Game in Central Asia*, London: I.B. Tauris.

—— (2002), *Jihad: The Rise of Militant Islam in Central Asia*, New Haven, CT and London: Yale University Press.

Rasmussen, Anne K. (1996), 'Theory and Practice at the "Arabic Org": Digital Technology in Contemporary Arab Music Performance', *Popular Music*, 15(3), 345–65.

—— (2001), 'The Qur'an in Indonesian Daily Life: The Public Project of Musical Oratory', *Ethnomusicology*, 45(1), 30–57.

Rice, Timothy (1994), *May It Fill Your Soul: Experiencing Bulgarian Music*, Chicago, IL: Chicago University Press.

—— (2001), 'Reflections on Music and Meaning: Metaphor, Signification and Control in the Bulgarian Case', *British Journal of Ethnomusicology* (special issue on Music and Meaning), 10(1), 19–38.

Ricoeur, Paul (1986), *Lectures on Ideology and Utopia*, ed. George H. Taylor, New York: Columbia University Press.

Rizgui, Sadok (1967), *Al-Aghāni al-Tūnisiyya (Les Chants Tunisiens)*, Tunis: al-Dār al-Tūnisiyya li'l-Nasr.

Rizk, Yunan Labib (2004), 'This is Cairo' (no. 529 in series: 'Al-Ahram: A Diwan of Contemporary Life'), *Al-Ahram Weekly*, 15–21 January 2004, 26.

Roberts, Sean (1998), 'Negotiating Locality, Islam, and National Culture in a Changing Borderland: The Revival of the *Mäshräp* Ritual among Young Uighur Men in the Ili Valley', *Central Asian Survey*, 17(4), 672–700.

Robertson, Carol E. (1987), 'Power and Gender in the Musical Experiences of Women', in Ellen Koskoff (ed.), *Women and Music in Cross-Cultural Perspective*, Urbana, IL: University of Illinois Press, pp. 225–44.

Robson, James (1938), *Tracts on Listening to Music*, London: Royal Asiatic Society.

Rosen, Barry M. (1973), 'An Awareness of Traditional Tajik Identity in Central Asia', in Edward Allworth (ed.), *The Nationality Question in Soviet Central Asia*, New York, Washington, DC and London: Praeger Publishers, pp. 61–72.

Rouget, Gilbert (1985), *Music and Trance*, Chicago, IL: Chicago University Press.

Roussillon, Alain (1998), 'Republican Egypt Interpreted: Revolution and Beyond', in M.W. Daly (ed.), *The Cambridge History of Egypt, Volume 2*, Cambridge: Cambridge University Press, pp. 334–93.

Roy, Olivier (2000), *The New Central Asia: The Creation of Nations*, London: I.B. Tauris. Originally published 1997.

Roy Choudhury, M.L. (1957), 'Music in Islam', *Journal of the Asiatic Society*, 23(2), 43–102.

Sa'dani, Mahmud al- (1996), *Alhan al-Sama'*, Cairo: Akhbar al-Yawm.

Safar, Sulton (1971), 'Bevatan', *Sado-i Sharq*, 3, Dushanbe: Union of Writers of Tajikistan, pp. 40–78.

Sa'id, Labib al- (1975), *The Recited Koran; A History of the First Recorded Version* (translated by Bernard Weiss, M.A. Rauf and Morroe Berger), Princeton, NJ: Darwin Press.

Sajoo, Amyn B. (ed.) (2002), *Civil Society in the Muslim World: Contemporary Perspectives*, London: I.B. Tauris.

Sakata, Hiromi Lorraine (1983), *Music in the Mind: The Concepts of Music and Musician in Afghanistan*, Kent, OH: Kent State University Press.

—— (1986), 'The Complementary Opposition of Music and Religion in Afghanistan', *World of Music*, 20(3), 33–41.

Salim, Majid (1993), 'Surudi Shohin' ('The Song of the Falcon'), *Adabiyot va San'at*, 34(818), 6.

Saussure, Ferdinand de (1986), *Cours de Linguistique Générale*, ed. Charles Bally and Albert Sechehaye, with the collaboration of Albert Riedlinger; translated and annotated by Roy Harris, La Salle, IL: Open Court.

Sayyid, Hiba al- (2003), 'Shuyukh al-Tilawa' ('Shaykhs of Qur'anic Recitation'), *Al-Idha'a wa al-Tilifizyun* (*Radio and Television Magazine*), no. 3581.

Schade-Poulson, Marc (1999), *Men and Popular Music in Algeria: The Social Significance of Raï*, Austin, TX: University of Texas Press.

Schaeffer-Davis, Susan (1983), *Patience and Power: Women's Lives in a Moroccan Village*, Cambridge, MA: Schenkman.

Scholes, Percy A. (ed.) (1995), 'Quakers and Music', in *The Oxford Companion to Music* (9th edition), Oxford: Oxford University Press, pp. 853–4.

Schuyler, Philip (1978), 'Moroccan Andalusian Music', *World of Music*, 78(1), 33–46.

—— (1981), 'Music and Meaning among the *Gnawa* Religious Brotherhood of Morocco', *World of Music*, 81(1), 3–11.

Scott, James C. (1990), *Domination and the Arts of Resistance: Hidden Transcripts*, New Haven, CT: Yale University Press.

Seroussi, Edwin (2003), 'Archivists of Memory: Written Folksong Collections of Twentieth-Century Sephardi Women', in Tullia Magrini (ed.), *Music and Gender: Perspectives from the Mediterranean*, Chicago, IL: University of Chicago Press, pp. 195–214.

Shahrani, Enayatullah (1973), 'The "Falaks" of the Mountains', *Afghanistan*, 26(1), 68–75.

Shakarmamadov, Nisor (1990), 'Reshapaivandi "Falak" – Qaidho dar Hoshiyai "Falak" Ci Ta'rikh Dorad?' ('The Roots of "Falak" – Remarks on "What is the History of 'Falak'?"'), *Adabiyot va San'at*, 20(649), 13.

Shakli, Mourad (1994), *La Chanson Tunisienne. Analyse Technique et Approche Sociologique*, Thèse de Musicologie, Université de Paris, Sorbonne, Paris IV.

Shalabi, Khayri (1997), 'Sawt al-Husari al-Sahrawi' ('The Desert Voice of al-Husari'), in Ibrahim Daoud (ed.), *Al-Qur'an fi Misr*, Cairo: Toot, pp. 57–68.

Shaw, Arnold (1995), 'Sinatrauma: The Proclamation of a New Era', in Steven Petkov and Leonard Mustazza (eds), *The Sinatra Reader*, Oxford: Oxford University Press, pp. 18–30.

Shay, Anthony (2000), 'The 6/8 Beat Goes On: Persian Popular Music from *Bazm-e Qajariyyeh* to Beverley Hills Garden Parties', in Walter Armbrust (ed.), *Mass Mediations: New Approaches to Popular Culture in the Middle East and Beyond*, Berkeley, CA: University of California Press, pp. 61–87.

Shayegan, Daryush (1997), *Cultural Schizophrenia: Islamic Societies Confronting the West*, Syracuse, NY: Syracuse University Press.

Shelemay, Kay Kaufman (1988), 'Together in the Field: Team Research among Syrian Jews in Brooklyn, New York', *Ethnomusicology*, 32(3), 369–84.

—— (1998), *Let Jasmine Rain Down: Song and Remembrance Among Syrian Jews*, Chicago, IL: University of Chicago Press.

—— (2001), *Soundscapes: Exploring Music in a Changing World*, New York: Norton.

Shemesh, Moshe (1996), *The Palestinian Entity, 1959–1974: Arab Politics and the PLO* (2nd revised edition), London: Frank Cass.

Shepherd, John (1977), 'The Musical Coding of Ideologies', in John Shepherd, Phil Virden, Graham Vulliamy and Trevor Wishart, *Whose Music? A Sociology of Musical Languages*, London: Latimer, pp. 69–124.

—— (1987), 'Music and Male Hegemony', in Richard Leppert and Susan McClary (eds), *Music and Society: The Politics of Composition, Performance and Reception*, Cambridge: Cambridge University Press, pp. 151–72.

—— (1991), *Music as Social Text*, Cambridge: Polity Press.

—— (1993), 'Value and Power in Music: An English Canadian Perspective', in Valda Blundell, John Shepherd and Ian Taylor (eds), *Relocating Cultural Studies: Developments in Theory and Research*, New York: Routledge, pp. 171–206.

——, Phil Virden, Graham Vulliamy and Trevor Wishart (1977), *Whose Music? A Sociology of Musical Languages*, London: Latimer.

Shiloah, Amnon (1992), *Jewish Musical Traditions*, Detroit, MI: Wayne State University Press.

—— (1995), *Music in the World of Islam: A Socio-Cultural Study*, Aldershot: Scolar Press.

al-Shorabji, al-Sayyid (2000), *Abd al-Halim Hafiz: Mishwar al-Majd wa al-'Azab*, Cairo: Maktaba al-Dar al-'Arabiyya al-Kitab.

Shoshan, Boaz (1993), *Popular Culture in Medieval Cairo*, Cambridge: Cambridge University Press.

Shrem, Gabriel (ed.) (1988), *Sheer Ushbahah Hallel Ve-Zimrah* (5th edition), Brooklyn, NY: Sephardic Heritage Foundation and Magen David Publication Society. 1st edition 1964.

Slobin, Mark (1970), 'Persian Folksong Texts from Afghan Badakhshan', *Iranian Studies*, 3(2), 91–103.

—— (1976), *Music in the Culture of Northern Afghanistan*, Tucson, AZ: University of Arizona Press.

—— (1996), 'Introduction', in Mark Slobin (ed.), *Retuning Culture: Musical Changes in Central and Eastern Europe*, Durham, NC: Duke University Press, pp. 1–13.

—— and Alexander Djumaev (2001), 'Tajikistan. Traditional Music', in Stanley Sadie (ed.), *The New Grove Dictionary of Music and Musicians, Volume 25*, London: Macmillan, pp. 14–18.

Solie, Ruth (1993), 'Introduction: On "Difference"', in Ruth Solie (ed.), *Musicology and Difference: Gender and Sexuality in Musical Scholarship*, Berkeley, CA: University of California Press, pp. 1–20.

SonoCairo (199x), *Masahif Murattala wa Mujawwada* (*Catalogue of Complete Qur'an Recordings*), SonoCairo, Ittihad al-Idha'a wa al-Tilifizyun.

Spinetti, Federico (2005), 'Open Borders. Tradition and Tajik Popular Music: Questions of Aesthetics, Identity and Political Economy', *Ethnomusicology Forum*, 14(2), 183–209.

Stapley, Kathryn M.G. (2002), 'Music of the Marginalised?', in Clive Holes (ed.), *Proceedings of the International Conference on Middle Eastern Popular Culture*, pp. 175–84.

Starkey, Paul (1998), 'Modern Egyptian Culture in the Arab World', in M.W. Daly (ed.), *The Cambridge History of Egypt, Volume 2*, Cambridge: Cambridge University Press, pp. 394–426.

Steger, Manfred B. (2003), *Globalization: A Very Short Introduction*, Oxford: Oxford University Press.

Stokes, Martin (1992), *The Arabesk Debate: Music and Musicians in Modern Turkey*, Oxford: Oxford University Press.

—— (ed.) (1994a), *Ethnicity, Identity and Music: The Musical Construction of Place*, Oxford: Berg.

—— (1994b), 'Introduction: Ethnicity, Identity and Music', in Martin Stokes (ed.), *Ethnicity, Identity and Music: The Musical Construction of Place*, Oxford: Berg, pp. 1–27.

—— (1994c), 'Turkish Arabesk and the City: Urban Popular Culture as Spatial Practice', in Akbar S. Ahmad and Hastings Donan (eds), *Islam, Globalization and Postmodernity*, London: Routledge, pp. 21–37.

—— (2002), 'Silver Sounds in the Inner Citadel? Reflections on Musicology and Islam', in Hastings Donan (ed.), *Interpreting Islam*, London: Sage, pp. 167–89.

—— (2003a), 'Discussant Comments', Panel on Popular Music in the Middle East, 48th Annual Meeting of the Society for Ethnomusicology, Miami, Florida, 2 October 2003.

—— (2003b), 'Globalization and the Politics of World Music', in Martin Clayton, Trevor Herbert and Richard Middleton (eds), *The Cultural Study of Music: A Critical Introduction*, New York: Routledge, pp. 297–308.

—— (2004), 'Music and the Global Order', *Annual Review of Anthropology*, 33, 47–72.

Stora, Benjamin (2002), *Algérie, Maroc: Histoires Parallèles, Destins Crossés*, Paris: Maisonneuve et Larose.

Strunk, Oliver (1952), *Source Readings in Music History From Classical Antiquity to the Romantic Era*, London: Faber.

Sullivan, Lawrence E. (ed.) (1997a), *Enchanting Powers: Music in the World's Religions*, Cambridge, MA: Harvard University Press.

—— (1997b), 'Enchanting Powers: An Introduction', in Lawrence E. Sullivan (ed.), *Enchanting Powers: Music in the World's Religions*, Cambridge, MA: Harvard University Press, pp. 1–14.

Sutton, Joseph A.D. (1988), *Aleppo Chronicles: The Story of the Unique Sephardeem of the Ancient Near East – In Their Own Words*, New York: Thayer Jacoby.

Tabarov, Sohib (1988), 'Andeshaho Roje' ba Dastovardhoi Hunarii Ovozkhoni Mashhur Odina Hoshimov' ('Thoughts on the Artistic Achievements of the Famous Singer Odina Hoshimov'), *Adabiyot va San'at*, 37(562), 5.

Talattof, Kamran (2000), *The Politics of Writing in Iran: A History of Modern Persian Literature*, New York: Syracuse University Press.

Tame, David (1984), *The Secret Power of Music*, Rochester, VT: Destiny Books.

Tapper, Richard (ed.) (2000), *Ayatollah Khomeini and the Modernization of Islamic Thought*, London: Centre for Near and Middle Eastern Studies, School of Oriental and African Studies.

Tarrock, Adam (2002), 'The Struggle for Reform in Iran', *New Political Science*, 24(3), 449–68.

Tawfiq, Mahmud (ed. and compiler) (199x), *al-Shaykh Muhammad Rif'at: Qithara al-Sama'* (*Shaykh Muhammad Rif'at: The Lyre of Heaven*), Cairo: al-Hadara al-'Arabiyya.

Taylor, Christopher Schurman (1989), 'The Cult of the Saints in Late Medieval Egypt', unpublished PhD thesis, Princeton University.

Taylor, Timothy D. (1997), *Global Pop: World Music, World Markets*, New York: Routledge.

—— (2001), *Strange Sounds: Music, Technology and Culture*, New York: Routledge.

—— (2007), *Beyond Exoticism, Western Music and the World*, Durham, NC and London: Duke University Press.

Temurzoda, Jum'akhon (1989), '"Falak" Ci Ta'rikh Dorad?', ('What is the History of "Falak"?'), *Adabiyot va San'at*, 43(620), 5.

—— (1990), 'Panj Namudi Falak' ('Five Types of Falak'), *Adabiyot va San'at*, 34(663), 14.

—— (1991), 'Ehsosi Falak' ('The Feeling of Falak'), *Adabiyot va San'at*, 6(687), 11.

Tenaille, Frank (2002), *Le Raï: De la Bartardise á la Reconnaissance International*, Paris: Cité de la Musique/Actes Sud.

Théberge, Paul (2003), 'Microphone', in *Continuum Encyclopedia of Popular Music of the World, Volume II: Performance and Production*, London: Continuum, pp. 245–7.

Tick, Judith (2001), 'Women in Music. I. Historiography. II. Western Classical Traditions in Europe and the USA', in Stanley Sadie (ed.), *The New Grove Dictionary of Music and Musicians*, Volume 27 (2nd edition), London: Macmillan, pp. 519–37.

Tirmidhi (2000), 'Sahih Tirmidhi', in *Hadith Encyclopedia* (CD-ROM), Cairo: Harf.

Tomlinson, Gary (1994), *Music in Renaissance Magic: Toward a Historiography of Others*, Chicago, IL: University of Chicago Press.

Toth, James (1994), 'Rural Workers and Egypt's National Development', *British Journal of Middle Eastern Studies*, 21(1), 38–56.

—— (2003), 'Islamism in Southern Egypt: A Case Study of a Radical Religious Movement', *International Journal of Middle East Studies*, 35, 547–72.

Trebinjac, Sabine (1995), 'Femme, Seule et Venue d'Ailleurs: Trois Atouts d'un Ethnomusicologue au Turkestan Chinois', *Cahiers de Musiques Traditionelles*, 8, 59–68.

—— (2000), *Le Pouvoir en Chantant: L'Art de Fabriquer une Musique Chinoise*, Nanterre: Société d'Ethnologie.

Turino, Thomas (1983), 'The Charango and the *Sirena*: Music, Magic, and the Power of Love', *Latin American Music Review*, 4(1), 81–119.

—— (1984), 'The Urban-Mestizo Charango Tradition in Southern Peru: A Statement of Shifting Identity', *Ethnomusicology*, 28(2), 253–70.

—— (1990), 'Structure, Context, and Strategy in Musical Ethnography', *Ethnomusicology*, 34(3), 399–412.

—— (1993), *Moving Away from Silence: Music of the Peruvian Altiplano and the Experience of Urban Migration*, Chicago, IL: University of Chicago Press.

—— (2000), *Nationalists, Cosmopolitans, and Popular Music in Zimbabwe*, Chicago, IL: University of Chicago Press.

Udovitch, Abraham L. and Lucette Valensi (1984), *The Last Arab Jews: The Communities of Jerba, Tunisia*, London: Harwood Academic.

Ulughzoda, Sotim (1977), *Riwoyat-i Sughdī (Sogdian Tale)*, Dushanbe: Adib.

Vahdat, Farzin (2002), *God and Juggernaut: Iran's Intellectual Encounter with Modernity*, Syracuse, NY: Syracuse University Press.

van den Berg, Gabrielle (2004), *Minstrel Poetry from the Pamir Mountains: A Study on the Songs and Poems of the Ismā'īlīs of Tajik Badakhshan*, Wiesbaden: Reichert Verlag.

—— and Jan van Belle (1997), 'The Performance of Poetry and Music by the Ismā'īlī People of Badakhshân: An Example of Madāh from the Shāhdara-Valley', *Persica*, 15, 49–76.

van Nieuwkerk, Karin (2003), 'On Religion, Gender, and Performing: Female Performers and Repentance in Egypt', in Tullia Magrini (ed.), *Music and Gender: Perspectives from the Mediterranean*, Chicago, IL: University of Chicago Press, pp. 267–86.

Varzi, Roxanne (2006), *Warring Souls: Youth, Media, and Martyrdom in Post-Revolutionary Iran*, Durham, NC: Duke University Press.

Vassiliev, Alexei (2000), *The History of Saudi Arabia*, New York: New York University Press.

Vatim, Jean (1987), 'Islamic Polemical Discourses in the Maghreb', in William R. Roff (ed.), *Islam and the Political Economy of Meaning*, London: Croom Helm, pp. 158–77.

Virolle, Marie (1995), *La Chanson Raï: De l'Algerie Profonde á la Scene Internationale*, Paris: Karthala.

Vitalis, Robert (2000), 'American Ambassador in Technicolor and Cinemascope: Hollywood and Revolution on the Nile', in Walter Armbrust (ed.), *Mass Mediations: New Approaches to Popular Culture in the Middle East and Beyond*, Berkeley, CA: University of California Press, pp. 269–91.

Walser, Robert (1993), *Running with the Devil: Power, Gender, and Madness in Heavy Metal Music*, Hanover, NH: Wesleyan University Press.

Ward, Brian (1998), *Just My Soul Responding: Rhythm and Blues, Black Consciousness and Race Relations*, London: UCL Press.

Waterbury, John (1970), *The Commander of the Faithful*, London: Weidenfield and Nicolson.

—— (1983), *The Egypt of Nasser and Sadat: The Political Economy of Two Regimes*, Princeton Studies on the Near East, Princeton, NJ: Princeton University Press.

Waterman, Christopher Alan (1990), *Jùjú: A Social History and Ethnography of an African Popular Music*, Chicago, IL: University of Chicago.

Waters, Anita (1985), *Race, Class and Political Symbols: Rastafari and Reggae in Jamaican Politics*, New Brunswick, NJ: Transaction Books.

Weber, William (1975), *Music and the Middle Class: The Social Structure of Concert Life in London, Paris and Vienna*, London: Croom Helm.

—— (1992), *The Rise of Musical Classics in Eighteenth-Century England: A Study in Canon, Ritual and Ideology*, Oxford: Clarendon Press.

Wicke, Peter (1990), *Rock Music: Culture, Aesthetics and Sociology*, Cambridge: Cambridge University Press. Originally published in German as *Rockmusik: zur Ästhetik und Soziologie eines Massenmediums*, 1987.

Wickham, Carrie Rosefsky (2002), *Mobilizing Islam: Religion, Activism, and Political Change in Egypt*, New York: Columbia University Press.

Williams, Raymond (1977), *Marxism and Literature*, Oxford: Oxford University Press.

Winter, Michael (1992), *Egyptian Society Under Ottoman Rule 1517–1798*, London: Routledge.

Xinjiang Weiwu'er Zizhiqu Wenhuating/Shinjang Uyghur Aptonom Rayonluq Mädiniyät Nazariti (1960), *Wei wu'er minjian gudian yinyue shi'er mukamu/ Uyghur Khalq Kilassik Muzikisi On Ikki Muqam* (*Uyghur Folk Classical Music: The Twelve Muqam*), Beijing: Yinyue chubanshe/Muzika Näshriyati, Millätlär Näshriyati.

Yanagisako, Sylvia and Carol Delaney (1995), *Naturalizing Power: Essays in Feminist Cultural Analysis*, New York: Routledge.

Yang Mu (1994), 'On the *Hua'er* Songs of North-Western China', *Yearbook for Traditional Music*, 26, 100–116.

—— (1998), 'Erotic Musical Activity in Multiethnic China', *Ethnomusicology*, 42(2), 199–264.

Yorov, Musohib Saidmurod (1988), 'Soate bo Odina Hoshim' ('An Hour with Odina Hoshim'), *Adabiyot va San'at*, 46(571), 1.

Youssefzadeh, Ameneh (2000), 'The Situation of Music in Iran since the Revolution: The Role of Official Organizations', *British Journal of Ethnomusicology*, 9(2), 35–61.

—— (2003), 'Music and Power: The Struggle between Religious Tendencies in Iran', Paper Presented at the 48th Annual Meeting of the Society for Ethnomusicology, Miami, Florida, October 5 2003.

—— (2004), 'Singing in a Theocracy: Female Musicians in Iran', in Marie Korpe (ed.), *Shoot the Singer!: Music Censorship Today*, New York: Zed Books, pp. 129–34.

Yusuf, Ahmad (1997), 'Nashaz al-Shaykh al-Hudhayfi' ('The Dissonance of Shaykh al-Hudhayfi'), in Ibrahim Daoud (ed.), *Al-Qur'an fi Misr*, Cairo: Toot, pp. 69–74.

Zarcone, Thierry (1999), 'Quand le Saint Légitime le Politique: Le Mausoleé de Afaq Khwaja à Kashgar', *Central Asian Survey*, 18(2), 225–42.

—— (2002), 'Sufi Lineages and Saint Veneration in 20th Century Eastern Turkestan and Contemporary Xinjiang', in Hasan Celâl Guzel, C. Cem Oguz and Osman Karatay (eds), *The Turks*, Istanbul: Yeni Turkiye Publications, pp. 534–41.

Zenner, Walter P. (1983), 'Syrian Jews in New York Twenty Years Ago', in Victor D. Sanua (ed.), *Fields of Offerings: Studies in Honor of Raphael Patai*, London and Toronto: Associated University Press, pp. 173–93.

—— (2000), *A Global Community: The Jews from Aleppo, Syria*, Detroit, MI: Wayne State University Press.

Zerubavel, Yael and Dianne Esses (1987), 'Reconstructions of the Past. Syrian Jewish Women and the Maintenance of Tradition', *Journal of American Folklore*, 100(398), 528–39.

Zhou Ji (1999), *Zhongguo Xinjiang Weiwu'erzu Yisilanjiao Liyi Yinyue* (*China, Xinjiang Uyghur Islamic Ritual Music*), Taibei: Xinwenfeng.

Zubaida, Sami (1992), 'Islam, The State and Democracy: Contrasting Conceptions of Society in Egypt', *MERIP Reports, no. 179: Islam, The State and Democracy*, 2–10.

Discography

Afghanistan. Rubāb et Dutār. Ustād Mohammad Rahim Khushnavaz et Gada Mohammad (1995), recorded under the direction of John Baily by OCORA (Radio France), Paris: OCORA, OCORA C560080.

'Ajmi, Ahmad al- (1996a), *al-Mushaf al-Murattal 10, min al-aya 13 Hud ila 86 Yusuf* (*The Recited Mushaf, from 13 Hud to 86 Yusuf*) (cassette recording), Cairo: Ushun.

—— (1996b), *al-Mushaf al-Murattal 11, min al-aya 87 Yusuf ila akhir al-Hijr* (*The Recited Mushaf, from 87 Yusuf to the End of al-Hijr*) (cassette recording), Cairo: Ushun.

Alizadeh, Hossein and Hamāvāyān Ensemble (1998), *Rāz-e No* ('New Secret'), Mahoor Institute of Culture and Art, CD-38.

Arian Band (2000), *Gol-e Aftābgardoon* (*The Sunflower*), Tehran: Tarane Sharghee Cultural & Artistic Company.

—— (2001), *Arian II – Va Ammā Eshgh ...* (*Arian II – And Now Love ...*), Tehran: Tarane Sharghee Cultural & Artistic Company.

—— (2004), *Tā Binahāyat* (*Till Eternity*), Tehran: Tarane Sharghee Cultural & Artistic Company.

—— (2008), *Bi To Bā To* (*Without You, With You*) (CD and DVD), Gemmy Music Records Company and Taraneh Sharghi Cultural & Artistic Company.

Bchiri, Yaacov (2001), *Tunisie. La Memoire des Juifs de Djerba*, Archives Internationales de Musique Populaire, Genève, AIMP LXIV.

El 'Azifet (n.d. c.1998), *El 'Azifet*, Direction Amina Srarfi, SOCA Music CD004, Laouina (Tunisia).

Gap Band (2004), *Gap*, (VCD), Tehran: Avay-e Nakisa.

Hafez, Abdel Halim (1983), *Abd al-Halim Hafiz ... wa Misr (1)/Abdel Halim Hafez ... Egypt (1)*, Soutelphan 1983/EMI Music Arabia 1996 0946 310547-2 3.

—— (1995), *Aghani Film 'Maw'id Gharam'/Songs from the Film 'Maweed Gharam'*, Soutelphan 1995/EMI Arabia 1996 0946 310597-2 8.

Hudhayfi, 'Ali 'Abd al-Rahman al- (1995), *Yusuf – al-Ra'd* (cassette recording), Cairo: Mu'assasat al-Risala li al-Intaj wa al-Tawzi' al-Islami.

Isma'il, Mustafa (1978), *Qari' Misr al-Awwal: Tilawat al-Shaykh Mustafa Isma'il, Ma Tayassar min Suratay Yusuf wa al-Haqqa* (*The First of Egyptian Reciters: Qur'anic Recitation of Shaykh Mustafa Isma'il, Chapters Yusuf and al-Haqqa*) (*mujawwad*) (cassette recording), Cairo: SonoCairo.

—— (1999), *Suratay Yusuf wa al-'Ankabut* (*murattal*) (cassette recording), Cairo: SonoCairo.

Kulthūm, Umm (1981), *al-Aṭlāl, Ḥaflah Kāmilah, Ṣawt al-Qāhirah*, cassette tape 81190.

Mäjnun, Abdulla (2003), *Mäjnun: Classical Traditions of the Uyghurs*, SOASIS 06.

Ministry of Culture, The People's Republic of China and The People's Government of the Xinjiang Uighur Autonomous Region, China (2002), *China Uighur Twelve Muqam Symposium Precious Souvenir for Collection*, Ürümchi: Xinjiang Yinxiang Chubanshe.

Music from the Oasis Towns of Central Asia. Uyghur Musicians of Xinjiang (2000), London: Globestyle, CDORBD 098.

On Ikki Muqam Tätqiqat Ilmiy Jämiyiti [OIMTIJ] (1994), *Uyghur On Ikki Muqam* (*The Uyghur Twelve Muqam*), Ürümchi: Shinjang Khälq Näshriyati.

—— (1997), *Uyghur On Ikki Muqam* (*The Uyghur Twelve Muqam*), Beijing: Minzu Chubanshe.

Part Music Group (n.d. *c.*2004), *Rakhs-e Mahtāb* (*Moonlight Dance*), Tehran: Tarannome Ashkmehr Cultural & Artistic Company.

Rama (2003), *Rama*, Tehran: Setareh Sahar Cultural & Artistic Company.

Sa'idi, Mahmud Abu al-Wafa al- (1999), *Yusuf* (cassette recording), Cairo: Sout El Tarab.

Tika Band, (n.d., *c.*2004), *Aftāb Mahtāb* (*Sunlight, Moonlight*), Tehran: Payam Cultural & Artistic Company.

Index